FALL BACK SKYWARD

THE FALL BACK SERIES
BOOK ONE

AUTUMN GREY

DEDICATION

We struggle.

We fall.

We rise.

We fight.

This book is dedicated to anyone who has fought, and is still fighting their inner demons.

Just remember that you are more than enough.

About the book:

Eleven years ago, I saved her. I loved her. But they took me away from her and locked me up. For two years, all I could think about was her. She consumed me. Took up every room in my head and gave me something to focus on, knowing I would see her soon.

Nine years ago, I watched her as she walked down the aisle and into the arms of a man who wasn't me. My brother. I left my home and never looked back.

Now, I'm staring at seven letters, each envelope stamped with one word in bold, red ink: **URGENT**.

I have no choice but to go back home. Seeing her will be the hardest thing I've ever had to do. But in order to reconcile with my past, I have to face my present. Even if the thought of seeing her, knowing that she is out of my reach, kills me.

I have no idea what awaits me, but I can only hope that the demons of my past will finally be buried and put to rest.

Due to possible triggering descriptions of self-harm, and some sexual situations this book is not recommended for anyone under the age of 17 years old

I've seen the inside of hell,
battled my demons
and clawed my way into the light.
Every scar on my skin has a story to tell.
Every scar makes me who I am today.
A survivor.

Eleanor Blake

PART ONE

PRESENT

CHAPTER ONE

Cole

"*I'm going to pretend you didn't just turn me down and try this again*," the woman sitting in the passenger seat signs before crawling across the console and trying to plant herself on my lap.

I jerk back, getting ready to shove her back to her seat. Too late. She's already straddling my hips and making herself comfortable.

What the hell? I can't believe this woman. Ever since Lawrence and Barnes Architects & Engineers was contracted for this residential project, she has been hitting on me. She was relentless the entire time we were in Boston.

She grinds herself on top of me. "*Come upstairs for a cup of coffee?*"

I reach for the door and flip it open, and then motion with my chin for her to leave the Suburban.

Of course, she doesn't.

"*So, you're mad at me now?*" she asks, leaning forward and nipping my jaw. Her fingers slide up the front of my T-shirt and halt on the right side of my chest. She tugs the nipple ring through the fabric there, and bites her lip. Her hands are too busy feeling me up so she leans back making sure I can see her lips, and says, "I've heard rumors around the office, Cole. I've heard you have a gift for making women see heaven."

I roll my eyes. Apparently, my one night of drunken misadventure five years ago, which I highly regret right now, made me a stallion in bed. Not that I mind. But messing around with the people I work with is not my thing.

Glancing up at the rear view mirror, I focus on pulling my shit together and catch a glimpse of my cat, Sirius, batting furiously at the metal bars of the carrier. I should open it and set him loose on this woman. I'm that desperate. I mean, what part of 'I'm not interested' doesn't she understand?

"Get the fuck out, Sam," I sign quickly, feeling my temper rising.

She stares at me blankly, her bottom lip pushed forward. Sam is the ASL interpreter the company insisted my colleague, Tate West, and I bring to Boston with us. I had perfected lip reading by the time I was eleven and my verbal communication is not bad, thanks to the speech therapy. I hardly ever need an interpreter anymore unless I'm attending a large meeting, and neither does Tate. He was born deaf to hearing parents as the result of a recessive gene, but he is just as good in ASL, lip reading and speech.

Sometimes a client feels more comfortable if an interpreter is present during meetings.

Right now, I'm exhausted after the five-hour drive. All I want is a good meal, beer and my bed. The past few weeks working on the project were exhausting. Now I'm hoping to grab some downtime.

This woman is not my type.

My chest tightens as the memory of the only person I consider "my type" flashes in my head. Her name a torturous whisper that has my chest aching, reminding me I'll never forget her no matter how hard I try.

Eleanor Blake, but she preferred her nickname, Nor.

Shit. I shouldn't go there. Nothing good comes out of it. She belongs to someone else now. Besides, why remember something that rips your heart out over and over again?

Already fed up with Sam's clinginess, I grab her by the hips and exit the car. After quickly depositing her on the sidewalk, I duck inside, meeting Sirius' furious green eyes, and snatch Sam's travel bag off the back seat. I shove it into her waiting arms and get back inside the car.

She flips me off while glaring at me.

Right before I close the door, I take a deep breath and glance at her, frustrated when the words don't leave my mouth. This happens when I get too emotional.

I raise my hands and sign, "*You are worth more than this, Sam. Don't sell yourself short.*"

I put the car in gear and drive off before she has a chance to speak. My only thoughts are of feeding Sirius and getting some sleep. Thank fuck it's Friday.

After parking the car outside my building, I grab my bag and the carrier, then lock the doors. I head for the main entrance and take the elevator to the third floor.

I unlock the door, step inside and kick it shut with my foot. I head toward the kitchen and drop the bag on the floor, then let Sirius out of his carrier and fill his bowls with food and water. I dig out the letters that I picked up from our private mailbox and set them on the counter.

When we moved to New York, Simon and I decided to rent a private mail box at the post office because we moved houses a couple of times during those first five years. We didn't bother to cancel the subscription after we finally settled in this flat.

I head to my office and settle on the swivel chair behind the desk. I skim through the mail in my hands and frown, staring at the seven letters with my name carefully scrawled in all too familiar handwritings on the right. One word stands out of all of them: URGENT. It's written in red and underlined three times. My heart beats faster as my gaze moves from Mom's handwriting to my dad's and finally to Nor's on the envelopes.

My hands curl into fists to stop them from shaking as possible scenarios of what might be wrong flash inside my head.

I received the first letter from Nor two months after I arrived in New York. I have no idea how she had gotten my private box address and I didn't care back then. I'd ripped it to shreds and thrown it away without reading it. She had continued to send more letters. Eventually, I asked Simon to get rid of them, because I couldn't stand the heartache every time they showed up in the mailbox.

Dread clouds my brain and I close my eyes, taking deep breaths. When I open my eyes again, I'm calm enough to deal with this without resulting to panic. I haven't spoken to my mom or anyone back home since that fateful day when my fucking heart was ripped out of my chest. Leaving my home and family had nearly killed me and the only things that helped me get through my despair were throwing myself into my school work, the two jobs I was working at that time and the gym to get out the hurt and aggression. My aim was to work hard, get a good job and pay my student loans.

Glancing down at the letters, I let my curiosity take over. I flex my fingers to dispel the tension trapped in them, then pick up the letter opener from my desk and carefully open the first one.

Dear Cole,

> *Where are you? Is everything okay? This is the fourth letter I've written to you. I haven't heard from you and I'm worried. Just, please. I need to talk to you. It's Josh. He is not fairing on very well. Get in touch as soon as you can.*

> *Love,*

> *Mom*

Fuck, no.

I toss the letter aside and snatch the next one. My heart is relentlessly pounding in my chest as the worst scenarios play in my head. Mom wouldn't write if this weren't serious. She knows the way I feel about Josh. About the place I left and never looked back at.

I hold my breath as I read the next one.

Son,

> *Get in touch with your mother or me as soon as you read this.*

Love,

Dad

I drop it and dive into the next one, which is dated December 28th. Scanning it fast, I feel my heart shatter inside my chest.

Nor.

I shoot to my feet, my fingers clenched around the paper.

Cole,

> *Please read this. I know that things between us aren't great and I don't know where to start. I never heard from you so I assume you never read the letters I sent you. I wouldn't be writing if it weren't important. It's Josh. He needs you. The doctors say he doesn't have much time left.*
>
> *I'm begging you, not for my sake, but for your brother's, Cole. Please. Come home.*
>
> *Nor.*

I grab the last letter on the table and rip the top open using my fingers. This one is dated January 20th. Three weeks ago. My mother's handwriting, usually confident and flowery, is shaky at best. I'm terrified of the words written in there and yet, I can't stop. I can't even think. My head is completely messed up.

Dear Cole,

> *I miss my son. I've spent nine years wondering if I'd ever see you again. I need to know you are okay. God, I know how things are between you and your brother but his health is deteriorating fast. He was admitted to St. James Memorial last week. He needs you, Cole. I hope to God this reaches you in time. I'm losing him. I can't lose you too. I just can't.*
>
> *Love,*
>
> *Mom*

Reaching up, I pull the beanie from my head and run a hand through my hair. Of all the scenarios in the world that would successfully drag me back home, I never expected this one. Whatever exhaustion I felt vanishes. My chest aches as dread finds its way through places I never knew existed before. I glance at the clock. It's almost midnight back home. There's no way I can wait until tomorrow.

I pull my phone out of my pocket, scroll down, stop on Simon's name, and open a new text message.

Me: **I'm going home tonight. Are you already in NY or still in Boston?**

The screen lights up a few seconds later.

Simon: **The fuck, man? I was buried deep in pussy. What do you mean you are going home? Florida?**

I would laugh if I could at his immediate response. He and I have known each other since kindergarten. When I moved to New York after leaving prison, he joined me a few months later.

I quickly type, **If you're distracted, that pussy is not worth a shit. Something came up and I need to leave immediately. I'll text you as soon as I can and let you know what's going on.**

His text message flashes on my screen three seconds later.

Simon: **I'll be there in twenty minutes. We need to talk.**

I frown down at the screen, nervousness creeping inside my chest. I'm not used to feeling like this and I don't like it. Worse, if Simon says we need to talk, then it's serious.

Rolling my head to ease the tension building at the nape of my neck, I start to pace unable to stay still. My body is wound so tight, I can feel it cracking in some places. I pause and groan in frustration. This isn't helping to lessen the panic I'm feeling.

I head to my room and strip off my jeans and shirt, and put on a pair of running shorts. Seconds later, I walk down the hall to the gym. I slip on my gloves and start taking out my emotions on the bag hanging from the ceiling.

Punch. Punch. Punch.

Sweat rolls down my face, my chest. Air locks and leaves my lungs. I feel alive, my head is clearing.

With one final punch, I pull off the gloves and toss them on the nearby mat in the corner. I exit the room, snatching a gray towel from the rack in the bathroom on my way to the kitchen to text Tate and let him know what's happening. The lamp in the living room blinks a few times, alerting me that someone is at the door. I look up and see Simon striding toward me. His short blond hair sticks out in every direction and his shirt is on inside out.

I don't know why he bothers to use the bell, given that he lives here and has his own key.

"*Dude. You can't just tell me shit like that while I'm getting laid,*" he signs, halting in front of me. I see the concern in his eyes behind those words. Unlike me, Simon has perfect hearing. I guess signing comes automatically for him when he and I communicate.

I nod my head to his shirt. He shrugs, smiling cockily, and takes off toward his room down the hall which is situated between mine and the gym room. He returns minutes later, clutching a bundle of letters held together by rubber bands in his hands. He stops in front of me, his gaze on the letters.

He frowns and shifts on his feet. "*Remember when you asked me to get rid of these? I never did. Sorry, man. I thought you might need to read them one day.*"

Simon thrusts them to my chest. I scowl down at them, and then up at my best friend. "I don't have time for this."

I turn around but a tap on my shoulder stops me.

"What's going on?" he asks when I focus on him again.

"This." I reach for the letters on the counter and give them to Simon.

He scans them quickly, his face paling fast. He raises his head and says, "I'm coming with you."

I shake my head. "I got this."

"Are you sure?"

I feel like a fucking toddler. Helpless. "I got this," I tell him again.

He runs a hand along his jaw, his eyes narrowed at me. "If you think I'll be sitting behind a desk and sucking ass all day while you have all the fun, you're fucking wrong."

I shake my head and chuckle, relieved he's making light of the situation though. I have fifteen hours of driving and not enough time to think or prepare myself for what's waiting for me when I reach home.

He jerks his chin to the bundle in my hands. "Do you think what's in there has something to do with this?"

I shrug. Right now, I have no fucking clue about anything. All I know is that my brother is in a hospital room, very sick, and the thought of never seeing him again terrifies me.

I need to find out what's in these letters, and be prepared for what awaits me back home.

I set them on the counter and my hands fumble around until the rubber bands are gone. I grab the blue envelope on top of the mound, carefully rip the top and pull out a letter. Something slides from within and flutters to the floor. I watch its descent, frowning at what looks like a birthday card. Crouching down, I pick it up and flick it open and I'm met with a picture of two identical girls, grinning at the camera. They can't be older than six years.

A touch on my arm pulls me away from the image. I look up to find Simon staring curiously at the card in my hand, and then meets my gaze.

"Who are they?" he asks.

I shake my head, return my focus to the picture and flip it around to scan for clues.

The words *'Cora and Joce Holloway. Six years old'* are scribbled on the back in Nor's handwriting.

I feel as if someone thrust a sharp object in my chest.

Nor and Josh have children? And why the hell did she see fit to shove that fact in my face? As if marrying my brother wasn't enough.

That thought sends pain spreading through my body. Throwing the card and picture on the counter, I grip the counter, my sight blurring with rage.

Knowing that Nor—the girl I'd loved and lost—and my brother have children is like having my heart broken all over again. They moved on with their lives, while I spent the last nine years of mine living in stasis.

Simon touches my arm again. I spin around to glare at him.

"Satisfied?" I spit out, jabbing a finger at the photo. "Fuck, Simon. This is the reason I never wanted to open those letters."

He's holding one of the letters in his hands, his eyes wide. He tries to say something but stops and drags a hand through his hair.

"Oh, man. The girls. . .Cora and Joce are your daughters. Nor and you. Not Josh," he says.

The words punch me in the gut, and I stumble back on impact. No.

He couldn't have said what I think he did. My eyes are playing tricks on me. "What did you just say?"

He slides the card I'd tossed on the counter seconds ago toward me. With my heart racing in my chest, I stare down, confusion then disbelief sweeping through me as my eyes catch the words on the card.

Hi Cole,

> *Cora and Joce celebrated their sixth birthday on Saturday. Cora reminds me so much of you. I want them to know their real father. I want them to call you 'Daddy' but how can they do that if you won't even reply back to my letters? I beg you to think about this, please.*

> *Love, Nor.*

How is that even possible?

I shake my head, forcing my mind to calculate the years we've been apart. The last time Nor and I were together.

Exactly nine years.

Jesus.

I've been a father all this time. I missed most of their childhood.

A lump forms in my throat and my muscles quiver as anguish and anger course through me.

Do they know about me?

I snatch the blue envelope it came in and scan for the mailing date. The black stamp indicates it was mailed three years ago. Suddenly I can't seem to catch my breath fast enough as I scatter the letters on the counter with shaking fingers, searching for the letter with the oldest date on it. Simon seems to read my mind and he rounds the counter to joins me in the search. It feels as if we've been searching forever when he holds a pink envelope out toward me. I reach for it and zero in on the stamp. This was sent nine years ago. I rip the top open and a color photo falls out on the counter. My gaze scanning the words on the letter while taking in every single word.

Dear Cole,

I hope to God you will read this letter because I have so much I want to tell you. I can't even start to tell you how sorry I am about what happened when you got released and came home six months ago. I've gone over so many ways of how I could have done things better, but every single one of them ends up with either you fatally wounded, something I know I wouldn't survive, or back in prison.

The reason I am writing to you is to let you know that, oh God. I should be telling you this face to face. I'm pregnant. This is what I was trying to tell you when you walked into St. Christopher's. I wish I tried harder, fought you harder through your anger. I wish I had been strong enough to disobey my dad and not marry your brother. My father had already hurt you so many times. I knew he had the ability to do worse. He warned me that if I disobeyed him you'd get hurt and I took him very seriously. I was going to save you, even if it meant making a decision that would not only alter the course of our lives, but, break my heart knowing I was breaking yours.

I know what it feels like to feel like you're dead. Numb and cold. And then I met you and I'd never felt more alive. More wanted. I felt that I belonged somewhere, with someone amazing. If obeying my dad was going to save you and keep my heart beating, I'd take that chance and I took it. Please don't blame Josh. He was doing what he thought was best for you to save you from my father.

Cole, please. Please get in touch with me. I want our children to know who their father is and I want you to know them.

Love,

Nor

I clutch the image of the babies to my chest. My brain tries to process everything I've learned the last few minutes. I shut my eyes tight, the memory of all the letters lying before me as well as the first one I ripped to pieces, flash inside my head.

Jesus. What have I done?

I've spent the past nine years hating two of the most important people in my life, Nor and my brother. I have two daughters and I've missed every moment of their lives.

And her father. There was no love lost between us, but forcing his daughter to marry Josh? That's some twisted shit.

My thoughts automatically wander back to the day I last saw Nor. She had tried to tell me something, but I was blinded by my anger and the weight of betrayal so I didn't stop to listen.

Simon appears in my line of vision. Wiping my wet cheeks, I raise my head to meet his gaze. His eyes widen, probably shocked to see the tears on my face.

I never cried when I lost Nor. I never cried when I left home. The pain of losing her was more than I could bare. I knew if I broke down and accepted that I had lost her, it would completely destroy me.

But this. . .everything is happening too fast. Every single emotion I've held onto these past nine years is trying to break free.

Simon hands me back the letters. *"I'll wrap things up here. I will be down there in five days tops. But right now, I have a woman who needs my attention."* He straightens and waggles his eyebrows then steps forward and gives me a one-armed hug before moving away from me. *"Have you told Tate yet?"*

"I was just about to text him when you walked in."

"Call me as soon as you get there," he signs.

I nod and follow him to the door. If I'm going back to the place I left nine years ago and swore never to return to, I need to man up. I need to face this.

The moment Simon leaves, I return to the living room and

quickly type a text to Tate. I grab my bag and scoop Sirius up from his spot where he's snuggled on the sofa and put him back in his carrier.

After gathering all the letters on the counter, I tuck them in the bag and zip it up. I lock up the house and head out. Once Sirius is settled in the back seat and the bag is in the trunk, I slide onto my seat, grip the wheel and stare out my window. I learned a long time ago that life is an unpredictable bitch. Constant one second, and utterly chaotic the next instant.

Several things I learned when I was locked away:

Keep your head down and carry on.

Set your priorities and stick to them.

When you get out, run the fuck away from that place and make sure never to return.

I'd set my priorities straight. I've known what I wanted and wasted no time getting it. I knew where I wanted my life to go and I've worked hard to get there.

Until now.

Until the letters.

My life is unraveling fast. I'm about to meet the girl who had promised her heart to me, then turned around and gave it to my brother. The girl I forced myself to forget. The girl who still holds my heart in her damn hands.

Fan-fucking-tastic.

I reel in my anger, focusing my rage on the one person I blame for this mess that doomed my future with Nor from the moment she and I met. Stephen, Nor's father. And now, according to the letter from Nor, he was also responsible for her and Josh getting married.

Fucking son of a bitch.

CHAPTER TWO

Cole

After dropping Sirius at the hotel I had booked during my short break at the motel last night, I drive to St. James Memorial and park the truck in the underground parking garage. My body aches from driving for hours. I woke up earlier this morning, restless. My head was cramped with visions of Josh lying in the hospital and the revelations in the letters Simon had been collecting. I was torn between texting my parents to ask them for Nor's address and driving straight to the hospital to see Josh. My need to see Josh, Cora and Joce clouded any rational thought and I found myself breaking a couple of traffic laws to get home faster, until I realized that ending up dead wouldn't help anyone.

Another thought entered my mind.

Was I ready to face them after years of ignoring their letters?

I shake my head, pushing aside those thoughts for now, and focus on Josh. How can someone as sturdy as my brother die? He always ate right and exercised. Whatever this is, I'm sure the doctors will find a way to sort it out. To save him.

I pull out the picture of Joce and Cora from my shirt pocket and then turn the overheard light on and study the two identical faces, committing every feature to memory. A sense of completion fills me, even though I haven't met them yet. Cora's mouth is quirked up on one side, a smile very similar to mine, with a dimple to complete that mischievous look. Joce, on the other hand, seems unprepared for the shot. She's wearing a cute little frown on her face, glaring at her sister. I'd imagine that's how I look when I frown.

My girls.

Putting the picture back in my pocket, I step out of the truck and head for the elevators. I have no idea where or which room Josh is in. I sent a text to my mother earlier today but I haven't heard from her. The elevator stops on the ground floor and I alight and shuffle to the nurses' station, counting on being lucky.

A nurse with black hair sprinkled with gray on her temple and crown, simultaneously speaks on the phone and types on her computer. I'm partly relieved. I still have time to get my head straight before I see Josh. I glance around the waiting room, trying to distract myself. Not that I succeed in any way. Seems like everywhere I look is filled with people pacing impatiently or agitated, others gathered in small groups in the waiting area.

Someone touches my arm. I turn around, startled.

"Can I help you?" the nurse asks, blinking at me behind black-rimmed glasses.

"I'm looking for Josh Holloway."

She eyes me with a little frown marring her features, a look similar to the one I notice on people when they first meet and talk to me. I've been told I have an unusual voice. I wouldn't know, though. I have no idea what my voice sounds like since I lost my hearing when I was five-years-old.

Her gaze drifts away from my face, following the tattoos peeking out from my T-shirt at the neck and then traveling down to my arms. Her lips tighten in disapproval. I really don't give a fuck what she thinks about me and my tattoos. People can be judgmental assholes.

I hold her gaze with my cold one, until she lowers hers to the computer screen and her fingers fly on the keyboard as a red flush fills her cheeks. Her lips move, but I can't read them given the angle of her face. She looks up when I don't answer her back, her mouth pressed into a thin line.

"Sorry. I didn't catch what you said." I gesture to my ears with my fingers. Her eyes widen, understanding flooding her face.

"Oh. I'm sorry for that. We have an interpreter—"

I hold up my hand and shake my head. "I can read lips." She nods and glances down at her fidgety fingers on the keyboard.

Great. I made her uncomfortable. "What were you saying before?" I ask, eager to move away from this awkwardness.

Her head comes up and she smiles. "Oh. Right. Are you family?"

I swallow around the lump in my throat. "I'm his brother."

She nods, types on her computer then looks up at me with something close to sympathy in her eyes. "Third floor. Oncology. Room 305."

My world comes to an abrupt stop.

My head is buzzing. The only word ringing through it is 'Oncology.'

A hand gently touches my arm again, tugging slightly. The nurse is staring at me, concern on her face. I think she asks me if I'm okay.

No. I'm not. Everything is reeling around me, and the hope I've been holding on to since I left New York fades a little.

No

God.

No.

The nurse says something, but I'm already turning around, my feet propelling me forward in no particular direction. I want to see my brother, but I'm scared of what I will find in that room.

How the hell am I going to face him after everything that has happened?

Then I remember Nor's words in that letter. *He doesn't have a lot of time left.*

I thrust my hands inside my jeans pockets and walk toward the elevators to search for my brother.

The room is quiet when I step inside. The curtains have been drawn to keep the light out. A bed is positioned close to the window with a thin form lying on it.

The faint light filtering through the blinds casts shadows on Josh's face, giving him an eerie look. His body has lost all its former football player physique. Sunken cheeks. Pale face.

Movement from the corner of my eye pulls me away from my brother. I look over my shoulder and suck in a breath.

Nor.

She's sleeping in a cot a couple of feet away. I hadn't seen it when I walked in, given the dimmed lighting. Her body is covered with a navy blanket. Pain drums inside my chest as I take her in. She looks so tiny and fragile, curled up with her hair splayed across the pillow. Her cheeks look hollow. Her eyebrows seem to have a permanent frown in them, a look that is both foreign and troubling.

Jesus Christ. She's still beautiful, despite the changes in her body.

My breathing quickens, and fire spreads in my veins as the love that has been simmering under my skin flares to life. I should have known I could never hate her, no matter how hard I tried.

Careful not to wake them up, I reach for a chair and place it next to Josh's bed. Once I'm seated, I pull out my phone and quickly type a text to Simon.

I'm here. It's not good, man.

He replies seconds later. **Where exactly?**

Me: **Oncology. St. James Memorial.**

He takes a bit longer to reply this time. **Fuck.**

My thoughts exactly.

I shove the phone back inside the pocket of my pants and adjust my weight on the chair and offer a silent prayer to the Main Guy above, begging for some kind of miracle to cure Josh.

CHAPTER THREE

Nor

STARTLED OUT OF ANOTHER UNPLEASANT DREAM, I OPEN MY EYES and shift my stiff body on the cot, trying to get into a comfortable position. I've been having these dreams for a while now; nightmares of Josh dying. Dreams about Cole. Sometimes they play out differently, giving me a glimpse of what Cole and I could have had if we had ended up together. At times they are horrible dreams that jolt me awake, shivering and sobbing.

The past nine years haven't been easy, but Josh, Cora and Joce made everything bearable. Everything worth living for.

And now Josh is dying, and there is nothing I can do to reverse that, and not enough words tell him how grateful I am for being there for me and the girls. For being my hero. For being an amazing dad and my best friend.

Josh's mom and dad, and I have been alternating during the past few weeks, making sure someone is always with him here at the hospital. At times my sisters, Elise and Elon, would offer to stay with him too. His youngest brother, Nick, sleeps over when he doesn't have a lot of classes the following day and mostly during the weekends. We have worked out a system that ensures one of us is always here at all times.

Finally, I sit up on the cot and grab my phone next to the pillow to check the time. Warmth radiates inside my chest when I'm met by the adorable faces of Cora and Joce, grinning at the camera. Since Elise doesn't have classes until this afternoon, she gladly offered to stay with them last night.

Swinging my feet off the bed, I climb to my feet and tug my dress down, fighting a yawn. I glance around the dim-lit room, my eyes narrowing in on the figure sitting on a chair next to Josh's bed. My gaze travels from the beanie-covered head lowered on the bed, to the hunched broad shoulders stretching the gray T-shirt. I blink several times, my heart skipping quite a few beats. My vision sways and my breath comes out faster and faster.

Cole?

My body hums with the kind of effect only he could ever evoke in me, verifying that it is him.

I start to walk forward but my steps falter. I'm breathless and my legs are suddenly nothing more than two slabs of lead cemented on the white floor.

Oh, God. He's here. He *is* really here.

I wipe the tears rolling down my cheeks. I'm worried that if I look away he might vanish into thin air. I continue to stare at the man I'd once loved, and still do, so much that my heart aches with the immensity of it all even nine-years later.

Cole lifts his head from the bed, and as if sensing me, he turns around.

I suck in a breath, and for just a few seconds, my heart stops its furious sprint in my chest. He straightens in his seat, his gaze searching my face with an intensity so raw, so fierce, so *hot* I'm wondering why I haven't dissolved to ashes where I'm standing. His expression softens and he's looking at me the way he used to, as though there's nothing in this world which is important to him right now. Just me and him.

He takes off his beanie and unfolds his tall frame from the chair.

Oh.

God.

He is still handsome, just like I remember him: square jaw, deep set gray eyes, generous lips, sharp cheekbones.

Did you get all my letters, is what I want to ask him. *Why didn't you write back?*

I don't, though. I have so many questions, each one of them fighting for precedence. Unable to hold back anymore, I rush forward toward him, ignoring the tension crackling the air.

I just want to hold him and make sure he's real.

His eyes widen right before I fling my body into his and wrap my arms around his waist, tucking my head into his chest.

He is real.

My heart soars as I inhale his scent deeply, shamelessly and desperately. Greedily.

Cole

Keep your head up and keep moving, bro.

I jolt awake as those words fade into my waking consciousness. Pain shoots from my neck, spreading along my arm and shoulders, caused by the angle I've been sleeping in. It takes a few seconds for my mind to gain awareness and realize where I am.

White room. Drawn curtains. An EKG monitor sits on the other side of the bed, some numbers displayed on the screen. Several wires are attached to the machine, disappearing on the sleeping patient on the bed.

Josh.

His chest rises and falls, his inhale longer than his exhale. His fingers, which are intertwined with mine, twitch every few seconds. The awkwardness I felt on my drive home, wondering how I'd feel when I finally faced him had disappeared. My hand had found his and held on to it fast. The fear of losing him overrode whatever I'd felt for him since the last time I saw him when he was standing in the front of the church, waiting for Nor to join him. All I see now is fragility. The sickness has sucked him dry, leaving protruding bones and jaundiced skin.

The words, *Keep your head up and keep moving, bro* are stuck in my head on repeat. They were my brother's mantra while growing up. He'd ruffle my hair and then say that every time we parted. Those words coupled with Nor's sweet face had been my lifeline when I was in prison.

I have been angry at him for so long, that the rage I've been carrying around all this time has overshadowed his heroic actions on the day he became my hero, my savior.

The day my world turned silent.

I was five years old when I was diagnosed with spinal meningitis. Josh and I were playing out on the porch that summer. I kept complaining that my head hurt. Everything seemed to be magnified tenfold. The daylight hurt my eyes. I felt drowsy, even though I'd slept over ten hours the night before. One moment I was crawling around, trying to race his toy car and the next I was on the ground, my body held prisoner by seizures. For that one second before my world turned into a series of unending spasms, I heard Josh call my name. I saw his face when he appeared in my line of vision, panicked. Later on, my mother told me that if it weren't for Josh, I would probably have died.

And now, he's lying on the bed. His life is ending even before he's had a chance to enjoy it to its fullest.

God.

He is only thirty-two. He hasn't lived his dreams yet.

I can't save him like he saved me.

I can't do shit other than sit here and watch him fucking die.

The hair on the nape of my neck rises in awareness. The force that had always been present between Nor and I surrounds me. I couldn't shake it off if I tried.

I take deep breaths, trying to control my racing heart. The thought of seeing Nor after all these years of separation had only fleetingly occurred to me. Honestly? I haven't had enough time to think about it. I've been too preoccupied dealing with memories of my past and trying to keep my shit together after seeing Josh.

I'm not a coward and I've never been one, but the thought of facing Nor terrifies me because;

1) I haven't see her in nine years. I've spent that time in a never-ending Hell, reliving every single moment of our life together. I never thought I'd ever see her again until my delusions were shattered the second I opened those seven letters about Josh dying. That, and my two little girls, solidified the decision to go home. But then, I would have returned home to Willow Hill even if it wasn't for the girls. This is Josh. My brother.

2) I have no idea how things will go as soon as I turn around. My head is completely messed up right now. The fear of losing Josh is a palpable driving force. I need something to anchor me. The woman standing behind me had been my anchor up until I saw her walking down the aisle toward my brother. I lost my footing, and since then I've been sinking into despair, searching for her in every face I meet.

I gently pull my fingers from Josh's then reach up and tug the beanie from my head. I stand up and turn around and my defenses crack at the corners. Her eyes widen and her lips part in surprise. My body jolts, reacting to the hope, hunger and love in her face.

Holy fuck. Are my eyes playing tricks on me? I never thought I'd see her look at me that way again.

Her face is a mirror of all the feelings I've locked away inside that special place in me.

Jesus. What happened to her?

The knee-length, floral red and white sleeveless dress hangs loosely on her tiny frame. Her arms seem long and gangly, but that may be because of all the weight she has lost. The scars on her arms are stark white against her skin. Dark circles mar the perfection that is her green eyes. I've always admired how her eyes seemed to look right through me. Right now, all I see is emptiness. Beyond that, she's still stunning, more beautiful than the last time I saw her. Her hair is bunched up in a messy bun at the nape of her neck with a few locks framing her heart-shaped face.

Tears fall freely down her cheeks and she doesn't bother to wipe them away. Then she rushes forward and slams her body into mine, wrapping her arms tightly around my waist.

My body is coiled tight, my senses overloaded by her scent. Her face is in the crook of my neck and her mouth is feathering warm air on my skin. The feel of her body violently shaking against mine, the tears seeping through my T-shirt—after years of being away from her, my body doesn't know how to respond to any of it. But my hands are still hanging at my sides.

What's happening?

This is awkward. I know she is hurting. I certainly wasn't expecting this kind of greeting from her. My brain yells, *Hug her back, you idiot*, but everything in me is ready to push her away. Reject to offer her comfort.

Then she moves her head, burrowing deeper into my chest. Her scent, that combination of vanilla and almond, slams into me and knocks the breath from my lungs.

Shit.

I can't do this. She is my biggest weakness and my greatest strength. But how can I *not* hold her when she's trembling like she is about to fall apart? When her pain is my pain?

This is not the Nor I knew, the girl I left behind. My Nor was fierce. Her life hadn't been easy, but she had been a fighter. This girl holding me is broken, surrounded by desolation.

I toss the beanie on the chair and wrap my arms around her. The feeling is so familiar, it physically hurts remembering how long it's been since I held her like this. I squeeze her tighter and bury my face in the crook of her neck just below her ear, my body seeking comfort and familiarity.

God. She smells fucking amazing.

Raw.

Real.

Home.

I should kick myself in the balls for thinking shit like this.

As though she's been waiting for my arms to hold her, her knees buckle. I scoop her up and stride across the room to the cot she was sleeping on and lower myself on to it. She sobs openly, her arms banded around my neck and her face burrowed in it. I hold her tighter as she curls her tiny body up on my lap. Right now, holding each other like this, we are two people grieving over someone we both love. Gone are the differences that drove us apart.

Just a brother and a wife comforting one another.

I rub my hand in circles along her back taming the storm raging inside her, until the sobs turn to little hiccups and her breathing evens out.

She stiffens and sits up on my lap. She seems to remember who I am. Who she is.

Our relationship.

She quickly swings her legs to one side. Her dress rides up her thighs in the process. My arms tighten around her on reflex as my gaze zooms in on the pink scars on her thighs. These scars look different than the white ones on her arms. She tries to pull her dress down quickly, her gaze averted from mine. Had she relapsed again after I left?

Obviously seeing my shock, her cheeks flush as she scrambles off my lap. I let her go as she stands up, wiping her face with the back of her hand. She leans down and grabs a pair of pink Keds from the foot of the bed and slips them on.

She's still a Keds kind of girl, even after all these years.

Her gaze darts around the room. Everywhere but at me, her chest rising and falling rapidly, but I cannot stop staring at her. My eyes can't get enough of her now that she's standing in front of me. I give her time to collect herself. Finally, she focuses those wide, beautiful eyes on me, searching my face. I have a feeling that if I mention the scars on her thighs, she will run. So I hold back and wait for the pain in my chest to subside. The air around us is weighted with awkwardness and unspoken thoughts. I hate this so damn much.

She bites her cheek, uncertainty flooding her features. Her lips part as if she wants to say something, but they fall closed again.

Say something.

My body is coiled tightly, waiting for her reaction.

Her gaze leaves my face, taking in the rest of me for the first time. They widen when they reach my arms and I know the moment she recognizes the words 'Silver Lining' intertwined within the red rose petals imprinted across my skin, an exact copy of one of her doodles. Her mouth parts on a breath as tears fill those eyes that have haunted me for years.

"*Cole.*"

"*Cole. . .*" she signs again, but pauses again. She lifts her right hand, the palm facing inward and moves it clockwise in front her face, ending the gesture with a closed hand. "*It's beautiful.*"

I pull the picture of our daughters from my shirt pocket and turn it around to face her.

Her gaze bounces between my hand and face. She exhales, her shoulders slumping forward as if a heavy weight has been lifted from them. "*You received the letters.*"

Before I can answer her, she glances way, focusing on something beyond me, then signs, "*Josh is awake.*"

She wipes her cheeks quickly with her palm, pastes a smile on her face and skirts around me. Turning around, I stare after her as she hurries toward the bed and sits on the chair I vacated just moments ago. Josh's features soften as she leans forward to cover his hand with hers. Their lips are moving but I can't read what they're saying, given the angle of their faces. Pain pierces my chest just watching them. She lifts her hand and strokes his face then gently touches her palm to his forehead as if checking him for fever.

Nor

"Hey, sleeping beauty. How are you feeling?" I ask, gently touching his face to check for fever. He grabs my hand and bats his lashes at me.

"Oh, my pretty prince, you came to rescue me," he says, his lips tugging in a teasing smile.

Tears spring to my eyes. I sob and chuckle at the same time. "I wish I could rescue you from this, Josh. I wish I could save you just like you saved me." I lift a hand and swipe the tears on my cheeks then clear my throat, then whisper, "Cole is here."

His eyes widen and his hand tightens around my wrist. "What? Where?"

I pull one of my hands from his grasp and lean back so he can get a clear view of Cole.

"Jesus. He really *is* here." His voice is a whisper, full of awe. His gaze moves from Cole and back to me. He searches my face for a few seconds before taking in a deep breath, his face taking on a serious look. "I need you to do something for me. I have been holding on to the hope that I'll see him before I go, even though I'd already made peace with myself. Cole is your dream. He has always been your dream—"

"Stop it, Josh," I plead with him, shaking my head. "Please. Stop."

"Shut up and listen to me, Eleanor."

Wiping my cheeks with my free hand, I shoot up from the chair, but his fingers around my wrist are like shackles, pulling me back to down.

"I love you. You and the girls have made me the happiest man on earth." He takes a deep breath. "Sometimes life throws you a curveball, just to test your limits. It happened to you and Cole. We never thought we'd ever see him again. Yet he's here. Shouldn't that count for something?" I nod and press my lips to stop them from trembling. "Promise me you'll be selfish for once in your life and do something for yourself."

I can't do this. Losing Josh, even though I knew it was coming, is still painful. "I need to go to the chapel."

"Darn it, Nor. Promise me this." His voice is urgent and his hold on me strong, despite his weak state. "Give me that, at least. It's my dying wish."

I glare down at him, tears still running down my face. I feel the anguish and anger inside me leave my bones as I stare into his pleading gaze. The genuine love shining through them comforts me. I nod and kiss his forehead. "I love you, Josh."

He lets go of my hand. I quickly dry my face before turning around to face Cole.

Cole

I shouldn't feel jealous. She is not mine. She is his wife now and has been for a while now.

I slip the picture back in my pocket and shove my hands in my pants pockets, feeling like an outsider. I have to leave before I do something stupid.

I cross the room heading for the door, but stop in my tracks when I feel a gentle touch on my arm, and look over my shoulder.

"Stay," Nor says, tugging my sleeve. Her other hand clutches my beanie tightly to her chest as if it might fly away. She follows my gaze and she licks her lips, her cheeks flushing. She wiggles her freckled nose in that cute way I adored so much and then hands it over to me.

I take it and put it on, then I glance over her head and meet Josh's weary eyes. He lifts his hand from the bed and waves at me, then lets it fall back on the sheet. He inhales, but it's cut short when a cough wracks through his body.

I walk back and hover at the foot of the bed, dread filling my chest with every cough. I refuse to allow my fear of losing him drive me into a panic, but watching him suffering like this drums the point home.

Fuck!

"*You're here,*" he signs when he's calm enough to move a part of his body. He can hardly sign the words, though he seems determined to do it. His usually vibrant blue eyes are dull with uncertainty as he stares at me with a hopeful, yet cautious expression.

I nod, watching as Nor hurries toward the bathroom without looking back. I pull my gaze back to Josh.

"*Thank you. Thank you for coming, bro.*" Josh signs, his brow is beaded with sweat from exertion.

I nod my head, a huge lump forming inside my throat.

Nor returns moments later, carrying a small white towel in her hands. I step back to give her space. She settles down on the chair and then leans forward and begins to wipe my brother's forehead, smiling softly. It's not genuine though. Her eyes are tight around the corners as if she's trying hard not to cry.

Josh's head rolls to the side to face Nor as he says something. He's staring at her like she is his whole world. She returns the look with. . .affection. The kind of look a sister gives to her brother.

As much as I hate to admit it, this gives me comfort. He genuinely *loves* her.

Nor kisses his forehead and stands up. She walks toward the door, but then stops and turns to face me. She doesn't say anything at all. We just stare at each other, reminding me of the very first day I saw her when they moved in next door. I hope to fuck my face is blank.

I can't afford to lay all my cards on the table. Show her how much she still affects me.

I know my presence affects her too. What I don't expect to see is the way her eyes soften when she looks at me. I'm not sure how to deal with that.

"*Thank you for coming. It's really good to see you,*" she signs. "*I'm sorry about earlier.*"

My jaw tightens involuntarily. *"He is my brother."*

She flinches at my words, a little frown forming between her eyebrows. She nods once. "I'll be at the chapel, if I'm needed." She lifts her chin in that defiant way that used to do crazy things to me and walks out of the room with her back straight and head held high.

I shouldn't let it get to me, but it does.

She dumped you for your brother.

That thought is like ice water poured over my head. I shove my balled fists into my pockets and focus on Josh, the new scars still haunting my mind.

We eye each other, the room filling with tension. I have no idea how to begin talking to him after years of no communication.

"You look like hell," I tell him.

He laughs. When he tries to sign again, his hands shake badly. He gives up and takes a deep breath. "If I knew you were coming, I would have worn my best tux and rolled out the red carpet."

His eyes are yellow around where the whites are supposed to be. He scans me, his gaze starting from my neck and down to my arms. They linger there for a long time before moving to my face. I see recognition burning in there.

"Great tattoos," he says, grinning. And for just a few seconds, his smile is easy, like I remember it.

I don't say anything. I don't feel like chatting about my goddamn tattoos when my brother looks like he's about to kick the bucket the next second. My head is empty right now and I'm not exactly sure what I want to talk about, but my ink is not it.

He grimaces and the smile disappears. The look on his face shifting to remorse, he averts his gaze to the vicinity above my right shoulder. Mine stays on him.

"Cole. . ." he starts to sign then stops, his chest rising and falling fast in exhaustion. His fingers slide across the bed and wrap around the control. He presses a button, adjusting the angle of his upper body a few degrees up.

He folds his hands on his lap. "I really don't know what to say. I'm sorry. I know it doesn't begin to cover what happened. I wish we had met under different circumstances—"

"What happened?" I cut him off, unable to hold my shit together. My hands start to shake as the same anger that had driven me out of Willow Hill hits me hard.

I shut my eyes and take a few calming breaths. I hate that my emotions are all over the place right now. One minute I'm angry and the next, I feel guilty as fuck. Terrified and apprehensive about meeting my parents. I'm not used to feeling this way. I have to calm down before I blow this up. I need answers, but I doubt letting my temper fuel this conversation will help achieve this.

I slowly open my eyes and glance at the ceiling, gritting my teeth. When I feel brave enough to face my brother and my nemesis, one of the people I'd literally kill for, I let my head fall forward, my eyes meeting his which are filled with guilt. I need to tread carefully around Josh.

"Let's talk about this later," I say, squeezing my neck with one hand.

His jaw clenches. "You don't get to feel sorry for me."

I sigh. "I didn't come back to sort out issues that happened a long time ago. I came here because Mom and Dad asked me to."

And because I can't stand the thought of losing you.

His mouth parts in surprise. Hurt crosses his features before he clenches his jaw and conceals it carefully.

"Nor wrote to me too."

His shoulders slump forward and relief spreads across his face. "So you know about the girls."

I rub by jaw with my hand and nod.

"Have you met them yet?"

"No."

His eyes widen in surprise. "Don't you want—"

My mouth opens and then closes when the words refuse to come out. I lift my hands and sign, "*I want to. Jesus. I want to meet them so fucking bad, but that can wait.*" I take a deep breath and admit, "*I needed to see you first. You are more important right now."*

His expression softens and tears fill his eyes. "They are pretty special."

I remember the picture in my pocket, warming my skin and smile. "I know."

We don't say anything for a few seconds. My head is a bit clearer after my admission. I want to tell him I missed him. I miss who we were.

I'm going to tell him. He needs to know before it's too late.

"Is Megs still around?" I ask, referring to Nor's childhood best friend.

I can't stop thinking of Nor. The stress is getting to her. She seems older than her twenty-nine years. When was the last time she left the hospital or has eaten anything? She needs a break from this place before this situation eats her whole. I might be angry, furious even, about the things that happened in our past, but that doesn't mean I will be a dick and watch her suffer. No one deserves this.

Josh's face clouds in confusion, probably wondering where I'm going with this. He nods.

"Do you have her number?"

He jerks his chin toward the bedside stand. I lean forward, open the drawer and take out his phone. Ignoring the weight of his stare, I scroll through the contact list. Nor wouldn't know when to quit even when her own exhaustion was staring her in the eye. She has always been the kind of person who, when she gives, she throws her entire fucking life into something. A part of me appreciates that. I'm not certain how big that part is, because I'm still trying to sort out the catastrophic mess of emotions storming inside my chest.

Nonetheless, it doesn't stop a smile from touching my lips.

That's Nor, going to great lengths to make sure everyone was comfortable.

I see movement in the corner of my eye and look up to see Josh waving his hand to catch my attention. "You're smiling."

I shut it down fast and continue to scroll through his phone.

When I find the number, I quickly type a text to Megs then hit send. I return the phone back inside the drawer.

I'm dying to ask him what type of cancer he has. But somehow I feel like if I voice the question, it kind of confirms that he is on death's door and that thought punches me hard in my gut.

I run a hand through my hair, sliding it down to rub my neck. I feel a dull headache forming in the back of my head, a product of the short night's sleep and long drive finally sinking in. That and this situation.

I make my way to the other side of the bed and lower myself onto the chair, drop my head in my hands, and blink back the tears. Fuck. I shouldn't display that kind of weakness in front of him. He needs a strong support system of family and friends surrounding him. Bawling my eyes out won't help shit.

He touches my arm and I lift my head to meet his steady gaze. Isn't he terrified of dying? I haven't seen fear in his eyes since he woke up. He has accepted this. Accepted that he is going to die.

"How can you look so unaffected by this?" I ask almost angrily. I'm not sure who I'm angry at. Cancer, Josh or me. Maybe all of them.

He shrugs. "I knew the end was coming. It was just a matter of time."

"When did you realize you had. . .you were sick?" I ask

"Six years ago. My pancreas finally flipped a finger at me. I'm on stage four." He pauses. Inhales deeply. "The first doctor who diagnosed me said I had only a few months left to live. I guess I was too stubborn to die." He grins.

He fucking grins.

Jesus. I want to kick something.

I shake my head, horrified and in awe of my brother. He should be scared. Instead, he's fearless, even when death is waiting, counting the days, hours, minutes, or even seconds to claim his soul.

"Do Mom and Dad know you came home?"

I shake my head, taking in the worried look on his face. I have no idea how to interpret it, so I ask, "Why?"

His expression clears and he grins. "They will freak out when they see you, especially Mom." He eyes my arms and neck where the tattoos are showing.

"I'm not twelve," I retort.

He laughs, his arm wrapped around his middle as if to support his body from bursting open. "I bet Mom will have something to say about that."

I had most of the tattoos done when I got to New York after leaving my home. Each word and every drawing on my skin was a memory. A reminder of what I lost. What I wanted to remember.

The mirth on his face vanishes, replaced by a somber look. His narrow chest expands as he takes in a long, deep breath. "I don't have a lot of time left. I need you to do something for me."

I should give him the respite he craves, given the desperate look on his face, but my mind and mouth have other plans. Before I can control the words burning my tongue, words I've asked myself a million times rush out. "Why, Josh? Why should I do you a favor, when you took what was mine? You ripped my life out from under me." I slow down and take deep breaths. "Give me a good reason why I should, Josh."

He doesn't look fazed by the words.

"Because Nor needs you, she's always needed you and she'll still need you long after I am gone. Please, Cole."

I open my mouth to talk but I pause, too worked up to speak. I grunt, frustrated.

Damn stupid words.

Heaving out a sigh, I raise my hands and I sign, *"Do you love her?"*

"Irrevocably," he says, his eyes fixed on mine and I see sincerity shining through them, but there's something else too.

Hopelessness.

Sadness.

Acceptance.

I exhale, my heart twisting hard in my chest so damn hard, I fear it might break free from its confines.

The next question causes my hands to shake as I raise them to sign. This is something I've wondered about so many times. *"Does she love you?"*

He drags a hand over his bald head, the look on his face bleak and says, "Not as much as I love her. Like I've always loved her."

I rip my gaze from his and frown down at my hands, trying to gain control of my wayward emotions. I'd promised myself during the drive home I'd play it cool until I got a handle on the situation.

Yeah, right. Like that would ever happen. Cool is a foreign emotion to me, especially when it comes to Nor. Thank God, Josh puts me out of my misery when he touches my arm.

"Nor took it very hard after what happened. She went back to self-harming, but she got better again with the help of a therapist. Having Cora and Joce also helped her a lot. She has never loved me like she loved you. Like she still loves you."

And just like that, pandemonium breaks out inside my head at his declaration.

She still loves me.

What kind of shit did that asshole of a father put them through? I have a clue but I have a feeling there's more. I open my mouth to ask him but he screws up his face in a grimace as he shifts his body on the bed.

CHAPTER FOUR

Cole

His face is covered in a sheen of sweat and his lips are pulled tight. His fingers are shaking as if he is going through a withdrawal.

"Shit. I hate this part."

Panic slams my chest. I shoot up from the chair and rush to his side . "What's wrong? Can I do anything? Call the nurse?"

He reaches for the remote control on his bed and presses the nurse button. "Pain. So fucking much."

Why didn't I notice this? I'm wrapped up in my own issues, too selfish to notice he's hurting.

"What can I do?" I ask again, my eyes blurry with tears.

He grins, but the smile resembles a frown instead. "Get me a unicorn. And fairy dust." His speech is much slower now. He sinks lower into the bed and closes his eyes. "If I'm leaving this world, I want to ride a unicorn. Cora believes unicorns are the best thing since Barbie dolls."

Those words jolt a fierce emotion in me, reminding me that I've missed nine years of my girls' lives.

"She sounds cool as shit," I say.

"They. . ." he breaths through his mouth. "They both are. Cora reminds me so much of you."

Before I can follow up on that comment, a nurse with a head full of short dark curls appears on the edge of my vision, dismantling my thoughts. She's holding a syringe in one hand. A cold shiver slithers down my spine and sweat breaks out on my forehead. I fucking hate syringes. After being poked and prodded when I was five, I developed a healthy abhorrence toward that shit.

She halts on the other side on the bed and my body relaxes, grateful for the distance between me and the needle. She starts working on the IV on Josh's arm, oblivious of my current state. Her mouth moves but I can't understand what she says. She raises her head to look at me.

"I'm nurse Peterson." She points at the name badge on her chest.

"Sorry. I didn't get what you said before. I'm Cole. Josh's brother."

Her cheeks flush. "Sorry—"

I raise my hand up to stop her. "No harm done. Just make the pain go away." I point to Josh with my chin.

She nods.

When she is done, she straightens and adjusts the sheets around Josh.

"How long does it take before he needs another dose?"

She purses her lips. "Depends on the patient and how much pain he or she has." She looks at my brother and smiles, then faces me. "Your brother is stubborn. We suggested a way for him to administer the drug himself but he refused."

She laughs when Josh winks at her. "He's a flirt this one." She shakes her head, turns and leaves.

I've never seen anyone in the throes of pain like Josh had been a few minutes ago. Is this what Nor has been facing everyday for the past six years? Watching him, knowing the only thing that can help him is medication?

Christ. This shit is scary.

"It's not so bad, you know."

I gape at him. "You're kidding me, right?"

Josh shrugs. "Some days are worse than others. I'm thankful I've gotten this far instead of those measly months the doctor predicted at first." He settles back on the pillows and steeples his fingers on top of his stomach on the sheet. "Dude, I asked Nor to go out and choose the most fucking beautiful coffin she can find. Something fit for this prince. She chose a badass coffin." His eyes slip shut, a look of pure bliss on his face. The medication must have taken full effect.

I stare at him. Open my mouth and snap it shut. Open it again.

Did that shit just spout out of his mouth? I'm fighting fucking hard not to bawl and he's talking about coffins as if he is chatting about the goddamned tuxedo he'll wear to a party.

Finally, I blink. This is typical Josh. I feel my laughter erupt from my gut and out of my mouth. It feels fucking amazing to laugh after the past forty-eight hours.

His lids snap open and he starts laughing too.

My mind momentarily drifts to Nor and the words he told me before, unable to let them go. According to Josh, Nor didn't love him as much as he loved her, yet, according to him, she has been living in the hospital, taking care of him.

I'm driving myself insane with these thoughts.

Cool air brushes the back of my neck alerting me that someone entered the room. I shift around and come face to face with Megs. Her face splits into a wide grin the moment our gazes lock.

"Hey." She waves, striding toward me with her arms outstretched. Leaving my chair, I start toward her and meet her in the middle of the room.

Megs is beautiful. Five foot four, brown eyes, brown skin and a lot of curves. The white dress she's wearing does nothing to hide them. She knows how to carry her height and body. She hasn't changed much. Simon told me she's going through a divorce. I have a feeling he kept tabs on her even after they broke up.

She eyes me up and down. *"It's good to see you, Cole,"* she says while signing. Her movements are still stilted, but she's gotten better at it since the last time I saw her.

My lips twitch. "I see you finally got the hang of ASL."

She laughs. "Yes, I did. I see you got inked. Damn, you look scary.

And hot." Her gaze drifts to the bed then back to me. Her face soft and sad, her loss so clear on her face. She faces me again. "How is he?"

I shake my head. "Weak. I need to speak to the doc."

Her gaze roams around the room, before turning back to me. "Nor?"

"She is at the chapel."

Megs nods, and shifts on her feet, biting her bottom lip. "When did you arrive?"

"About an hour ago." I rub my neck. I'm not good at small talk so I get right to the point. "Could you take Nor away from here at least for a few hours."

She appraises me as she tugs the strap of her handbag over her shoulder, and nods, smiling softly. "Sure. Catch up later?"

"You bet." I dig my phone out of my pocket. "I'll give you my number, in case you need to call me."

She nods, handing me her phone.

After exchanging our contacts, she turns to leave but stops and turns around to look at me. "It's really good to see you. I hope we'll have some time to catch up."

I don't respond to that. I know if I do, I might end up asking her what went down nine years ago, because, obviously, she is still Nor's best friend. She definitely knows.

But this is not her shit to tell.

"Simon will be here in a couple of days," I tell her.

She seems frozen by the news for a few seconds. Then she tucks a strand of black hair behind her ear with shaking fingers.

"When?"

"Five days. Give or take."

"Awesome," she says and grimaces. She spins around and hurries out the door.

Just as I'm about to leave the room to search for coffee, a tall man with graying hair and a white lab coat walks in the room.

His gaze moves to my brother and then back to me. My stomach feels like it's made of concrete as I watch him halt in front of me. He sticks his hand out in greeting and speaks, but his lips move fast I can't read them. I clasp his outstretched hand then pull mine back.

"Could you please speak a bit slower?" I ask, shoving my hands inside my pants pockets.

He blinks at me in confusion.

"Unless you know ASL," I add, pointing to my ears.

All right, Cole. Stop being a smartass.

Understanding dawns in his eyes. He presses a fist against his mouth and coughs in obvious discomfort. I've seen this many times. The moment someone realizes I'm deaf, they get all nervous and shit. I stopped taking offense years ago.

"I'm Dr Heinemann. Are you family?"

I nod. "Cole Holloway. His younger brother."

"Can we talk outside?" He jerks his thumb toward the door.

I nod curtly and glance at the bed, before heading for the door, without checking if Dr Heinemann is following me but I feel his presence on my back. My body has learned how to recognize people around me, sense their objectives. I turn to face him. He indicates with his hand in the direction down the hallway urging me to follow him. I do, and we end up in a well-lit office.

I sit on the offered seat and lean forward watching as he rounds his desk and settles on the leather swivel chair across from me. My gaze strays around the room long enough to take in shelves filled to the brim with books and the stethoscope on his desk before focusing on him again. He leans forward, elbows propped on the hard wood surface, and takes a deep breath. His eyes are studying the folder in front of him. His chest rises on a deep inhale and he raises his ice-blue eyes to mine. Steeling myself, I nod for him to continue.

CHAPTER FIVE

Cole

FORTY-FIVE MINUTES LATER, I WALK OUT OF DR HEINEMANN'S office. My head heavy and my thoughts beating against each other. He was honest enough to tell me the truth when I asked him to lay it on me. Josh might not even make it the few weeks they predicted. He's too far gone. Chemo is no longer an option. He threw around a whole lot of medical jargon, and by the time I finally took my first deep breath, I was lightheaded. What I know now is, the cancer is no longer contained in his pancreas. The only thing being done now is to make sure he is comfortable and the pain is handled with medication. He is under hospice care to ease him into the goddamn greedy hands of death.

I stop in front of Josh's room. My head's pounding. My chest feels like a fucking void and nothing I can do at the moment will fill it.

I can't face my brother looking like this. Feeling like this.

I stalk down the hallway in search of the bathrooms. Just as I am about to follow the instructions indicating where they are, someone grabs my shoulder, spinning me around. My body tenses, hand bunched into a fist, raised. This became a knee-jerk reaction during my time in prison. You learned to be fast or someone else would be faster than you.

I blink through my hazy stare and finally focus on the familiar faces in front of me. Time stands still as I stare at my parents, unable to move. Dad has more gray hair than the last time I saw him, his eyes bracketed with crow's feet. Mom's hair is short. She looks thinner and has bags under her eyes.

God, I've missed them.

"Cole." My mom utters my name, tears rolling down her cheeks and time suddenly moves forward. I wrap my arms around her shoulders, pulling her to me. I close my eyes and bask in the comfort of her arms. Something I desperately need right now.

Fucking tears won't quit.

When I open my eyes again, I meet dad's gray ones, filled with so much emotion. He's clearly trying to hide the pain and grief of losing his child by smiling. It doesn't work. His eyes swimming in tears betray him.

Mom pulls back, holding me at arm's length as she studies me, her gaze lingering on the tattoos. She's sobbing freely as she slides her hands up to cup my face. Dad places his hands on Mom's shoulders, and gently pushes her aside, as if she were a fragile china doll. There was a point I thought they'd end up filing for divorce. I'm glad that things have gotten better since I left Florida. He still handles her like she is the most precious thing in the world. The gentleness fades as he comes at me with all of his two hundred pounds of strength. I'm bigger, though, and heavier. About twenty pounds heavier so I absorb the impact and reciprocate the embrace. I might have toughened up in prison. I might be able to face the world's fiercest storm. But when it comes to these two people standing in front of me, I feel like I'm five all over again, protected by their love and strength.

How have I managed to go so long without this?

Dad leans back to stare at me.

"Son." I read the word on his lips.

I swallow the ball of tension threatening to rip my throat open, and look at the ceiling, blinking back the tears. When I'm sure I can handle myself without clutching my mom's skirt and hiding behind it like a three-year-old, I return my parents' gaze.

"*Did you see him?*" Mom signs, automatically slipping into ASL instead of speaking. This was a habit of ours.

I nod once. "*I spoke to the doctor too.*"

Her gaze roams my face as if she's looking for answers. Her thumb brushes the tear rolling down my cheek and then she drops her hand. "*We've missed you so much. Don't ever shut us out like that again, Cole. Do you know how worried we were about you? Nine years without a word. . .*"

She breaks down and clutches onto my shirt, crying into my chest.

"I'm so sorry, Mom," I say, pressing my lips to her hair and meeting my dad's angry gaze above my mom's head. And right here, I know it was very wrong of me to shut them out. I had let my emotions take over and chose to leave everything I knew behind, including the people who loved me the most.

Who does that? I'm a selfish, son of a bitch.

God.

"Let's not do this here," my father says, gently rubbing my mom's shoulder. She frees herself from my arm, opens her handbag and rummages inside for something. Dad, the ever-loving gentleman he is, covers her trembling hand with his and tucks a white cloth handkerchief in it. Then he pulls Mom into his arms and gives her a kiss on her forehead.

Pain cuts through my chest. I remember when I was an enthusiastic nineteen-year-old boy full of romantic dreams, which Nor had stealthily injected in me. When my life was so bleak, I hoped Nor and I would mirror my mom and dad. They have a kind of love that breaks down dams and lasts forever. Nor and I had that. But it obviously wasn't supposed to last forever.

"Is Nor in there?" Mom asks.

I shake my head and tell them that Megs picked her up earlier on.

"Did you and Josh chat? You know. . .about everything?"

I frown. "Everything? You mean Cora and Joce?"

They exhale in unison and exchange a look of relief. Mom nods. "Have you met them yet?"

I shake my head. "I wanted to head out after seeing Josh. He's sleeping now so—"

Mom takes my hands in hers. "Where are you staying? Come stay with us. Please."

I should politely refuse and offer an excuse because I still need time to work out everything in my mind without anyone getting in my head. But at the same time, I need them so much it fucking hurts. I nod and I'm rewarded with the most brilliant smile ever. "I've missed you and Dad."

She cups my face in her hands and kisses my cheek. Then she digs around inside her handbag and pulls out a bunch of keys. "You will need these."

After saying our goodbyes, I take the elevator down to the parking lot. My head is pounding, sending excruciating pain down my spine. Once I'm seated inside the truck, I tug the beanie from my head, open the glove compartment and grab the bottle of painkillers I keep in there for emergencies. I twist the cap and pop two inside my mouth, recap it and toss it back. I chase them down with the bottle of water sitting in the cup holder on the console and then lean my head back on the head rest. I close my eyes and wait for the medication to do its magic.

I jolt awake suddenly, feeling as if a heavy weight is pressing on my chest. Taking deep breaths, I squint at my watch. I've been asleep for almost thirty minutes. My head feels much better although my neck is cramped from the awkward position.

After checking my phone for text messages—most of them from Tate, checking how everything is going—I roll my neck to ease the tension there, and then start the car. I have no idea where Nor lives. Plus I don't know if the girls know who I am to them.

I drag my fingers through my hair as nervousness fills my chest. I can't do this without Nor. If I'm going to meet them, I want her around. I'm excited and worried in equal measures. What if I don't make a good impression? I don't want Cora and Joce to look back one day and think that their father was a nervous wreck. Or worse.

I peel out of the parking spot and drive to the hotel.

CHAPTER SIX

Cole

AFTER TAKING A SHOWER AND PACKING MY BAGS, I HEAD DOWN TO reception with Sirius safely inside the carrier, check out and leave the hotel. I'm pushing almost fifty-two hours without sleep. I hadn't slept a lot the night before I left Boston.

I'd woken earlier than usual to double-check the floor plans for the Boston Project. Our client, Mr Kiplinger—a stubborn son of a bitch—suddenly changed his mind about the door placements and extending some rooms at the last minute. Tate had entrusted me to work the floor plans. I'd been more than happy to do it. Knowing that he trusted me enough to leave it in my hands boosted my confidence. After editing the plan in the drafting software to fit the client's instructions, which took almost half the night, I met him and Simon for breakfast the following morning to go over the plans again. And still, after the meeting, the client seemed disgruntled about something else. Eventually, Tate informed him to call our office for another appointment once he decided exactly what he wanted. Mr Kiplinger seemed to sober up after that.

Tate, the project manager—who took me under his wing when I started interning at the firm during my second year—and Simon have worked together on a few projects in the past, including the Boston

project. Tate and I met while I was volunteering at a Deaf Awareness fundraiser. He was doing pro bono work at the Western Heights
School and Center for the Deaf to make the facilities more hard-of-
hearing student oriented. We had gotten along very well because we
had a common goal. After being turned down by several companies
for their internship programs, both Simon and Tate vouched for me
and I was accepted as an architect intern at Lawrence and Barnes. No
one batted an eyelash when Tate mentioned he'd show me the ropes,
which was a good thing. Sometimes people get awkward, not sure
how to react or talk to someone who is hard of hearing.

To impress the interviewer further, I'd presented a 3D model
of a low-cost beachfront house I'd worked on the previous summer,
hoping it would help them solidify their decision to hire me. Also
having worked in my dad's firm as a teen added some weight to my
portfolio. I spent most of my free time in the studio to accrue work
experience hours needed for the architectural program. If everything
goes as planned, I should be ready to register for the licensure exams
in a year or so.

Sleeping is not a priority right now, though. My head is full of
unprocessed thoughts and things I have to come to terms with.

I take a deep breath and concentrate on getting to my destination
without causing any accidents.

Fifteen minutes later, I park the truck outside my parents' house.
My gaze drifts to the house next to it, as though some force is pulling
me toward it. Memories of the time spent here on that roof hit me
hard.

Fuck.

I can't breathe.

I grip the wheel and wait for the feeling to pass. Then I fling my
door open, grab the carrier and my bag. I stride toward the house I
grew up in, keeping my eyes averted from Nor's childhood home.

The door flies open. My little brother—I'd know that shaggy hair
of his anywhere—Nick, dashes out, barreling toward me. He skids to
a halt and throws his arms around me.

Whoa.

I set the bag and carrier down, and then wrap my arms around his shoulders.

He pulls back and lifts his hands, and signs, *"It's so good to see you, bro. Mom called to let me know you would be dropping by."*

"You should stop growing so the rest of us can catch up," I tease him.

He laughs. *"As if I would. I need to be able to look down on you all."* He glances down, then back at me. *"Who is this little guy?"*

"Sirius." The cat opens its eyes and meows in greeting. Sometimes I think this cat is half human.

Nick grabs the box from the ground and nods for me to follow him. I place a hand on his shoulder to get his attention. He stops and turns around.

"Slow down. How are you holding up?"

The smile on his face fades. He shifts on his feet, averting his eyes from mine and then blinks several times to keep the tears at bay.

"I'm trying. We're all trying." He fixes his gaze on mine and grins tiredly. "It's all about hope, right? That's something we can't afford to give up on."

He and I know that Josh's death is inevitable. Hope is like a red flag, waving in the distance. If I let myself reach for it, it will sway and all I will end up with in my hands is air.

"Don't do this, Nick. Please."

His shoulders slump forward. He blinks furiously, working his jaw. "I can't afford not to. I can't think of Josh being gone. He's my big brother for shit's sake."

"Come here."

I meet him halfway and he falls in my arms.

"Look at me," I command and he obeys, blinking tear-filled blue eyes at me. "I'm here now, all right?"

"You weren't here. You left." His nostrils flare in anger.

"You know why I left, Nick. You do, right?"

He glares at me, his jaw clenched. With a quick nod, he averts his gaze and swipes the wetness on his cheek with the back of his free hand. My hands flex beside me, fighting the urge to comfort him, but I hold back. He needs some time to work out what he is going through right now.

He rolls his shoulders, meeting my gaze again but now the anger is gone. "It fucking sucks, you know? That bastard ruined everyone's life around here." He jabs a finger toward the house next to ours.

I glance again at Nor's house, grinding my teeth. My blood boils in my veins just thinking about that asshole and I yank my gaze away back to face my brother.

"He's not around. No one knows where he is. Good riddance," he says, obviously noticing my anger. "No one lives there anymore."

I raise a brow. "Nor's mother?"

He shakes his head. "Divorced his sorry ass. She lives with some dude in Phoenix. You hungry? I can whip up something for you."

Good for her.

I nod answering his question. I can't even remember the last time I ate. "Thank fuck you asked."

Nick flashes me a smile and heads to the door. I follow him inside the house, embracing the familiarity of the place I left years ago.

Nothing has changed in here. The same brown couch with pillows of various colors arranged neatly on it, heavy wood antique table, vintage lamp hanging from the ceiling. . .all mismatched furniture from over nine years ago. The house still smells like home, warm food and security. The mantle on top of the fireplace is filled with pictures. Some of them are new. A few are of Nor and Josh with two red-headed girls sitting on their laps and grinning at the camera. I don't allow myself to stay there too long, though. I climb upstairs with my bag in hand and head to my room.

About twenty minutes later, I head back downstairs, hoping to catch up with Nick. He's leaning on the marble kitchen counter, pouring milk into a bowl for Sirius, who's greedily lapping at the sides. I glance around the kitchen with pride, taking in the elegant yet homey feel of it. When I was eighteen, my dad and I worked on upgrading this room as a gift from him to my mom for their twenty-third wedding anniversary.

I watch my little brother, his head bent toward the counter, his focus on the task of putting together a sandwich.

Shit. I've missed most of his teen years.

"How's school? What's your major?"

He lifts his gaze from the chicken sandwich he is preparing for me. "Hospital management. Florida State. It's okay so far." He pushes the plate toward me, then folds his hands on his chest and stares at me.

I take a bite of the sandwich, chew and swallow. "This is really good. You should start your own sandwich shop or something."

He grins proudly. "Thanks. It's in my five-year plan."

"Very ambitious," I say taking another huge bite.

My phone vibrates inside my pocket. I hold the sandwich with one hand and dig my phone out and swipe the screen to read the message.

Megs: **My shift at the hospital starts soon. Nor wants to go back to Josh.**

Me: **No. Distract her. I'm on the way.**

I know it's probably not my place anymore, but I can't help but feel protective of Nor.

After letting Nick know where I'm going, I grab a bottle of water from the fridge and head out to my truck, while chewing on the last piece of my meal.

I arrive at Spinner's cafe ten minutes later and spend the next three searching for a spot to park my truck. The smell of coffee and pastries immediately welcomes me as I step through the glass door. The cafe has maintained its fifties retro look, which is one of the things I loved about this place. Although I don't see any familiar faces, being inside here brings back so many memories.

I spot Megs and Nor, sitting in a booth in the furthest corner of the room. I walk past the green door with the words 'Book Nook' on it. The wooden floor vibrates beneath my feet in rhythmic beats from the song playing on the red vintage jukebox placed against the wall near the counter, with blue lights flickering on and off in intervals.

Megs waves when she sees me. Nor's head snaps up and she stiffens when our eyes meet. She whips around to glare at her friend and says something to Megs.

When I get to the table, I ask, "Ready to leave?"

Megs nods and flashes me a smile, relieved and then quickly snatches her purse from the table and stands up. I raise a brow at Nor. Her lips move as she mutters something under her breath before dragging her feet wearily. I notice again how thin she is. If I wasn't deaf, I'm sure I'd have heard a few bones rattle against each other, having nothing to support them.

I head for the cashier's counter and pay for their tab, despite Megs' protests, and then follow them out. Megs stands on the tip of her toes to kiss my cheek and says that she's about to start her shift at the hospital. She gives Nor a quick hug and tells her she'll call her later.

Nor spares me a nervous glance and signs, "*She'll drop me at the hospital,*" before shuffling after her friend.

Hell, no.

My fingers wrap around her upper arm, pulling her back to my side. She jerks her head up, her eyes widening in surprise. I nod to my truck parked a few blocks down. She looks over her shoulder to Megs, but she's already seated in her car.

She jerks her arm from my grip. "I need to go back to the hospital. I'll go get some rest as soon as Ben and Maggie get there."

"My parents are already there. You need to eat and get some rest. I'm taking you home."

Her eyes flare with anger, her cheeks filling with color. Her indignation seems to boost some energy inside her. She straightens to her full height of five feet, hardly hitting my chin, and looking like a very pissed off fairy.

I scowl down at her and jerk my chin toward the truck. "Let's go."

Her shoulders slump in defeat. She turns to follow me, stumbling twice and then pulling her small frame back upright.

Christ, she can hardly carry her own weight she's so exhausted. Without any warning, I scoop her up in my arms and cradle her to my chest.

Her lips part in surprise. "What the hell, Cole? Put me down."

"If you don't stop it, I'm going to toss you over my shoulder." I glare at her.

She squirms, fighting for me to release her, but finally gives up and wraps her arms around my neck to minimize her body from being jostled. A few seconds later, she leans her head on my shoulder.

I bite back a groan as her scent slams into me.

Her hair is about an inch from my nose. I can't resist the pull to her any longer. I lower my head, breathing her in. I feel some kind of peace I haven't experienced in a long time settle over me, which makes me angry at myself for allowing that to happen.

I lengthen my strides, eager to get to the truck and put some distance between us. I halt in front of the Suburban and balance her in my arms which is no huge feat, given how light she is. I dig out my keys from my jeans pocket. After opening the car door, I duck in and sit her on the seat then stand back as she buckles the belt with fidgety fingers. I shut the door, round the car and slide onto my seat. Then I realize I have no idea where she lives. I angle my body to face her at the same time she peeks up at me.

"What's your address?"

She yawns. "We live in my grandma's house."

My gaze automatically goes to the flower shop across from the cafe. I shove the key into the ignition and dart a glance at her. "What happened to Phoebe's?"

She sighs and shuts her eyes for a few seconds. They flutter open again. There's so much pain in them it hurts just to stare into their green depths.

"I run it now. Grandma Phoebe passed away a few years ago."

My fingers itch to tuck those strands of hair behind her ear. Pull her to my chest. Comfort her.

Instead, I tighten my hold on the wheel. "I'm sorry."

She stares into my eyes for a few seconds. I can see questions locked in there, fighting to break free. It's a wonder she hasn't exploded yet with whatever she's holding inside her chest.

"Why didn't you reply to my letters, Cole?" Her eyes are bright with tears. "I don't blame you for not wanting to have anything to do with me. I'd probably have done the same thing if I were in your shoes. . ." She pauses and inhales deeply. "I wanted them to know you so badly."

I try and fail miserably to think of a suitable excuse. "I'm sorry. I was wrong to ignore the letters."

Her features soften immediately and she lifts her hands from her lap and signs, "*I'm not blaming you. I just need to understand. Please make me understand.*" She stops and rubs her eyes with the heel of her hand. "*I got the private mail box address you were sharing with Simon from his mom. She also gave me your home address. I wrote you letters, hoping to get a reply from you. But I never received any letters. Josh flew to New York to search for you, but when he got to the address, the landlord informed him that you had moved houses.*"

I drag my fingers through my hair, tugging it back in frustration. I can't bring myself to tell her how much I hated her and Josh. How much I craved her smile, her touch every night, and then hated her all over again in the morning. I would rather she thinks I'm a jerk, but I can't hurt her like that.

I rub my forehead, feeling drained. "*Tell me what to expect when we get to your house. Please.*"

She shakes her head and quickly wipes the tears on her cheeks. "*They think Josh is their father. I've tried so many times to tell them the truth over the years, but with every passing month, year I didn't hear from you, doubts filled me. What if you weren't interested in being part of the girls' lives? How could I explain that to Cora and Joce? Your mother thought it would be good for them to learn ASL. She always believed you'd come back. I continued to send the letters, batting away at the fears though. I knew you received them. I made sure I sent them through*" *certified mail to make sure they got to you.*

"Maybe I'm selfish for not telling the girls the truth. I wanted them to grow up in a home where they felt loved and wanted. I grew up wondering if my father loved me and my sisters, or if he was living in regret for having us. Oh, God. you will never know how sorry I am for the way things turned out."

Silence falls between us.

I understand what she is saying. I know where she is coming from and I know the truth in her words. Her father was a sad excuse for a DNA donor.

Fuck. I can't think right now. So much has happened, misunderstandings and missed opportunities, which could have been easily solved if I hadn't been so stubborn.

I turn my focus on the road as I back out of the parking spot. Her fingers touch my forearm. Fire ignites where her small hand is pressed to my skin, spreading all over my body. Rekindling the dark places I've hidden away from myself. It's distracting. It's dangerous. And right now unwanted, even though everything in me screams in need. Wanting more. Wanting less.

I shake her hand off and send her a quick glare. "Don't touch me."

I see her shrink away from me from the corner of my eye.

I sigh, cursing myself for the harsh words. Her touch combined with the way she looked at me in the hospital and everything she said has me on edge. My body is coiled tight, and even an innocent touch from her can set me off. I don't need any kind of distractions right now. I can't afford to tangle myself up in emotions that will only end up hurting me. Us.

By the time I pull up in front of the house, Nor has already dozed off in her seat. I study her face, so peaceful and carefree in sleep. Her mouth is parted and her eyes flicker behind the lids. A small frown appears on her head. Her lips move quickly, then stop before she settles back into sleep.

I shake my head to get rid of those stupid feelings balled up in my chest and focus my gaze on the two-story house. Clenching my hands around the wheel, I inhale deeply to calm my fucking heart. I'm about to meet my daughters, who don't know that I'm their father. SHIT. I understand Nor's point of view, but it still hurts like a motherfucker. I wish the girls and I were meeting under different circumstances.

I get out of the truck. After scooping her up from the seat, I adjust her in my arms, kick the door shut and stride up the little path that leads to the house. Every step, bringing me closer to my daughters. The door flies open all of a sudden. Nor's sister, Elise ducks her head out, eyes wide when she sees me, followed by a huge grin. She pushes the pink dyed strands of hair away from her face.

Good to know she hasn't lost her sunny disposition. Nor will definitely need her sister if. . .when Josh leaves us.

"Oh my gosh. Cole! When did you arrive?" Her entire body radiates joy. That smile disappears when she sees her sister in my arms. "Is she okay?"

I glance at Nor. "She's fucking exhausted. She needs to lie down for a few hours."

Elise ushers me in. I follow her upstairs and down a hallway with polished wooden floors and walls painted in a soft pink, completely different from the floral wallpapered walls her grandmother had when I last visited this house. We enter a room, which I assume is Nor's. A double bed sits in the middle of it and I stride forward and carefully lay Nor on top of the bed. I slip her shoes off, reach for the folded blanket at the foot of the bed and cover her petite frame.

Standing inside this room, knowing that Josh and Nor spent their time in here, Josh touching her, Nor groaning in pleasure, tears me apart. I startle when Elise touches my shoulder, then she's pulling me into a hug.

"It's so good to see you Cole."

I smile at her as we walk out of the room. "Same here." We head back downstairs and into the kitchen where my steps falter and my heart literally stops beating at the sight in front of me. The lump in my throat is growing bigger by the second.

Joce and Cora.

My daughters.

I inhale deeply, that action kick starting my heart and it beats fast. So fast I feel like I'm losing my breath.

The picture in my pocket didn't do them justice.

Elise once again touches my arm, her eyes full of understanding, and it makes me feel that she somehow knows what's running through my head. She stares into my eyes as if to warn me or pass on an important message. "Girls, I'd like you to meet Cole."

The girls stop whatever they're doing and look up, and then walk towards us, their eyes all sorts of curious.

"*I know who he is. Uncle Cole,*" one of the girls signs, grinning wide. "*Mom and Dad talked so much about you but they never said you'd be so tall.*"

In that second, I die a million deaths. My fucking heart crashes to my feet, shattering into a million worthless pieces.

Uncle Cole.

I flex my hands at my sides as regret threatens to choke me. I ignored all those letters Nor sent me because of my stupid pride and rage. Then anger fills my veins. How could I have known we had kids together? I don't even know where to find my balance on this issue.

Seeing them with my own eyes, it hits me all over again how identical and pretty they are; their waist length red hair, bright gray eyes, all the way down to the cute dimples on the right side of their cheeks.

"That's Jocelyn over there." Elise touches her hand on the shoulder of the girl clutching a copy of *Charlotte's Web* close to her chest. "And that's Cora." She gestures at the hyper girl, who is hopping on her feet, hardly containing her excitement.

I dart a glance between them and see the subtle difference. Joce is slightly taller than Cora. I sigh, relieved that I'm able to tell the difference between my daughters.

Jocelyn shakes my hand and signs, "*Mom and Dad call me Joce, so you can call me that too. It's great to meet you Uncle Cole.*"

"*It's very nice to meet you, Joce,*" I tell her. Her lips lift into a small smile, then she shuffles toward the couch and sits down primly. Then Cora throws herself at me with her entire weight, hugging my waist. And in that moment, every negative emotion fades. I'm filled with wonder and awe and love as I hold my daughter.

Elise turns to me and says, "The girls are amazing at signing."

I nod, completely floored. My family thought about me even though I'd turned my back on them. "They are so good at it. It's amazing."

After the introductions are over, I step back and Elise says something to Joce and Cora. They nod solemnly in return. She tells me that she asked them not to disturb Nor.

Cora grabs my hand all of a sudden and pulls me toward the living room, where a small desk stands next to the floor-to-ceiling windows. Dropping my hand, she opens the first drawer and pulls out a sketchbook and starts flipping through the pages.

She pauses and peers up at me. *"Mama praises you a lot. She says you can draw like a wizard. I told her I want to be like you when I grow up."* She points at the sketch of a butterfly so similar to the one I drew a long time ago and gave to Nor on her seventeenth birthday.

Cora's drawings are really good. Probably much better than mine were when I was her age.

"I asked her if I could keep it," she says shyly, her ears and cheeks turning pink. *"I hope I will be as good as you one day."*

"Can I see that?"

She nods. I bend down, our heads almost touching and flip through her book.

My fascination soon turns into something else. Gone is the uncertainty I felt before, replaced by admiration and pride, and a certain feeling of connection to this lovely girl who is staring at me as if I hung the moon in the sky. I raise my head and look around the room as a feeling close to kinship flows through me. Joce is still sitting with her hands folded in her lap on the couch, her gaze intense, studying me. And once again, those gray eyes leave me breathless. My heart is attaching itself to Cora and Joce. Fast.

CHAPTER SEVEN

A HAND TAPS ME SOFTLY ON MY SHOULDER. I RAISE MY HEAD AND meet Elise's gaze. Gone is the smile, replaced by a grim look. Her face is pale and her bottom lip quivers slightly.

That look on her face sends chills through my blood. "Are you okay?"

She shakes her head, her gaze darting between Cora and Joce, then mouths, "We need to talk." I follow her as she heads for the kitchen. "Your mom called. It's Josh. He's taken a turn for the worse. His body is shutting down faster than the doctors anticipated." Tears fill her eyes and roll down her cheeks. "He was asking for you."

Fuck. "I need to get to the hospital. Now."

She nods quickly, and spares a glance over my shoulder toward the twins. "I'll wake Nor. I can't tell them—" She stops and swipes her palm on her cheeks.

"I'll wait down here," I tell her.

I start to pace, my hands clenched into fists on my side. I hope we get to the hospital on time. I notice Cora waving to catch my attention from the corner of my eye. I stop and face her.

"*Is everything okay*?" she signs. I glance at Joce, sitting stiffly on the couch her entire focus on me.

What the hell do I tell them? I have no idea how much they know about Josh's condition or what Nor told them. How do I tell them that the father they have known all their lives is dying? How do I break my daughters' hearts without destroying mine?

Taking a deep breath, I walk to the couch and gesture for Cora to join us.

I clear my throat and then reach out and take each of their hands in mine. They don't pull away so I figure they are okay with the contact.

"Do you know why your daddy is in the hospital?" I glance at their faces to gauge their reaction.

Joce nods solemnly. "Mama says he is very sick."

I look at Cora. Gone is the bouncy girl I met half an hour ago. Her eyes fill with tears and her bottom lip quivers as she nods.

I feel my eyes burn with suppressed tears, imagining they have lived with this knowledge for a while now.

"Grandma Maggie called. Your daddy wants to see us. All of us."

Their tiny faces brighten immediately and I have no idea how to tell them that Josh might be asking to see us for the last time. I just can't do it.

Unable to hold back any longer, I slip both of my arms around their waists and hug them. "I think you two are the bravest girls I've ever met. Keep your heads up and keep on moving," I tell them when we pull apart.

"Daddy always says that," Cora says, wiping her cheeks. Her gaze moves over my shoulder. "Aunt Elise, Uncle Cole says daddy wants to see us."

I shift my body to face Elise and I see Nor trailing behind her sister, the shadows around her eyes look darker.

"*Yes, he does,*" Elise signs, shooting me a grateful look. "*Come on, little darlings.*"

I drop my hands and the girls dash toward Nor. Her face transforms from worry to delight as she smooths the girls' hair and then kisses their foreheads. She looks my way from over the top of our daughters' heads, nodding subtly before turning and herding them out the door. Dragging my fingers through my hair, I stand up and follow, my feet heavy with trepidation.

We finally arrive at the hospital and rush to the waiting area where Mom, Dad and Nick are seated, focused on Dr. Heinemann as he speaks. Megs stands beside him, her hands shoved inside the pockets of her blue scrubs. Mom seems to have aged since I last saw her this morning. She's holding Dad's hand tightly. I don't realize I've been staring in their direction for a long time until Mom stands up and walks toward me.

"I forgot to ask for your number. Josh was asking for you. Even weak with pain and drowsy from the medication they gave him, he kept murmuring your name over and over."

I swallow hard and nod.

The doctor walks toward us and Mom stops talking, and faces the doctor with a hopeful look on her face. It breaks my heart to see her like this. Dr Heinemann looks grim, his lips drawn in a thin line. He starts to speak and I have to watch his lips intently so I don't miss a word.

"He wants to see all of you but insists to speak to his brother first and then his wife and children." He glances at me. "In normal occasions, we advise no more than two visitors at a time. But in this case, we'll make an exception."

I trail after the doctor, shoving my clammy hands into the pockets of my pants. We stop outside Josh's room, and after the doctor advises me to keep the conversation between me and my brother light, he walks away.

Light? Is he kidding?

Shaking my head, I push the door open. The atmosphere has shifted since I was here earlier today. It's heavier, as if death is hovering just around the corner, waiting to snatch him up at any time.

CHAPTER EIGHT

Josh

FIVE CRACKS. THERE ARE FIVE CRACKS ON THE CEILING. I COULD close my eyes and tell you exactly where they are positioned.

I've been lying in this bed for far too long. My only source of entertainment —when the pain becomes unbearable, when regret comes flooding in—is to focus on those cracks.

The nurse gave me a shot of pain medication before she left. My body feels lethargic. Painless. It's finally giving up, though. I've been holding on for too long, waiting for Cole. Now, I can finally let go. I never knew a person could put death on hold by sheer will, but I think I succeeded in doing that. Or God somehow answered my prayers.

Whichever.

I'm grateful my parents and Nor contacted him when they did. I wanted to be the one to tell him I was dying. I wanted to talk to him before I left this world. Ask him to give Nor the benefit of the doubt. I never set out to hurt Cole. I never contemplated marrying Nor, until the day I stepped through the front door of her house and saw her father's furious face so full of vengeance.

Yes. I wanted her the moment she moved in next door. I was twenty-one and a savvy flirt. I'd lie in bed at night and think about the girl with innocent green eyes, a dimple and a constant look of pain in her stare. Just looking into her eyes, I knew. The scars on her body proved it. I knew she'd had a difficult past. I wanted to protect her. Wipe away the bad and give her a clean slate.

I never did though. She already belonged to someone else.

My brother.

Nor was Cole's from the second he laid eyes on her. The connection was powerful. Every time she walked into a room, or Cole's gaze was on her, his face would soften and his lips pulled into a smile. Every time Cole looked at Nor, she'd bloom under his stare.

I'd never seen my brother's attention claimed by a girl the way it was by Nor. His life had drastically changed when he became sick, leading to his hearing loss. He'd always been so serious, his nose constantly buried in books, or drawing. Then Nor dropped into our lives. And everything changed.

What Nor and I did to him is unforgiveable. I'm not sure we had a choice in the matter though. Sometimes we make the hardest of choices, hoping that one day we will be granted forgiveness. As much as I'd like to put my mind to rest, tell him what happened on the day he came home from prison, I can't. Nor insists it's her cross to bear. She blames herself for landing him in prison in the first place. I promised her I'd keep my mouth shut.

I have one more chance to convince him not to give up on her. He still owns her heart, even though he doesn't know it.

The door silently opens and Cole steps inside, his gaze finding mine. He slips his beanie off his head, shoves his hands inside his pockets and walks toward me.

I sigh and settle back into my pillows.

He has to listen to me. If he doesn't, I'll just have to use the dying card. Cruel, I know. But what choice do I have if he doesn't cooperate?

CHAPTER NINE

Cole

Josh lowers his eyes from the ceiling when I walk in. His fingers are intertwined on his stomach, the thumbs twitching every so often.

Taking a deep breath, I stop at the foot of his bed and just stare at him, feeling helpless as fuck. His weary eyes shift to look over my shoulder before returning back to my face.

"Nor and the girls?"

I clear my throat and have to look away, focusing instead on what's going on outside the window in Josh's room. The curtains have been drawn and the orange light of the setting sun filters through the glass. A flock of birds fly by, swooping low in unison before disappearing out of sight. "They are waiting outside."

His shoulders droop as if relieved. Wetting his cracked lips, he lifts his hand and waves me toward the bed weakly, like a king urging his subject to come closer.

I roll my eyes, and I have to fight the urge to laugh. "Yes, your high assholeness." I sit on the chair that has become a fixture next to the bed.

He smirks, but flinches when he moves slightly to adjust his body. "I might as well take advantage of this. Besides, you can't deny I look good ordering your ass around."

I chuckle, shaking my head.

He shrugs. "They shot me with more painkillers, dude. I'm high as a kite right now." He grins lopsidedly.

He looks down at his intertwined fingers and when he raises his head back up, the bliss on his face has been replaced with an urgent, desperate look. "We need to talk before Nor and the girls come in here." He takes a deep breath and I wait, my hands automatically fisting on my thighs. "Doc says my body is shutting down." His speech has considerably slowed down in the few minutes I've been in here. "I can feel it. So I need to talk to you before I'm too weak to say shit."

"You just had to go out with a bang, didn't you?" I ask, blinking hard to stop the damn tears from falling.

His shoulders shake as he chuckles. "It was the only way to get you to listen."

He tries to sit upright, but his body buckles beneath his meager weight. I stand up and help him, adjusting the pillows to support his head and back, then start pacing beside his bed without taking my focus off of him. I'm too anxious to sit down.

Questions are fighting for release in my chest but one look at Josh makes me stop. I watch his head roll back and his eyes fall shut. His face contorts as if he's in pain, and when he opens his eyes again, they are damp with tears.

His chest expands and contracts as he struggles to take air into his lungs. Finally, he runs his tongue along his cracked lips, and levels his gaze at me.

"Remember when Nor moved in next door?" Josh waits until I nod before he continues. "I have never seen you look at anyone like that, Cole. You looked at her like she was your world, like you had the ability to look into her past, her pain, her future. Your future. With little ColeNor brats waddling around in diapers.

"Please. . .just don't judge her. Listen to her first, okay? You know Nor. You know her heart. And you *know* she would've never done anything to hurt you. She would have done everything in her power to keep you safe, just like you would have for her, which you did. You two are simply crazy. You'd rather get killed while trying to save each other." His face is flushed from exertion. A bout of coughing interrupts his words. "She's still in love with you."

His chest is rising and falling fast. "Take care of her and the girls. Please promise me that, Cole. Be there for her. Our girls will need you when I'm gone. Nor has been waiting a lifetime for you. If there's anyone to blame, please blame me."

"Okay. Okay. I blame you, okay? Just calm down, please. I'll take care of her," I say desperately, but then the words I just committed to resound in my ears. "No. No. Nor is your wife. You can't ask me to do that. I'll make sure they're okay. Every day. But my life is in New York, Josh. I can't. . ." I try and fail to gather my words. My thoughts. This is insane. He is insane.

Wiping my eyes, I glance back to the bed, to the body that was once muscular. Healthy. Strong. Now mere bones held together by skin.

I shuffle back to his bedside and reclaim my seat. Lifting my hands, I sign, "*God, Josh. She is your wife—*"

He jerks forward using most of his strength and grabs my hand, clutching it in desperation. "Only in name and by law. But her heart. . .it has never belonged to anyone but you. She still loves you. Always has. I want someone. . .not just anyone. . .you. I want you to be there when I'm gone. I want you, no. . .I need you to be the one she falls back on when I'm gone. Please."

I blink hard as tears burn the corners of my eyes.

Why did I hold onto my anger for so long? I've missed so many opportunities; time I would have spent with the people I love.

He squeezes my hand, his eyes intense. "I know what you are thinking. Don't live your life in regret and blame. The past happened and there's nothing you or I can do to change that."

Josh drops my hand and curls into a ball as a series of coughs threaten to tear his already wasted body into pieces.

God, no!

I lunge for the nurse call button and press it repeatedly, my eyes fixed on him. My heart's in my throat as I stare helplessly, unable to do anything to ease his suffering.

Soon, nurses pour into the room. Someone pushes me aside, but I'm too dazed to protest or even hold my own weight. I stumble back several steps until my back hits a wall. I feel as though I'm watching everything that is happening in front of me from outside my body. Suddenly, there is a commotion that has nothing to do with the nurses trying to save my brother, and everything to do with Josh fighting them. Instinctively, I rush to the bed only to find him thrashing, his wide eyes filled with absolute desperation. I zoom in on his lips, but he's sentences are interrupted by brutal jolts from his body.

"Where. . .he? I need. . .him. Now!"

One of the nurses says something but my sole focus is on Josh. I shoulder my way through the throng of people and yell, "I'm here, bro. I'm here."

The frantic look in his eyes ceases for just a few seconds when he sees me. "I love you, Cole."

His upper body slumps back on the bed in exhaustion, but that isn't what sends more tears running down my face.

No.

It's the peaceful smile stretching his mouth. I stand there, frozen to my spot, watching as his shallow breaths slow to a stop.

His eyes stay open as life fades from them, leaving them empty. My gaze flies to the telemetry monitor next to his bed, and I watch as the numbers drop until a continuous flat line appears. I keep staring at it, waiting for the line to change its pattern.

Nothing.

Everything stops. I see the nurses exchange grim looks and then shake their heads. I blink, lifting my gaze to the window, noticing the yellow and golden jagged lining as the sun sinks beyond the skies.

Taking in a shuddering breath, I stagger out of the room. I stand in the hallway, pain ripping through me. My hands curl into fists, and I slam them on the wall.

Fuck. Fuck, fuck!

Someone touches my arm.

"Just leave me the fuck alone."

More tugging. I jerk my head up and glare at the intruder.

Nor's eyes widen as she searches my face. "Josh?"

I try to bring some kind of control to my emotions, my heart dying as I take in Nor's expectant stare, and shake my head. It's all I can give her.

She covers her mouth with a hand as tears roll down her face. I shift around to grab her in a hug and I see Cora and Joce staring up at me from behind their mother, their eyes round and lips trembling.

"No," Joce says, shaking her head. "My daddy can't be dead. You're a liar. He is not dead. Dad. . ."

I can't take it anymore. In a little over fifty-five hours, I've lost my brother and found out I'm a father. And still, nothing makes a single bit of sense.

Something gently tugs the back of my shirt. I stop mid-stride and look over my shoulder. Little Cora is looking at me through red eyes, tears falling down her eyes.

"*Please don't go*," she signs. "*Please.*"

Fear, loss, and panic fill her small features. Turning around, I drop to my knees, wrap my arms around her and hold her close. Her body trembles as her arms circle my neck.

I shut my eyes tight. I wish I could take away this fucking pain crippling her body. I tuck a thumb under her chin, lift it up and wait until she meets my gaze. "I'm not leaving. I promise."

I have no idea how to console my own daughter. How will I be a good father to these precious girls, if the thought of doing something wrong cripples me? I've spent the last thirty years just taking care of me. How will I know what they need? What if I mess up being a dad?

Christ. I can't afford to think like that. I will do everything in my power to be the father they deserve. The best father I can be.

When I open my eyes again, Nor and Joce are huddled together, Nor's hand moving in circles on our daughter's back to soothe her. I climb to my feet, taking Cora with me, and bridge the space between us, slipping my arm around Nor. I pull her and Joce to my chest.

I pull back and swallow hard. I'm not going to cry in front them. Right now, it's about them. I kiss each of their foreheads. Nor's lips are pressed in a straight line, her lashes wet and her eyes bright with tears she's trying to hold back—for Cora and Joce's sake, I'm sure.

"We need to go back to tell—" I hesitate and clear my throat. My parents and Nick. They need to know. They didn't even get a chance to say goodbye. Nor and the girls didn't either.

Joce, my quiet, sweet daughter tightens her fingers on my T-shirt as though she never wants to let go. I glance up at Nor. She nods, smiling softly and I watch as one tear, then a second one rolls down her face.

She smooths Joce's hair first, then Cora's, in a comforting gesture, but her focus is on me. "Thank you for coming back home and for being here for the girls. And me."

Those words hit me right in my chest, warming me. Feeling needed.

Balancing Cora on one arm, I crouch and lift her sister with my free arm and adjust them against my body. They both tuck their heads in the crook of my neck. A sense of completion fills my chest as I walk down the hallway toward the waiting area.

I can't control what happened to Josh. I can't even begin to process it right now. All I can do is keep moving, because if I stop to think about it, the grief will swallow me whole. Focusing on the girls is what I need to do. I will make sure I'm here for them.

The rest will have to wait.

PART TWO

PAST

Being deeply loved by someone gives you strength,
while loving someone deeply gives you courage.
~ Lao Tzu

CHAPTER TEN

Nor

The moment the moving truck pulls up in front of the two-story house with a navy blue painted exterior on Pineway Drive, I flip the door handle open. I grab the last of the lemon drops from the plastic bag and pop it inside my mouth and then hop out, eager to leave the confined space I've been sharing with my family for the last six hours. That was the last time my dad stopped to refill the tank. Dad flat out refused to make more than one stop. He said we needed to be in Willow Hill before nightfall.

I look around while shaking my legs to get rid of the stiffness there, then stare at the house in front of me. It's similar to the ones on this street. The front lawn is a bit shabby, though. The grass is missing in some areas and there are no flowers to boast of. With a little TLC, though, it could flourish.

I don't care as long as we have a place to live and sleep. I hope that Dad doesn't get another promotion because it would mean us moving again.

Behind the house is a line of trees, which I guess is the Pineway Woods. I googled the location before we moved here to Willow Hill, Florida. Thank goodness for Google Earth, as I now have more information about this town.

Population: 68,023

Next popular destination: Jacksonville and Gainesville.

I turn around, ready to open the trunk, but stop when something catches my attention out of the corner of my eye.

Not something. Someone.

Two boys are standing on the front lawn of the house next to the one we're moving in to. The only difference between the two houses is the exterior, since theirs is gray in color.

One of the boys is a foot taller and looks older. Older than me anyway, but not by much. He's wearing an easy smile on his face, tossing a basketball between his hands. Even from here, I can see his eyes are a brilliant blue, like the Caribbean. He waves in our general direction in greeting and I reciprocate. The second boy lingers a step back, as though he doesn't want to be noticed.

I notice everything about him, though. The black beanie on his head, the black wife-beater, the way the shorts hug his hips, his wide shoulders, his lanky form, angular jaw, full lips and lastly, his deep set gray eyes. There is nothing Caribbean in them. They are stormy, like his features. His gaze on me is intense and searching. When he hones in on my forearms, they widen, probably taking in the scars there. I swear I hear his sharp intake of breath from where I'm standing. He lifts those stormy grays to my face. I don't see pity, just a million questions and something else I've never seen in the eyes of the opposite sex before.

Interest. Awareness. Its swiftness and fierceness as it sweeps through me, leaves me shaking in my sky-blue Keds.

God.

Is it even possible for someone to look at you as if they totally get you? Someone you had no idea existed until the very moment you met?

Clenching my jaw, I inhale, somehow finding the strength to glare at the boy who has managed to make me shiver. I cross my arms on my chest and raise a brow, challenging his stare. He narrows those astounding eyes at me, but I'm not about to give him an inch of me. I already gave him too much when my body betrayed how his perusal affected me. I doubt I have the ability to even walk right now. Honestly, he's intimidating as hell. I feel drawn to him, which is insane. We just met. Things like this don't happen in the real world. They don't happen to me.

Or do they?

I'm insane, which is why I need to keep my distance from him.

Stormy Eyes has given a whole new meaning to the word interesting.

"Hello boys!" my mother chirps from somewhere behind me, effectively drawing my attention away from Stormy Eyes.

"Darn it, Caroline. Do you have to yell like that?" Dad's voice is like a whip, slashing through the air, sending a chill down my spine.

Mom inhales sharply and falls silent for a few seconds. I peer over my shoulder at her and my heart aches all over again. I still don't understand why she stays with him. I keep hoping that one day she will pack up and leave, taking me and my sisters with her.

Her gaze drops to the floor and I know she's shoving those words inside the little box that has my father's name on it. The box where all the yelling, snarling and insults live. The only place she can store them in order to keep our family together. There's one thing I've learned in my seventeen years on this earth: the hand that feeds you can quickly turn to be the one that destroys you. Sticks and stones may break bones, but words have the power to crush a person's spirit.

Mom clears her throat and forces a cheery smile, hiding her broken spirit behind a bright facade.

"How are you?" she asks the two boys in a lower tone.

Blue Eyes tucks the ball under his left arm and gestures with his hands toward Stormy Eyes. His hands move in fluid movements, and I realize he's saying something. With his hands. They are using ASL to communicate with each other. Blue Eyes tosses the ball on their lawn and the boys make their way toward us. Stormy Eyes hangs back a little when they stop in front of us.

"These are my daughters, Elon, Elise and Eleanor," my mom says, smiling wide. "I'm Caroline and that is my husband Stephen."

I wiggle my fingers in a wave and mumble unintelligibly, "Nor." They stare at me blankly and I realize they probably didn't understand what I said. Gah! Why do I get nervous when I meet new people? I huff a breath of frustration and clear my throat. "You can call me Nor."

My dad's gaze moves between the two boys before settling on Stormy Eyes. He narrows his eyes and his lips tighten as if he's irritated. How can he be put out by someone he met only five seconds ago?

Blue Eyes clears his throat and says, "It's great to meet you all. Welcome to the neighborhood." He smiles nervously, obviously shaken by my dad's stern perusal, even though it mostly wasn't directed at him.

He's hot, especially with the dark locks of hair falling on his forehead like that. "I'm Josh Holloway and that's my brother, Cole," he says while signing at the same time in Cole's direction. Then he jabs a thumb over his shoulder, indicating the boy sitting on their porch surrounded by toy cars and says, "and that's our younger brother, Nick." Nick waves at us, but my attention is once again stolen by Stormy Eyes.

Cole.

Cole.

Cole.

The name suits him. It's mysterious just like its owner.

Cole is staring at me again with those eyes that seem to say nothing and everything at the same time. He's touching me without even being close to me. Sounds silly, right? I can't even believe that thought passed through my head because admitting it actually means a couple of physics laws are being broken right this second. But then, I've never experienced such a strong pull towards another person before.

His gaze darts to my chest and I look down. Heat floods my face. Crap.

The first three buttons of my dress have popped open, revealing my white bra and too much boob and skin. My fingers fly up and fasten the damn things and then I peek at Cole. He coughs, his cheeks and ears flushing, and averts his eyes.

"Need help taking the boxes inside?" Josh asks, his gaze moving between my mom and dad and the truck full of boxes. "My brother and I would be happy to help."

"That would be lovely," Mom says, at the same time my dad turns around, ignoring Josh's words. He grabs a box from the truck and stalks toward the front door.

Josh faces his brother and signs. Cole glances at the truck, then the house and nods. He exhales long and hard, as though he has been holding *his* breath for ages, grabs a box from Josh's hands and strides toward my new home.

I take deep breaths to ease the giddiness infecting my brain. My stomach tightens and my boobs do this tingling thing. I can totally empathize with my girls. Cole's focus on them is the most attention they've gotten since. . .well, ever. Unless you count my hands, body wash and my washing sponge. I had a boyfriend a while back. Our relationship lasted a month. His stare wasn't anywhere close to being as potent as Cole's.

"Drool-alert. You need to wipe your mouth, sis," my fourteen-year-old sister, Elise, whispers beside me with a giggle before she walks toward the house.

I laugh and follow her, carrying two small boxes, and almost topple over when Josh bounds out of the house.

"It's great to have a redhead in our neighborhood." Josh flashes me a bright smile and winks, then walks back out to the moving truck.

I set the boxes on the porch and wait for Cole to come out. I want to get a good look at his butt. It's cute in those cargo shorts he's wearing. It's not saggy at all, just tight, grabable. Just because I'm keeping my distance doesn't mean I can't look.

The thought of seeing him makes my heart beat irregularly and my palms clammy. Definitely not attractive.

What the hell is wrong with me? This is the first guy to cast a look anywhere close to resembling interest and I'm behaving like an idiot.

"New neighbors," a woman says in a sultry voice.

Startled, I turn around to face a woman with dark hair and blue eyes whose feature are strikingly similar to Josh and Cole's. As she walks up the path leading to our house, she freezes mid step and pales as her gaze meets my dad's. My father stiffens and I swear I hear him gasp, but I might be wrong. My father never gasps. Nothing fazes him. Nothing ever shakes the almighty Lieutenant Blake.

But this woman's voice did.

His shoulders lift as he takes a deep breath, recollecting himself one piece at a time, before turning to face the newcomer.

"Stephen?" Her voice is almost a whisper as she utters that name. They know each other?

"Maggie," my father says her name with familiarity. Reverence. The hard, dominant edge of his voice gone. "How have you been?"

He doesn't sound surprised at all to see her. Maggie, on the other hand, looks like she's about to faint.

"You moved. . .here?"

He straightens, his lips pulling into an easy smile. The look is so alien on his face, it's disturbing. "We just got here." He turns to look at me and clears his throat. I've never seen him nervous. A red flag is waving madly inside my head.

Who is Maggie to him?

"Eleanor, go inside. I'll be there in a second." The hard edge in his voice returns, and with it, the coldness that always sends me running. The faded scar running diagonally across his right cheek tightens as he narrows his eyes at me in warning when I fail to follow his orders.

My curiosity prompts me to swivel on my heel and directly face Maggie, momentarily ignoring my father. It's a stupid move and I might pay for this later, given the muscle twitching on my father's hard jaw. I'm too intrigued to care about the repercussions. Maggie eyes me warily, clutching her heaving chest with one hand. Her fingers fiddling with the silver necklace around her neck with the other.

I retrace my steps down the path and stop in front of Maggie. "I'm Nor." I stick my hand out to her in greeting.

She hesitates at first, her gaze shifting briefly to my dad and then back to me, nervously. "Margaret Holloway."

I step aside when Mom joins us. They shake hands, but I don't miss the tension, which has heightened rather quickly in the past five seconds.

Turning away, my thoughts spinning, I head back to the porch then grab the two boxes and straighten.

"Oomph!" A set of hands grab my shoulders to stop my backward descent. "Watch where you're—" I manage to utter the words, but my body does that annoying shivering thing again, making me aware of the body plastered to the front of me.

"Sorry. Are you okay?"

The shock of hearing him speak jolts me upright, bringing me face to chest with him. His voice has a somewhat husky, breathy quality to it, and it softly curls around some consonants. I can't really describe it, but I can definitely say it needs a little getting used to.

God. He is tall. And his gaze is completely focused on my mouth.

"Eleanor?" Cole says.

I look away, flustered by his attention and mumble, "I'm good."

I feel his hand on my cheek, turning me to face him, the entire span of his palm covering the left side of my face and right there, I decide I love his hands. Big and strong and calloused. Those hands are made for doing things like carrying heavy stuff and gently cupping faces.

"I need to see your lips to understand what you're saying. Are you okay?"

Oh crap.

"Sorry. Yes, I am." I quickly take a step back, moving away from his space so I can bring my racing heart under control. "Thanks for . . .um. . .breaking my fall."

He nods and drops his hands before spinning around and striding purposefully down the porch, his hands clenched into fists at his sides. He leaps over the little fence that separates our houses and disappears through his front door.

CHAPTER ELEVEN

Cole

I NEED TO GET MY SHIT TOGETHER. HOW CAN A GIRL I'VE NEVER MET before shake me to my very core like Nor does?

I take off toward the little white fence which separates our houses and hop over it, leaving Mom, Josh and Nick to get acquainted with our new neighbors. Besides, I'm not sure what to think of the way Nor's dad, Stephen, was staring at me. Scary as shit. I wonder what he said to Nor's mom. She clearly seems afraid of him.

Right off the bat, I don't like him. But that doesn't stop my fascination with his daughter.

Nor.

Other than their height, she resembles her mother right down to the freckles on her nose and the red hair. It's jarring how similar they look. She's the shortest of the three sisters.

Once I'm inside my room, I shuffle to the window and just stand there, hoping to catch a glimpse of her.

I'm not disappointed.

She steps out of the door with Josh in tow. He's leaning close, staring at her. Smiling easily. Checking her out. *Shit.* He's flirting with her. I know his moves and I know when he's interested in someone. I notice him blatantly checking out her rack, and then pretending to cough into his folded fist. I roll my eyes in irritation.

I can't blame him. Nor has the most amazing tits I've ever seen on a girl. I lick my lips, my throat suddenly parched and bang my head on the wall twice to get my thoughts in line. If Mom got wind of my thoughts, she'd glare in disapproval that I forgot my manners. But Jesus. . .my eyes couldn't stop gawking at her bra and the soft rise of her boobs.

Nor laughs at something Josh says. If there was a time I'd have wished to be able to hear a sound, it would be now. I would have sold my soul to the devil to hear her voice. Her laughter. I settle for watching her speak to Josh. The way she slants her head to the side as she listens to him, giving him all her attention. I stare transfixed at how her hair falls over her eyes, and then her hand, fragile and small, sweeps it off her face.

My eyes take in her little, hot body. She can't be more than five feet tall.

The breeze sweeps the yellow dress she's wearing, tangling it around her hips and ass, framing her curves.

Holy. Shit.

New neighbor boner alert.

I've never met a girl like her before. She makes me feel both guarded and aroused at the same time.

My gaze drifts to her arms as she lifts them up above her head in a stretch.

I can't get those white scars I spotted out of my head. She didn't seem self-conscience about them until she saw me staring at her arms like a fool. The look she sent me froze me in place. It was fierce and challenging, especially the defiant lift of her chin. It has been a while since a girl got that reaction out of me.

I didn't have anything to say, though. My brain had been trying to understand what I'd seen. I've never met anyone who harmed themselves. What would make her hurt herself?

Josh says something to Nor, wearing a stupid grin on his face. I want to grab it and rip it from his face. She smiles at him, that little dimple I noticed before on her right cheek making an appearance. She pushes the hair off her face and quickly slaps her skirt down when a stronger breeze blows it up.

Jesus. I'm jealous of my brother. Jealous of the breeze. I wish I was the wind so I can have the pleasure of touching her. Ripple gently on her skin.

Touch her? Where the hell did that come from? I have known her for all of three minutes and now I'm having all these thoughts about touching her invading my brain. I need to get a grip on whatever this is.

Shoving those thoughts away, I sigh and rub my forehead with my palm. I saw the fascinated look on her face when Josh turned to sign to me, but I couldn't tell what she was thinking. I'm not about to assume she's interested in me. I've been down that road before. Made fun of because of my 'weird voice'—whatever that means—and gotten burned. It didn't stop me from speaking, but I swore if I ever got involved with a girl, I'd make sure she accepted me with all my faults. I'm not about to get involved with this girl or any other girl for that matter.

Stepping away from the window, I walk over to my desk. On top of it sits my sketch book, trace paper, pens and pencils, and scales. The latter was a birthday gift from my parents when I turned seventeen last year.

I drag out the chair and sit down and flip through the pages of my sketchbook until I find my current project. I want to show it to my dad, but need to attempt a few final touches before it's ready. I have been drawing for as long as I can remember. Two years ago, I took a five week drafting course during summer, which was being offered at Eastern Lake University to students who wanted to pursue a Bachelor in Architecture program.

My dad is my mentor. He has been working and encouraging me since he realized where my passion lies and that I had a talent for drawing when I was ten. And to motivate me, my father has been using my sketches—after making improvements on them—to send out proposals to real estate developers. This gave me more confidence and made me believe that my work wasn't bad at all.

I blink at my current project—a four story town house—in front of me and blow air through my mouth. It has a long way to go before it's done.

I close my eyes and all I can see are the green eyes and red hair of the new girl next door. Opening my eyes, I toss the pencil on the desk and yank the beanie from my head. I run my fingers through my hair, frustration knotting inside my chest like an angry beast.

Two hours ago, this girl didn't exist in my life. Not even as a figment of my imagination.

Now, she's this huge distraction to me. She's larger than life, even though she's hardly five feet tall.

She reminds me of a snowflake, but the look on her face when she caught me gawking at the scars on her arms and shoulders, told me she was nothing close to a snowflake. It was fierce, almost angry. Challenging. Immediately, Shakespeare's quote comes to mind: And though she be but little, she is fierce.

I sensed right away that Nor has had more than her share of the kind of shit that life throws your way.

The scars prove that she overcame whatever challenges she went through.

I can't stop thinking about her.

I don't want to think about her.

I prefer my normal, but from the moment I caught her staring at me, I knew that normal would be a memory I'd remember fondly months from now.

This girl is trouble.

She is chaos.

She is perfect.

CHAPTER TWELVE

Nor

By the time I wake up the following day, my dad has already left for work. He was scheduled to start his new job today at the police station. As much as I would like to sleep in, I want to start ticking off the things on my to-do list, which include surveying the lawn to check on where I'd like to plant flowers, and unpacking the boxes in my room. I plan to visit my grandma because I haven't seen her in ages. I promised her that I'd visit her when we got here. She'd promised me she would gift me a few lotus flowers as well as carnations and roses for my little gardening projects.

After taking a shower, I slip on a knee-length yellow halter dress. I glance at the mirror on the vanity in front of me, my gaze automatically moving to the white scars on my arms, shining like a beacon. I don't feel the same twinge of guilt or embarrassment I felt a year ago. If there's one thing the past year has taught me, it's that my past, no matter how troubled or perfect it was, doesn't define my future. It doesn't define me.

I am who I am, and who I want to be. I am more than enough.

I've also learned that, even though my mind is in a better place right now, it doesn't stop the craving for the immense rush I used to feel, having a sharp object pressed on my skin. I just have to fight hard and avoid possible triggers that would send me tumbling down the thousand steps I've ascended thus far. Taking a deep breath, I focus on the wall across from me, where a poster of a doodle I worked on a few months ago hangs. The words *self love* stare back at me, reminding me to love myself first, an inspiring quote my therapist in Ohio used to repeat over and over until those words imprinted themselves on my heart.

I pluck a lemon drop from the bowl on my desk, pop it inside my mouth and cross the room to my gramophone on top of my desk. It was a gift from my Grandpa from my mom's side. My grandparents and my mother's twin sibling, Sabine, died in a cabin fire on Christmas ten years ago in their cabin in Hawthorne. After several investigations, the reports confirmed it was caused by a candle they probably forgot to put out. Their death affected my mom so much, sometimes it's a miracle she gets out of bed. Yesterday was a good day for her.

Grandpa and I shared the love of old records, and Sinatra. After grabbing a Sinatra record from the pile on my desk, I place it on the gramophone. By the time I climb down the stairs humming Frank Sinatra's *Strangers in the Night* under my breath, I'm grinning, ready to start my day.

Boxes are still piled up next to the walls in the living room. A few are open, with newspapers used to wrap our stuff scattered on the floor. Voices drift from the kitchen, pulling me toward the room. Elise is going on about heading out to buy the stuff she needs for her next project. For a fourteen-year-old girl, she's a ball of energy, positivity and ideas. Elon is finishing up her bowl of cheerios, with earphones tucked into each ear. Her head bobs to whatever music is playing on the iPod stashed inside the pocket of her shorts. Mom is standing at the sink, fiddling with the dishtowel in her hands, while staring vacantly out the window.

Oh God, no.

I know that look on her face. The look that screams, 'I'm about to tumble down the rabbit hole' where she stays for days and the only thing that perks her up is medication. Before we left Ohio, my mother had had bouts of absentmindedness. It has gotten worse over the past couple of years. My mom used to tell me stories about her career as a ballet dancer. She was nineteen when she met Dad and fell madly in love with him. The minute he proposed, she accepted and never looked back. I always had a feeling this wasn't the truth. Especially when I'd find her pirouetting and singing, looking beautiful and untouchable and happy. Now, I can feel her slowly retreating back to the place she had been living in before we moved. I thought things would be better once we got here.

Elon plucks the ear buds from her ears then carefully places them on the table, making sure the buds are perfectly aligned to each other. Only then does she stand up and carry the bowl to the sink. She wraps her arms around Mom in a hug. Mom startles as if she's waking up from a dream. She drops the cloth on the counter and turns to return my sister's embrace.

"Oh my baby!" She shuts her eyes but not before a few tears escape. When she opens them again, they are back to their usual vibrant green. Clear. She pulls back and kisses Elon's cheek. She waves Elise and me over and we huddle together.

This feels good. Perfect. I feel their warmth and love seep inside me and lock it in the place where memories live. These are the rare moments I treasure.

We break apart and I raise to my tip toes and reach for a mug inside the cupboards above me and then fill it with coffee from the pot. The skin on the back of my neck prickles and I look up to find mom staring at me. Her gaze darts to the counter and mine does the same.

"I'm over that, mom," I say, eyeing the knife, glinting against the sun light spilling through the kitchen window.

She nods, but looks away without saying a word. I hate when people do that. It makes me feel as though I'm being judged for the things I did in the past.

Sighing, I take a seat on one of the chairs around the table and we talk about what we will be doing today. Thirty minutes later, I refill my mug and head out the door to survey the front yard in preparation of the flowers I'm planning on planting there.

I squint up at the cloudless June sky and fan my face with one hand. Oh God. The heat around here is just too much. It's hardly ten o'clock, but it feels like it's past midday. Strolling along the little white fence that separates our house and Cole's, I notice a white ladder on the side goes directly to the roof outside my room. Maybe the previous owner had a thing for climbing through windows. I've never done that in my life so I'm left with images of forbidden, adventurous nights.

I sneak a look at the Holloway house. There's no activity whatsoever. Maybe they have a thing for sleeping in until after midday.

Taking a sip from my cup, I scour for a clue as to which one is Cole's room. I'm utterly fascinated by that boy. I have no idea where the interest is coming from. All I know is that his quiet intensity captivates me like nothing else ever has.

"Hey there!" a cheery voice greets me, pulling me away from studying the house where my current obsession resides.

I jolt upright and see a girl around my age on the front lawn of the house across the street. The Walkers as per the name on the mailbox. She tosses the long braid of hair over her shoulder. Her brown skin glows against the sunlight. She waves and grins wide. I wave back, smiling. Her disposition is infectious.

"I'm Megs!" she yells from across the street. "Great to meet you!"

Jesus. The girl will wake up the neighborhood.

She turns and talks to someone inside her house, and then tosses a braid over her shoulder again and walks toward me. I meet her in the middle, with our white little fence separating us.

"Eleanor. Nor. Whatever you want to call me." I hold out my free hand toward her.

"Megan. But I prefer Megs." She holds my gaze for a few heartbeats before shaking it. "You're gonna give the boys a run for their money with that red hair of yours." She winks at me causing a giggle to abruptly escape from my lips.

"The boys, huh?" I ask, my gaze automatically going to the Holloway's house as though some kind of force is pulling me to it.

Megs chuckles. "So you've met the boys next door, yeah?" My cup is suddenly snatched from my hand.

"Tasty." She smacks her lips together. "You and I will get along very well. There is this little cafe-book-nook that plays music from a jukebox I know you'll just love and they serve really good coffee. You and me, yeah?"

Whoa. How did she do that without bursting a lung or something?

She hands me the cup.

"Are those real?" she asks, staring at my chest.

My cheeks heat up. I was a late bloomer, so when my boobs finally came in, they arrived with a bang. "Yeah. Want to give them a test drive?" I joke.

She laughs, then says, "Sure." Her hands shoot forward without warning and latch on to my boobs. Before I can jump back, she's squeezing them tentatively as if she's choosing fruit at the market.

"Yep. Round and suckable."

What? My cheeks heat up at her words. "What?"

"These are awesome. A guy could live on these alone. Mine are saggy tits." She sighs. "I call dibs on yours if you ever get tired of them."

I laugh. I just met this girl and she's managed to make me laugh within five minutes of knowing her.

"So which one are you interested in?" she asks, nodding toward the Holloway house.

"Um. . ."

"Okay. Let me give you a run-down. So, the one with the blue eyes, football player body, wide shoulders, tall and sort of playful? That's Josh. The one with the gray eyes, beanie, toned all over and hot? That's Cole. Very intense. Not my type. . .but. . .give me Josh, and you and I will be best friends forever." She grins.

I'm trying so hard not to grin. This girl is a ball of sunshine wrapped in light blue jean shorty shorts and a yellow top. "Okay. So, playful Josh and intense Cole. Got it. Which one is older?"

"Josh is twenty-one. He goes to Florida State, and Cole is eighteen. He will be attending Eastern Lake University in fall and wants to major in Architecture. I hear Architects are very creative." She winks at me and grins.

I laugh. "I wouldn't know that."

"I bet you're interested now, eh?"

I giggle. God, this girl is a hoot.

The sound of a door shutting pulls me away from Megs. I twist around toward the Holloway house and my jaw drops. My heart does its sprinting thing inside my chest. He's wearing a pair of running shorts, shoes and. . .nothing. His abs flex with every swing of his arm.

Lord have mercy.

He shoots a glance our way and waves, and then he's jogging down the street in determined steps.

"What do you think?" I can hear the smile in Megs' voice. I drag my gaze from Cole's enticing back and face Megs.

"Um. . .he is very thought provoking."

Hah! As if I have any lingering thoughts after seeing Mr. Shirtless leave his house.

Someone shouts her name from across the street.

"That's my mom. We're going to the mall. Wanna join us?"

I shake my head. "You and I are going to get along quite well, Megs. And I wish I could join you, but we still have a lot of unpacking to do."

Her gaze lowers to my wrists, up my forearms. She frowns. "Are those—" she cuts herself off and blinks at me nervously.

Shit.

"Sorry. It's none of my business." She leans forward, catching me off-guard and hugs me. Then pulls back just as fast as she'd snatched me.

"I could drop by later and help you out if you want."

I nod, relieved she's still standing across the fence and still wants to come and help us unpack. "I would love that."

She waves as she turns around and jogs toward her house, leaving me feeling as if a little hurricane just swept through me, leaving me reeling.

I gulp down the coffee and walk around the perimeter of the lawn, surveying the grounds.

CHAPTER THIRTEEN

Nor

I bolt upright on the bed. My eyes dart around my room. My heart races inside my chest as the sound of the rolling thunder fades in the distance. Lightning flashes across the sky several times outside my window, momentarily lighting up my room. All I want to do is bury myself under the covers and hide from the world. Dragging the sheets up to my chin, I shut my eyes tight and wrap my arms around my midriff to ward off the chills and shivers racking my body. My T-shirt is drenched with sweat and sticks to my body. Sweat that has nothing to do with the humidity and everything to do with memories from my past.

Lightning strikes again and I whimper, my eyes flying open. Closing them is never a good idea because all I end up seeing is my dad's face, twisted in an ugly expression as he yells at Mom. I was five years old the first time I saw my father hit my mother. The sound of thunder, and my father's angry voice, had woken me up. I tiptoed down the stairs and sat on the step with my hands clutched around the wooden bars, watching the horrible scene unfold. Lightning struck outside, illuminating my parents in the living room. Dad's arm raised with his fist ready to strike. Mom's body was curled up on the floor, her arms braced over her head to protect herself, right before Dad's fist began landing on her back repeatedly. It was also the last time I saw him hit her. Either my mom learned how to hide the bruises well or my dad never did it again, but that moment was forever imprinted in my brain.

I take a long, shuddering breath and exhale, pushing the sheet off my body.

Damn Florida weather and its sudden thunderstorms. I hate feeling helpless and scared.

Swinging my legs off the bed, I climb to my feet, pull the T-shirt over my head, and toss it in the corner. I head to my dresser, grab a clean tank and scuttle out of the room before the next round of thunder. Right across the hall from mine is my mom's room and the one at the furthest end of the hallway, near the bathroom, is my dad's. Elise's stands between a guest room and Elon's.

I stop in front of Elon's door, which is next to mine, turn the door knob and enter. The next roll of thunder has me sprinting in the dark toward Elon's bed, stumbling and trying to right myself. My knee hits the side of the bed and I double over as pain stabs that spot repeatedly and mercilessly.

"Stupid son of a cross-eyed dragon!" I curse furiously while rubbing my knee.

"Nor?" Elon's surprised voice, croaky from sleep, pulls me out of my stupor. I glance up but I'm only able to see the outline of her head in the dark. "What are you doing?"

I straighten and crawl on the bed. "Can I sleep with you? It's raining outside. . ."

I don't need to finish the sentence because she knows that storms scare me. She nods quickly, scoots toward the wall and pats the empty space beside her. Once I slip under the sheets, I whisper, "Thank you."

I feel her hand move down my arm and stop when she finds my fingers.

"Always," she whispers back, linking our fingers together.

Seconds later, her breathing steadies and my heart finally settles into its normal rhythm.

I probably should be embarrassed. I'm the older sister. I'm supposed to be the one offering refuge to my nine-year-old sister. I stopped feeling embarrassed when I realized that my sisters accepted me with all my oddities and scars.

Finally, I close my eyes, feeling at peace.

The next time I wake up, it's twenty minutes past eight in the morning. I clutch my chest, trying to breathe through the tightness trapped there, but I feel as though my lungs are dying from lack of oxygen. My body shutting down, every part of it turning numb.

Oh God.

I hate losing control over my own body. I hate that, years later, the memory of my dad's angry face illuminated by lighting still triggers fear inside me, sending me into full panic mode.

With one last glance at Elon sprawled across the bed, softly snoring, I slip out of the bed, careful not to jostle it too much and tiptoe out of the room. When I reach mine, I change into my running shorts and head downstairs. The house is silent, so I assume my mother and Elise are still asleep. After shoving my feet inside a pair of tennis shoes, I rush out the front door, hungry to find the relief running gives me. Humid heat slams into me the moment I step outside. The ground is dry with no evidence of last night's storm. As soon as my feet hit the sidewalk, I'm off in a furious sprint, feeling the muscles in my legs snap into action.

Finally, I can breathe.

CHAPTER FOURTEEN

Cole

STEPPING OUT OF THE FRONT DOOR OF MY HOUSE, MY ATTENTION IS drawn toward the Blake's house, like it has been since Nor moved in, automatically finding Nor's room. There's a white ladder on the side of the house that leads to her roof, which was built by the elderly couple who owned it previously. That room belonged to their son, who moved out almost ten years ago.

I've seen Nor climb out the window at exactly ten o'clock every night since she moved in next door. She settles in on the jutting roof and lies there, contemplating the night sky. Half an hour later, she clambers back inside her room and disappears from sight.

Waiting for her every night has become an addiction to me and I can't shake it off. She fascinates me, this girl, for reasons I cannot explain. What does she see when she stares at the sky?

I stride toward my car, open the door and toss the sketch pad and pencil case on the passenger seat. Then I slide in the front seat, forcing my mind to stop obsessing over the girl next door. Dad is meeting a prospective client downtown, who is looking for a firm to do a complete overhaul on an old residential complex. He opted to go with my dad's company, BH Architects & Builders, instead of contracting different firms to do the job. He founded his company ten years ago. It has come a long way from operating in the little room he'd built in our backyard, to renting a plush office in town. I've never seen anyone work so hard in my life. After many late, sleepless nights in the office, it finally paid off. BH Architects is now one of the top ten architectural firms in Florida. I hope to join him one day, which is why I will be attending Eastern Lake University, starting this fall to study architecture.

I pause when I see movement in my peripheral vision. I turn around just in time to see Nor, looking cute yet still sexy in a white T-shirt and bright pink running shorts, race out of her front door and sprint down the street as though Hell Hounds are after her ass.

I glance from the door and then back to her tiny frame moving farther away from me.

What's going on?

Worried that something must be wrong, I start the car and peal out of the parking spot. Gripping the wheel with both hands, I duck my head, searching the road ahead for her red hair and pink running shorts.

Where the hell did she go?

I slow down the car to a cruising pace and look around for any signs of Nor. I pull up on the shoulder of the deserted road and hop out of the car, my gaze scouring the woods. I'm about to give up when I catch a glimpse of pink through the trees on the path that leads to St. Christopher's Church on the other side of the street.

I can spare a few minutes to check on her so I get back inside the car, drive around the woods and pull up in front of the church. One of the brown wooden doors is slightly ajar.

What the hell am I doing? If Nor is in there, she definitely doesn't need me invading her space.

Nevertheless, I find myself stepping out of the car. My feet lead the way toward the concrete path, flanked with shrubs and flowers on either side. I pause when I reach the top of the stairs, reading the notice behind the glass board.

Confessions are in session.

I remove the beanie from my head and duck through the door, squinting in the softly lit interior. The church is deserted, save for Nor. She's sitting on the pew in the first row. Her head is arched back as if she's focusing on the ceiling. My heart twists inside my chest as I watch her lonesome figure. Everything inside me tells me to go to her, overruling the promise I made to myself not so long ago to stay away from her. Her shoulders visibly loosen as if a weight has been lifted off of them. I give in to the urge to walk inside.

When I reach the front row, I sit down on the bench and scoot toward her. She doesn't move. In fact, nothing about her indicates she knows I'm here. Her gaze is focused on the altar a few feet away. She blinks, lowers her head and I notice her lips moving but I can't understand what she is saying. She turns her head to look at me and her eyes widen. I feel as if I've been punched in the gut. Gone is the fire that momentarily flashed in her eyes when we first meet, it's been replaced by a sadness so deep, I'm fighting hard to not look away. I just want to put my arms around her and comfort her. My fingers itch to trace the gentle curve of her jaw.

Shit. My emotions are all over the place, sitting next to this girl.

I take a deep breath. Big mistake. Her scent—a mixture of sweat, a subtle hint of vanilla and sweet almonds—seduces my senses, causing a growl to rise up my throat.

Nor jerks a little, her gaze moving to my mouth.

Shit. I need to learn to control myself around her.

I clear my throat, and her eyes find mine again.

"Sorry," she says. "I asked you something. I forgot about your. . ." she trails off, a flush spreading across her cheeks, and points to her ears. She takes a deep breath and exhales. When she bites her bottom lip between her teeth, that little dimple on her cheek appears.

"What are you doing here?" she asks, her fingers clenched around the Bible, the sharp corner pressed with force on her thigh, given the indent on her skin.

Isn't she feeling any pain?

"You left your house running like a bat from hell and I got curious."

"So you followed me?"

"Yes," I say, my gaze wandering to the book in her hands and then back to her, starting to feel worried. Maybe she has that condition where people are immune to pain? I nod to her lap. "I think the Bible needs a breather," I tease, hoping to invoke a smile from her and hopefully see that little dimple again.

Her gaze drops to her lap and her jaw tightens as if in pain. Did she just wince?

Raising my hand, I curl it on top of hers and the second our skin touches something like fire charges through my veins and down my spine, jolting me upright. I snatch my hand away from hers at the same time Nor startles and swings her gaze back to mine, her eyes wider than before and her mouth parts. The Bible slips from her hand and drops to the floor.

Holy shit! What was that?

She shoots to her feet and tugs the edge of her T-shirt down, looking everywhere but at me. Confused as fuck, I stand and walk out in the aisle before turning to face her. She leans down, grabs the Bible from the floor and places it on the pew in front of her.

"Hey. Would you like me to drop you somewhere?" I ask.

Her fingers stop fidgeting with her T-shirt and her head snaps up in my direction. "Aren't you supposed to be on your way to. . .um. . .wherever you go every morning?"

My eyebrows shoot up and my gaze sharpens on her, taking in every little detail of her face.

"It's just a passing observation," she says, raising her chin defiantly, which is cute as shit.

My lips twitch, fighting a smile. Oh, little Miss Freckled Nose has been watching me just like I've been watching her.

"It's not important." The lie slips from my mouth so easily it gives me pause.

The look in her eyes fades a little, replaced by a spark I can't put my finger on, until I see her lips quirk in a soft smile. "I'm low on energy, considering I was running like a bat from hell. I could use a lift."

Her smile. . .Jesus. If that smile makes me feel like I'm high, I wonder what seeing her laugh would do to me. Oh wait. I already did. But she was laughing with Josh. I kind of want her to laugh with me, no matter how lame the joke might be.

Dude, cool it. Take her home and stop all this sappiness.

Taking my own advice, I shove the beanie back on my head once we walk out of St. Christopher's and lead the way to my car. I open the passenger door, grab the sketches, toss them in the back seat, and then move aside for her to settle on the passenger seat.

The atmosphere in the car is filled with that same energy I've felt every time I'm close to Nor. It rolls over my skin, causing the hair on my arms and neck to rise in awareness. Every time I sneak a look at Nor, her face is trained out the window.

Can she feel it? Maybe this is all in my head. I should be happy, shouldn't I? I promised to stay out of her hair and not tangle with her emotionally.

Then why do I feel disappointed? Why do I crave for her to turn and look at me with those vibrant green eyes?

Shaking my head, confused by my own feelings, I pull up in front of her house, and literally run to her side to open her door.

Jesus, Cole. Couldn't you be any more subtle?

Nor steps out of the car and tips up to look at me, one eye slightly squinted against the glare from the sun.

She licks her lips, looking nervous. Then she lifts her right hand to her chin and moves it forward in my direction, smiling shyly. "Thank you." She bites her bottom lip, rocking on her feet. "Thanks for the lift. And for checking on me at the church."

She tucks a lock of hair behind her ear which has escaped the bun on her head.

My lips pull into a smile, floored. Just when I thought I couldn't be more intrigued by this girl, she surprises me by using sign language.

I nod once and turn to leave, afraid I'll end up saying something stupid, just like the weird way my body has been reacting to her. Once inside the car, I glance out the window, watching as Nor walks to her door, opens it and disappears without looking back.

Shoving those confusing feelings aside, I get back on the road and drive to BH Architects.

CHAPTER FIFTEEN

Friday morning I wake up early. I was stunned to see him walk inside St. Christopher's yesterday.

I haven't seen Cole since he dropped me off. Every time that memory crosses my mind, my chest feels light and my body warms up. If I close my eyes now, I can see his lips quirked slightly in a smile and his chaotic mid-length chocolate brown hair. No wonder he feels the need to tame it by wearing a beanie, it obeys its own laws. I like it though. It looks silky soft.

I can't get over the surprise and delight on his face when I signed 'Thank you'. That single look increased my determination to learn more just so that I can see it again.

"Hey Nor."

My head pops out of the closet and I spin around to find Megs sitting on the window ledge, holding two Styrofoam cups.

"Coffee?" She shoves one of the cups toward me and my heart skips a beat as the smell of coffee tickles my nose. "Elise let me in."

I snatch it from her hands and inhale the scent. "Oh my God, you're a godsend. Thank you."

She takes a sip from her cup while scanning my room, her gaze landing on my doodle notebook on the floor beside my bed. "Can I see that?" She points at it with her free hand.

I bite the inside of my cheek. Would it seem rude to refuse? No one, other than my sisters, have ever seen the inside of that book.

She hops down from the windowsill and hurries toward me. She touches my shoulder with one hand and says softly, "Hey. It's okay. You don't have to show me. I've always wanted to doodle and I was curious when I saw yours."

This girl has seen my scars. I expected her to cringe, turn and walk away from me. Instead, she hugged me, which kind of threw me for a loop. She's here today. It all has to mean something, right?

"I've never had a best friend, so I don't know how to do this."

"You don't have to do anything. Just be yourself."

I am who I am. The past doesn't define me. I smile at her. "Right." I jerk my chin toward the bed. "Some of the stuff in there is not. . .for the faint hearted," I warn her.

"I don't scare easily."

I cross the room, pick the book up off the floor and hold it out to her. She takes it before lowering herself to sit cross-legged on the floor. My heart beats faster every time she flips the page, wondering what she is thinking. She pauses, clutching her cup with one hand as she stares at the drawing of an arm, the sharp edge of a razor cutting through it. The word 'relief' written in block letters screaming from the page with little skulls surrounding it. I wait for her to say something, but her eyes are trained on the page. She turns the page. The words 'courage' and 'self-love' are linked together. A flower pattern drawn repeatedly, surrounding the words.

She exhales and lifts her gaze. "These are stunning. You could totally sell them as coloring books. Take advantage of the trend."

I shake my head. "They are too personal."

She seems to sense my discomfort. She shuts the book and tosses it on the bed. "I had a very hard time when my parents divorced, I was ten-years-old," she announces abruptly, catching me off guard. "It took me a couple of therapy sessions, and a lot of time, to accept that the two people I loved the most in the whole world, weren't together anymore."

"Oh, Megs. I'm sorry." I want to hug her badly, but I hesitate for no apparent reason. I'm not used to hugging people other than my mom, Grandma Phoebes and my sisters.

She shrugs. "It was for the best, I guess. They couldn't make it work. I don't think it's fair for people to stay together if all they cause each other is misery and regrets. My dad remarried and now lives in California. Mom is still single and happy. I'm okay with that."

Yeah. I like this girl.

Before taking a sip of her coffee, she shoots a playful look at me from the rim of her cup.

"What?" I ask her. It feels good to just hang out with a girl my age, have someone who checks up on me, brings coffee and most of all, is interested in what I have to say. I hope I don't mess this up.

Megs lowers her cup and holds it to her chest. "Spill."

"Spill what?" Am I missing something?

She rolls her eyes and grins. "I saw Cole drop you off with his car right in front of your house."

Oh, that. My stomach does its usual butterflies-fluttering thing and my cheeks warm at the memory of his hand on mine. Finding that little church while on my run was an amazing discovery. We aren't a church-going family by any means, but it's the one place that quiets my turbulent thoughts. Just me and a Higher Power. I believe there is someone greater than me. There just has to be.

I cringe, remembering the rush I got when I pressed the sharp edge of the Bible on my thigh. God, I'm messed up. Plus I sort of admitted that I noticed he goes somewhere every morning. I've noticed more than that though. The way he walks confidently, the way the muscles on his shoulders flex when he moves. . .Ladies and gentlemen, I'd like to accept my sort-of-stalker-y award now.

I clear my throat and avert my gaze. "I went for a run and ended up at St. Christopher's Church. That's where he found me and offered to give me a lift."

Mischief enters her face. "So, he stalked you?"

I laugh. "I'm not stalk-worthy."

She shakes her head, a huge smile gracing her face as if she knows something I don't. "Not from what I've heard."

"Heard? From who? Oh my god! What are you talking about?" My giddy feeling turns to nervousness.

"Relax. Cole and his best friend, who is also my boyfriend, Simon, have been talking. Your name came up. Cole got all twitchy in a cute way. I've never seen him act that way, which means you affect him more than he wants to admit."

The air locked in my chest bursts out of my parted lips in a rush. Cole has been talking about me? And why does that make me want to fly through the roof in joy? "Um. . .what did he say?"

"He said you're pretty. He also mentioned that you sit on your roof every night, which seems to fascinate Cole a lot. Then Simon asked Cole if he needed help asking you out. Cole got all prickly and asked him to stay away from you. It was fun to watch, though. I can't remember the last time someone claimed his attention like you seem to have done."

And I swear my heart has sprouted little wings and is trying to break free from my chest and fly.

"So, what are your plans for today?" I ask, changing the subject, too flustered to continue with the previous conversation. I need to consume that information in small doses in the private sanctuary of my bed. At night.

She chuckles. "Too much?"

I clutch the coffee cup, hoping the caffeine will give me the strength I need to open up to Megs. It's what friends do, right?

"I'm not used to it." Her brows scrunch up in confusion. "I've only had one boyfriend. He lasted a month and took flight when he eventually saw the scars."

Her face softens and her gaze lowers to my arms. "Do you still. . .do it? Cut?"

I shake my head. "I haven't done it in a while, but sometimes I'm tempted. That's why I run or doodle. I binge on ice cream too." I smile at her, hoping the latter diffuses the situation.

She laughs. "We should have an ice cream and movies night soon."

We decide that we'll take Elon and Elise to the mall just to look around and get them out of the house. We chat about my new school and I realize we'll be attending the same high school. She and I will be graduating next year. Megs already has her life planned out ahead of her. She wants to be a nurse and her plan is to get a nursing degree.

Me? I haven't decided yet. It's either Music Therapy or Psychology. I want to be able to help people who have gone through what I did.

Maybe I can ask Josh to teach me a few things in sign language, just in case Cole and I meet again. I know he reads lips perfectly, but if feels good to throw him off his game.

Josh.

He's been looking for any excuse he can get to drop by my house. I don't want to encourage him in any way that will give him false hope about me being interested in him.

After Megs leaves, I walk to the window and duck my head out just as Josh's laughter drifts toward me. He's on their lawn, tossing a football with Nick. When Nick manages to catch it, he whoops and giggles.

Josh glances up as if sensing me, and waves. "Want to join us?" The sun rays bounce off his perfectly styled hair.

I shake my head. "Maybe another day. You two have fun." His shoulders slump forward in disappointment. "I need a favor, though."

He grins wide and winks. "Anything for you, darlin'." I roll my eyes at his blatant flirting and press my lips together, fighting a smile. He crouches down to be eye level with Nick. They talk for a few moments, and then his little brother nods, turns and takes off toward the front door.

"You didn't need to send him away."

He shrugs his broad shoulders. "I just wanted to make sure you had my full attention."

I laugh. "Stop flirting, Josh." He shrugs again and slants his head to the side. "I'm thinking about. . .can you teach me how to sign, just a few words?"

I swear his shoulders slump down a bit and disappointment flashes across his face before it vanishes. It's replaced by a smile. "Sure."

"Perfect. Tomorrow at eleven o'clock?"

He nods just as a black pick-up truck with blaring music drives up the street and stops in front of his house. He turns around and waves at whoever is sitting behind the tinted windows before facing me again.

"Awesome. Can't wait to start our lessons." He winks again.

"Seriously, stop doing that."

"You love it when I flirt with you." He laughs, walking backwards. "Rule number one in ASL: Eyes and facial expressions are important. Your eyes and that sweet blush on your cheeks say a lot. You're enjoying my flirting."

I laugh, shaking my head. I kind of do, because I know it's harmless flirting. Besides, I've already set my sights on someone else. "You're incorrigible."

A tall woman with blonde, wavy hair steps out of the driver's seat and calls his name. Josh spins around and stalks over to her, scoops her off the ground and kisses her, pinning her to the car.

Another guy with dark hair steps out, interrupting the kissing session. After the one-armed hug and a round of back-thumping with their fists, they get inside the car. The driver does a U-turn, missing the Walker's mailbox by barely an inch, before racing down the street and out of sight in all its music-blaring glory.

I leave my room and head to my mother's to check on her. She sits in a rocking chair humming along to Yiruma's *River Flows in You* that's playing from the CD player on the desk next to the window. Her eyes focus on me as soon as I block her view of the garden. A soft smile stretches across her face.

"You remind me of your grandmother, honey. The freckles on your nose, the way you tilt your head to the side."

And you remind me of my mother, the woman I looked up to when

I was a child.

I wish I could tell her that, but I know the aftermath would be catastrophic. The last time I said something like that to her. She had fallen deeper into despair, shutting everyone out. My dad refused to take her to see the doctor. When he eventually did, she got medication and started therapy to help her through the depression that had started, I suspect, long before we were born.

So instead, I say, "Grandma Phoebe asked about you when I spoke to her on the phone earlier today. Want to pay her a visit with me?"

Her smile fades. She sits up and starts fretting with her hair. "Do you think I look okay?"

I grab her hands and twine her fingers with mine. "You look perfect. Just a little lipstick and voila!" I beam at her.

Her nervous movements stop. She stares at me, tears in her eyes. Her gaze drops to my wrists, "I'm—you don't deserve this. You've been so strong and here I am—"

"Mom." She shakes her head furiously, tears brimming in her eyes. "Mom. Just focus on getting well, okay?"

Finally, the tears fall. She sobs soundlessly. Tears of the horrors she has probably gone through living under my dad's iron hand. Unaccomplished dreams. Missed opportunities with her daughters.

After she calms down, we sit there holding hands and I tell her about Cole. There is not much to tell though. By the time I leave her room, she has already retreated into her shell. I'm not even sure she heard anything I said.

"I love you, Mom," I whisper and kiss her cheek before leaving the room and walking out the front door.

I lower myself onto the swing on the porch and drop my head in my hands. I'm trying hard not to feel the weight of seeing my mother on a downward spiral. I wish I could help her.

Just a few hours until Dad comes home. Or not. He has gone back to his old habits like he did in Ohio; spending most of his time at the office. I'm not naive so I don't believe he spends his nights there.

Personally, I prefer if he doesn't come home at all. At least this way, I don't have to worry about his temper or what he might do when he's angry.

After dinner, Elon and Elise clean up while I sit with my mother, urging her to eat. After a few spoonfuls from her plate, she pushes it away.

"Go, baby," she says. "You don't need to take care of me."

I really do. I nod and stand up, then kiss her forehead. "I'll be back later. Want to play a bit on the piano with me? We could let Elon and Elise jump around on the sofas," I say softly, smiling, hoping my words will spark something inside her. Spark the kind of light I haven't seen in a while.

She nods, smiling. I leave the room and, for the millionth time, wish my mother had pursued her career and never met my father. But where would my sisters and I be if that would have happened?

When I get to my room, I grab a handful of lemon drops from the table and lie down on my bed to listen to Queen's *Bohemian Rhapsody* on the gramophone, while waiting on my usual star-gazing hour. At exactly ten o'clock, I snatch my pillow from my bed and head for window, like I've been doing since we moved here, and settle on the roof, glad to have a place where I can watch the stars like I did in Ohio. My thoughts and problems vanish, replaced by the beauty of the star-filled dark sky.

This.

This is everything. Just me and the quiet night with the occasional honk of a car horn in the distance. Just me and the stars. When I close my eyes, I see the galaxy behind my eyelids; bursts of purple and blue. So mesmerizing. Stunning.

Cole

"*Why are you in such a hurry, bro?*" Josh signs when he meets me in the hallway.

"*I am just going out for a walk,*" I reply, the image of Nor still fresh in my head. The minute I saw her crawl out of her window, I felt this crazy urge to join her.

Josh glances at his watch, then looks up at me, a knowing grin splitting his face. "*Yeah, right.*"

"*What?*" I ask, feeling irritated but at the same time, wanting to wipe that stupid grin off his face.

"*She is on the roof. Just admit it, Cole. You can't resist the pull.*" He slaps me on my shoulder without warning, causing me to stumble forward. Apart from our similar heights, Josh has more bulk, which is a product of his training regimen. My body is made up of lean muscle that I have built up through the past few years, working construction in my dad's company on weekends and school holidays. That and the occasional run.

I rub the nape of my neck and clench my jaw, feeling awkward. Should I admit that I feel differently toward Nor? That something about her just calls to me?

I scratch my head and turn to face him. The teasing look is gone from my brother's face, replaced by a contemplative look.

He tucks his hands inside the pockets of his shorts. "It's okay, you know. You don't need to hold back. I've seen you sneak looks at the Blake's House. I've also seen the look on your face whenever you see her."

I won't ask him what he means. "I thought you were interested in her. I've seen you flirting with her."

He shakes his head. "*It's harmless. She asked me if I could teach her how to sign, which kind of knocked my ego down a few notches. Look, I know chicks haven't been too good to you. If you feel something for her, no matter how small, just follow your instincts. Porn will only go so far.*" He smirks at me.

"*Jack ass.*" I blow out a breath. "*I don't want to make a fool of myself.*"

His eyebrows shoot up. "*What is the worst thing that can happen?*"

"*Scare her by blurting out some random shit.*" I run a hand down my face. Jesus. That would be the end of me.

He claps me on my shoulder. "When you feel like some random shit is about to leave your mouth, just stop talking and sign. Easy," he jokes. "Oh hey. About those scars on her. . .she might be going through stuff and maybe she still cuts. Doesn't that scare you?"

I scowl at him. "What are you, the Devil's advocate? Didn't you just tell me to go for it?"

"Yes," he admits without shame. "I like her. But I love you, bro."

I glance at the watch on my wrist and then look at the stairs. "No. Okay? I saw the scars, but I also saw beyond that. I saw pain and loneliness. She intrigues me."

He finally steps aside, letting me pass. "Then don't worry about making a fool of yourself."

"Thanks, bro." I grab him in our usual one-arm hug and spin around, but he grips my arm, stopping me.

"*Take risks. Keep your head up and keep going, right?*" He advises.

"*Right.*" I bound down the stairs, his words filling my head. I wave to my parents, who are sitting in the living room, working on a crossword puzzle. Seconds later, my feet are carrying me across the lawn and to the fence that separates our houses. I leap over it and jog toward the white ladder on the side. I grab it with clammy fingers, my heart racing in my chest at the thought of being near her again.

Christ. I need to calm down.

Taking a few calming breaths, I grab the top rung of the ladder and climb the rest of the way to the roof. She doesn't stir and I'm not sure if she heard my footsteps or sensed my presence. I shuffle ahead, stop and lie down next to her.

Then I let out the breath trapped in my chest.

Nor

The air around me shifts, like atoms rearranging themselves to accommodate a potent, powerful entity. My eyes snap open. I swing my head around to my right and there, lying next to me calmly as though it's something completely normal, is Cole Holloway.

I bolt upright and turn to face him. "How did you get up here?" He doesn't respond. Then I remember that he can't hear me. I touch his arm, making sure he can see my lips. Thank goodness the moon is full tonight. He tilts his head to the side to look at me. "How did you get up here?"

He points to the side of the building. I follow his finger and see the white ladder poking at the roof. Ah, I'd completely forgotten about it.

He turns his head and faces the sky. Holding my breath, I study his profile; his sharp nose and angular jaw. A faint scent of musk cologne drifts toward me, making the hair on the nape of my neck stand on end.

Dragging my gaze from his face, I look up at the infinite dark sky and I smile. Every part of me is centered on him. His movements. Every rise and fall of his chest doubles my heart beat until the only sound that fills my senses is my pulse pounding in my ears.

Thump.

Thump.

Thump.

Seconds, minutes, probably hours go by. Centuries could pass. Seasons could come and go, but I wouldn't notice, because this is the most spellbinding moment I've ever experienced in my seventeen years on this earth.

Something fleetingly touches the back of my hand, startling me.

There it is again. A soft touch along the side of my pinkie. My skin is on fire now. My heart is in my throat and my lungs are nowhere near working right. The touch is firm now. Deliberate. He hooks his pinkie around mine and tugs gently. Then he exhales hard, and I swear the roof moves beneath our bodies. Suddenly, the finger uncoils from mine, leaving me cold. I blink several times before twisting, turning my head to the side to look at him.

Did I imagine that touch?

I glance down and see that his hand is curled into a fist at his side. He sits up, then turns slightly to the side to face me. His face is framed in shadows so I can't see it clearly. A shiver skitters down my back as he leans forward without warning until I feel his quick breath fan my lips, his eyes on my mouth the entire time. He takes a tendril of the hair fanned around my head and rubs it between his fingers, his eyes not leaving mine. I'm captivated by his eyes, his overwhelming presence. I should scold him for being too forward and getting into my space, but I can't. I'm mesmerized by the inhales and exhales passing through his parted lips.

He lets go of my hair and climbs to his feet with the agility and swiftness of a panther. Between one breath and the next, he's gone, disappearing into the night as quietly as he came. Taking with him a tiny piece of my heart. As odd as it sounds, I feel a certain connection to this quiet boy.

I attempt to prop my upper body on my elbows so I can watch him as he walks back to his house, but they feel too jelly-like. I settle back on the roof, grinning and listening to the muffled crunch of his shoes on the grass until it fades.

CHAPTER SIXTEEN

Cole

IT HAS BEEN THREE DAYS SINCE I FIRST JOINED NOR ON THE ROOF. I've been going every night ever since.

I step from the bathroom, while ruffling my wet hair with one hand and head to my room. After grabbing a T-shirt from the dresser, I slip it on and stride to the window. I'd never given star-gazing a thought until after the night I lay next to Nor on the roof of her house. It was an eye-opening moment, especially when I took a chance to touch her. I wanted to see if that connection between us was still there. I wasn't disappointed. Now, I can't seem to stop invading her space every night.

It's almost ten o'clock. My breath catches every few seconds, knowing I'll see her soon. This reaction has become like a natural reflex. I still have to work up the nerve to talk to her, something I haven't done since that day in St. Christopher's. I need to feel her fingers shake again when mine brush against hers. It feels damn good, knowing I can do that to her with just a simple touch.

The lights flicker a few times, alerting me that someone is on the other side of the door. I glance around quickly to make sure everything is in its place, but realize my porn stash which is overdue for returning at the video library, peeks from under the sketch book. I lunge forward, grab it and shove it inside the drawer.

"Come in," I say, combing my hair with my fingers.

Mom ducks her head around the door and smiles. Her eyebrows rise as she takes me in before signing, "*Hot date tonight?*"

I roll my eyes, fighting a smile.

Before I can answer her, she continues, "*You like her don't you? She's pretty. Very pretty.*"

"*How can I like her when I don't even know her?*"

Mom folds her arms on her chest. "You know her."

"*Know who?*" My father's tall, bulky frame enters the room, his fingers signing the words. His gray eyes twinkle and I know he is ready to launch into some sort of advice-rant, like he usually does, when he corners Josh. "The girl next door?"

Mom nods. They exchange a look then turn to me and I know they've been talking about my sudden interest in Nor.

I pull my hands from my pockets. "*You have got this all wrong. It is just—*"

"*Honey?*" Mom cuts me off. "*Go and have fun.*"

I scratch my head and give up on convincing them. Dad slides his arm around my mom's shoulder and swivels her around while kissing the top of her head before tugging her out of the room. I stare at the door for a few seconds after they've gone realizing I've never seen my parents act any other way. It's always appeared as if they can't get enough of each other.

I hope I'll have that one day.

I sneak another look out the window just in time to see Nor duck her head out the window, look at the skies and then disappear back inside the room. The clouds hang low in the sky today. There's no chance they will clear soon. I stride out of my room, down the stairs and step out into the humid air. A soft breeze sweeps across my face, bringing with it the scent of rain.

I jog across the lawn, do my usual hop over the fence routine, and jog up the porch steps. I take quick breaths to calm my racing heart, and then ring the bell. The door opens a few moments later and the air stalls in my lungs as I stare into brown eyes set in a scowling face. Eyes that belong to Nor's father. His mouth tightens, forming a white line. His hand on the door frame flexes as if he's fighting to rid himself of a wild emotion. I'm suddenly reminded of the look on his face when he saw me the day they moved in.

Shit. I don't even know what I did to deserve his anger. Maybe he didn't like the way I was staring at Nor the day they moved in. He must think I'm creepy.

"Good evening, Sir," I say, hoping my voice and my face reflect confidence, because it sure as shit isn't what I'm feeling right now.

"What do you want?" His mouth forms a sneer. Maybe this is his normal disposition.

"Can I talk to Eleanor for a minute? I realize it's late but I need to talk to her for a few seconds."

His hand drops from the door frame, and he steps forward. Nothing about his posture yells 'friendly'. I should move, but my feet feel like lead.

His mouth twists into an ugly scowl and I have to try harder than normal to read his lips. "Stay away from my daughter. She doesn't need the likes of you ruining her life."

The likes of me? What does that even mean?

Before I can contemplate those words, he disappears back inside the house and slams the door in my face.

Seriously, what the hell?

Spinning around, I clench my hands into fists as I shuffle away from the porch, confused and angry about his assumptions about me.

CHAPTER SEVENTEEN

Nor

After filling my bowl with vanilla ice cream, I grab the pieces of peeled orange from the kitchen counter and stir them in. I was kind of bummed when I checked the skies and saw the dark clouds. I hope ice cream will help chase away the star-gazing blues.

Satisfied with the amount and consistency, I leave the kitchen, bypassing the living room where my dad is watching a crime TV show, and climb the stairs to my room. I went to check in on Mom in her room a few minutes ago. She and my dad don't share the same room. I can't even remember the last time they did.

I change directions and enter my sister's room. She is sitting on a stool next to the window, her eyes closed in concentration and the bow in her hand moving effortlessly across the strings of the cello. Everything in here is color coded and neat. A medal, shaped like a G-clef, stands on the shelf above her desk, flanked by several books on music. She has a thing for orderliness.

The music stops and she huffs in frustration. She places the bow on the desk, grabs a pen and scribbles furiously on a notepad. She tucks her hair behind her ear and picks up the bow once again.

"E?" I call out. Her head snaps up. "Why don't you get some sleep? You can practice tomorrow. It's pretty late right now."

She shakes her head. "I want to be ready for when schools open. The teacher back in Ohio said we should always be competitive and learn every chance we get."

I shift on my feet, worried that my father will stomp upstairs and yell at her. It wouldn't be the first time. "I have an idea. We could watch a movie on my laptop and eat ice cream. You can choose the DVD."

She shakes her head and starts packing her stuff in the cello case.

"Did you know Elise has a cat in her room?" she announces without looking at me.

"What? Where did she find a cat?" I ask, hurrying out of the door in search of confirmation. Elise has a penchant for rescuing animals, something that irritates my dad to no end.

Before Elon can answer, my father's raised voice reaches me. He sounds even angrier than usual. Changing directions, I hurry downstairs coming to an abrupt halt at the bottom and gape in shock when I see Cole standing at the door.

My dad moves forward in a threatening stance, but Cole doesn't back away. I applaud him for his bravery and fear for him for his stupidity. He should run away.

"Stay away from my daughter. She doesn't need the likes of you ruining her life." These words are spoken in a shout, but Cole doesn't cringe. I'm partly happy he can't hear him. The chill in his voice is enough to make even the strongest of men scuttle away in fear.

Dad steps back and slams the door in his face. He spins around and stops me mid-turn with his words.

"Eleanor," he snarls. I straighten and spin around to face him and my heart drops to my stomach at the look of anger and disapproval he is directing my way. I hold the bowl in my hand tighter. "Do you need to tell me something?"

I quickly shake my head.

Two steps and he's glaring at me from the bottom of the stairs. "Stay away from that boy. Do you hear me?"

I grip the bowl tighter and do something stupid. One single word falls out of my lips in a quivering whisper. "Why?"

His face darkens, rage rolling across it like thunder in a cloudy sky. "Don't question me, Eleanor. I'm your father. You will do as I say, do you understand me?"

I nod quickly, eager to get away from him. Seventeen years on this earth, and he still scares the living crap out of me.

With one last warning glare, he turns and storms back into the living room. I exhale and dash back upstairs and into my room. I shut the door behind me and lean on it, taking deep breaths.

Crap. Crap. Crap.

Lifting the spoon from the bowl, I scoop a large helping of ice cream and shove it in my mouth, the urge to feel something other than fear and loss of control immense. I shut my eyes tight as the coldness from the ice cream sweeps through me, numbing those desires, those demons that remind me how good the sharp whisper of a razor on my skin feels. The demons that send images of the sight of blood dripping from my skin, greedy for the rush.

My eyelids flip open at the sound of a knock on my window. Cole is kneeling on the roof, his eyes intense on my slumped form by the door.

I stand up and push away from the door, then hurry to the window. God, did he see me in my state of weakness?

"What are you doing here?" I ask, making sure he can see my lips.

He continues to study me closely. What is he thinking behind those gray eyes? We haven't talked again since the day he brought me home from St. Christopher's, yet, he is here, staring at me. Something flashes across his face. He blinks, breaking the connection.

"Would you like to go for a walk? I figured since the chances of gazing at the stars are null, we could do something else," he finally says, and a shiver dances down my spine at the sound of his voice.

I glance nervously over my shoulder to the door, and then back to Cole. "My dad. . .aren't you afraid of him? I heard what he said to you."

He shakes his head. "His words make me angry, but he doesn't scare me."

Cole is officially my hero. Even after being yelled at and insulted, here he is here. At my window.

"A walk," I repeat, tasting the words on my tongue. I look down at the bowl of ice cream, then back to Cole. "Sounds like a good idea. I need to change though."

Holy crap! I'm not wearing a bra and my boobs are literally waving at Cole. I cough, choking on that discovery.

His gaze lowers to my chest as if he read my mind, staying there a few seconds too long. He glances up at me. His Adam's apple bobs up and down as he swallows violently. He lifts a hand and scratches his head, which I'm just noticing is beanie free.

My cheeks are on fire. "I need to change. Want to come in?" I ask, then turn around, tripping on my own feet in my haste to hide my flustered face.

"You don't need to change on my account," he says. I jerk my head around just in time to see amusement dancing in his eyes.

I laugh and roll my eyes. "No peeking."

Oh wow. I'm feeling quite brave, letting Cole inside my room after the scene downstairs. Being a rebel is such a rush. Knowing my dad would burst a vein if he found out about what I'm up to, acts as the driving force to my debut into rebelliousness.

Besides, Cole fascinates me. Doesn't hurt that he's so hot and his lips look like something I'd like to taste.

Er. . .back to the point.

I place the bowl of ice cream on my desk, hurry to the door and flip the lock, before walking to the dresser. After picking out a black knee-length dress and bra, I turn around, wondering if Cole is still standing outside the window after blabbering my hasty invitation.

He's not. God, is he ever not.

Cole is standing next to my desk, with his hip leaned on one corner, his focus on my doodle book. He turns a page, and continues to study my work. Drawings and words written in moments of pain and peace. My soul is in those pages.

Crap. What is he thinking? I'm just starting to know what normal feels like, and I don't want anything taking that away from me. Even though I'm certain he knows my scars are from self-harming, the things in that book are my inner thoughts. My inner demons unleashed.

He turns another page and something flutters to the floor. He lifts his gaze from the book and straightens when he sees me watching him.

"That's private," I tell him, annoyed at myself for leaving that book on my desk, instead of under the pillow. Annoyed at him for poking around without asking me first.

He looks worriedly at me. "I'm sorry." He bends down to scoop up the fallen paper then looks at me again. "This is beautiful."

My gaze drops to the paper, a string of scribbled words surrounded by hearts drawn in Zentangle patterns. "The past does not define me."

I swallow and close my eyes, trying to bring my conflicted feelings under control. A gentle touch on my shoulder forces me to open my eyes and meet Cole's gentle ones, which seem to understand what I'm feeling.

"I didn't mean to snoop around. The book was lying open on the desk and I couldn't resist." He hands me the book, but holds onto the Zentangle doodle and continues to study it.

I touch his arm. "You can keep that one." I'm not even sure why I told him that. I just know that I want him to have something from me. Something that reminds him of me.

His eyebrows shoot up in surprise. "Really?"

"Yes. Really. I swear I don't mind."

He beams at me and I melt. That look on his face is magnificent and worth the little doodle sacrifice. "Thank you." He folds it carefully and slips it into the front pocket of his shorts, walking back to the desk. "Ready?" he asks, turning around.

I shake my head and lift my finger and tell him to give me a minute. But his eyes are fixed on me. One of his hands is tucked inside a pocket while the other is holding the spoon—my spoon—shoving it into his mouth. Eating ice cream has never looked so sexy.

He licks the spoon and I die.

"Turn around," I say, motioning with my index finger in a circular motion, then wave my clothes in the air.

He dips the spoon inside the bowl and shoves a large scoop of ice cream inside his mouth before he obediently obeys my request. My attention is split in two: listening for sounds outside my door and making sure Cole doesn't sneak a peek.

I straighten my dress, take a deep breath and walk toward Cole.

I touch him on his arm and he turns around. "I'm ready."

His mouth parts as he looks at me from head to toe, and then back up. He doesn't say a word, but I see the appreciative look in his eyes. He puts the spoon in the bowl, leans forward and brushes his thumb across my bottom lip, lingering at the corner of my mouth.

"Ice cream." That's all he says before he spins around and strides toward the window, leaving me shivering in his wake.

Biting my cheek to fight a grin, I unlock the door and then trail after Cole out through the window. This is so clandestine and the possibility of being discovered makes my heart race in excitement and a little bit of panic. Dad would definitely ground me for years if he found me sneaking off with Cole.

Once Cole and I are standing on the lawn, he takes my hand in his, linking our fingers together, and tugs me forward. With one final glance toward my house, I trot after him. He lets go of my hand when we reach the fence, swings his long legs over it, and motions for me to move closer.

"I could just use the—" Heat bursts through my skin where his strong, big hands circle my waist and scoop me up over the fence as if I weigh nothing. By the time my feet touch the ground, I'm giddy, fighting for breath, enjoying the rush. He holds me against his body, staring into my eyes.

His fingers leave my waist and link with mine again. He leads the way to the back of his house, opening a small gate that leads to the woods. We continue to walk deeper into the woods. It feels as though we've been walking for hours when suddenly he stops in between two trees. Cole drops my hand, walks the short distance to the first tree and fumbles around a small shrub until, seconds later, the entire place is illuminated by lights. His finger motions above our heads, a proud smile on his face. I look up and gasp as I stare at the structure above us. A tree house.

I look at him. "Oh my God. It's beautiful. I've never seen anything like it before." I scan my surroundings, searching for the source of electricity, but find none. "How do you power the lights?"

"Solar power." He points up again with a finger. I squint up and glimpse an outline of a flat object, but I can't figure out what it is. "Solar panels," he says, as if reading my mind. He walks to the tree covered in vines, fumbles around and suddenly the area is lit up in what looks like a million light bulbs, strung together.

My gaze comes down again. "Oh my God! This is so cool," I whisper to myself.

"Come on," he says, gesturing with his hand and pointing to the ladder. "I'll go up first."

He grips the first rung on the wooden ladder and hoists himself up. My eyes pop wider, zeroing in on his behind.

I don't know much about backsides, but that one right up there is Class A.

He reaches the top step, looks over his shoulder and waves for me to come up. Moments later, I'm crawling inside the lit-up interior of the tree house and scrambling to sit up. I glance around, taking in the polished wood floors, shelves littered with what looks like text books, pencils and pens lying in a corner on the wooden floor. I turn to face Cole.

"This place is amazing," I say, pulling my knees up and wrapping my hands around my legs.

He flashes me a boyish grin and begins to sign and speak at the same time, "*Thank you. It's my thinking spot. I designed the house and my friend, Simon, helped me with the lighting."*

Hm. Maybe I should switch my sign language teachers and ask him if he can teach me instead of Josh.

He scratches his jaw and looks around. He lowers himself on the spot directly across from me. We stare at each other for long seconds until it starts to feel awkward.

"I'm sorry about my dad."

He shrugs. "You don't have to apologize for him."

I shake my head, tightening my arms around my knees. "He was so mean to you."

"It doesn't bother me. Really." His jaw tightens. My dad's words must have affected him more than he is admitting.

I dig around inside my head, desperate to change the subject. "Megs told me you will be attending Eastern Lake in fall?" He nods, the taut look on his face fading. His gaze lingers on my mouth and I snag my bottom lip between my teeth, heat filling my cheeks. I'm not used to having someone's entire focus on me like the way Cole looks at me.

God. His eyes are just so intense!

He continues to stare at my lips, waiting for the next words to pour out. His Adam apple bobs up and down as he swallows, then takes a deep breath.

I clear my throat. "How are the classes taught? Do they have an interpreter?"

I admit I've been very curious since Megs told me about it, but we never got around to talking more about it.

He nods again. "They have a special needs department, and they will provide an interpreter, which is really great."

"I hope you don't mind me asking. What happened? How did you. . .um. . ." I point to my ears, feeling awkward for even asking.

His lips quirk at the side in his usual almost smile. "I don't mind talking about it. Bacterial Meningitis. I was five. Josh literally saved my life." He blows out a breath. "It was extremely difficult adjusting from hearing to hard of hearing."

"Oh gosh. I'm sorry," I say. I can't even imagine what he went through after the hearing loss. One day everything is okay and the next he's adjusting to his new life. "That must have been hard for you and your family."

He nods. "Yes. My mother home schooled me for about two years before she finally gave in to my badgering. I wouldn't stop asking her to enroll me in a school. Any school. Eventually, she signed me up in Simon's school in third grade. Being in a mainstream school as a hard of hearing student was not easy. My parents couldn't afford an interpreter, especially with the extra lip reading classes and speech therapy they were already paying for. I learned to rely on myself. I would ask the teachers for reading materials in advance. That is how I survived elementary through high school." He slants his head to the side, one side of his mouth tipping up. "I usually don't talk about this, mainly because not many people are interested in my life."

Wow. I can't believe that this quiet boy trusted me enough to open up to me. Why was I feeling weird about it?

"I've heard there is an electronic device that helps with the sense of sound. I can't remember the name—"

"Cochlear implant," he says, and that breathy, soft rounding in some syllables tickles my sense. "They cost a lot. We couldn't afford it."

We continue to chat about my life in Ohio, the reason we moved here, my new school which I'll be attending in fall, his family—which sounds amazing and very different from mine. Before we realize it, we are somehow sitting one inch from each other. Conversation fades as tension takes up the space around us. His hand moves from his side and takes mine, turning it as he looks at my arms. He brushes his thumb across the raised skin, the tip of his finger lingering there.

"Does it hurt?"

I shake my head. The visible wounds don't hurt as much as the invisible ones do.

Cole lifts his hand again as if he can't help himself and hovers it around my cheek. I hold my breath and wait. Wait to feel his touch send that thrill all through my body. His head dips a little, his eyes never leaving mine and he wets his lips before he exhales.

Kiss me, I beg silently. *Kiss me.*

He tucks the hair behind my ear instead then pulls back and I feel like someone dumped a bucket of ice down my shirt. Thunder rolls in the distance and my entire body stiffens.

"I need to go home," I shoot to my feet and dash toward the entrance and begin my descent down the tree.

The sound of Cole's footsteps reach me as soon as my feet hit the ground. I straighten and when I look up, Cole is standing beside me, looking perplexed. He searches my face for answers, I think. But I'm not ready to give them to him. Taking a deep breath, he looks at the sky before returning his confused stare to me, taking my hand and beginning our dash through the trees, toward home.

We reach the clearing just as fat drops of rain begin to hit my head. Cole tugs me forward to the fence, leaps over and circles my waist with his hands, lifting me up as he did before. I halt at the bottom of the ladder and whirl around to face Cole, our chests heaving with exertion.

I tilt my head up, blinking as the raindrops fall down faster and faster. "Thank you." He continues to stare down at me, and I'm not sure if he caught the words from my lips. It's too dark to see anything. I grab his hand and place his palm against my lips, and do the only thing I can think of that might make him understand what I'm saying. I mouth the words, "Thank you."

His thumb brushes my cheek before he slides his hands to my hips and spins me around to face the ladder. His fingers dig into my skin as if he doesn't want to let go before loosening and giving me a gentle push toward the ladder. I scramble up and when I reach the top, I swing one leg over the roof followed by the next, then glance down at him.

After a quick nod, he spins around and jogs across the lawn, does his usual leap-over-the-fence thing and strides toward his front door. Only then do I turn around and crawl through my window as thunder rolls and lightning strikes across the sky. I pull the window down and walk to the dresser to change my wet clothing, while contemplating my evening to keep my fear at bay. After years of feeling invisible, it feels great knowing that someone sees me, even when I think they aren't looking.

CHAPTER EIGHTEEN

Nor

I NEED TO GET A JOB. MY SAVINGS HAVE RUN LOW. MAYBE MEGS knows where I can get a part-time job. I'll be meeting her as soon as I drop Mom at my grandma's house. Elon is over at Cole's house, playing video games with Nick. She and Nick are the same age and they seem to be getting along quite well. I've seen how he looks at her. The poor boy is crushing on my sister. Elise went to visit a girl she met at the community swimming pool. Three days ago, she and I drove to the local animal shelter to drop off the cat she'd rescued. Apparently, Elise had been hiding the poor thing in her room for nearly two days before Elon mentioned it. The cat didn't have a collar so we had no choice but to take it there. My dad would have hit the roof if he'd found out about it. I'd seen that happen so many times when we were in Ohio.

Honestly, I'm not sure there is a single thing in this world that would make my dad happy. I can't even remember the last time I saw him smile, or saw him hug my sisters or me.

Grandma called me to ask if my mom and I could visit her at her house instead of the flower shop. She asked if Elon and Elise would be coming too. I told her the girls had plans and they'd visit the next time. Grandma's hip is starting to bother her again so she stayed home today. She had a hip fracture surgery a few years ago when she tripped and fell down the stairs from the roof terrace. The pain medication helps, but it makes her tired.

After parking the old Station Wagon my father bought for my mom when we got here, Mom and I exit the car and walk up the path leading to the beautiful white house with vines crawling up the walls. She seems much better today so I thought I'd bring her with me, hopefully leaving the four walls of our house would improve her mood.

After a round of hugs, Grandma insists on sitting on the terrace and she leads the way up a flight of stairs. Mom and I trail after Grandma, unable to dissuade her. The smell of roses and jasmine welcome us as soon as we get to the top. The space around us is a paradise for any plant-lover, and I can feel my body relax just being here. Flowers in pots are placed strategically along the walls, a wind chime sings softly to the sound of the breeze. The fire pit in the middle of the terrace is cleaned within an inch of its life and fresh wood sits beside it.

I walk toward the black metal railing at the edge of the terrace and take in the view overlooking a creek. The light splash of water against rocks soothing in the quiet air. No wonder Grandma insists on spending more time here than inside the house. The last time we visited my grandmother was when my grandfather passed away years ago. He was a tall, intimidating and non-compromising man who fought in the Vietnam War. General Blake wasn't a man to be underestimated. Sometimes I wonder if he is the reason my dad turned out to be the way he is.

I shift around to face my grandmother when she calls my name. She hasn't aged a lot since I last saw her. Her black hair is peppered with white. Her blue eyes are similar to my father's, except hers are kinder, and laugh lines fan the corners. I'm glad her husband's character didn't change her.

She pats the space next to her on the orange-brown lounge seat. I walk over and join her. "How are you? I mean, how are you, really?"

Unable to hold her direct gaze, I drop mine to our hands and take a deep breath. "I'm getting there. My last session with the therapist was more than a year ago. That's a huge plus, right?" I look up at her and smile.

She studies me, searching for the truth in my words. Then she laughs softly, the worry creases around her mouth disappearing. "Yes. It's a very big plus as long as you feel strong without seeing a therapist. I never stopped praying for you. Your mother and sisters. Especially your father."

Her eyes cloud over. "Did he say he'll visit me?" she asks hopefully.

"Oh yes, I forgot to mention that," Mom says a bit too enthusiastically. "He has a lot going on at the station. But he said he'll visit you as soon as things calm down."

Grandma smiles. She knows that Mom is making excuses for my dad like she always does to lessen any kind of tension.

Mom stands up and goes back downstairs, murmuring something about making a snack.

Grandma watches my mom until she disappears from view before she turns to face me. "Well, I'm extremely glad to hear you're doing well, darling. How is your mama? I always worry about you all."

"She's. . .um. . .some days she's doing really great. Like today. And sometimes she gets lost in her own world." I blow out a breath through my mouth. "We're here now. Not far away from you."

She hugs me and we pull apart just as Mom returns, carrying a plate of fruit and cheese, smiling. She reminds me of the girl in her photos who had everything to look forward to before she met my father.

Ugh! These are the kind of thoughts that plunged my life to hell. I can't afford to go there now. Not when my sisters need me and definitely not when my mother breaks apart at the slightest little thing.

Shoving those thoughts away, I kiss my grandmother on the cheek and walk toward Mom, sitting on one of the cushioned wood seats under an awning covered in vines and blooming flowers.

I hug and kiss her on her smooth cheek. "Have a great time with Grandma. I will pick you up later."

"Sweetheart, you mentioned on the phone that you were looking for a job?" Grandma says, stopping me mid-step.

"Yes. Desperately."

"I need help at the flower shop," she says as she winks at me, knowing how much I enjoy working with flowers. I'm bouncing on my heels and clapping when she adds, "I already have someone who drops by two to three times a week to help with big deliveries and anything that requires heavy lifting.

"Also, I was wondering if you'd like to help out at the Lily Rose senior center once in a week. One of the women who plays the piano in our music group hasn't been feeling too well. The pay isn't much, though. If you don't mind working with us old ladies, it would be great to have a pretty, young face around. I thought maybe you'd like to earn a little more money. We would only need you for two hours on Thursdays."

Unable to contain my excitement any longer, I leap forward and hug her. "Thank you, thank you! I was on my way to town to see if I could find a part-time job for the summer."

She laughs and kisses my forehead. "I can't wait to show you off to my friends." She beams at me, looking at me with pride. "Go on, now. I'll prepare the flowers and pack them in a box for you."

I wave at her and head for the stairs that lead to the kitchen.

My mom told me that after Grandma retired as a nurse, she went back to college and took some courses for Senior Care. Now she works at Lily Rose Senior Day Care & Recreational Center once per week, every Thursday for two hours.

I park the car outside an old, quaint cafe directly opposite from my grandmother's flower shop, Phoebe's Enchanted Garden. I glance through my window to read the sign swinging gently in the summer breeze.

Spinners Book Emporium & Cafe.

I grin when Megs steps out through the glass door, a huge smile on her face. "You coming or what?"

I nod, grab my purse, jump out of the car, and then race toward the door.

"Holy crap! The heat around here is killing me. I kind of miss Ohio," I tell Megs, hurrying up in an attempt to escape the heat. She grabs my hand and drags me inside the cafe. Cool air engulfs me immediately once we're inside. I love the café's fifties retro look: a jukebox at the corner, black and white tiles, red diner booth sets. Even the wait staff is wearing little frilly red and white checked aprons.

"The summers here are pure torture. Come on. I've been waiting for you! You need to taste this. It's orgasmic."

A chuckle reaches me from where I'm standing. Megs rolls her eyes and sighs dramatically, before turning to face the tall blond boy sauntering towards us, a little pink apron wrapped around his waist.

He runs his long fingers through his overgrown hair and flashes me a cocky grin. "It's a talent. My hands have that kind of gift."

"Such a large ego," Megs says.

"The bigger the ego, the bigger the dick." He winks.

Megs narrows her eyes and props her hands on her hips. "Been there. Tapped that. It's not that impressive."

Blond Boy smirks. "Two hours ago you were worshipping my dick reverently. Didn't you say it's God's gift to womankind?"

She rolls her eyes again. "Just serve us our coffee, Mr. Frilly Apron, or I will write a bad review to Mr. Spinner."

"I'm his James Bond. Secret weapon. He can't afford to fire me." He smirks. "And he's my uncle. He wouldn't fire his only nephew."

He swaggers to the counter, leaps to the other side, then spins around and focuses those hazel eyes on me. His gaze momentarily wanders to my arms. They widen and he clears his throat before looking up at me. My stomach flutters nervously as I wait for his verdict. He's Megs' friend and I really want him to like me.

I hold my breath as an awkward tension fills our conversation.

He licks his lips. "Green eyes. Red hair. Pixie-tall. Um. Let me guess. Cole's hot new neighbor?" He grins, and reaches up for two mugs from the little cupboard on the side and then narrows his eyes. "I'm still waiting for you to sprout little gossamer wings and fly. You do have wings, don't you? And a pouch full of fairy dust?"

My breath rushes out of my mouth and I laugh. As much as I'm trying to be brave about working on this new me, I'm still terrified of being judged. Of rejection. "Be very careful, Blondie, or I might blind you with a dash of my glittery fairy dust."

His eyebrows shoot up. "Blondie? Of all the names out there, you chose Blondie?"

"Oh, what do you want me to call you?" I tease.

"Edwards," he says in a deep voice. "Simon Edwards." He slides a mug of coffee in front of me and another to Megs, and then stands back and stares at us expectantly. I love the faint taste of nutmeg and vanilla flavoring he added in the coffee.

"Good coffee, Edwards. Simon Edwards," I say.

He grins. "I like you, Keds. Your boy is in there." He points to the doorway that has a little board with the words "Book Nook" on the door.

"My boy?" I ask him, glancing down at my navy blue sneakers with little yellow and white hearts on them.

"Cole. Go ahead," he says quietly. And with that, he turns to focus on the little ball of fire that is Megs.

"Oh, before you go, would you like to check out this amazing clothing store just a few blocks from here. They have discounts like all the time. You game?" Megs asks, tapping a finger on the side of her mug to the rhythm of the The Chiffon's *One Fine Day*, playing on the jukebox.

I nod and smile. I'm not really in a hurry to tell her that I don't have money to spend on clothing at the moment. I try to save up every cent I get and use it only when absolutely necessary. I used to work in a candy shop on the weekends in Ohio. The pay wasn't great, but it served me well during emergencies.

When Mom married my dad, her life became all about being a mom and a housewife. She never went to college, which is something she really regrets. She once confided in me that my sisters and I have a college fund, courtesy of her and her parents. No one else other than her and me or my sisters could withdraw money from the account. The money would only be released to us if and when we started college. Dad gives my sisters and I pocket money. It's not a lot, so we have to make do with what we have. Admitting this to Megs is embarrassing, which is why I let the forced smile linger on my face and turn to study the little shop while trying to work up the courage to walk inside the book nook.

Standing up, I inch toward the book nook. My step falters when a group of boys and girls sitting in a booth a few feet away, stare in my direction and begin to whisper among themselves, while pointing at my arms. I bite the inside of my cheek and drop my gaze to the floor to block the judgmental looks.

"I'm more than enough," I mutter under my breath. "Nothing else matters." I whisper these words over and over to drown out their murmurs and gawking.

I've been working hard to nurture the new me. Hiding from people and feeling ashamed doesn't help me achieve that.

Raising my chin, I look up, meeting each and every one of their gazes. My momentary bravery might be stupid. Confronting them could end up hurting me even more than their stares, if they decide to use words as their weapon. But I have accepted what I did. I'm not going to stand by and let anyone make me feel like I'm a freak of nature.

"If you have something to say, say it because it's rude to stare," I say in the most polite voice I can muster.

They drop their gazes one by one.

Relief bursts through me when a few whispered "sorry" reach me where I'm standing, nervous and unsure what my next step should be.

I glance back at the door before me, suddenly feeling hot and as if my stomach is full of butterflies. I don't even know why I'm nervous. It's not like we don't see each other every day. Or I haven't stopped having inappropriate thoughts about his hands touching me, and his mouth kissing me. Heat fans my face. Gah! He will know what I'm thinking as soon as I step inside the room.

I straighten, pluck a lemon drop from my purse and pop it in my mouth. And then I push the 'Book Nook' door slightly and duck my head.

Cole is sitting in the corner next to the window, the light streaming in. His shoulders hunched over the sketch book, bottom lip snagged between his teeth as his hand moves swiftly across the page. He is wearing his trademark beanie. A copy of *Peter Pan* sits on the table. The edges are frayed and the cover is wrinkled and slightly faded. A collection of crumpled papers, pens and what looks like rulers.

I walk back to the counter.

"Did you say hi?" Megs grins at me.

I shake my head. "He seems busy." I gulp down my coffee and place the empty mug on the vintage Formica counter.

Megs grabs my shoulders and spins me around. "Breath in. Out. Now go in there and talk to that boy."

I stumble forward before righting myself and send a pretend-glare over my shoulder at Megs. She gives me a thumbs up and winks, and I turn to face the book nook again.

I wish I could read this boy. One moment he is sweeping me into the woods, showing me his tree house and opening up to me, the next he is quiet. Almost too thoughtful. I wonder what goes through his mind when he's lying next to me on the roof. I remember how his thumb felt against my skin, the warm air fanning my lips when he dipped his head closer to my face. I was so sure he wanted to kiss me.

My life has been full of uncertainties. I just wish I was certain of this thing with Cole. I'm going to find out, one way or another. I want to feel like I belong somewhere. And I'm hoping he will agree to teach me how to sign.

The moment I step inside, I halt and stare around the room. The walls are lined with shelves filled with books to the brim. Four rows of bookcases stand in the middle of the room. Two-seaters are arranged across the room, giving it a cozy feeling. A few kids are perched on the seats, reading or chatting in low voices while others sit on the chairs, heads bent low over desks, working studiously. The music from the other side of the wall doesn't leak into the room, so I assume some kind of soundproofing system has been installed to keep the noise out.

I turn to face Cole, and as if he senses me, he raises his head and his eyes widen slightly. He's been invading my space constantly since we moved in next door to his house, and now I'm invading his.

Cole

The second Nor steps though the door, my body snaps in awareness. Only one person has the ability to do that to me. The one girl I've been fantasizing about for a while now. I was so close to kissing her when I took her to my tree house. I can't seem to stop staring at her mouth, especially when she says my name. That bottom lip, fuller than the top one. Every time I close my eyes, I imagine how her mouth would feel against mine. I just want to kiss her. That's all. Kiss her and touch her skin. I've given up pretending that I'm not interested in her, because I am. I'm admitting it shamelessly. Our nightly star-gazing is the highlight of my day.

Right after our trip to the tree house, I lay in bed, thinking about my evening. She was easy to talk to, and she *listened*. The longer we talked, the more her eyes came alive, chasing away the shadows and pain from their depths. Other than her dad being the king of douche-dicks, that evening had been in my top five of all times. I can't stop thinking about all the ways I could erase the constant look of pain in her eyes.

And now, she's standing in front of me, watching my every move with her big, innocent eyes. She's pulling me into their lushness, and she doesn't even know it.

I'm in trouble, and I welcome it willingly.

Clearly, I'm obsessed.

My gaze moves to her mouth as I wait patiently for her to say something.

Cole is still staring at me. Maybe I should have settled for our nightly star-gazing session and let him come to me when he was ready.

I shake my head to clear those thoughts. I'm here now. The need to talk to Cole, to be close to him, has surpassed all rational thought. It's probably not healthy, but I *need* to. My desire turned into a craving that night when he came to the roof and hooked his pinkie around mine.

I step closer, braving his stare. The only thing that betrays his nerves is the way his fingers fiddle with his beanie on the table.

I wave at him. "Hi."

He nods once, but doesn't smile back. His eyes are fixed on me, watching intently.

I bite my bottom lip and glance down at my hands, feeling a little nervous. Lately, Josh hasn't been around a lot. I've resorted to learning a few signs by searching the various sites dedicated to teaching ASL online.

I bend my fingers to form a curve and bring them to my middle with the knuckles touching and then roll them forward and point at him, smiling and say, "How are you?"

He blinks and the corner of his mouth tips up in my favorite almost smile.

Success! I've managed to get that addictive smile and also surprise him.

I pull out the chair across from him and sit down, enjoying that look on his face. I glance at the notebook in front of him. It's full of what looks like geometric drawings. Elegant and beautiful and very complicated. I feel a vein explode somewhere inside my head. My eyes are drawn back to the notebook and the hand gripping a pencil. They are beautiful fingers. Long, strong, capable of inducing so many emotions in me with just a simple touch. They are artistic fingers.

"Thought you might need this, Keds."

I jerk my head up and see Simon place a glass of ginger ale in front of me.

"It's on the house," he announces with a wink.

He turns and signs something to Cole. Cole's lips twitch as if he's fighting a smile and shoves his middle finger in Simon's face.

Simon laughs and leaves the room, shaking his head. Cole is back to watching me like he's seeing me for the first time, taking every feature in before focusing on my mouth. I browse through the limited ASL knowledge in my head for something witty or clever and fail miserably.

Angling my face to make sure he can see my mouth, I sign at the same time as I say, "I enjoy talking to you."

His gaze leaves my hands and returns to my face. He clears his throat, his lips twitching.

Yep. That probably didn't come out right.

I clear my throat and wait until his focus narrows on my lips. "I enjoy talking to you, but you never talk a lot. You come to my roof, lie down next to me, breathe my air and watch the stars. But you never talk to me."

He grabs the pen and turns a fresh page on his sketch book and scribbles some words on it. And then flips it around and slides it toward me.

You're a terrible signer.

Heat crawls up my cheeks and I look up at him. He's smiling now. Grinning, actually. It's the most beautiful thing I've ever seen.

He pulls the notebook back and writes on it again before pushing it back to me.

Use your mouth and speak slowly. I love to watch you while you speak.

Holy hell!

"You do?" Those are the only words capable of leaving my mouth. My brain cells. . .gone. *Poof!*

He nods, his gaze still fixed on my mouth. I lick my lips, the courage that acted as fuel when I walked over a few minutes ago has vanished.

He scrawls on the book, **Something got your tongue?**

"More like Cole got my tongue," I mutter under my breath. The boy sitting two feet away from us snickers.

Crap. I didn't mean to say that out loud.

Something brushes against my knee. I jolt upright as the impact of it rushes through me.

Oh God, his knee is touching mine. Maybe it was accidental?

Yeah, right. I've known Cole for a while now. Nothing about his actions are accidental or innocent. They are measured. Deliberate. Precise.

He applies pressure where our bodies touch. I'm no longer Eleanor. I'm a girl who's hanging on by a thread, waiting to burst into flames. The movement stops and air finally finds its way back into my lungs. I should move my leg, put a stop to this torture. But I can't. There's a force that tethers my body to his. I want to find out more about it because. . .I just need to.

Period.

Time to regroup. Why was I here again?

"Why do you come to my rooftop every night?"

His gaze leaves my mouth and holds mine captive.

He folds his arms on his chest and tips his head to the side. "Do you want me to stop?"

The thought of not having Cole's body next to mine at ten o'clock every night makes my chest twist in pain. But I need to know.

"Why do you come to my rooftop every night?"

"Why do *you* lay on your roof every night?"

I sigh and smile. I can't help it. "Because the sky is a dark canvas of endless dreams and fantasies, just waiting to be discovered. When I'm lying there, tossing my thoughts to the sky, it's just me and the stars. Bliss. Peace."

His stare intensifies, studying my face for several seconds. He blinks and says, "I'm a huge fan of astronomy."

I roll my eyes, enjoying this banter a lot.

"And you can't do that on your roof because. . ." I raise my brows and purse my lips.

His wide shoulders roll in a lazy shrug, but he doesn't answer.

I lean closer and his arms drop, the nonchalant pose gone. His scent slams into me and I have to fight hard not to launch my body across the table and wrap myself around him for eternity. The muscles on his forearm tense as he grabs the beanie with his free hand from the table. He clenches it in his fist as though holding on to the hat gives him something to keep himself from drowning in the tension surrounding us. I know this because that's what I'm feeling right now, like I'm being pulled toward something I've never felt before. Something indescribable. Something phenomenal.

His Adam's apple bobs up and down.

Do I make him nervous? Or is there something else going on behind those stormy gray eyes?

I lift my chin, aiming to goad him further. "Why do you come to my rooftop every night?"

He stares at me for a long time, longer than it should be legally allowed for one person to stare at another.

He closes his eyes, those long spiky lashes casting shadows on his cheeks, and exhales shakily as though he's forcing air out of his lungs. His eyes flicker open and he stares down at the notepad. His grip on the pencil is tight. He might snap it any minute now. He lets go of the beanie and runs his fingers down his hair before hunching down and writing fast. Once he's done, he slides the notebook in my direction then leans back in his chair and stares at me.

My heart's beating out of my chest as I drop my eyes from his to the words written in a careless scrawl.

Can I let you in on a little secret? I've imagined for a while now how your mouth would feel pressed against mine. That bot-

tom lip between my teeth. I've wondered if you'd moan if I kissed you, how your body would feel flush to mine. I've fantasized about so many things about you, but most of all, I've wondered what you taste like. Sweet and innocent as you look.

Holy hell! How am I even sitting down?

Body: Liquid

Brain cells: I'm searching my head to determine if I have any functioning ones left. I'm ninety-nine percent certain they melted like butter after reading those words.

Heart: It's not even mine anymore. He owns it. It's perched on his lap, panting like an eager puppy waiting to be petted.

Soul: He owns that too.

Ovaries: I'm not sure mine have recuperated since I first laid eyes on Cole.

I haven't taken a sip of my drink since Simon brought it over. I grab the glass like a lifeline and gulp down half of its contents in one swoop.

When I set it back on the table, my throat is still parched. I'm still hot and my heart is beating fast.

"If that's how you feel," I say and gesture to the note, "then why haven't you kissed me yet?" I blurt out.

Gosh, Nor. Desperate much?

"I wanted to kiss you every time we were together, but I couldn't. Do you know why?" He leans forward and brushes his knuckles against the back of my hand and says, "Anticipation."

That word is everything that is Cole Holloway. I'm never sure what he's thinking behind those gray eyes. Will he smile at me? Frown? Not say anything at all?

Cole pulls his hand back, his gaze never leaving mine. He pins my knee with his against the soft curve of the seat.

Once.

Once is enough to set my soul ablaze, fiercer and hotter than ever before.

I cough and breathe and cough again, trying to get my body back under control before saying, "I came to see you because I want you to do something for me."

One dark eyebrow goes up and he sinks further into his chair. He folds his arms on his chest.

I lift my hands and sign, "*I want to learn how to sign.*"

CHAPTER NINETEEN

Nor

HIS SHOULDERS START TO SHAKE RIGHT BEFORE HE GRINS WIDE.

"Yeah, yeah get it off your chest," I murmur under my breath. I made him laugh even though whatever I signed was ridiculously wrong. It kind of feels good to know I can do that to him.

Oh man, his smile belongs in a freakin' toothpaste commercial.

The mirth in his eyes fades a bit. He scribbles on his trusty notepad again. **You just asked me if I want to take a piss**.

I gape at him. "I did?"

This only pushes him to laugh harder, and oh man. His laugh is throaty so it's definitely worth messing up the signs.

"No. I'm just teasing you."

I pretend to scowl at him but end up grinning. I'm liking this playful side of him. It's addictive and unexpected.

I'm not ready to stop playing this game. I grab the notebook and write, **Teach me** and then straighten in my chair, crossing my arms on my chest. When he looks up from the notepad, he's no longer smiling.

I raise a brow at him, challenging him and point my finger to the words I wrote. His stare drops lower to my chest. I follow his gaze and see my boobs, pressing against my dress, pushing up from my folded arms.

"Really, Cole?!" He's such a guy!

He shrugs.

"I thought Josh was teaching you." His shoulders tense, his jaw clenches.

"I want you to teach me."

He nods once, that little smile appearing once again. His body visibly relaxes.

Downing the rest of my ginger ale, I place the glass on the table and wipe my mouth with the back of my hand. He drops the pen on the table, the sound bouncing around the silent room.

He holds his hands out with the palms facing up, draws his fingers toward him as if they're grabbing something, and then curls his hands into fists, puts one on top of the other and does this counterclockwise grinding motion.

Um. . .

He bites his bottom lip and repeats the gesture while saying loudly, "Wanna get coffee?"

I raise my hands and copy what he just did. I know I'm messing it up big time when he smirks, scoots his chair closer and grabs my hands to walk me through the steps.

His hands are touching mine now. I can't think. I can't breathe. I swear my brain has short-circuited. I'm useless.

He drops his fingers from mine and asks me to repeat. I do it but mess the steps up again because my skin is tingling where his hands were. He's patient though. In fact, it seems like he's enjoying this a little too much.

"*Thank you*," I sign.

He nods and says, "The pleasure is all mine."

Why do I feel those five little words hold more meaning than meets the eye?

Cole stands up from his chair, lifts his arms up in a stretch and my fantasy about ever seeing a part of his skin other than his face and arms comes to life. His T-shirt rides up and reveals a slip of his stomach. He's toned, probably from building houses and lifting things in his dad's construction company.

God.

Are those abs real?

Right before the shirt slides back down, I catch a glimpse of a tattoo on the right side of his rib. His smirks when he sees where my attention is. He steps around the small desk, takes my hand from my lap and tugs me up. Once I'm standing, he hooks his pinkie finger around mine, turns around and strides toward the back of the room where the majority of the shelves are. Everyone seems preoccupied with whatever they are doing. Feeling braver with each step, I follow him. I'm helpless not to. It's like Cole is a wind charmer and I'm the wind. Whichever way he blows, I'm there, following him, unable to resist his call.

We stop at the back of the room in a spot hidden behind two book cases. He gazes down at me with that look of his that makes me wonder what he's thinking about.

"Can I see your tattoo?" Man, I'm on a roll today.

He nods.

Tentatively, I lift his shirt. The muscles beneath his skin tense as if anticipating my touch. His eyes go from gray to stormy in two seconds flat. I tear my eyes from his and scoot closer to read the inscription:

The moment you doubt whether you can fly, you cease forever to be able to do it.

Placing my fingers against his abs, I trace the quote with my thumb and he sucks in a breath. I jerk my head up to look at him. His eyes are sealed and his breathing is ragged. I touch his shoulder and his eyes flip open.

"It's beautiful."

I drop his shirt and we stand there, staring at each other. He takes a step forward and my legs follow his lead, closing the space between us. He stares at my mouth again, his eyes darkening, seemingly fascinated by my lips. I'm dying to test his theory and give him a taste of what my mouth feels like because I want to know what *his* tastes like.

I raise to my tiptoes. His eyes widen, darker and hungrier than before, but my Cole, the boy I've come to know, doesn't make a move. I press my lips to his, then let my tongue taste his bottom lip. I've imagined doing this a million times. Kissing him. Tasting him. But I've never done something like this until this moment. Never initiated a kiss. Something about Cole makes me want to beat down my fear and try things I've never done before.

He doesn't disappoint. His mouth parts on a breath, and his tongue meets mine in a quick caress before retreating back. I drop to the soles of my feet and tilt my head up. God, he is tall.

Does he want to grab me, kiss me again? Or push me away? I can't read him. All I know is that his eyes are like thunder and lightning on a dark velvet night. A part of me is terrified and the other is excited because I know that when he finally really kisses me, I won't want to emerge from the storm he will create.

Finally, he slides one hand around my waist and pulls me close. He rests his forehead against mine before lowering his head to the crook of my neck. His other arm comes around my back, pulling me close. He hugs me tight, then his hold loosens, and just when I think he's about to let me go, his arms tighten again, firmer than before. Like he's not ready to let me go. Like he wants our bodies to meld into each other. God, I want that too.

He lifts his head and brushes his thumb along my bottom lip. A groan rumbles in his chest and that is the only warning I get as his lips crush into mine, swallowing my squeal of surprise.

"Fuck, Snowflake. If I had known kissing you would be this intoxicating, I would have claimed this perfect mouth sooner. But I was a coward. I need to kiss you," he says, pulling back slightly. The words are a little unclear, affected by the same hurricane that's destroying my thoughts inside me. "I've wanted to kiss you since I saw you glare at me from your front lawn. You've crawled under my skin so deep, I have to kiss you to seal you in. Never leave."

Did he just call me Snowflake?

Holy crap. "Were you afraid of kissing me?"

He blinks. His hands loosen their hold. He seems hesitant to say anything, but I see the moment he decides to let me in.

He nods. "I wasn't ready for you. I wasn't ready to get myself tangled up with you. Girls break you. I've been broken before. I planned to stay away from you, but fuck. Nor. I keep coming back to that roof every night. Every fucking night. And now you're here, in my space. What have you done to me?"

My knees buckle and my hands shoot out to grab his arms for support. Before my body hits the floor, he grips my upper arms hoisting me up and his hips press forward, supporting my weight at the same time that my back connects with a hard surface. Then he slides his hands under my knees, hooking my legs around his waist, locking me in completely. My heart's thumping hard against his chest. I wish I had more than two sets of hands so I could touch him all over at once like I've imagined doing. I settle for sinking my fingers into his thick hair and pulling him down toward my mouth, but I don't need to. He's already leaning down to me.

When his trembling fingers connect with my body, the hesitation I'd felt when he first joined me on my roof is gone. His hands are all over me, brutal and greedy. One hand slides up my neck and lifts my hair over to one shoulder. His fingers splay on my throat, soaking up the vibrations from my groans.

"Is this okay?" he asks. "I want to feel the sounds you make on my skin."

I nod in understanding. I have no idea what I'm doing, so I let him guide me because I know he won't hurt me. I trust him, even though that's an emotion reserved for very special people.

Just before his mouth crashes down on mine, he groans, a sound that's a cross between torment and desire. I moan and the last thing I see are his stormy eyes as they darken further. Then he's kissing me, driving me wild with kisses that taste like mint, hope and storm. Gravity can't hold me down, I'm so high I'm touching the sky without my feet leaving the ground. His mouth moves, shaping into mine, his hands desperate and needy. Demanding and unrelenting. I'm like clay in his hands and I don't care. He can shape me into whatever he wants. Whatever he needs me to be as long as he doesn't stop making me feel like I'm kissing heaven. It's overwhelming.

Pure torture.

Exquisite.

Perfection.

It's everything that is Cole Holloway, a quiet yet powerful storm, which could wreck me.

Break me.

Mend me.

I swear this boy will be the death of me.

His hand leaves the nape of my neck and now he's cupping my cheeks, slowing the kiss, taming the hurricane currently destroying every little fragment that makes me who I am. I open my eyes and lean my head back, as his mouth slides down my neck, across my collarbone, before he pulls back to stare at me.

"Hi," he pants.

"Hi," I reply, twirling the hair curling on his neck. I bury my face in his chest. Feel his heart beating frantically to the same rhythm as mine.

I close my eyes and smile.

I could live on that kiss alone.

Cole cups the side of my neck, caressing my jaw with his thumbs as he searches my face. His eyes are filled with something akin to be-wilderment, bordering on wonder. And then he shakes his head and kisses my forehead.

"Thank you." He mouths the words on my skin and I can feel them imprint themselves in my soul. The soul that he owns.

Unhooking my legs from around his taut waist, I slide down his body, and suck in a breath as his erection pushes against my stomach. I land on shaking feet. Cole doesn't let me go yet. He readjusts my dress, then deftly brushes my hair back with his fingers before pulling me back into his arms, wrapping them around me. Cole doesn't just hug me, though. He has a way of holding me, and just when I think he's about to drop his arms and let me go, they tighten around me. Firm yet gentle. I love it. I'm sure he invented this kind of hug.

A Cole kind of hug.

He ducks his head to meet my gaze and asks, "Can you walk?"

I jerk my head up and feel heat burst on my cheeks at the look on his face. I'm afraid if I open my mouth to speak, I might start whooping in joy.

I nod and grin. "Dude. You're lethal." I still can't believe this quiet boy kissed the living crap out of me. The quiet ones are always the most dangerous, I guess.

One side of his mouth tips up. I'm beginning to get addicted to that smile of his. He steps back and shoves those hands that tilted my world off its axis inside his pockets.

Cole kissed me.

Cole hugged me.

Cole kissed me.

"See you later." *And hopefully we'll create a storm of kisses again.*

I wave and turn around, literally skipping out of the room and ignoring the freckled boy gaping at us. With Cole's taste still fresh on my tongue, I press my fingers on my lips and grin.

He tastes like what my dreams are made of. I like it.

"That look suits you," Megs announces, startling me out of my thoughts.

I glance up and see her smiling wide. She and Simon exchange a look. Simon scowls, darts a look in the direction I came from, then back at me.

"Damn it," he says, shoving his hand inside the back pocket of his shorts and pulling out his wallet. He pulls out a ten-dollar bill and slaps it on the counter toward Megs, who is now laughing hard.

"What's going on?" I ask, feeling the heat in my cheeks fade a little.

"I told him Cole would kiss the shit out of you. Simon said he wouldn't. We placed a bet and I won. How could Cole not kiss you when he gets this moony look in his eyes whenever your name pops up in a conversation?" She winks, grabs the money on the counter and tucks it inside her bra.

I don't even know how to react to this, but the look on Simon's face is priceless. A giggle sneaks out of my mouth, followed by another one. Soon Megs and I are laughing hard. Simon's lips twitch as he fights a smile. When I finally stop, Megs walks toward me and hugs me too tight.

"It's so good to see you laugh, Nor," she whispers in my neck.

I hug her tighter, basking in this friendship. "I promise to laugh more often then," I say, pulling back.

"That shit would be hot if you two didn't look as if you're having a soap opera moment," Simon says from the other side of the counter.

We turn to look at him as he waggles his eyebrows.

I chuckle and shake my head, too happy to even form any kind of reply. "I'm ready to check out those dresses you were talking about."

"Awesome." She sashays around the counter. Simon grins like he can't stop himself, his face lit up with his feelings for Megs. Grabbing her hand, he drags her to an alcove which is mostly hidden from the public, shackles her wrists with one of his hands and slides them above her head before he kisses her. Oh my God, he kisses her like he wants to consume her whole.

My face starts to heat again at this passionate display, so I yell, "I'll be in the car, Megs," while turning around and heading out the door.

Once I'm seated inside my mom's old Station Wagon, it hits me that Cole probably wasn't just giving me a lesson in ASL. He asked me out for coffee.

Well, at least I hope he did.

I roll down the window to let out the heat in the car and wait for my friend, and my thoughts go back to what happened in the book nook. I shiver all over again, feeling a tingly-warm feeling settle low in my stomach.

I've always wondered what steamy, heart pounding kisses feel like. Cole knocked the ball out of the park with that kiss.

CHAPTER TWENTY

Monday morning, I jerk awake at the sound of a bird chipping merrily outside my window. I turn my head to check the time on the clock on my nightstand and fly out of bed.

Crap!

It's nine-thirty in the morning. I'm starting my job at my grandma's shop today and I'm supposed to be there in ten minutes.

I slip on knee-length sky blue dress and adjust the straps on my shoulders, my mind on last night. Last night's star-gazing session was incredible. Cole held my hand in his the entire time and when we finally climbed down from the roof, he kissed me so long, so soft, so hard that I stayed up for hours just thinking about it. It's as if the kiss behind the shelves at the book nook unlocked something in me, in us. We couldn't keep our hands off each other when we were close.

A tap on the window pulls me out of my thoughts. I turn around to find Cole standing there. My heart drums its usual *thud thud thud* inside my chest and heat fills my cheeks, absorbing the way his gaze travels down my body like he wants to crawl through the window and ravish me.

"Hey," I wave, wondering why my knees feel like jelly but I'm still standing here.

"Come here," he says. Somehow, I float across the room to the window, and he enters my room.

As soon as I reach his side, he takes my face into his hands, and stares into my eyes for long seconds before dipping his head and pressing his lips to mine. My eyes automatically fall shut as the soft innocent kiss quickly changes into a passionate one as our tongues tangle and teeth clash. My hands find their way to his neck, and further up, to tug the beanie aside a bit and sink my fingers into his thick, soft hair.

The kiss ends too soon. The sound of our ragged breathing fills the room. I open my eyes and watch as he takes a deep breath, before his eyes slowly open.

"Do you want me to drop you at Phoebe's? I looked out my window and saw your mom's car still parked outside. I figured you hadn't left and so I am here to offer my chauffeur services."

I nod, thoroughly excited about sharing space with him in the car. "Let me just get my purse and phone."

His fingers linger on mine a little longer before he shakes his head as if he is lost in a dream and pulls them away. Cole crawls out the window again to wait for me in his car. He has been using the window since the confrontation with my dad. If there's something I'm grateful for, it's that my dad is rarely home, but that doesn't mean that we aren't careful.

After quickly checking on mom in her room and find her sleeping, I pop in to say bye to Elon and Elise, letting them know how long I'll be gone and to call me if they need anything. I bound downstairs and out the door. Cole is waiting next to his car in his usual parking spot, holding the passenger door open for me. Once I'm seated, he rounds the car to his side and slides in on his seat. Seconds later, he pulls out of the spot and drives off, with our fingers already linked together on his thigh.

When we arrive at Phoebe's, he walks me to the door and we stop. I turn around to face him.

"What time will you be done? Maybe we can continue with those sign language classes I promised you."

Yes! More Cole time. "In four hours. Or. . ." I pull out my phone from my purse. "You can give me your number and I'll text you."

He glances down at the phone and says, "Right, why didn't I

think of that?" Then he chuckles. The sound is breathy, sexy, husky.

After exchanging numbers, I turn, heading for the glass door with the "Open" sign on it, but a hand wraps around my wrist, spinning me around. I gasp and before I can say a word, his mouth is once again on mine, parting my mouth and exploring me in a gentle sweep of his tongue. Reminding me of what I'm looking forward to when my shift here is done.

Then he nips my bottom lip before he pulls back, straightening to his full height. "See you in four hours."

God.

Cole. I have no words, really.

As soon as he leaves, I push open the door and float inside the shop.

"Now that is what I call a good bye kiss," Grandma says with a chuckle. I glance up and see her sitting in a chair next to her desk.

I stop next to her and toss my purse on the chair across from the desk, suddenly feeling shy. I lean down to kiss her cheek and straighten. "I'm happy."

"Is that the Holloway boy?"

I nod, taking in my surroundings and breathing in the mixed scents of roses, lilacs, gardenia and some flowers I don't even know, placed strategically around the room.

"Yep. That's Cole." Even his name makes me shiver.

She is quiet for a few seconds, and I turn to face her. "Do you know him?"

She nods. "His mother and your father were inseparable in their teens. They grew up together. Maggie lived a few houses away from ours."

Oh wow. This explains the way he was looking at Cole's mom on the day we arrived. It doesn't answer why he hates Cole though, a thought that makes my head hurt every time I think about it.

"What happened? Why did they break up?"

She shrugs. "I'm not entirely sure. Maggie came to see me before she went off to college. She wanted to talk. She told me that she couldn't handle Stephen's 'obsessive ways'. Her words, not mine. Your father can be quite intense."

Don't I know it.

She inhales deeply as though she is about to let me in on a secret. "Cole is a good boy. Very hardworking. He reminds me of my Thomas."

I stare at her, confused.

"My son."

Wait, *what*? My father has a brother? How come I've never met him? And no one talks about him?

My grandmother blinks, her eyes filling with tears. "He was my first born child, your father's older brother. I got very sick when I was pregnant with Thomas, which affected his hearing. He was born deaf. He passed away a few years ago. I don't talk about it, it's a very difficult topic for me. I've held onto it for so long. Seeing the Holloway boy brought back those memories.

"Your father and Thomas never got along very well, because of Thomas's. . .um. . .lifestyle." She wipes her cheeks and tries to smile, but fails miserably when a sob escapes her lips. "He was gay, something my husband and later on, Stephen, didn't approve of."

My mind is reeling with this information. "Does Mom know?"

She shakes her head. "I have no idea if Stephen ever told her. Every family has a secret and this was ours, mainly because of the way he died."

I scoot around the table, drop on my knees in front of her, and wrap my arms around her. I had a relative, an uncle, who I never even knew existed. Does my father ever have any positive feelings for anyone? This is just. . .insane.

I pull back and rest my bottom on my heels. "How did he die?"

She rolls her head back and stares at the ceiling, tears running down the side of her face now. I climb to my feet and rush to the counter where the cash register sits, grab the box of tissues, and hurry back to her. I pluck one out and press it into her hand. She dabs her cheeks and eyes with the tissue, before focusing on me again. I want to tell her that she doesn't need to talk about it, but the need to know is overpowering.

"He. . .um. . .he killed himself right after he broke up with his boyfriend."

Oh my God.

I lean forward and pull her into my arms, as my own tears roll down my cheeks, joining her in mourning someone I never had the pleasure of meeting.

I'm not even sure how this day turned from one filled with swoon-worthy kisses, walking-on-sunshine moments to one of confessions. Seeing Cole must have triggered Grandma's memories, ripping open barely healed wounds.

"Have you ever talked to someone about this?" I ask, pulling back and walking around the desk. I lift the chair and set it on the floor next to hers so our knees are touching.

She nods. "The psychologist at work. It took me a long time to accept the consequences of not standing up for my baby. For Thomas."

We continue chatting about the past. Customers come in, buy what they need and leave. I can't help but think that my family is really messed up.

Eventually, we get on to the orientation. Grandma explains to me what requires urgent attention, which is arranging the carnations in various buckets in the corner. The owner will pick up their order before closing time. I end up texting Cole to inform him that I need more time. Grandma orders us Chinese for lunch from the restaurant next door. I'm not hungry despite not having breakfast this morning.

Six hours later, Cole pops in to pick me up and drive me home. I'm not even surprised when my grandmother converses with him in sign language after the introductions are over.

"Where did your grandmother learn how to sign like that?" he asks, on the way to his car.

I tell him about Thomas, his father, and how he died. I leave out the part where my father hated his own brother. I need to mull over that information first, and if I'm being honest with myself, I'm a little bit scared that Cole will look at me differently. Surely, Dad's prejudices wouldn't be clouding his mind, judging Cole, would he?

As soon as Cole drops me home and he kisses me senseless, we agree to meet at our usual place, and I walk toward my house. There is so much I don't know about my dad, and the more I discover about him, the more I realize he is practically a stranger. I can't shake off this uneasiness creeping down my spine.

CHAPTER TWENTY-ONE

Nor

TODAY IS MY FIRST DAY OF WORKING WITH MY GRANDMA AT LILY Rose and I'm running a little late. I swear if someone asks me what my super power is, I'll tell them, running late.

I hop out of the Station Wagon, grab my purse and dash through the sliding glass doors at exactly ten o'clock in the morning. I ask the lady at the reception where Albert Hall is, then hurry down the hall. Grandma is already here. The chairs have been arranged in a circle, which I assume, will make interacting easier. I kiss her cheek and she hands me folders, and tells me that they contain songs she uses for the sessions. After placing a folder on each empty chair, she asks me if I would like to practice on the piano, get reacquainted with some of the tunes. I grab a copy of the music sheet and scan it. The first song on the list is "Frosty The Snowman."

Ten minutes later, an elderly couple walk in slowly, the man pushing the wheelchair for his wife. More people trickle in until all the seats have been taken.

I spend the next forty-five minutes singing and playing the piano. I swear it is the most fun I've had in a while.

When the session is over, I excuse myself and head out into the hall, searching for the bathroom. I pause when I see a short, burly man arguing with an elderly woman. Their facial features are similar so I assume she is his mother. He drags a hand down his face in obvious frustration. The older woman's face is red, her hands shaking in agitation. He turns around again, repeats his name and tells the woman he is her son. She shakes her head and yells, saying she doesn't have a son. This goes on for a few seconds. One of the day workers steps forward, says something to the man with a stern face, before turning to focus on the frantic woman.

Curious, I inch closer to the man. "Is everything okay, Sir?"

He startles and snaps his troubled gaze to mine. His face is flushed and he is swallowing hard, unable to get words out of his mouth. He shakes his head. I excuse myself, grab a plastic cup and fill it with water from the water cooler in the reception area, then head back and give the man the cup. He downs the water and sets the cup on the table.

"Thanks."

I nod and turn to leave.

"She doesn't know who I am," he says, sounding lost. I spin around and face him.

"She thinks I'm a stranger. She can't remember her dead husband or me, or my brother." He rubs his forehead and crushes the cup in his fist.

I imagine my mother forgetting who I am and pain stabs inside my chest. My heart aches for this man.

"I'm Eleanor Blake." I offer my hand in greeting, which he accepts.

"Eric Taylor." He pulls back his hand.

I glance over my shoulder. Grandma is still inside the hall. She probably needs a little longer before she is done with what she is doing. I clear my throat and search the reception area. It's like the staff have gone MIA.

God, what do I do? I've never seen an adult freak out—other than my mom—so this is quite frightening. I turn back to face Mr. Taylor and notice tears, probably born of frustration, shimmer in the corner of his eyes. I shift on my feet nervously. I can't just leave him looking like this.

"Sir, um. . .Mr. Taylor. Would you like to talk about it?"

He shakes his head again. Then nods, expels a breath and lowers himself on the seat next to him. His body is coiled tight around the shoulders and his hands are balled into fists. He bumps them against each other, his eyes focused on the floor. With one last look over my shoulder, I round the table and sit across from him with my hands folded on my lap. I hope Grandma will be done soon.

He presses a fist against his mouth. "Why does this happen? Why does this disease steal memories?" He's looking at me although I have a feeling his focus is not on me at all, but rather stuck in the distant past as he talks about their life. The time when he started noticing her forget the small things, and eventually the bigger things, like his son and her husband. By the time he is done, my heart is breaking for him and his mother, and I understand his frustration and panic. He stops speaking, but continues to stare at the floor. Grandma's voice drifts toward me. I turn around to see her hugging one of the women who work here, then starting to walk in my direction.

Thank God. I don't have answers for Mr. Taylor. I don't think anyone is in a position to provide the answers he desperately seeks, but since Grandma is more knowledgeable than me, she might be able to help him more than I did. She stops next to me and they start to chat. I realize she and Mr. Taylor know each other and probably have for a long time, since his mom has been visiting the center for a few weeks now.

By the time we part ways with Mr. Taylor, the look of frustration from before is gone.

Outside the center, I hug Grandma and promise to talk to her soon before heading for my car while switching on my phone. A message pops up.

Cole: You done yet?

I reach my car and stop, smiling.

Me: Just finished. On the way home.

Cole: Hurry. I've missed you.

I dig my keys out of my purse, open the car and hop on the driver's seat, grinning wide.

I love that Cole never hides his feelings for me.

CHAPTER TWENTY-TWO

Cole

"You guys need to tone that shit down," I say without looking at Simon and Megs, opting to speak instead of sign for Megs benefit.

Simon is an only child. His mom is a lawyer and his dad works in consulting for a public relations firm. Both his parents are hardly ever home, so he spends most of his time in Spinners Cafe, Megs' house and my place. He and I had plans to shoot some zombies on my Playstation. We did for a while. Then Megs called to ask if she could come over and Simon's concentration went to hell.

They have been making out on the two-seater in my room for the past thirty minutes, while I've been obsessively hopping between the window and my bed, waiting for Nor to come home from the center. My hand is starting to cramp from checking my phone for her text message so many times.

I glance up from the latest thriller novel that I bought last week to the couple writhing on the couch to my right and I feel my eyes burn.

Jesus.

Simon's hand is two seconds away from pulling down Megs panties, given the way her skirt is bunched up on her ass.

I grab the bookmark on the bed and mark the page before shutting the book. "*That is it. Get out of my room.*"

Simon's head pops up above Megs' chest. He pulls his hands from her body long enough to sign, "*Leave the room if we are bothering you.*"

"*Get your ass off my couch, Asshole. If I wanted to watch porn, I would watch my own collection.*"

He flips me off, sinks his fingers into Megs' hair and kisses her neck.

Where the hell is Nor? I need to get out of this hell. I can't stop thinking about her. My heart speeds up when I think of her and my hands tremble, dying to touch her.

My phone vibrates. I pull it out of my pocket and click on the little envelope on my screen.

Nor: **Just finished. On the way home**.

Hell-fucking-yes.

Me: **Hurry.**

My fingers poise above the screen. Would I look too desperate if I told her I missed her?

Whatever.

Me: **Hurry. I've missed you.**

Nor: **Should I come over?**

Me: **Yes**.

We've been spending more time in my house lately. It's safer that way.

I press send and grin at my phone. Shit. I'm completely obsessed with this girl. No wonder Josh can't seem to stop teasing me.

I toss my phone on the bed and spend the next few minutes peeling Simon and Megs from my couch and tossing them out of my room.

Nor

It's fifteen minutes to midday by the time I park my car in my usual spot outside my house. I grab my purse, hop out of the car and run up the path leading to my house. I'm meeting Cole soon, and knowing him, he'll be striding out his front door and leaping over the fence to get to me. I've gotten used to his intensity so I'm always ready for him.

With one last glance at Cole's house, I enter mine. *More than a feeling* by Boston blares from upstairs, shaking the floor boards beneath my feet. The sound of the cello joins Boston, it's sorrowful, yet alluring melody filling the space. I follow the throbbing beats to Elise's room before I stop, and duck my head through the door. Elise is sitting on top of her bed, holding a pencil in each hand, playing a pretend drum while rocking her head vigorously back and forth, while Elon's eyes are closed, a soft smile on her face.

"Turn down the music, guys." When they don't seem like they heard me, I cross the room and turn down the volume. As much as I love to see them like this, we still have to think of our mother.

"Hey!" Elise yells, her hands frozen mid-play.

"Too loud. I love you, girls. But if you don't stop I'll be forced to take you over my knee."

Elise snorts loudly and Elon rolls her eyes, shaking her head.

"Have you eaten lunch yet? And mom?"

They nod.

"Mom said she wanted to get some rest." Elon says, biting her lip and staring at Elise. "Maybe we should do this tomorrow."

Elise shrugs and hops down from the bed. I leave the room, and after taking my cell phone from my purse, I toss it on my bed and go back downstairs. After grabbing a quick bite of the pizza one of my sisters must have ordered, I settle on the bench in front of the Bosendorfer in living room and quick shoot a text to Cole to let him know I'll be at his house in ten minutes.

My mom started teaching me how to play the piano at the age of three. We would play frequently, especially when Dad wasn't home because he hated it and said the sound got on his nerves. Now, I play whenever I get a chance. Music is one of those things that helped me through the tough times.

I search my mind for a song I know will soothe her, one of her favorites, Yiruma's *River Flows in You.*

Placing my hands over the black and white keys, I close my eyes and let the chords play from my mind to my fingers. I continue playing, completely lost in its high and low soft tones. I hardly notice I'm not alone in the room. That is, until I feel air brush my arm. I open my eyes and blink. Cole is standing across from me, his hands splayed on the black gleaming surface of the piano. My fingers falter, stumbling on the keys and end up sounding like someone banged on them. I let my fingers trail off.

I glance around wondering how he got inside the house and for just a second, I panic. Cole has never been in here before. His visits are restricted to my bedroom only. What if Dad finds him in here? I jerk back to look at the clock and breath out, relieved. We still have a few hours until he comes home. If he comes home.

"Elise let me in while she was on her way out. I checked to see if your dad's car was outside before I snuck in."

Wow. I didn't even hear my sister leave.

"Are you okay?" he signs and speaks the words. He's been teaching me a few words when we aren't making out like crazy. Some of them I learned on YouTube.

Swallowing my nerves, I nod and go to him. I push on my tiptoes and press my lips against his in a kiss. He sucks in a breath, moaning softly before he pulls back and narrows his eyes at me.

"What?" I ask, as I drop to the soles of my feet.

"I've spent most of my life learning how to read people. I've spent the last few weeks learning to read you. What's wrong?"

I remember the way my father yelled at him, glaring at him with so much hate. Then grandma's story about Thomas and my father's hate for his own brother.

"My father doesn't like you," I say, carefully watching his face for a reaction.

"I know," he says. He doesn't look bothered at all. "I'm messing around with his daughter. Of course he doesn't like me. It won't stop me from liking you or wanting to kiss the shit out of you whenever I think of you. Which is every single fucking second of the day."

I shake my head, wondering if I should speak out loud my suspicions that my father not liking him is not caused by a mere irritation over a boy making a pass at his daughter. It's more than that. I can't really put a finger on what it is. My dad never liked my boyfriend in Ohio, but at least he was decent about it. Well, as decent as my father can be, which is glaring at a person until they scurry away in fear.

The scars on my arms prickle and I put my hands on them, running my nails along my skin to lessen the itch. "We have to be careful, okay?"

Cole's eyebrows dip, his eyes holding mine, studying me. He lays his hands on mine, halting my progress and then lefts them, replacing them with his. He rubs his palms up and down my arms, in slow, deliberate motions and my mind explodes into a thousand different sensations. "We will be careful." He tucks a lock of hair behind my ear and then tucks a thumb under my chin. "Chin up, beautiful.

"I have no idea what I did to piss him off, but when he told me to stay away from you, I intended to heed his warning. I was walking past your window when I realized I couldn't do it. I could not ignore the pull I felt between us in St. Christopher's."

I shrug off the uneasiness inside my chest. He kisses my forehead, and then turns me around and sits on the bench in front of the piano, pulling me on his lap. He sweeps my hair to the side and places kisses along the length of my neck, and down the side of my arm. I shiver, gasp, fight for air and my heart flips around inside my chest. I press my thighs together, and I swear he knows what he is doing to me, if that chuckle is any indication.

Shifting on his lap, I turn to face him. He groans and I can feel him getting hard under me.

"Should I sit over there?" I point at the space on the bench next to him.

He shakes his head and gestures for me to play.

I scroll through my mind, thinking of my favorite songs. Something to express what I'm feeling, what I feel for this boy. I can't believe how strong my feelings for him have become in such a short time. He hasn't voiced his feelings yet but I'm falling hard for him, which scares the crap out of me. The only people who have the ability to evoke these feelings inside me are my sisters, my mom and Grandma. And now Cole, but with him, it's different. Everything about him lights me on fire. His kiss, his touch, and the way he looks at me.

I let my fingers hover on the keyboard, and then slowly lower them onto the keys. He slides his hand to the nape of my neck, his hold possessive, before resting his chin on my shoulder.

Humming softly, I start off with the notes of Dionne Warwick's *This Girl's in Love with you*. I learned to play this by ear after my grandma Phoebe sent an old record of Dionne Warwick's to me for my birthday three years ago.

I let the last notes of the song trail off, singing the last of the lyrics softly. I'm quite relieved because Cole can't see my face. He can't read what I'm feeling and neither can he read my lips. I let my breathing slow down before turning to face him.

"So?" I let a smile cover the state of havoc I'm feeling inside. "Did you like it?"

His throat moves as he swallows hard, still staring at me as if I'm something. . .*special*.

"What?" I ask, squirming on his lap.

He brushes a finger along my throat. "I could feel you. What was the song about?"

I snag the corner of my lip and close the lid of the piano.

"It's about a girl confessing to a man that she loves him." I speak aloud the first few lyrics then stop when I get to the chorus. He gestures for me to continue. And I do, speaking the words of the chorus then pause.

He wraps his fingers around my wrists and peppers my skin with open mouth kisses on the scars.

Oh, God.

I'm not just falling for him. I've already fallen and I'm just waiting for him to catch up. I hope he feels the same way as I do.

His hands drop from my wrists and wrap around my bottom, pulling me to him. He presses a kiss on my stomach. Heat shoots between my legs at that simple, tender gesture. He looks up at me, a slow smile stretching across his face. His fingers shake as they move down my dress, under it and on to my thighs, skipping my underwear and circle my waist.

I need more. I need his mouth on more of my skin. I grab one of his hands and my dress drops back in place. I dart a look at the clock. We have over three hours before Dad comes home. If he comes home at all. "If you're going to attempt hitting third base, we need some privacy." And he follows me, his hand trembling in mine but the grin on his face. . .Jesus. It's beautiful and confident with a trace of shyness. You'd think I promised him the moon and exceeded his expectations by delivering the galaxy on a silver platter.

Once we stumble inside my room, I flip the lock and pull Cole toward my bed. The sound of our quick breathing fills the room, mingling with the hurried sound of our muffled footsteps on the wood. My knees hit the edge of the bed and I turn around to face him, tug the beanie from his head and toss it on the bed.

"I love touching your hair. So soft," I say making sure he can see my lips.

He grabs my chin between his thumb and index finger and looks into my eyes. "I have been dying to see you today. God. Snowflake. I just need to kiss you. Let me kiss you."

His mouth is on mine, kissing me hard. Desperately. My fingers grip his hair while looking for something to hold onto. His hands grip my waist and flip me around. He lowers himself on the bed and pulls me to him without losing the connection between us. I love the way he desires me. I don't care that he hasn't said those three little words, but I feel like I belong with him. To him. My hands leave his hair, exploring the hard muscles on his back, his chest, his abs. I feel his muscles tense beneath my fingers when I move them further down, skimming the edge of his shorts. He sits upright without warning and rolls me over so that I'm lying on my back and he's straddling me. His shaking fingers travel down, take the edge of my dress, and slowly pulls it up. He pauses and looks at me. We've never gone this far before and I'm nervous, but I want him to touch me so bad. Biting my lip, I raise my chin and nod. The dress is up and over my head before I can blink, which makes me giggle.

I grab the edge of his shirt and tug it up. He hooks his fingers around the edge and slides it over his head.

I. Can't. Breathe.

I meet his gaze. "You're beautiful."

He laughs. "Thanks, I guess." His eyes drop to my chest.

I touch his arm and his eyes swing back up to mine, dark, hungry. But the urge to cross my arms on my chest is getting stronger. "Say something."

He licks his lips and swallows, returning his gaze back to my chest. "Jesus. Beautiful."

I'll take that.

His hand moves to his pants and I glance down to see him adjust the bulge they barely contain. My cheeks heat when he catches me watching.

"Um. . .have you ever done this before? Been intimate with a girl?"

He shakes his head. "You?"

"With a girl?" I can't resist teasing him. "No. Not with a guy either."

His mouth spreads into a wide grin as he bends down.

"Um. Cole." I sink my fingers in his hair and tug his head up from my shoulder. He stares down at me with hooded eyes. "I'm nervous."

He sits up immediately, but he doesn't put any distance between our bodies. "I'm nervous too."

I bite the inside of my cheek. "But you look so sure of what you are doing."

"Your body is like my guide. I know where to touch you or kiss you by watching how you react to me and listening to what my hands tell me. I touch you the way I want to be touched."

Oh wow.

He leans down and kisses the top of my right breast making this humming sound that vibrates into my skin. I shiver, whimpering.

He lifts his head. "Is this okay?"

I nod, smiling. "I love what you're doing so far."

He dips his head back and does the same thing with my left breast. I hold my breath and close my eyes, wondering where his lips will kiss me next.

His hands squeeze my breasts and he buries his face between them, his hot breath fanning my skin. His mouth moves down, tracing his tongue along my ribs, and nips at the slight rise of my stomach. My eyes fly open and my hips buck off the bed.

"Oh God, oh God, oh God," I chant under my breath.

I bite my lip when I feel his lips skim the edge of my panties, moan when he blows a breath on my navel, groan and wiggle when he sucks on my skin there. My eyes fly open and I bolt upright when I feel a finger trace the material of my panties between my legs.

His head comes up and he bites his lip, running the tip of the finger back and forth in that place that burns for his touch. My head falls back and my body thrashes on the bed. It's too much. I feel everything, everywhere.

"Is this okay?" His speech is slower and the words are barely audible, coated by lust. His hands pull back just as I start to feel this tingling feeling building up inside me.

My eyes flip open and I lift my head to look at him between my legs. "What happened? Why did you pull back?" I ask panting.

He looks unsure, it's touching and extremely cute that he cares that much about my needs. But I want that finger back. I need to feel that magic again. I reach out, grab his hand and pull it back between my legs.

"Please?"

Confidence floods back into his features. He snags his bottom lip between his teeth and picks up where he left off. His movements are a mix of rough and too gentle now and I know he's just as nervous and I am.

I wrap my hand around his finger and guide him, showing him what feels good.

Something is building inside me, and I can't control it. Cole seems to read my body because that finger rubs faster, pressing harder. His lips kiss my inner thigh, nip a bit and with just one last push of his finger, my eyes close and I'm flying without wings, riding on what feels like a wave made up of so many emotions I could actually cry. My breathing calms slowly as I come back down from my high, and when I feel the swipe of a finger on my cheek, I open my eyes and stare into the most beautiful face in the world.

"Fuck. That was stunning." He brushes my cheek with his thumb and then the other one.

Crap. I didn't mean to cry. Why am I crying? It was the most perfect thing I've ever experienced.

"Wow. Your fingers. . .oh God." I bury my face in my hands, too happy, feeling different than the girl who walked inside this room ten minutes ago. If his fingers can drive me wild like that, the thought of him inside me sends all kinds of images flashing through my head.

He tugs my fingers away and grins wide. "You came. And you are welcome," he says with a smug smile.

My eyes widen, staring at the proud look on his face. "You're cocky."

"Thank you." He groans and rolls to lie on my side, and turns to face me as he uses his hand to massage himself. "I need to go home and take care of him."

"I could help you with. . .um. . .Batman. . .if you showed me what to do."

His hand stops moving and he stares at me incredulously. "Batman?"

Oh God. "Yes." His shoulders start to shake in laughter as he moves to sit up then turns to look at me. "I just don't have words for you right now."

He rolls out of bed and grabs his shirt from the floor, slipping it over his head. "We'll have to work on showing you how to make me feel better." He winks and walks to the bed where I'm lying, feeling as if my body doesn't have a single bone left to hold it together. He plants his hands on either side of my head and leans down to kiss me softly. Gently. He pulls back and stares down at me. "I need to run. I promised my dad I would drop by at his office to help with the construction he has going. See you at ten?"

I raise my hands and link them behind his neck and pull him down for a kiss. "Silver lining. Knowing I'll see you soon is my silver lining. Thank you for what you just did for me. I lo—" I bite my tongue so fast to halt those words from my lips. "I will miss you."

He narrows his eyes on me, but he doesn't call me out on my little slip. "Silver lining. I like that."

I rise on my elbow to watch him stride to the window and disappear from sight. My eyes close automatically and I lose myself in a blissful sleep.

I jerk awake to the sound of pounding on my door and a deep, angry voice calling my name.

Dad.

What the hell? I bolt upright and hop out of the bed, feeling a bit disoriented.

Crap. The door is locked. I forgot to unlock it after Cole left.

I glance down at my body. Shit. I'm still naked, save for my bra and panties. I scan the floor wildly and find my dress at the foot of the bed. After slipping it on, I smooth my hair while dashing to the door, unlock it and swing it open.

"Why is your door locked?" His gaze scans the inside of my room suspiciously.

Crap. I scramble for an excuse, anything to make him go away. "I wasn't feeling too well when I came in from the center. I locked the door so I could take a nap without interruptions."

His scowl recedes a little and his eyes land on me. "Your grandmother asked me to bring some flowers for you. She mentioned you needed some for the garden. She forgot to give them to you the last time you were there."

I nod, my shoulders sagging in relief. "Thank you. I'll get to it right now."

I skirt around him, scurrying down the hallway and toward the stairs, eager to put distance between us.

"Eleanor?"

Chills run down my spine at the coldness of his voice. I turn around slowly to face him and I suck in a breath when I see what he's holding. My body sways and my hand shoots to the side, grabbing the wall for support.

"What is this?" He takes a step forward, Cole's beanie gripped in his hand.

I've never fainted before, but today might be my first time. I watch him advance closer, his eyebrows dipped in a menacing glare. I press my shoulder on the wall and wrap my arms around my middle tightly to stop from itching the scars on my arms.

"Was *he* in your room?"

I can't deny it, given the evidence in his hand, so I choose to keep my mouth shut. He pounces forward with his arm raised and I drop on the floor, curling into a ball to protect myself and wait for the blow to land, but it doesn't come. I raise my head a little, shivering on the floor and look up. He's looming over me, that fist curled at his side and instead of the furious expression on his face, I find something else. This look is completely foreign to me, it takes me a while to find the name for it. Resignation, mingled with another emotion I can't describe. Pity? Sympathy? Love?

"Why do you choose to disobey me, Eleanor?"

What the hell is happening to my father?

The look is gone without warning. He bunches the beanie in his hands and throws it in my face. "If he can't stay away from you, I guess I will have to look for a way to make him stay away." He spins on his heel and stomps down the stairs without a backward glance, without even throwing a look towards my mom's room.

A whimper finds its way to me, followed by the sounds of feet padding on the wood.

"Nor! Are you okay?" Elise asks, wrapping her arms around me. "I hate him so much. He yelled at Elon because she forgot to turn off the sprinkler on the lawn."

"Really. I'm fine," I say, pulling myself up from the floor while clutching the beanie to my chest. I need to warn Cole before my dad gets to him. I'd be stupid not to heed his warning. "I'm sorry he yelled at you and Elon." I hug her tight for a few seconds then pull back and wipe the tears streaming down her face. "Want to help me work on the lawn? Grandma sent a few flowers we could plant around the fence."

She nods. Before we head downstairs, I go back to my room and shove the beanie under my pillow. The tip of my fingers graze the cool metal of the penknife. I wrap my fingers around it, relishing the pain from the edges digging into my skin.

Growing up, I'd thought about reporting him to child services so many times, but I always held back. There was no way I was going to let anyone take away the people I love. Mom would probably end up in an institution. My sisters would be torn away from me and placed in the system. I'd heard some terrifying stories from a few kids in school back in Ohio, and that enforced my decision to keep quiet.

I would rather brave my dad, buy some time until I am old enough to move out, taking my sisters and mother with me. Which means going to college, working hard and getting a good job. He won't be able to touch or yell at us.

Until then, I breathe in and breathe out. Repeat.

CHAPTER TWENTY-THREE

IT HAS BEEN TWO DAYS SINCE I LAST SAW COLE AND IT HAS BEEN pure torture. I feel as though my dad is watching me at every turn. Paranoid, I know.

Since I told him what my dad said we have been laying low, no face to face communications, just texting. To make matters worse, Megs flew to California to spend some time with her dad.

Grandma opted to leave the shop closed today. She took Elon and Elise for a shopping trip to Jacksonville. I will drop by later to pick them up at her house.

My phone vibrates on the desk, pulling me out of my thoughts.

I smile when I see Megs' name flashing on the screen. I press the button to answer.

"Oh my gosh! I've missed you. When are you coming back?" I ask, pulling my legs up on the chair and wrapping one arm around them.

She laughs. "Wow, I should stay away more often. It's good to know you missed me. What's up? You and Stormy Eyes still having naughty sex all over the place?"

I choke on a laugh. "We haven't had sex yet. And no. It's been a little crazy over here." I tell her what happened when my dad found

Cole's beanie.

"Holy shit! I'm sorry. I can't imagine how hard it is for both of you. I haven't seen Simon for a while and it's driving me insane," she says in a soft voice. "Your dad is such a dick. What's his deal?"

"Other than that he has some sort of misplaced prejudice against Cole because his brother was deaf, I have no idea. Do you think it has something to do with his relationship with Cole's mom?" I ask, since I already told her what Grandma told me weeks ago.

"Do you think?"

I sigh.

"Do me a favor, okay? Text Cole. Go out and have fun. Don't let your dad spoil this for you. You two are the happiest when you are together. Life is too short. Promise me you'll do that."

I smile at her words. "I will. I'm just scared for him. But. . .ugh. I miss him so much."

"Text him. Babes, I have to run. Text me and let me know how it goes. Love you."

"I love you, too."

After ending the call, I scroll down my phone contacts and stop at Cole's name.

Me: I want to break some rules. Want to join me?

I stare at the phone, waiting for his reply, But nothing comes through. I head to the window to check if his car is in its usual spot. It is. Could he have gone for a run? As far as I know, he runs every morning. Or maybe he's working on his drawings or something.

I bound downstairs and slip on a pair of blue flip flops and head out of the house. Stopping in front of Cole's front door, I ring the bell and a voice yells that the door is open. I step inside the house and see Nick playing on the game console in the living room. He pauses the game and waves. "Hey Nor. You want to play with me?" Nick squints up at me, jiggling the controller in his hands.

"Where's your brother?" I ask, walking toward him.

"Which one?" he asks. "Cole is in his room and Josh went to Portland to visit Uncle Ray."

I smile at him and sneak a glance toward the stairs, eager to surprise him, but Nick turns those cute blue eyes on me and my resistance crumbles. He hands me the extra controller and adjusts the settings for two players. He explains the rules, which buttons to press for what action, the world he created. He looks at me with one eye closed and asks, "Got it?"

I grin and nod. "I'm about to kick your butt."

"Hah! In your dreams, Snowflake."

I blink at him, shocked to hear him use that name.

"What? Cole calls you that. It's cute. I like it." He grins and turns back to focus on the screen. He moves the toggle around emitting a crashing sound from the screen. "Are we going to play or not?"

"Yeah. Sure." He kind of threw me off for a second.

We begin playing. He whoops and pumps a fist in the air after our team annihilates a few of the guards from the other team we are playing against. We continue playing. The sounds of swords boom as a wizard swings his magic wand and points towards another wizard.

He says something like "I like you," but I'm not sure I heard him correctly.

"What?" I shout so he can hear me over that noise.

"I like you!" He shouts at the top of his voice, his eyes never leaving the action happening in front of us.

I take a quick look at this adorable nine-year-old with dark hair and blue eyes. I'm three seconds from floating on air. I hadn't realized how much Nick's opinion mattered. "I like you too."

"Can I come and play with Elon?" He blinks up at me. Nick is crushing hard on Elon and uses any excuse he can to come over. Unfortunately, I don't think she feels the same way.

"Maybe you can call her to check if she's home first, yeah?"

He nods. "I'll take some of Mom's cookies. She'll love them."

"I'm sure she will." I peek at the stairs again. "Hey. I'll be right back."

I drop the controller, make my way up the stairs and stop in front of a closed door. There's no sound coming from the other side of the door. Maybe he isn't in his room. I retrace my steps to the stairs, but freeze when a low groan reaches me from inside Cole's room. I backtrack, open the door and step inside. I squint through the sunlight streaming in and glance around the room. My gaze zeroes in on Cole, sitting on the chair next to the desk with his shorts pulled down to his strong thighs. His head is thrown back and moans leave his parted lips. Following the movement below his chest, I watch as his hand palms his. . .whoa. His hips buck, his palm sliding up and down in deliberate strokes.

I rip my eyes from the sight before me, feeling a hot flush sweep through me. I'm shaking and my knees feel weak. I take a step back so I can give him some privacy but stumble on my feet. I grab the door frame, breathing hard. When I look up again, Cole is still immersed in his own pleasure. His groans grow louder and my name slips through his lips. I right myself, lock the door and tiptoe toward him, mesmerized by the look of pure bliss on his face. I stop in front of him, my eyes darting around and narrowing in on the computer screen on the desk. My throat feels dry as I gawk at the video playing silently, the couple writhing on the bed. The man is taking the woman from behind in powerful thrusts. The woman arches her body, her mouth open in pleasure and the man continues to pump his hips, veins popping on his neck. Heat dances in my belly and tingles shoot between my legs. The man pulls out and holds his erection while his partner turns around. She drops on her knees in front of him. One of his hands leave his huge—like really huge—stiff penis and grips the back of the woman's head, guiding her down on him. I stare, fascinated and wondering if he will fit inside her mouth. Wonders of all wonders, he does.

Would Cole let me do that to him?

I squeeze my thighs, incredibly aroused at the thought of him in my mouth.

I swallow hard, sneak a quick glance at Cole and my heart stops beating. He's biting his bottom lip, his eyes fixed on me; wide, dilated, dark. I should feel embarrassed for being caught watching, but

I don't. A look of uncertainty flashes across his face. It fades just as quickly as it had appeared. Then he peels one of his hands from his impressive erection, reaches for my hand and pulls me down to his face. His touch is hot, and his breath even hotter as it fans my mouth right before he grasps the back of my head and kisses me with reckless abandon. He separates our mouths, taking my fingers. He places them on top of the hand pumping him harder and harder. Then he covers mine with his and continues to slide them up and down. I go to my knees without breaking eye or skin contact and just watch his face, fascinated. I feel wetness between my legs just looking at him jerk off. He pumps his hand faster, his hips jolt quicker, and our breathing sounds hasher in my ears. He stiffens and his eyes fall shut, his jaw clenched. A low growl rips through his mouth.

I've never seen a more beautiful vision in my life.

Something warm touches my skin. I glance down and see white, thick liquid shoot from his Batman. Before I can move my hand, his fingers unfold from mine and he grabs a few tissues from the box on top of his desk. I pull back my arm and let him clean himself.

Oh.

God.

I need to start watching porn. Or maybe just watch Cole when he does his thing.

He stands up and pulls his shorts up, then clicks his mouse next to the computer. The video disappears from the screen. He straightens and runs his fingers through his hair. "That was unexpected."

Is he blushing?

I clear my throat, feeling a bit awkward now that the action is over. "Sorry for the interruption. I texted you. I decided to drop by when I didn't hear from you."

His eyes dart around the room, before finding mine again. "I'll just go and grab a shower. Can you wait for me?"

I nod my head.

He nods and strides out of the room. I collapse onto his bed, falling on my back and throwing a hand over my eyes as I replay the entire episode in my head.

Cole returns ten minutes later. I uncover my eyes and sit up, trailing him with my gaze as he walks to the dresser and takes out a T-shirt. He moves toward me and pulls me up with his hands around my arms.

"*Hi*," he signs.

"*Hi.*" I raise to my tiptoes and press my lips to his to break the tension. "That was intense."

He laughs. "Yes, it was. Are we back to seeing each other again?"

"*Yes*," I sign.

"*Good.*"

He walks to his desk and grabs his car keys, then takes my hand. He unlocks the door and we climb down the stairs and head for the front door.

"Don't forget to ask Elon!" Nick shouts as Cole heads toward the door, with me trailing behind him.

I give Nick a thumbs up, just as Maggie walks in from the kitchen. She stumbles when she sees me, and quickly rights herself. I make her nervous, and I have no idea why.

"*Hi Eleanor.*" She speaks and signs the words.

"Hey, Mrs. Holloway."

"Please call me Maggie, okay? You're literally joined at the hip with my son."

Cole throws his head back and groans, making his mom chuckle. He starts to sign quickly, causing her to laugh harder.

"*It's so good to see you happy, Sweetheart*," she tells Cole, then turns to me. "*Thank you for making him happy.*"

I smile. "*He's amazing.*"

Cole grins at me, his ears reddening a little.

She turns to face her son. "I have something for your dad. Let me get it." She goes to the kitchen and returns, carrying a bag. The scent of freshly baked cookies waft from inside.

Outside by the car, Cole waits until my seatbelt is fastened then rounds the car to his seat.

"Where are we going?" I ask

"My dad asked me to drop by his office. He is meeting with a real estate developer, who is looking to work with BH Architects for a future project. I enjoy sitting in during the meetings as an observer to learn how things work."

"What about Josh?"

He shakes his head. "My brother wants to play professional football. This is all I have ever wanted to do."

When we get to his father's office, Cole leads me inside. One part of the wall has been knocked down. A few men wearing helmets and carrying tool belts mill around the outer office. Cole's dad is hunched over on his desk, studying some complicated diagrams in front of him. He looks up when we walk in and then greets us. I really like his friendly face, genuine smile and kind gray eyes.

After initial greetings, I settle myself on a couch to wait for Cole. He and his father head out to one of the conference rooms to meet with their client. I pull my phone out and spend a few minutes texting Megs.

I put the phone beside me and close my eyes, enjoying the silence. I jolt awake and realize I fell asleep. Somehow I'm no longer curled up as I was before I fell asleep, but stretched out on the couch. Sitting up, I slip on my sneakers and head out in search of my boyfriend and find him chatting with a few workers near the construction.

Oh, God. He looks hot, wearing an orange helmet, black wife-beater, jeans and boots. A tool belt hugs his waist and sweat trickles down the side of his face. He tucks the hammer in one of the loops before grabbing the drill from the floor and sets to work joining the wood panels. I've never seen him at work before. He seems so engrossed in what he's doing, his entire focus on his work. And let me tell you, if Cole makes his mission to focus on something, he gives it his everything.

He stops drilling and as he senses me, turns in my direction. I make a show of staring at him from head to toe slowly, then lick my lips. His face breaks into a roguish smile. I shift on my feet to curb the heat settling low in my tummy.

Another half hour passes before Cole is done with his work. He tells me that I was sleeping so peacefully, he didn't want to wake me up, so he joined the construction crew working on extending the offices. The outer wall on one wing had been knocked down, most of the foundation work was already done. By the time Cole cleans up, it's late afternoon. I ask him if he could drive me to my grandma's to pick up my sisters.

Lately, I've been thinking about finally telling him about my past. He's been very patient with me. Am I ready to share with him that part of me?

"Grandma has this amazing roof terrace. We can do popcorn and movies."

"As long as they are subtitled, I'm game." He yawns and rubs his eyes with his fingers.

"Or we can do it tomorrow." I smile. I'm relieved by my own suggestion and this time I hope he says yes.

He shakes his head. "I want to spend some time with you. I missed you." He frowns. "Aren't you scared of what your dad will do?"

"I am. But I want this too. I can't let him control my life like that. I have the right to spend my time with anyone I want."

After calling Grandma to let her know that Cole and I are on the way to her place, I give him directions to my grandmother's house.

I ring the bell once to let her know I'm here and then use the key she gave me when I first visited her with my mom. She looks up from the television, a glass of red wine poised against her lips and smiles. I'm also a little surprised to see Mr. Taylor sitting across from her. She told me that he has been checking on her often, but I didn't realize they had become this close.

After the greetings and introduction, I gather what Cole and I need, then head toward the stairs that lead to the terrace.

"Your sisters are in the guest room, Eleanor. They seemed exhausted after our trip. They could stay here for the night. I could use the company." She smiles, in my direction. It's a sad, yet wistful smile.

"Sure. I'm sure they'll be happy to sleep over."

"It's so good to see you two again," she signs and speaks the words for my benefit. *"You kids have fun. Yell if you need me."*

Ten minutes later, "The Wedding Date" is on the projector with the captions displaying on the screen. Cole is lying on his side and I snuggle into his chest. I move the popcorn in front of me where he can reach it easily before taking a handful and beginning to feed him. He licks the salt off my fingers then drops his head to my neck and breathes me in. He shifts, pressing his hips forward and I feel how much he wants me. Warmth simmers low in my belly, remembering how he looked when I walked in his room earlier today.

I bite my lip and try to bring those feelings under control. I want him to know more about me. My past. But I can't do that if my brain is filled with lusty thoughts.

I shift around to face him, making sure the lights above us illuminate my face so he can see my mouth. I open my mouth to speak, but close it again, unable to find the right words to start this conversation.

Taking a deep breath, I brush the tip of my thumb in circles on his palm.

Cole

Nor sighs, her focus leaving the starlit sky and shifting to me.

"What's wrong?" I sign, slowly so she can follow my movements. She has been getting better at it, when we aren't too distracted by fooling around.

She raises her hands and the front of her dress shifts, displaying the soft swell of her breasts peeking through a purple lace bra.

Shit. I can't stop staring. I flex my fingers and swallow hard.

She'd better spit out what's bothering her. I'm about bursting and seriously, her boobs are just calling to me to bury my face in them. The
last two days being away from her have been pure torture. She was
already scared after her dad's threats, so I didn't want to add more
pressure. But now, I want to make up for lost time.

She waves a hand in my face and points to hers, scowling, but I
can see a smile lurking behind that cute expression.

"My face is up here, jackass."

"I can't help it." I grin at her and wink. She swats my shoulder
and laughs. I really wish I could hear the sound of her laugh. "So
what's wrong?"

"Do you ever feel as though your life is not enough? That there
is more out there? You want more?"

I blink back the lust crowding my vision, reminding myself to
be a little bit patient.

"What do you want?" Jesus. Would she smack me if I took a bite
on that pale skin peeking out on top of her dress?

She bites her bottom lip between her teeth, still frowning as if
she is deep in thought. "I want the moon."

I would give her the fucking galaxy if she'd look at me the way
she did earlier today when our gazes met across my room. I'll never
forget the desire on her face as she watched me jerking off. I felt embarrassed for like three seconds. Then I noticed the quick rise and
fall of her chest and realized that she was just as aroused as I was. .

I sigh and shift on the seat to adjust the front of my pants to accommodate my dick. Looks like dry humping will have to wait. This
girl has the power to make me sprout a boner in the span of a few
seconds. "Yes. I feel that sometimes. There is so much out there for
us to explore. I can't wait to do all those things with you."

She doesn't say anything for several minutes.

"My father is a heartless asshole."

Those words rip me out of my thoughts about boners, tits and
conquering the world with Nor by my side.

I agree with her completely. Her father a gigantic douche, who can't seem to appreciate how amazing and strong his daughter is.

I graze her cheek with my knuckles and nod for her to continue.

CHAPTER TWENTY-FOUR

Nor

My heart is racing fast at my confession. I've never said those words out loud because I've always been scared he would somehow know what I said and bring his wrath down upon me.

Cole's eyes are fixed on my mouth, waiting for my next words.

"My father never wanted to marry my mother. He never wanted me. Us."

He blows out a long breath and pushes a lock of hair off my forehead. "Why do you say that?"

I wipe my clammy palms down my dress. "Because he confessed it to me one night when he came home drunk."

His arms tighten around me, his body tense.

"My parents had been having problems for as long as I could remember. I used to feel like if I was strong enough for both of them, they wouldn't fight so much. Maybe my dad would come home from work every night, instead of going away for days. At one point, my mother got off kilter and went down a dark hole. My bed time stories weren't made of princes saving princesses from evil step-mothers or high towers. They consisted of Mom and Dad fighting, or sometimes, when my mom was high on her medication, she would cook dinner. Then she'd tuck me in bed at night and tell me how she and Dad met when they were nineteen. Her ballet career was on the rise. But apparently my dad swept her off her feet and she couldn't see anything beyond him. They were engaged shortly and then got married. Mom was pregnant with me. According to her, he was in love with another woman. She knew when they met, but she chose to stay with him anyway. She was hopelessly in love with him and hoped her love for him would be strong enough to make him *see* her."

How do I tell him about his mom and my dad? How will that change us? I don't want to lose him. He is quickly becoming an important part of my life. I just have to find a way to tell him and hopefully he stays.

I gulp for air. I'm not sure I can make it through what I'm about to tell him. Cole scoots down, stretching his long frame out on the couch and lays his head on my lap, adjusting his body to make sure he can read my lips. Then he takes my hand, kisses the scars on my inner wrist and does the same to the other one. That little gesture gives me strength to continue.

"He broke my mother's heart. He said that she gave him no choice when she got pregnant with me. He made her feel worthless. She started getting easily distracted, becoming absentminded almost all the time. My sisters. . .oh God. Elon was only four and Elise nine when my mother had her first complete breakdown.

"One afternoon I came home from school and found Mom in her room, lying on the floor in her own vomit. Elon was in her playpen across my mom's bed and Elise was not yet home from school. I just stood there, staring at her numbly. Suddenly something inside me stirred to life and panic set in. I ran to her side and touched her face. It was cold. So cold. I stood up, picked up Elon and went downstairs to call 911, then I sat down on the couch in the living room, rocking my little sister back and forth. I guess the shock of seeing my mom lying on the floor numbed me to any feeling. The next time I looked up, Elon was playing with my hair clip and people were running around inside the house. I don't even know how they got inside. Dad appeared in front of me with Elise in tow. That was the first time I saw him look anything other than angry or indifferent. He looked grief-stricken. Dad took Elon from my arms and motioned for me to follow him. We stopped at the bottom of the stairs as the paramedics negotiated the stretcher with my mother on it, an oxygen mask strapped over her nose. Anyway, Dad left us in the hands of our neighbor, Mrs. Jennings, and followed the ambulance with his car to the hospital. He didn't even hug me or my sisters or comfort us with words. He just *left*."

Cole lets go of my hands and sits up, facing me before reaching for my hands again.

I want him to hold me so badly, but if he does, then he won't be able to read my lips.

"I don't remember how I got to the bathroom upstairs. All I know is that, I was standing in front of the mirror, staring at myself. I was the cause of all these problems. If my mother hadn't become pregnant with me, Dad wouldn't have felt forced to marry her. I hadn't even cried. I asked myself who I was, and why I couldn't even cry for my own mother. I wanted to feel something to stop the numbness that had turned me into a robot. I pinched my arm but it wasn't enough to startle my emotions. My hand reached for Dad's shaving razor, pressed it on my right forearm and slid it across. The pain shot through me, making me lean forward on the sink. Blood pebbled again my skin. Finally, I felt something. I felt alive. The events of the past hour hit me hard. I dropped the razor on the sink as my knees gave way and I crumpled on the floor. When I finally left the bathroom, my feet guided me to my dad's computer where I searched on the internet. I wasn't even sure what I was searching for, but suddenly, I had so many answers about things I didn't know and instead of walking away, cutting became my escape. It was my guilty pleasure.

"I got better at pretending. I would smile when my parents were around, chatter aimlessly, but inside, especially when I got nothing in return, I'd feel a part of me die. Every night, I'd drop to my knees and pray for some kind of miracle or magic that would mend whatever rough patch my parents were going through. I felt as if I was drowning with no chance of coming up for air."

Cole doesn't say anything. His eyes are transfixed on my lips, absorbing every word that falls out of my mouth. The movie and popcorn long forgotten. He asks for some clarification on words he didn't catch because I was speaking too fast. My stomach is tight and filled with tension.

"The first person to notice was my high school counselor during our quarterly progress evaluation. My grades were perfect, but I had withdrawn from all activities. I stopped hanging out with my friends because I was afraid they would shun me if they found out that our family was a mess. I was also afraid they would find out what I hid beneath my long sleeve sweaters and blouses.

The counselor called a meeting with my mother. My father was hardly ever at home. It took me a very long time to get my life together. A lot of therapy sessions. My mother seemed to get her act together for a while. But my father's constant absence and his temper didn't help.

Rumors started to circulate around school about what happened with my mother. In two days everyone was talking about how she tried to commit suicide. I couldn't bear facing my former classmates. I transferred to another school, not that it made things better. Eventually, my father came home one night and announced he had found another job. A promotion and so we moved here."

He closes his eyes, a muscle ticking furiously in his jaw. When he opens them again, his lashes are wet with tears that haven't fallen yet. "Did it help? Cutting yourself?"

I wince and lick my lips. That word—cutting—sounds so harsh, coming from that mouth that makes me forget who I am. "Yes. For a while, it did. Until I cut myself too deep, desperate to gain some sort of control over everything that was happening. The next time I woke up, I was in a hospital bed."

The admission makes me nauseous. When I woke up in the hospital, I saw my father standing beside me. He'd been staring at me softly, a look full of remorse etched on his face. But the second he realized I was conscious, his face had immediately hardened and he asked me why, what was wrong with me. He said that being a Blake is not for the weak.

I shake my head quickly remembering the harsh words that fell from his lips. "I wasn't trying to commit suicide. I just wanted to feel something. I felt as if I was losing control of everything. I was so desperate."

He lifts a hand to wipe my face. I hadn't known I was crying until I felt his thumb brush my cheek.

"Crap. Sorry," I say, quickly wiping my face with the back of my hand. "I'm such a mess."

He takes my chin between his thumb and index finger in a firm hold. "I don't care. You are my beautiful mess."

I sob and laugh in one breath. "Beautiful? I'm covered with tears and snot."

"Yes. Your face is puffy and your eyes are red, but you've never looked more beautiful." He points at me and then holds his hand flat with the palm facing him. He moves his hand from his forehead and ends at the chin while pulling his fingers together, and says, "You are beautiful."

"*Thank you*," I sign and speak the words.

I know I probably look weak basking in those words and my previous statement about tears and snot sounded needy, but if his hands offer me the solace I crave, then I'll gladly welcome it. I tug the black beanie from his head and toss it on the couch before I tangle my fingers into his soft hair. His eyes fall shut immediately and a moan escapes his parted lips.

He opens his eyes again and stares at me through heavy-lidded eyes. His thumb brushes my jaw and I close my eyes, soaking up the heat, the reverent adoration flowing from him and into my skin. I take it all in with a hunger so wild it's a physical pain. Then he pulls my head down to him and kisses me. What starts out as a sweet kiss transitions into a battle of teeth and tongue. Hands greedy for a touch, bodies fighting to get closer. His fingers leave my face and wrap around the nape of my neck, gripping me tight. A low growl pushes through his lips and into mine.

Holy hell.

How is it I'd lived without his mouth on mine all these years, and the second he kisses me I feel as if he has always been there, kissing me, comforting me, claiming me. Desiring me.

Pain shoots through my spine, reminding me of my awkward position. I tug his hair and he moans, nipping my bottom lip before pulling back. Our hard breathing mingles as our hearts fight to calm down. His hands dive into my hair, sifting through the tresses, his mouth pulled at the sides in my favorite smile.

"How long has it been?" He's playing with a strand of my hair, wrapping it around his finger, but his eyes are still on mine.

My brain is still trying to recover so it takes me a while to catch up with his question. "Do you mean since I completely stopped cutting myself?" He doesn't cringe at me using that word. He nods, his stare as rapt as it was before.

"Almost three years now."

I pause and inhale deeply. I could lie to him, pretend I'm strong. Pretend the mere sight of a knife or a fork, anything that has the power to give me relief, doesn't tempt me. I've come this far now. He deserves to know everything.

"I've relapsed once in those three years. One day I came home after a bad day at school. Everyone was going to this party they had been invited to. I wasn't part of a clique and didn't have a friend who was friends with the popular kids."

When I'm done, I take a deep breath. My body feels lighter after the admission, but at the same time, apprehension coils deep inside me. I'm still waiting for him to recoil away from me and leave.

But he doesn't. He wraps his arm around my shoulder and pulls me to him. His gaze is soft and full of admiration, even laced with tears, as he leans to kiss my forehead, my cheek. He looks at me like I'm the most perfect thing in his world, despite the scars that mark my body, despite my insecurities. He looks at me with stars in his eyes.

We spend the rest of the evening just hanging out on the terrace.

Later that night, Cole meets me on the roof. We spend the next thirty minutes with my hand in his. I've never felt so content in my life. I stand up and so does he. We go to my room. . .he kisses me again, his hand slipping under my shirt.

"So you just wanted to grope me? Cole, I'm disappointed."

He laughs, his hands shamelessly bunching my shirt up to my neck and he nuzzles his face between my breasts. He kisses my skin, his warm breath causing heat to skitter down my body, then makes a sound close to a hum under his breath, closing his eyes.

After he leaves, I change into my pajamas and sit down on my chair while pulling out my doodling notebook. I grab the pens on the table ready to scribble, but something catches the corner of my eye. My heart races as I reach over and slide the letter titled, "*Open when you feel like crying*" off the corner of my desk. My stomach does this somersaulting thing as I take in Cole's careless scrawl.

"It's okay to cry. It doesn't make you weak. It means you've held onto the pain for too long. It means you are strong enough to let go and it makes me love you even more. I want to be there to hold you when your world is falling apart. Maybe I won't be able to put it back together, but I sure as hell will try."

Remember the silver lining. ;)

Cole.

CHAPTER TWENTY-FIVE

Nor

I TURNED EIGHTEEN ON AUGUST SIXTEENTH. I CELEBRATED THE better part of that day with my sisters and Mom, snuggled on her bed in her room. Later that night on the roof, Cole brought a cupcake for me with one candle on top of it and a drawing of a butterfly in flight, with a special note on the back of it. "*Find your wings and fly.*" He also gave me a necklace with two beautiful pendants on it: a round galaxy, made up of a dome glass which is painted in blue-green and red colors beneath it with glitter for stars, and an anchor. It was beautiful and a thoughtful gift, and I adore it so much. I couldn't have asked for a better birthday.

Megs flew back home from California a week before school started. I contemplated if I should wear a blouse with long sleeves to cover my arms, but decided against it. Everyone would know about the scars sooner or later. I preferred the latter and to get it out of the way.

After dropping Elon and Elise at school, I drove to mine. My first day went better than I expected. Word spread around that there was a new girl in school—a cutter. Most people stared in the hallways and during lunch, and in every class I attended, which made my skin itch and the urge to run, immense. It wasn't easy.

Right after school, I was wonderfully surprised to find Cole, Simon and Megs waiting for me outside in the school parking lot next to the Station Wagon. I'd never felt so relieved and happy in my whole life. It made me wonder how I'd survived all this time without friends.

The first week of school crawled by, people continued to stare, but after a while they got bored, I guess.

Cole and I were chatting about our life goals last night. I still have no idea what I really want to do. There are so many options to choose from.

Today is the first time Cole didn't show up on the roof since we moved here. Watching the night sky has become our thing. I've already sent him several texts but he hasn't replied.

I walk to the window and duck my head out. No one seems to be home in The Holloway house. It has been that way for hours and I'm starting to feel nervous. None of their cars are parked outside the house. Uneasiness slithers down my spine. I can't shake off the feeling that something is wrong.

Before I met Cole, I would've rolled my eyes if someone told me that another person could become your whole world within the blink of an eye. Now I know and understand that a person can be a stranger one second, nothing but a fantasy, and the next, knock your world off its axis and claim every breath from your lungs with his existence.

At around ten-thirty p.m., I hear the sound of a car pulling to a stop, snapping me out of my thoughts. I scramble up and carefully balance myself on the tiles. My heart flips around inside my chest as I dash to the window.

I glance at the Holloway house. Maggie is walking briskly toward the porch, her head bowed. Suddenly, she stiffens and looks around. I follow her gaze and see dad's car pulling in to a stop outside our house. He jumps out of the car and jogs across the lawn toward her. Maggie snaps into action, clutches her purse under her arm and literally dashes to the front door. She stops to unlock her door, darting a glance over her shoulder while fumbling with the keys in her hands. Dad catches up to her, reaches out for her arm and spins her around. He leans closer, speaking in a low voice. She yanks her arm from his grip in an attempt to move away from him, but he doesn't give her space. He stalks after her and positions his body in front of her, blocking her escape.

"You shouldn't be here, Stephen," she says in a shrilly, quivering voice. She shoots a glance in the direction of our house, then back to my father.

"Fuck. Listen to me, Maggie," he snaps at her, gripping both of her arms. "You keep ignoring me. Every. Single. Time."

She sighs, and stops fighting him. "You and I have nothing to talk about. Please don't make this more difficult than it already is. Our children get along very well. Don't destroy that."

Crap crap crap.

I hold my breath and wait.

No one says anything for several seconds. Seconds that feel like a bomb is ticking, ready to explode.

"What did you just say?"

She sighs in exasperation. "Let the past be what it is, Stephen. I'm happy with Ben—"

"Your son and my daughter. Together." He sounds like a robot.

"Yes." She pauses. "Didn't you know they were together?"

He laughs, but it's cold and forced. "Well, well." Those two words send chills all over my body.

He straightens and waves a hand in the air as if dismissing what Maggie told him about Cole and me. He steps closer, caging her in. "This is about you and me, Maggie. You and me. You still feel something for me. We are forever."

She plants her hands on his chest and shoves him back. "Go home and take care of your family. They need you, especially your wife."

"Maggie." He spits out her name. "I told you why I moved here. You're not in love with Ben and you never have been. You went back to him to get back at me. Admit it, damn it. You still love me."

She shakes her head quickly. "No. I don't. I've told you so many times."

He shakes his head violently, his eyes wide. I know that look. Pure madness and determination. "You've always been mine and I have always been yours. We promised, remember?"

"We were young for God's sake." I hear the panic in her voice.

My body is frozen in place, rendered immobile. My dad is *really, really* insane. His fixation on Maggie is not normal.

"Yes. But we meant every word. I told you you belonged to me, yet you still went and whored yourself to him."

She raises her hand and slaps him across the face, the sound echoing in the quiet night. "Don't you ever talk to me like that again." Her entire body is vibrating with anger now. "Don't ever touch me again either, Stephen. Ever. Move aside. Now."

He clenches his hands at his sides but doesn't move. I've never heard anyone speak to my father like that. She doesn't seem intimidated by the fact that my dad is two seconds from ripping her head off her neck.

She gives him a wide berth and hurries to the door. Keys clank loudly in the quiet night as she fidgets with them and the lock. Finally, the door unlocks. She steps inside and it slams shut in his face.

Dad spins around and stalks to his car. I duck away from the window and only come up when the sound of his car racing down the street fades. The night is blanketed in the aftermath of what just happened.

I toss and turn in bed for hours, different thoughts whipping around inside my head. What I witnessed tonight answers many questions about why my father looks at Maggie as if she's everything he's ever wanted. She IS everything he's ever wanted. My dad is still in love with Maggie.

Scratch that.

He is obsessed with her.

I pull my phone from beside my pillow and type out a text to Megs, then delete it. Then type it again. I press "send" before I chicken out. I need to get it off my chest, otherwise I won't be able to sleep tonight. I set the phone on the pillow, waiting for her to answer. My eyes finally give in to exhaustion. I sigh, turn on my side and fall asleep.

I snap awake to the feel of my bed dipping down, then my hair being pushed off my forehead. I stiffen and gag on the pungent smell of liquor-soaked breath slamming into me. The bedside lamp is still on, but I can see a shadow reflected on my wall.

Dad. His head is bent low. The sounds coming from him are...God...this is not my dad. He's...crying? No, he's bawling. Keening sounds are coming out of his chest as if his entire world is crashing. He's mumbling unintelligibly under his breath between sobs.

This is so out of character for him. But I can't afford to lower my guard.

He sniffs, then I feel a hand on my hair again.

"Caroline, I wish I loved you enough. I wish I loved you like I love her." I've never heard my father speak in such a voice. It's broken, lonely. Wistful.

Oh God.

Everyone tells me I look like my mom. But surely my father can tell the difference. Surely he can tell that he is in the wrong room, at least.

God, please make him leave.

But he doesn't. The last time my dad came into my room like this, we were in Ohio. My life was complete crap and I used to find relief in cutting myself, desperate for some sort of control.

One night he came home drunk and had a horrible fight with my mother. She asked him where he was spending most of his days and nights. He'd left her in the living room and headed for the stairs. He stopped in the hallway before storming into my room. He started to curse me, saying I was as useless as my mother, his face marred with angry lines.

Hate.

One second he was yelling at me. Yelling and shaking out of me any hope I had for sleeping that night. I will never forget what happened after that. It was the first time he hit me. He backhanded me, sending me tumbling across the room. Then he drunkenly lumbered toward me. But I was young and fast, and despite the pain tearing me apart, I crawled to my dresser and opened the drawer where I kept the kit containing razors and rubbing alcohol and I yanked it out. It slipped from my hands and clattered on the floor. I found what I needed to defend myself. I clutched the razor between my thumb and index finger, ignoring the pain as it cut through my skin. I waited for him to advance. He came swinging his fist at me. I swiped my hand in front of me, catching him on his left cheek with the razor. It wasn't too deep to cause any lasting damage, but it was enough to make him freeze. He shot me a hateful look and staggered out of the room. After he left, I ran to the door, slammed it shut and locked it. I threw the razor covered in his blood on the floor and grabbed a clean one from the confines of my kit. Leaning back against the wall with tears falling down my face, I extended my arm and ran the razor against my skin letting it sink in. The relief had been immense, the feel of pain rushing through me, making me feel alive, the sight of red against my skin. . .

Ever since that night, I've never let my guard down. I've never stopped concealing some sort of weapon under my pillow. Cheetahs don't change their spots. My dad is who he is, rotten to the core. And right now, my hand is itching to slip under the pillow and take hold of the penknife.

But I wait.

The bed shifts with his weight. I can't breathe. My lungs are burning and spots appear in front of my vision.

Then I feel it. The slight movement of the sheet shifting away on my back, the hard fingers pressing my back. Lower.

Oh God, no.

He continues his journey, murmuring about making it up to "Caroline" and promising to be a good father. I shove my hand under my pillow and grip the penknife. I jump out of bed. My fingers fumble with the blade before flipping around to face him. The scariest man I've ever met. The monster who hides in plain sight.

His eyes blink open through their liquor-induced haze, and he blinks rapidly as his vision adjusts. He must realize who I am and recognition floods his face. His eyes widen, then narrow as they move from my face to the knife in my hand.

I'm not a victim. I'm more than my past. I promised myself I'd never be a victim again. Not by my hand or anyone else's.

"Get out of my room. Right. Now." I don't even recognize my own voice. I expected it to quiver, given the terror ripping through me.

He climbs to his feet as fast as he can in his inebriated state. The shock leaves his face and his mouth folds downward in a sneer.

He looks around the room before returning his loathing gaze to me. "Well, if it isn't the little abomination that calls itself my daughter." He eyes my arms then looks at me. He wipes his hands on his shirt as if having touched me disgusts him.

A shudder rocks my body and my hand shakes at his words. Tears burn my eyes and I blink them back furiously. He is not worth my tears.

I thrust my chin forward in defiance. "You made me the way I am. I don't care if you think I'm Satan's child. Get. Out. Of. My. Room. Or I'll call the police!"

He looks at me and grins, the look on his face filled with malicious intent. "Call the police? Go ahead, daughter. Call them."

Shit. He's the police. But they can't all be like him. I refuse to believe that they're all like him.

My hand is shaking so badly I can barely grip the knife properly.

He backs out of the room, his eyes on me the entire time. "So, you and that freak kid next door are still seeing each other." He narrows his eyes. "You continue to defy me, Eleanor." He turns and stumbles out the door.

This is bad.

As soon as he leaves, I rush to my door and slam it shut, locking it. I lean on it. My pulse is pounding in my ears. I try to catch my breath to stop the thudding of my heart long enough to listen to his heavy footsteps. I sigh, relieved he's heading downstairs and not into his room, or worse, my sisters' rooms. The front door opens and slams shut. I slide down to the floor, draw my knees up and drop my head to my knees.

Jesus. Christ. What the hell?

If he hadn't left, I'd have hurt him. I was so close to shoving the penknife in his hand and marking a part of his body like I did all those years ago.

The adrenaline is waring off and with it, questions and doubts slam into me. What if he'd decided to use his strength against me? Would I have been able to defend myself? At this point, I know I disgust him with my scars and he blames me for ruining his life. Every time I think I've succeed in kicking those doubts out of my head, something happens to bring them back.

My phone beeps on the bed but my feet can't move from where I am. It beeps a few more times before I crawl across the floor and up on the bed. I swipe the screen and see three messages from Cole flashing on the screen.

I replace the penknife back under the pillow and set the phone down. There's no way I'm going to answer his texts. I can't formulate any words right now, and knowing Cole, his heart overrules his mind when he feels like the people he loves are threatened.

I climb to my feet and dash to the bathroom. I feel dirty. I want to scrub the feel of his hand off my body.

After turning the shower to hot, I grab a wash cloth and stagger into the space filled with steam.

By the time I leave the bathroom, wearing my pajamas and a towel around my head, I feel raw and numb. I need to feel something. Anything. I need to stop feeling as if I'm dead. I know what happens when my body craves the rush. I have tried so hard not to relapse, but I'm starting to feel the walls that stand between sanity and insanity, cracking. I need Cole. He makes me feel another kind of rush.

Cole is sitting on my bed, his elbows propped on his knees, when I walk into my room. My steps falter at first. Relief sweeps through me when I see that he is okay. I cross the room and drop to my knees in front of him, wrapping my arms around him. He hugs me back, but the way he is holding me feels different. It's tighter than usual, as if he doesn't want to let me go. He pulls back and kisses my forehead, then nuzzles his face in the crook of my neck.

"What's wrong?" he asks, when he pulls back to stare at me.

I shake my head. "Nothing. I'm tired." I start rubbing my hair dry with the towel.

"Are you mad at me?"

I frown and shake my head. "I'm not mad at you."

"Then what's wrong? Why won't you look at me?" he says.

Because I'm afraid you will see right through me. I divert my gaze before I can say those words out aloud and run my hands along my arms to calm my prickling skin.

I wish my mother wasn't as sick or still hopelessly in love with my father. I wish I was old enough to move out of this house and take my sisters and mom with me.

"I'm not leaving until you tell me what's wrong." He climbs on the bed and scoots back to the wooden headboard. "Come here."

I walk toward him fighting the urge to throw myself in his arms, but stop at the foot of the bed and suck in a breath as I take in his slouched form. Something is off with him. His eyes are rimmed with red as if he has been crying, and his shoulders are hunched forward. How did I not notice this when I walked into the room?

"Is everything okay?" I ask, hoping to get a glimpse of what is bothering him.

He scrubs his hands down his face. He signs and speaks the words, *"I just came home from the hospital."*

"Are you all right?" I inspect him with my eyes, but he seems perfectly okay. But his eyebrows are folded in a worry frown and his eyes are tight around the corners.

I take a deep breath, pushing my problems aside.

He shakes his head again. "Josh. We received a call three hours ago from his football coach, telling us that they had to rush him to the hospital—St. James Memorial. He has been having recurring pancreatitis for almost three years. We thought he had gotten better, but we were wrong. This time it was worse than the other times."

I crawl on the bed toward him and pull him into a hug, and then lean back and take his hands in mine. "Oh gosh. I'm so sorry. Is he going to be okay?"

He removes one hand from mine and rubs his neck. "I don't know. I mean. . .yes. I hope so. The doctor wanted to keep him in the hospital a bit longer to monitor him until tomorrow. They put him on I.V. medications to lessen the irritation."

Tears fill his eyes and he clenches his jaw. "I can't lose him."

I slide my palms to his cheeks and fix my gaze on his. "You won't lose him. He is going to be all right. You hear me?"

He sniffs and blinks several times. "He had better be or I will kick his ass. The idiot hasn't been following his diet."

He inhales deeply, and as his chest deflates he sinks deeper into the bed. "It's your turn. Talk to me. I won't be able to sleep tonight if I don't know what is wrong."

I sigh. Knowing Cole, he won't leave this alone. So I tell him what happened, omitting the part where my dad and his mom were arguing. I'm not touching that issue right now.

By the time I'm done, Cole's body is rigid and his face wears a hard expression. Beautiful. Hard. Unforgiving.

He loosens his hands around my neck. "Did he do anything to you?"

"No!" I say, shaking my head. "No. He didn't."

He exhales, then pulls me to him. He kisses my forehead, and just holds me until I feel my body calm down.

I pull back a little and look up at him. "I felt all this rage inside me, Cole. I am afraid if he had gone further, I would have hurt him really badly. Like really hurt him."

His gaze widens in surprise or shock at my admission.

"I have done it before. That scar on his cheek. . .I did that to him when I was thirteen." I proceed to tell him what happened.

This is a make or break moment. My heart is bleeding raw emotions and there is no way to stop the flow. If Cole is meant to stay he will stay. I'd rather deal with the devastation in one go, than drag it out until later. He needs to know my brand of crazy.

"I'm so tired of blaming myself. Of him blaming me for something I had no control of. I needed, and still need, to get control of my life at some point without using pain as a way to have it. I promised myself I wouldn't let him do any more damage to me. I don't want my sisters to go through what my mother and I went through. So yes, I'm not above hurting him." I bury my face in my hands and mumble, suddenly terrified of my own mind, "Am I crazy to feel this way?"

Cole cups my chin and tugs it up. "What did you say?"

"It feels wrong to admit something like that out aloud. Does that put you off? You must be shocked at least." I add the last part because the boy is just sitting there calmly as if my admission is the most natural thing in the world.

Suddenly, he smiles at me and cups my face in his palms, brushing a thumb over my bottom lip. He stares into my eyes for what feels like forever, drinking in my face with just a look.

Then he drops his hands from my face. "No. You are the bravest girl I've ever met. I don't know how you do it. I'm in awe. Yes, your mind is a chaotic place. But you know what? I want to be the one who calms your mind."

I lift his hand to my lips and kiss his palm. "You need to go home and get some sleep," I say, and then press my forehead against his.

"I'm staying here."

This time I don't protest. I need him. I also have a feeling it will take a monumental effort to uproot him from my room. My father is not here, and knowing him, he probably won't be returning home tonight.

I climb out of the bed and lock my door, then rejoin him on the bed, curling my body into his. He slides his hand until it meets mine and links our fingers, then pushes my hair to one side with his other hand. He tucks his face into my neck and kisses me.

We stay like this, his breath feathering the hair on the nape of my neck and his fingers gripping mine as though he never wants to let go.

When I wake up in the morning, Cole is no longer by my side and the space he was laying on last night is cold.

CHAPTER TWENTY-SIX

"How old are you again?" I ask Megs, while lying on her bed Thursday after school.

I move my gaze from the white ceiling to the doily on the night stand and the two on the dressers. "Even my grandmother doesn't have that many doilies."

"Oh *pssh*. You're just jealous." She huffs and I laugh. "My Grams has a thing for doilies. Anyway. Stop avoiding my question. You need to talk to Cole. He's going crazy."

The hand holding the nail polish brush stops. I looks at her. "What if I carry that obsessive gene? What if I'm like my dad? Gosh, I don't know." I finally voice my fears.

"Listen, Nor. You are nothing like your dad. You care about the people you love. You don't have a mean bone in your body." She falls quiet for a few seconds, then says, "Does he know how you feel?"

I sit up quickly and stare at her. "My feelings?"

She laughs. "Yes. You love him."

"Is it *that* obvious?" Oh. God. Has Cole seen whatever Megs sees when she looks at me?

She nods, closing the cap of the hot pink nail polish bottle and puts it on top of the nightstand and then stretches her legs and wiggles her toes. "You two gravitate towards each other like nothing I've ever seen before. Have you asked him to be your date at the Winter Formal?"

I bite the inside of my cheek and shake my head. I should be excited about attending a school dance for the first time in my life. Instead, I'm worried that if I tell Cole about my dad and his mom, I might jinx *us*.

Crap. I feel as if the room is getting smaller and my breath is coming out in little bursts of air. I stand up and quickly hug Megs before dashing for the door. "I love you. I will let you know once I ask him," I yell over my shoulder, while heading for the stairs. A hand grabs my upper arm before my foot hits the bottom step, halting me abruptly. I turn around to face Megs, her eyes soft.

"Call me, okay? I love you and all your weirdness." She wraps her arms around me without asking me why I bolted out of her room. Without looking at me like I'm crazy. I return her embrace, my eyes prickling with tears and my heart aching with profound gratitude.

This. This is how it feels to have someone understand you, even though they've never walked a day in your shoes.

"I love you so much," I whisper. "Thank you." I feel like I've known Megs my entire life. I can't imagine my life without this girl in it. Just as I cannot imagine my life without Cole. Both of them understand me and feed my soul on different levels.

As soon as her arms drop away from my body, I shove my feet into the flip-flops, unlock the front door and jog the rest of the way to mine before bounding up the stairs. My breath is ragged and my chest hurts as I enter my room. I strip off my dress and put on my running shorts, grab some money to buy ice cream and head out for a run just as Cole's car pulls into his parking spot outside his house. I stop and watch him get out of the car, and my fingers shake at the mere thought of sinking them into his hair. My body shivers, wanting him to hold me. I can keep the little secret about our parents a bit longer—until I speak to his mom—but I don't have the power to walk away from him. He closes the distance between us in long strides and immediately cups my face. Before I can open my mouth, his lips are claiming mine in a ruthless, desperate kiss. My arms wrap around his neck and I'm three seconds from climbing into his skin, ignoring the thoughts whipping around in my head that I shouldn't kiss him like he is the air and I'm dying, dying, dying. His scent with a hint of sweat wraps around me, comforting me.

Cole hums under his breath as the kiss slows down, his fingers gentle as he tucks wisps of hair behind my ear. He raises his head, questions in his eyes.

I drop my hands from his arms. "*Do you want to join me for a run?*" I sign while speaking the words out aloud. He nods and opens his mouth, but I place my finger on his lips to stop him. "No questions, please. I'm sorry for worrying you, but I just need a little more time, okay?"

He studies me, his eyebrows scrunched up in a frown. I hate doing this to him, but this is something his mom should tell him. And if she doesn't, I will take matters in my own hands. He exhales in resignation, drags his fingers through his hair and nods again.

We end up at St. Christopher's, and we walk in past the little board, announcing that a Fr. Joseph is taking confessions. And just for a second, I wonder if Fr. Joseph would be shocked by the state of my thoughts. Is plotting ways my dad could die a sin? Is it the same as committing murder?

Cole's hand presses on my lower back, as he urges me to get inside the church, successfully pulling me out of my thoughts. As soon as my backside hits the bench in the first row, I exhale and close my eyes.

God, I'm so ashamed of those thoughts. Make him go away, please. Just make him disappear. Opening my eyes, I link my fingers with Cole's and lean my head on his shoulder. He kisses my forehead and slides his free hand around my shoulders, holding me close as we wait for my riotous thoughts to settle.

Cole

Thank fuck it's Friday. Just a few more minutes until this lecture is over. This week has been torture. My mind has been preoccupied during the entire class. I can't stop thinking about Josh lying on that hospital bed. He looked so fucking fragile. Now that he is home, Mom is making sure he follows his diet at least for the duration that he will be home.

My mind keeps going back to Nor and what happened a few nights ago.

My fist itched, wanting in on some action. This morning, when I saw her dad—that son of a bitch—leave their house, I was three seconds from charging at him and giving him a piece of my mind using my fist.

Christ.

I can't stand the sight of him. I want Nor out of that house.

Scratch that.

I want Stephen out of that house. The thought of him living with them, terrorizing his entire family with his words and actions makes me want to hurt him so badly. A few weeks ago, Nor told me that she'd often thought about reporting him to children's social services. The only thing that held her back was her fear of being separated from her sisters and mother.

I shut my eyes tightly and inhale deeply, pulling my last memory of her into my mind. The way she seemed to avoid my eye when we're talking, the hesitant touches as if she's afraid to touch me, but that became desperate as if fighting to tell me something. I've seen the red marks on her skin where her fingers pinch her arms, or the way she scratches her scars. I've been studying her since she and I got close so I know something is bothering her.

Why won't she talk to me?

My eyes open in time to see the professor finish scribbling '*How does Roman technology influence us today'* on the white board, right below the words '*Technology and Revolution in Roman Architecture*' then turns and glances around giving the class a meaningful look, which halts us from packing our books in our bags. He starts to talk and I grab my notebook and a pen, my gaze moving to the interpreter. I flip through the pages and quickly glance down to make sure I'm writing on a blank page, then look up again.

"*Write five hundred words. This assignment is to be sent to my email by eleven thirty at night on Thursday. That gives you a week before Thanksgiving to get it done.*"

He turns and walks to his desk and begins to put his books into his leather bag.

Simon is waiting for me outside the lecture hall. We had planned to go for a run on the university's track. He attends his undergraduate lectures at Montgomery campus, located two miles from here. The reason I choose Eastern Lake while I was applying for the Architectural program in colleges was that, it's close to home and they have a special needs class.

We are changed and warming up ten minutes later. Simon touches my arm to get my attention.

"*How is Josh?*" he signs.

"*Better. He was discharged from the hospital yesterday.*" My brother seemed put off, when the doctor sternly told him that this time he should take his orders about the low-fat diet very strictly. He explained the high risks associated with multiple acute pancreatitis flares, which include cancer. That seemed to sober him up fast.

"*Do you want to talk about what's crawled up your ass?*" he signs, jogging in place.

I bring my arms down from the stretch and rub my jaw, feeling frustration coil in my gut. "*Something is going on with Nor, man. I can feel it. I have asked her but she says everything is fine.*"

"*You mean something else, other than her asshole of a father coming to her room? Dude. That shit would mess with anyone.*"

I nod. "*I feel as if there is more going on.*"

He stops and slaps my shoulder all of a sudden, catching me off guard. I turn to glare at him after righting myself.

"*Let us forget our man cards for just a second and pull on frilly pink panties because I feel this conversation needs confessing of feelings and shit.*" He grins and pretends that he is pulling a pair of underwear up his legs. "*How do you feel about Nor?*"

I drop my gaze to the ground, contemplating his words and I realize that I don't even need to think about it. What I feel for Nor is something I can't even explain. The depth of that emotion terrifies me. The thought of losing her makes me break into a sweat.

"*Man to man. Just thinking I might lose her does all these crazy things to me. I don't think I could handle it.*"

"*Then you know what you have to do.*" He starts jogging in place again.

I nod. It's becoming increasingly clear what I need to do after evaluating my feelings for her. I have to get her to talk to me.

"*Good. Let us reclaim our man cards quickly before I start bawling all over the place. My little spitfire is waiting for me at home.*" He starts to run off, but I grab his arm. He turns around to face me.

I smirk. "*Speaking of feelings. What about you and Megs?*"

He spreads his hands out on either side of his body and says, "Simple. I'm crazy in love with that girl," and then he takes off down the track without looking back.

Shaking my head, I smile and trail after my best friend.

CHAPTER TWENTY-SEVEN

Nor

SUNDAY MORNING, I WAKE UP TO THE SMELL OF BACON AND PANCAKES wafting into my room. My stomach grumbles as I swing my legs from the bed, wondering if Elise decided to surprise us with breakfast, something she was quite fond of doing in Ohio.

When I reach downstairs, I follow the voices drifting from the kitchen. I stop and take in the sight in front of me. Mom is standing by the oven, flipping pancakes and humming under her breath. She's dressed in a pair of yoga pants and T-shirt, her hair swept up in a neat ponytail. It's been a while since I saw her like this. Her mood could switch back any second. Elon is sitting on Cole's right side and Elise on the left, watching his fingers intently as he signs.

I spin around, and hold my breath, hoping that my dad isn't home. Things could turn very ugly if he finds Cole here.

"Mom?" I call. She looks over her shoulder at the same time my sisters' turn to face me. "What is Cole doing here? If Dad finds him here—"

"Your father is not home," she says in a soft voice. "I found your boyfriend climbing the ladder to your room and invited him in for breakfast."

Her words send relief coursing through me allowing my feet to finally move and I hurry forward just as Cole, realizing my siblings' attention is no longer on him, turns to face me.

"*Hi,*" I sign,

"*Hey, Snowflake. Your mom invited me in for breakfast.*" He grins and climbs to his feet, his mouth aimed for my lips but changes his mind and hugs me tight. My hug, the Cole kind of hug. He clears his throat and darts a look at my mom, but her attention is on the pan.

"Wow, you two might be talking about us and we wouldn't know," Elise says, a little frown marring her forehead.

Pulling away from Cole, I laugh and go to my mother. I snatch a slice of bacon from the plate on the counter and take a bite.

"Everything smells really good," I hike up onto my tiptoes to kiss her cheek, which she returns with a smile. "Thank you for allowing Cole to come over for breakfast."

She flips a pancake before turning to face me. "He seemed very eager to see you. We can't have him sneaking around, can we?" she teases, smiling. "Don't let the past get in your way. Maggie, your father and I, we are all in the past. I see the way Cole looks at you. Are you happy?" I nod, shoving the bacon in my mouth. "He's a handsome boy." She falls silent for a few seconds. I have a feeling she wants to say something so I wait in the silence. "Elise told me what happened between Cole and your father. I've never seen you so happy, honey. I know that you and Cole are still young and no one knows what the future holds. You'll need to fight for Cole. Don't let him destroy your life like he did mine. Promise me that, honey. Promise me."

I huff and whisper, making sure my voice doesn't carry across the room. "I don't get it. Why don't you just leave? You said it's complicated but seriously? I can't think of anything that would force you to stay."

She winces and closes her eyes, taking deep breathes. "Just promise me."

I sigh in frustration, but end up wrapping my hands around her waist. "I promise."

After breakfast, Cole proposes that he and I head for a swim at the local community swimming pool, which is heated in the months after summer when the temperatures drop.

As soon as he leaves to get his stuff, I pack mine, kiss and hug my sisters and Mom. I head for the door. When I reach the Holloway compound, I see Josh is already on the passenger seat in Cole's car. Cole told me last evening, after our run that his brother was doing much better. He was discharged from the hospital and will go back to school in a couple of days. Cole arrives a few minutes later and we drive off.

Cole's head breaks out of the water and he swims toward where am I with smooth strokes of his arms. He turns to glare at a dark-haired boy, who has been swimming close to me on and off since I stepped into the pool. The look on my boyfriend's face is enough to send the boy wading backwards, his arms raised in surrender. I chuckle under my breath, remembering the other boys Cole has told off when he saw them staring at me.

He is in a protective mood today.

Cole reaches me and cages me in with his arms on both sides of my body before he leans forward to kiss my neck. He pins me with his body, pushing his pelvis against me and I shiver.

God.

It still amazes me that I do this to Cole. Arouse him. Cause his breath to stall in his chest. . .it's such a powerful feeling.

He removes his hands from the wall behind me. "*I love your mouth,*" he signs, his eyes on my mouth then dropping lower to my chest, which is hardly visible above the water. "*I imagine those lips on my skin, driving me wild.*" He mouths the words at the same time as signing them, since I'm still catching up with my lessons.

His fingers wrap around my waist, then skim the edge of my bikini panties with bold, deliberate strokes.

"Oh!" My cheeks are hot, my body on fire and my eyes scanning around me. "What are you doing? We can't do that here, Cole."

"Unless you prefer to talk and tell me what is going on with you, I'll just let my hands do the talking."

I shake my head and push his chest. "That's not fair, you big brute."

He chuckles and shakes his head, and I swim around him while making sure my two piece is still intact before climbing the ladder out of the pool.

I shake the water from my hair, then look over my shoulder when I feel Cole's eyes on me. His eyebrows are bunched in a frown, his lips pursed.

I force a smile and point to the lounge chairs on the other side of the pool, letting him know I'm heading there.

"You're hot."

I twist around, searching for the owner of the voice. I can't remember the last time anyone said those words to me, which is why I'm curious and want to get a look at the person who said them. Two boys sit on the lounge chairs close to the pool, who earlier had approached me inside the pool—making rude remarks about what they would do to my body. Cole almost got into a fight with them. I guess they got scared when Josh showed up. The guy with blond, straight hair eyes me from head to toe, his gaze lingering a little too long on my chest and wets his lips.

Creep.

I spin around and continue my little journey. My steps falter when I hear the same voice say, "Too bad her arms are ugly. Did Daddy and Mommy not love you enough? Freak."

I suck in a breath and swivel around to face them, the magnitude of the cruelty in those words causing me to breathe fast. I take a few steps toward them. I'm not even sure what I want to do, which stops me cold in my tracks. I flex my fingers and walk toward them.

"Do we know each other?" I ask.

They exchange a nervous look.

"Do you want to get to know us?" Blondie asks, darting a look at his friend and shaking on his seat. He grins, seeming to get a kick out of his suggestive remarks.

I walk closer. "Is that what your mother taught you? To call people names? Does it make you feel brave? Or powerful?"

"Oh hey, now, ginger. Don't get your tits in a twist. If you don't want a piece of this," he waves down his body. "Go on now. Run along to your freak boyfriend."

I force my lips into a smirk and raise my brows. "At least I have a boyfriend. What about you, Blondie? Do you have a girlfriend? Or are you just frustrated because at the end of the day, you jerk off to some imaginary girlfriend?"

His nostrils flare and he shoots up from his seat. His friend grabs his hand, pulling him back.

I turn and walk away, feeling triumphant. I reach my chair and grab the towel, then wrap it around myself. I don't know what is more exhausting: defending myself and my scars or walking away.

I stretch my body out on the chair and close my eyes. A cool hand wraps around my knee and my eyes flip open, meeting Cole's. His eyebrows dipped in a worried look.

"*Are you okay?*" He signs.

I force my lips into a smile and nod. He doesn't seem convinced. He glances around the pool then brings those beautiful eyes, framed with long spiky lashes to me.

"*Are you sure? I saw you talking to those dickheads.*"

"It's nothing I couldn't handle. Come sit with me."

He sighs, grabs a towel to dry himself then lays it on his chair and sits down. He takes my hand in his hand and links our fingers together, brushing his thumb on the back of mine. Cole is so good to me it's overwhelming sometimes, in a good way.

Don't blow this up, Nor.

I'm already doing that because I'm keeping things from him.

I pull my hand from his. "*I'll be right back,*" I sign, standing and grabbing the towel from the chair.

I dart around a few chairs, heading for the changing rooms. Before I reach the entrance, a hand wraps around my wrist, spinning me around. I'm breathing hard, fighting hard not to cry.

He drops my hand. "You are shivering. What's wrong?"

"You guys okay?" Josh jogs toward us out of nowhere.

Cole starts to pace in obvious frustration while signing fluidly and fast. I can't make out some of the words. A few seconds into their conversation, Josh looks at me. He opens his mouth to say something but stops and drags his fingers through his hair.

"He's asking why you ran away." Josh darts a look at Cole. "It's hard for him to speak when he's frustrated."

I rub my hands down my arms, suddenly feeling cold. "I wasn't running away. I just needed to use the bathroom." My voice shakes a little.

I turn around but Cole grabs my wrist again and cages me between the wall behind me and his body. My head hits his chin and I can hardly see anything beyond his broad shoulders.

"Wow, he's got it bad for you." Josh chuckles from somewhere behind Cole. Then he appears in my line of vision. "I've seen that look before. It means you're not going anywhere until he gets some answers."

I glare at him. Instead of being even slightly intimidated by my *I will take you down* look, he chuckles again gleefully. "What? This is the best entertainment I've had in weeks. I've never seen my baby brother go all He-Man over a girl."

Cole signs again, his eyes never leaving mine.

"What did those jerks say to you?" asks Josh.

I sigh, my gaze wandering to Blondie and his friend. His focus is on us, watching intently. I can't tell him what grease face over there said. After the scene in the pool earlier on, he doesn't need more provocation to set off his fuse.

"Sometimes it's hard to see people looking at my scars and know they're judging me."

I feel Cole's gaze move from mine and figure he is focused on

Josh for translation. He tucks his thumb under my chin and tilts it up. I lift my eyes to his.

"He's not judging you," Josh says softly.

"I know." I blink hard to chase away the tears threatening to spill and try to wiggle from his hold, but he increases the pressure, making me raise up on my tiptoes to escape his touch in self-preservation. God, this is torture. My cheeks and body heat up. Our thighs are touching, skin on skin. "I'm just being silly. Maybe we should just leave."

Cole's hands circle my waist, sliding up to the sides of my breasts and end up framing my face.

Josh makes a gagging sound and says, "I'm out. I don't need to see you two going all soft porn."

I chuckle, a sound caught between a choked cry and a laugh.

He takes my hand in his free one and brings my wrist to his lips. He places an open-mouth kiss on the skin there, then blows air, his eyes fixed on mine.

"Have I told you how brave I think you are, Snowflake? You'd have scars on your face and I wouldn't even notice. Being strong doesn't necessarily mean doing things so the world can see how brave you are and applaud. It's how you win the battle that matters. That is what makes you strong."

I swallow hard. I try to find the words to express what his words mean to me, but fail miserably.

"Thank you," I say, smiling.

"Thank *you* for the silver lining."

I laugh, unable to keep the joy inside me anymore. His smile is slow to appear but when it finally does, it's powerful and sexy.

"Are we good?"

"Yeah, we're good."

He takes my hand and leads me back to our lounge chair, takes a seat and pulls me down. He cups a hand on my cheek, while rubbing the other one down my arm. I love his hands. They are big and the skin on the palms is rough, likely from the hard labor he does at his father's construction company. But the way he's holding my face in his palms, I can't believe they're the same hands that hold sharp and heavy tools like nails, saws and hammers.

His finger traces a path along my nose, my shoulders and finally my forearms. "Everything. I. . .see. . .everything. You are breathtaking."

I can't breathe. Cole reached inside me and stole the air from my lungs and now I'm drowning, while at the same time basking in his words. For a guy who never says much, he managed to rock me off my axis with just seven words.

"Cole. . ." I can't find the words to express what I'm feeling. How much his words affect me. "Thank you."

I throw one leg over his, sitting astride his lap, and wiggling until I feel his erection snuggled between my legs. He groans, grabs my shoulder and crushes his lips to mine. His tongue urges my lips to part impatiently and I'd be stupid to refuse him because the same fire that's burning inside him is setting my body ablaze.

He lets go of me and slightly leans back, the look on his face fierce. He points at himself, crosses his arms over his chest and then points at me. I know what the sign means, because I've spent the past few weeks practicing over and over. He repeats the same gesture, his mouth tipped at the corners in that almost smile now. "*I love you.*"

Air whooshes out of my lungs. My heart flips inside my chest, as I take in the honest to God emotions shining in his eyes. The eyes that seem to see my fears, chaos and insecurities and the girl who just wants to be loved. To be told that she is beautiful. A little crazy sometimes. Sitting here on his lap, I feel like a princess. Cole has just stripped away my proverbial tattered clothes, dressed me in a beautiful gown and put a crown on my head.

I'm Cinderella and I don't need anything else in the world. Just him and me.

What started as curiosity on my part has grown into something huge. Love. Sometimes it's so overwhelming it scares me. I've wanted to tell him how I feel for a while now. What I feel for him.

But then doubts swoop in. Feeling like this, having someone who pays attention to me like Cole does is unreal. It's like living in a dream. My wildest fantasy. An illusion. I'm terrified I'll wake up and it will all be gone. My heart is too invested in Cole. So I've kept my mouth shut and just reveled in it.

"Nor?"

I snap out of my thoughts, and offer him a shaky smile. For a moment, the confidence I've built up over the past few years wavers and I start babbling, "I'm a mess sometimes. I live inside my head too much. I. . .I—" I pause to gather my thoughts. "I don't care. I've been falling for you since that first night on the roof. I can't explain it, but it happened."

I realize that his confession changes everything. He needs to know the truth. My truth. "Being in love with me is a risk." I tell him.

He grasps my chin with his fingers and urges me to look at him. "I. Don't. Care. I'm in love with you and all the little quirks that make up who you are. Your chaotic mind, your insecurities, your big heart. You think you're not perfect but you are perfection to me."

He narrows his eyes at me and drops his hands from my chin running his long fingers through his tousled hair. "Everyone has scars, whether they're on the surface of our bodies or on the inside, hidden in our souls. We've just gotten good at hiding them. Give me a chance to love you. All of you. I want those parts you've hidden so deep inside you. . .those parts you think are unworthy of me loving. I want those. I crave them. I can't promise to fix you but I promise to be there when you need me. I just want to be there to hold you when you cry."

Tears roll down my face. He tucks me against him and wraps his hands around me so tight, I feel everything in me piece together.

"That's the most breathtaking thing anyone has ever said to me, Cole. And Yes. Oh God. I love you. I love you, too. I was so scared of telling you."

"Don't ever be afraid to tell me what's on your mind. We're in this together. Silver lining, right?"

I nod and then laugh. "We got to 'I love you' even though we have never been on a date."

He raises a brow. "We have been on a date. Several dates. Every minute we spend together is a special date. The roof, the cafe, St. Christopher's."

Boom. There goes my heart again.

A whistle cuts through the air, jolting me from the kiss. God, what's gotten into me? I've never been the kind of girl to kiss in public, not that I'd ever done it before.

I lean back and close my eyes, pressing my forehead to his.

"Ahoi, you two freaks. Deaf and dumb, and a cutter." My body stiffens. God, why can't they just leave us alone?

"What?" he asks when he feels my body's reaction.

I shake my head. "Let's go home."

Cole must sense trouble because his nostrils flare, his mouth tightens and he rips his gaze from mine, darting it around the pool area.

His gaze is hard, uncompromising. *"What did he say to you? And don't tell me it's nothing. If you don't tell me, I will go and ask him myself. We are not leaving until I know what he said."* His fingers are a bit too fast, so he has to say some words aloud, which seems to aggravate him even more.

Tears prick the back of my eyes. I take Cole's face in my hands and force him to look at me. "Not worth it. Silver lining, remember?"

I bite my cheek, scrambling for something to say that will hopefully ease the storm brewing on his face.

"I want the truth, Nor," he signs-speaks.

I sigh. "He called us 'freaks.'"

Cole grabs my hips, lifts me off his lap and sits me on the lounge chair. He stalks toward the two guys, the muscles on his back bunching and flexing with every movement.

Scrambling to my feet, I dash after him, hoping to intercept him.

"What do you want, Deaf Boy? Can you hear me?" The idiot with the black hair shouts, sneering at Cole.

Oh God. Where is Josh?

I search around the pool, praying under my breath for him to appear. I have a feeling, given the dangerous vibes coming off Cole in droves and cracking the air around us, I won't be able to stop him. I turn back to Cole and tap him on his shoulder to catch his attention, but he shrugs my finger off his body. He reaches down and grabs one of the guys by his throat. Black Haired idiot is slightly taller than Cole, but my boyfriend packs more muscle. He hauls him up and drags him back until they hit a wall. I've never seen him like this before and it's frightening. Someone yells there is a fight going down. Yet, no one intervenes. I feel like I've left my body and am now watching everything from a distance, unable to control it.

Josh suddenly appears before me. A whoosh of air leaves my chest as he dashes to his brother's side. Somehow he manages to make Cole let go, but Blondie springs to his feet, probably thinking Josh is here to help his brother by kicking his friend's ass. He raises a fist, ready to take down Cole. Rage like I have never felt grips me by the throat. It drives me forward with my hand locked in a fist. I swing back and aim for the boy's jaw but end up slamming into his shoulder. He blinks at me stunned and before I can think twice, I jump on his back, locking my arms around his neck. He swings around in circles, trying to dislodge me, but I'm smaller and my grip is surprisingly strong. Someone plucks me off Blondie's back. I kick and squirm reaching out for the jerk in front of me who is busy rubbing his chin. I must have clocked him one.

"Calm down, Nor," Josh whispers in my ear. I stop fighting and look over my shoulder. He's grinning wide and shaking his head. "Jesus. You're a little ball of fire, aren't you?"

I huff and attempt to wiggle out of his arms, but he tightens his hold on me.

"Cole won't be very happy if you end up getting hurt. So between a pissed off Eleanor and a raging Cole, I choose him."

I stop fighting him and watch Cole prowling up and down, his chest rising and falling fast. One of the lifeguards is standing in front of him, trying to keep him from pouncing on the guy with the dark hair, who is now sitting on the floor, rubbing his neck. He's jaw is already sporting a red mark where Cole's fist connected with his face.

Shit. If he presses charges, Cole will be in trouble. Then I remember that my father is part of the Willow Hill police force.

Crap!

Panic steals my ability to breath. I point at the two boys and yell to the lifeguard, telling him they started it.

"He knows," Josh murmurs, finally dropping his hands from my waist. "Are you calm, Nor?"

I nod glancing around the pool. People are laughing and others are pointing at the two boys, Blondie is glaring at me from behind the lifeguard's shoulder.

"You're going to pay for this," the black-haired boy croaks. "I'm going to press charges."

The lifeguard swings around to glare at him. "You will *not* press any charges." His voice is scary low, making the boy cower under the full weight of it. "You started it. You press charges and you will have me to deal with. Come on, get out of here, you little piece of shit."

The boys scramble to their feet, and head for the lockers with their heads hanging.

The lifeguard turns to face us, sparing Cole a look. "You okay?"

Cole gives him a curt nod, a muscle ticking furiously in his clenched jaw.

"Let me know if they cause any more trouble," Lifeguard says, his eyebrows raised. "Jesus, how old are you again? Where did you learn to fight like that?" He shakes his head and walks away, looking over his shoulder once.

Cole wipes the blood seeping from the gash on his top lip with the back of his hand and then signs, "*You okay*?"

I nod. "*You*?"

He nods.

"Let's go home, then. We've had enough excitement for one day," I say.

When we pull up in front of the Holloway house, Cole turns on the overheard light and shifts on the seat to face me. His mouth tips at the corners. "You jumped on the guy's back? You're a little more savage than I thought. I like it."

I swat his chest as he laughs deeply.

"My little savage Snowflake. Dainty on the outside, but a fighter on the inside."

This time I laugh. I don't really have anything to say because I'm basking in his words. I tilt my head up, making sure he can see my mouth. "Thank you for standing up for me."

"They can talk shit about me. I don't care. I'm used to it. But when it comes to you, I'm not above hurting anyone. I don't care who they are."

"You can't prevent people from talking, Cole. You can't fight all my battles. I'm learning to stand up for myself and that is what matters."

"It doesn't mean I won't try." He clenches his jaw. "I don't want you to fight them alone. I want to be at your side when you do."

"I would love that. Thank you, Cole."

"*You two make me proud*," Josh sign-speaks before hopping out of the car and sauntering toward his front door.

Cole and I follow suit. He walks me to my door and pulls me into a tight hug.

"*See you at ten,*" he signs.

I bite the corner of my lip. "One more thing. Will you be my date for the Winter Formal?"

He shifts on his feet a bit, looking uncomfortable. "Crowds are not my thing. I feel overwhelmed when people try to talk to me."

"Oh, I'm sorry." I can't even begin to imagine how that feels for him.

"You should go. Don't miss it because of me," he says, raising his hands to cup my face in his palms.

I shake my head and wrap my fingers around his wrists. "I'd rather spend the evening with you."

He opens his mouth, ready to argue but I stop him with my finger against his lips. His face softens as he studies me. The worried look on his face fades, replaced by a boyish grin spreading across his face. "I have two left feet. Are you okay with that?"

"Are you sure?"

"I changed my mind, just in case some weird guy decides to ask you to the dance. I will be devastated. And the thought of you in someone else's arms, while I am in my room waiting for you to come home, kills me. If you want to go to the Formal, I am your date."

I laugh, push myself on my tiptoes and press my lips to his in a kiss. I pull back and release his wrists and sign, "*Thank you.*"

"*Anything for you,*" he signs, then says aloud, "You are turning me inside out, Snowflake."

Laughing, I break away from his hold and turn to walk toward my house. *I love you so much it physically hurts to be away from you even for a second, Cole,* I whisper inside my head.

CHAPTER TWENTY-EIGHT

Nor

THE DAYS FOLLOWING MY DAD AND MAGGIE'S ARGUMENT HAVE BEEN some of the most difficult ones that I've had in a long time. Cole knows something is wrong. I've seen the way he looks at me, waiting patiently for me to open up. And I will.

Today, Cole and I are double dating with Simon and Megs. It's our first date and I'm pretty excited about it. She mentioned there was this new posh Italian restaurant that she has been dying to go visit. I'm not exactly sure what I should wear, which is why I'm standing in front of my closet, staring at my meager wardrobe collection. I duck inside and unhook the heavy lace, mint green dress from the clothes hanger, straighten the black bow-tie around the waist to give it more fluff and lay it on the bed. I dash out of the room and head downstairs to grab my Keds, but freeze when I hear Dad's raised voice. I retrace my steps, my heart thudding inside my chest and stop outside my mom's room. I lean forward and press my ear on the door.

"I really need the money, Carol. Please." His voice is low now, pleading. "I'll pay it back. I promise, I will."

"How can you ask me to lend you money from our daughters' college fund? I can't do that to them," Mom says in a barely audible voice. "This money is for their future."

Dad roars, followed by a thud. I jump back from the door, my eyes wide.

"You useless bitch. That was *our* money. If it weren't for those worthless little shits, it could have been ours."

"Don't you dare talk about my daughters like that," Mom says in a raised voice. I've never heard her speak to my father like that. "You know very well my mom and dad set up that account for them. I chipped in from my own savings. You never bothered to help out. So don't go around blaming them for your own stupidity."

Silence follows my mother's words. I wait, holding my breath. What kind of trouble is he in?

The door flies open without warning. Dad almost knocks me down as he storms out of the room. I stumble away to avoid being trampled, and press my back on the wall behind me.

He glares at me, and I swear I've never seen so much loathing in anyone's eyes. "You and your sisters are nothing but pain in my life. You ruined everything for me."

Fear and anger scorch my veins, but the latter wins out. I fist my hands at my sides. "Then why don't you leave?"

His eyes widen at my insolence. "Because your pathetic mother is like a leech, stuck on me and sucking me dry." He narrows his glare at me. "Look at you, standing there, confronting me. You fall apart and cut yourself instead of facing a challenge like a true Blake. You make me sick. My own blood wouldn't be as weak as you."

He turns and stomps down the stairs. Tears burn my eyes as his words rip apart the confidence and resistance I've spent the last year building up.

My own blood wouldn't be as weak as you.

"Honey?" My mom's voice breaks through the deafening crash of my flailing emotions as they try to find something to hold onto.

My feet turn to face her, but my body is too heavy.

"Why do you stay with him? Why can't you leave him?" I plead.

"It's. . .it's complicated."

"What could be more complicated than this?" I yell, sobbing.

"You know what? I can't do this, Mom." I shuffle down the stairs and race out the door barefoot. Dad's car is already gone by the time my foot hits the hard ground on the sidewalk. I let my instincts take over as I race to find the comfort I desperately need, welcoming the sharp pain from the gravel on my bare skin.

When I finally get back home, the soles of my feet are raw, but I feel much better than when I left. I head to the shower, making sure to avoid my mother. I resent her for her stubbornness and whatever stupid reason she has as to why she still stays with a man, a monster, who has made his mission in life to make everyone around him miserable.

After dressing in my pretty dress and sneakers, I put on the necklace Cole gave me for my birthday and head downstairs to the kitchen. I empty the jar we use for grocery shopping money, and leave.

I wander along the aisles, adding what we need in the cart. I have two more hours until our double date. I pull out my phone and text Megs, asking her if it's okay to chill at her place before we leave. I need the distraction and someone to talk to before I drive myself crazy. She texts me back to let me know that she's at Spinners cafe and will be heading home soon.

I turn down an aisle heading for the tampon section and look up from my list. My step falters as I come face to face with packs of disposable shavers on a shelf. I should be able to look at them without fear. Blood roars in my ears and my scars start to itch, shooting tingles to my toes. I remember how good I used to feel when that sharp pain on my skin took over.

The sense of control. My hands start to shake with need and I have to ball them into fists as I fight the urge. My body vibrates, eager for that fix. People continue to mill around me. A woman's voice asks me if I am okay. I nod, fighting for breath. Fighting for control. I close my eyes and see myself in a tunnel and the light that will save me is that pack of razors.

My own blood wouldn't be as weak as you.

I'm not weak. I'm not weak. I'm not weak.

I open my eyes, and stare ahead. I can walk past this shelf without turning into my former self, craving for a fix. Maybe if I just touch the pack, I'll feel better. I reach for the shelf, but something holds me back. There is a war in me; angels versus demons, fighting to own me. I'm in my own personal Hell and only I can get myself out of it.

My own blood wouldn't be as weak as you.

I'm stronger than this and I'll prove him wrong.

Suddenly, my feet are moving. I abandon my shopping cart and sprint toward the exit, blindly swerving around the other shoppers.

I burst through the doors and run to my car. My hands are still shaking too much. I can't fit the key to the lock. A strange sound is coming from my chest, and I can't stop it.

"Ma'am? Are you okay?" A man's voice says. I shake my head, tears rolling down my face.

"Work, damn it," I hiss, trying to over and over to shove the key into the lock.

Turning around, I slump back on the car and slide to the ground, the keys gripped tightly in my hand. I drag my legs up and drop my face on top of my knees. I breathe in and out for several moments. Tears stream down my face and my chest aches. It's not as bad as it was when I was inside the store. A sweet kind of pain presses on my palm, making me momentarily focus. I lift my head from my knees and unfold my hand. The car keys tumble to the ground and the rush fades. I grab them from the ground and extend my arm, then drag the sharp edge on my skin. Adrenaline shoots through me. A sense of euphoria sings through the blood in my veins as I watch a few drops of blood pop up in the jagged cut.

Closing my eyes, I let my head fall back as I ride that feeling. It's short lived though. It doesn't make me feel as if I can conquer the world. It makes me feel guilty. It makes me feel as though I've let my-self down. I hate myself for breaking my own promise.

My fingers start to shake as I realize what I have done. I grab the edge of my dress and scrub my arm clean of the blood.

Shoving my hand in my purse, I pull out my phone and scroll through the names on my contact list and stop when my former ther-apist's name pops on the screen. I press the call button and wait for her to pick up. It rings three times before diverting to voice mail.

I breathe through my mouth, fighting to fill my lungs with air.

Breathe, Eleanor. Breathe. Freaking breathe.

I shut my eyes tight, fighting the darkness looming around the edges of my consciousness. "Dr. Thorsten? Um. . .It's me. . .El—" I stop and take a deep breath again using my mouth, and release it through my nose. "Eleanor Blake. You said if I ever needed to talk to you, I could call anytime?"

I wipe my cheeks with the back of my hand. "I need to talk to you so badly. I did something today and I'm scared I'm about to relapse. I can't—I don't want to go back to being that girl. Please. Please call me back." I raise my head and disconnect the call.

The darkness inside me is like a yawning chasm, eager to swal-low me whole. I grip the phone tighter in one hand and scroll through my contacts again and stop on Cole's name. I hesitate, because I have no idea how he will react when he sees me like this. He knows me as the strong girl who fought and is still fighting her demons. I think about calling Grandma, but I can't let her see me like this either. And neither can my sisters.

I find Megs' name and call her. It rings once but I disconnect it quickly.

Despite my deepest fears and the guilt ravaging my soul, the only person I want to see right now is the same person I'm afraid I'll end up losing the minute he sees me in this condition.

No one else but him.

Cole.

My Cole, even though the reason for my breakdown involves

our parents and whatever secrets lie between them. The weight of it is dragging me down. Every emotion inside me is flailing, searching for something to latch on to. I'm seconds away from reverting to that helpless little girl that found release inflicting pain on herself. Cole has never seen me at my worst, because the angels in me keep the demons at bay whenever he's around me. He's the only person I've ever admitted to about the things I'd gladly take to my grave, my truest fears and the fact that I'd harm my own father to stop him from hurting my family. To save Cole.

But am I ready to tell him about my dad and his mom?

I wipe my cheeks with the back of my hand and quickly shoot a text to Megs with shaking fingers.

Me: **Please come and get me. Stuck in front of Wal-Mart**.

I press send. I can't bring myself to tell her the truth over a text.

Seconds pass. What if she doesn't have her phone with her?

One minute passes. I know this because I'm squinting at the phone, waiting. Tears blur my eyesight. I hate how weak I am right now. I look like a junkie in need of her next fix.

My phone lights up as a text comes through.

Megs: **On my way.**

Five minutes later, the sound of tires on tarmac claim my attention. Megs' Prius drives by slowly, her eyes darting out the window, searching for me. She spots me, reverses and slides into the parking space across from me. I managed to climb to my feet to wait for her. It's enough that I look pathetic in the first place anyway.

She jumps out of the car, grinning. At the same time, Cole steps out of the other door and Simon too. I groan, inwardly.

Shit.

Megs' grin disappears as she gets closer before dashing to my side with her arms outstretched ready to hug me.

"What happened, love?" she whispers as she hugs me tightly.

"I didn't want him to see me like this."

"You know how he is when it comes to you. I was about to leave when I received your text. He jumped in my car before I could stop him," she says quickly.

Cole is zeroing in on us and he looks at me with shock and sorrow. I probably look like a complete mess.

He pulls me from Megs' arms and envelops me in his. I close my eyes, letting the feel of his body soothe me. When I open them again, Simon is standing next to Megs, his hands shoved inside his Capri pants, speaking to Megs in a low voice.

Cole pulls back. He holds out his hand and says, "Keys."

I blink at him, confused.

He points to my car. I nod and place them on his palm. He signs something to Simon, who nods and says, "We'll see you guys later," then takes Megs' hand and drags her toward the car. Cole opens my car and jerks his chin for me to get in.

After telling Megs I will call her as soon as I get home, I get in the car. Cole follows me and slides in the driver's seat. This Cole is kind of scary. He's determined.

When we arrive at our neighborhood, instead of taking me to my house, he kisses my forehead and leads us to his. Nick is on the porch, playing race cars with a friend of his. After saying a muffled hello to them, we head inside the house. Maggie's voice drifts from the kitchen. She's talking on the phone.

Shit.

She is the last person I want to see today. I drag my feet on the carpet and Cole stops and raises his brows at me as if to ask "What's wrong?" But I can't tell him yet. I need a little more time.

Cole tugs me by the hand upstairs to the bathroom and locks the door. He turns on the shower, turns to me, and motions for me to lift my arms.

"I can undress myself," I say quietly, but making sure he can read my lips.

He keeps his gaze on my face and shakes his head.

I sigh and take a deep breath, then lift my arms. He makes efficient work of undressing me and when he's done, he nods toward the shower. I step inside and he pulls the doors closed. When I'm done I linger a bit longer, hoping Cole will eventually leave the bathroom. I finally give up and slide open the door. Cole is holding the towel out for me and wraps it around me, rubbing my body dry. He unhooks a T-shirt from his shoulder that I hadn't noticed before and slides it over my head. Finally he leads me to his room, drops my hand and scrambles on his bed before urging me to go to him.

I blink back tears, and shake my head. "I'm sorry you had to see that."

"I'm not sorry."

Finally, the tears I've been holding onto fall down my cheeks. "I'm a mess, Cole. I can't. . ." I suck in a deep breath. "I keep promising myself I'll be better next time. God, I need to leave. You don't want me like this."

He scrambles out of the bed and grabs my shoulders. "I don't care, Nor. Just come to bed. Let me hold you, all right?"

Those words breakdown the wall I've been erecting since I was in the shower. I fall into his arms and let him lead me to the bed. He gathers me in his arms. "It's okay, Nor. I'm here."

I lean back to look into his eyes. "I was standing in front of the shelves with razor blades. The urge to buy them was so strong. God, I'm weak."

"You did not buy the razors. You won the fight." He glances down at the red marks on my forearm where I dug the car keys in. "You stopped yourself. Don't stop fighting, Snowflake. Fight whatever demons keep you awake at night. Just don't stop fighting."

Our lips are almost touching. I can feel his breath fanning the skin around my mouth. Sliding my hands to cup his face, I press my lips to his. A kiss seeking comfort. He kisses me back, softly at first and sighs under his breath, a cross between a moan and a groan. He cups my face with one hand, and wraps the other around the nape of my neck, pulling me closer. Holding me captive. I move and latch my legs around his hips momentarily disconnecting our mouths but not for long. His hand leaves my face, slides down my neck, the side of my breast and down lower. He lifts the edge of my dress and wraps his fingers around my lower back, holding me against his body.

A light blinks feverishly behind my closed eyes. I open them to see the little alarm light on the nightstand lighting up to indicate someone is knocking on Cole's door. I scramble off Cole's lap just as his mom walks into the room. My face is flaming as her gaze narrows on me and then her son.

"Staying within limits, okay?" She asks loudly at the same time signing. She has this rule that the boys can take girls to their room but never go beyond kissing.

Cole nods and looks at me, his face flushed and eyes dark. I can't meet his eyes. I can't meet Maggie's eyes and not because she caught us kissing up a storm.

I swing my legs out of the bed and stagger upright. "*I have to go,*" I sign while saying the words out loud. "*See you later?*"

Cole moves from the bed as if to follow me, but I shake my head. His eyebrows are furrowed as he studies my every move. I know he's looking at me because I know the feel of his eyes.

CHAPTER TWENTY-NINE

Nor

Last night when I came back home from Cole's house, I came to a conclusion: I was going to have to talk to Maggie. My notebook is filled with a million words. I've been trying to get it all out. Music isn't helping me as much as it did before. Yesterday's near breakdown was my undoing and it made me realize that there was no way I was going to allow myself to go off the deep end. I wasn't going to carry other people's burdens. I was already carrying my own.

I have one mission today. I pretend I'm sick today so I can handle this.

Standing at my window, I watch Cole get into his car and drive away. Seconds later, a black truck pulls in front of the Holloway's house playing loud hip hop music. Josh, with an overnight bag slung over his shoulder, dashes from the front door and waves to his mom who is standing on the front porch before he jogs toward the car. After a round of greetings, Josh gets in the truck.. Seconds later, it speeds off down the street and disappears around the corner.

I rush downstairs and out of the door. Two minutes later, I'm standing in front of the Holloway's front door. I take deep breaths to calm my racing heart and quickly wipe the sweat now beading on my forehead.

Am I going to do this? Confront Cole's mother about whatever I saw on her lawn? God, why does it feel like I'm about to cross a line, that I might change things exponentially? I spin around and climb down the steps, then stop and ball my hands into fists.

I can't live like this. I feel drained all the time and if I don't get to the root of this, I might relapse.

There is no way I'm going to let that happen. I have too much to lose.

Shaking my hands at my side, I whirl around and ring the bell before I can bail. I hear the sound of muffled footsteps coming toward me from the other side of the door. I hold my breath, waiting, and when the door opens, Maggie blinks, and her eyes widen slightly.

"Eleanor." Her gaze darts over my shoulder before returning back to me. "Why aren't you in school? Cole left—"

"Actually, I wanted to talk to you."

Her eyebrows shoot up but she seems to recover fast. "I'm about to take Nick to school. Can it wait until later?"

I shake my head. "No, I just need a few minutes."

She nods and steps aside, allowing me entrance.

Once inside, she gestures for me to sit on the couch but I shake my head. I'm too nervous to stay put in one place.

She clears her throat and raises a brow. Her hands are clasped in front of her tightly.

Right. My grandmother has a saying that goes something like, Choose your battles well. If you know you cannot handle it, then walk away.

I chose this battle. The only thing that terrifies me is that I have no idea which condition I will come out of it in.

Without further pre-empt, I blurt out, "I saw you and my father arguing on your lawn two weeks ago."

Her face blanches and her mouth falls open then closes again. "What?"

"Are you and my father having an affair?"

She gasps, then sits down on the couch, dropping her face in her hands. "Why would you think that?"

"I heard you and my dad talking."

She wipes a trembling hand over her brow. "No. Your father and I are not having an affair."

"Then why were you arguing?" I insist, feeling my panic start to rise.

She leans back and stares at me. "It's none of your business, Eleanor."

I start to pace. "Mrs. Holloway. It's my business. My mother is in that house right now lost in her own world. My sisters have no idea what is happening and I. . .oh God, I can't do this anymore. I can't handle it.

"It might not be any of my business, but, it's eating me inside out. I'm going to be honest with you. My mom used to think that my dad was her entire world. She still does. She hasn't accepted the fact that he doesn't love her anymore. It has destroyed her. It's destroying my family. Me." I stretch out my hands toward her. "This. I don't want to go down this road again. Two days ago, I almost relapsed after I had gone for so long without self-harming. Cole keeps asking me what is wrong. I care about him very much. But I can see his heart breaking whenever he looks at me, because I can't bear to look at him when I know I'm keeping a secret from him. So please, Maggie, tell me the truth. Please. I need to be able to sort this out in my head."

She stares at me the entire time, her gaze moving from my wrists to my face, a soft look on her face. Then she straightens on the couch and takes a deep breath, releasing it in a long shuddering breath.

"Your father and I practically grew up together. We did everything together. His parents and mine were friends. We lived next door to each other. We went to school together. We were inseparable. So naturally, we fell in love. He was the sweetest, most caring person I had ever met. But he had such a hard life at home. His father was a general in the army. He was strict to the point of cruel, and always demanded more than one hundred percent from his son. But his cruelty exceeded even his norm when he found out that Stephen's brother,

Thomas, was gay."

I remember my grandmother mentioning him but I let her talk.

"Thomas was the most handsome boy I'd ever met. And the most cheerful person. But he was also born deaf." She licks her lips. "In an attempt to make sure Stephen didn't turn out like his older brother, Thomas, their father became even more demanding to the extent that he beat him up. At this time, he'd already thrown Thomas, who was fifteen at that time, out of the home. Even their mother's words and protection didn't help.

"Anyway, Stephen hated your grandfather so much. He asked me to run away with him, but I refused. I loved him very much, but I couldn't leave my family. And I told him exactly that. He was extremely enraged. I'd never seen him like that, which made me realize that I probably didn't know him like I thought I did. Things fell apart and we broke up. I got accepted to a college out of state and I left him here in Florida. Years later he tracked me down, but by that time, I was already engaged to Benjamin."

I rub my clammy hands down my dress. "And now, we are living next door to you."

She nods. "A few years into my marriage with Ben, things weren't going so well. Ben was preoccupied most of the time with starting his own business and I was raising Josh, mostly alone. Ben was out of town for long periods of times. He was distracted. Our love seemed to have diminished and my marriage was rocky, with no chance of saving it especially after Ben confessed to me later on that he'd been having an affair. We were heading for divorce. Just around that time, your father came to town for a seminar hosted by the state's police department. He was a police detective at that time. Old feelings for him resurfaced and I ran to him for comfort."

"But my dad. . .he was still married to my mom."

"He told me that he'd divorced her. Because things didn't work and that he'd never been able to forget me." She drops her face in her hands and inhales deeply. "I was so stupid to believe him."

I stare at her, completely confused on what I'm supposed to do now. Hug her or stay put and wait it out? "What happened next?"

"I realized your father hadn't changed. He was the same man. Hot tempered and sometimes cruel. Also Benjamin approached me and pleaded with me, told me that he didn't want to lose me. My life had always been the kind I'd dreamed about with Benjamin, an exceptionally amazing father and husband, apart from that affair. I wasn't proud of what I did. But at the same time, I wanted Josh to grow up with his own father. I wasn't perfect either. So I went back to my husband. One month later, I realized I was pregnant with Cole. Around that time, I received a call from a woman who told me that she was Stephen's wife and I should stop destroying her marriage. I was shocked. The next time your father called to convince me to come back to him, that he'd change, I told him I couldn't because I was pregnant. That Benjamin and I had decided to work on our marriage. He was angry. He cursed me on the phone. I told him to never contact me again and to go home and work on his marriage."

Flash backs of the time my father came home from one of his long trips flash in my mind. The words he'd used to belittle my mother, makes me realize he was doing this long before I was born. The look on his face when he'd looked at me. Now his words are his weapon and he has a talent for unleashing them. Sometimes I wonder if physical abuse would have been better than words that left scars on my soul.

She stands up and walks to the kitchen, and returns with a glass of raspberry juice with a slice of lemon in it. After thanking her, she sits on the couch again, and clasps her hands in front of her.

I clasp my hands around the glass and bite the inside of my cheek, and mutter distractedly, "He hates Cole so much."

Her head snaps back, her eyebrows dipping low. "He hates Cole?"

I look up from my glass and meet her shocked gaze. I nod.

"Has he done anything to hurt him?"

I shake my head. She looks so stunned by my revelation that I'm not sure how to answer that. "No." She breaths out and her shoulders loosen in relief. "I would never let anything happen to him, Mrs. Holloway." My words are a solemn promise. Because, really, Cole is my life.

She stands up from the couch and heads for the kitchen again and I sip the raspberry juice in my hands, trying to process the conversation we just had. Minutes pass, and I notice Cole's mom hasn't returned. I glance at the clock. I've been here almost an hour. I got the info I wanted.

I set the glass on the table and follow her to the kitchen. Her hands are planted on the marble counter of the kitchen island, and her head is bowed down. Her shoulders shake silently as if she's crying.

I take a step closer. She sniffs and lifts her head, and I'm met with blue eyes similar to Josh's. I feel the animosity I had toward her slowly ebb away. Standing before me is a woman who is caught between the past and the present. The air is still loaded with the revelation. I bridge the gap between us and wrap my arms around her. She has been good to me and my sister's since we moved here and treated us almost like we were her own children. I hate to see her hurting.

"I'm sorry, Mrs. Holloway."

She returns my embrace, but only for a few minutes before she steps away. She wipes her palms over her face to hide the hurt swallowing her whole.

"I'm terrified of what Stephen might do," she says in a low voice. "Maybe you and Cole should break things off."

What?! That's not what I was expecting to hear at all. "Why?"

She takes another step back and leans on the sink behind her. "Nothing good will come of this."

I shake my head and start scratching on the scars on my forearms. Suddenly I feel as if ants are crawling all over my skin. "I can't. Please don't ask me to give up Cole."

Her eyes soften. "I might have an idea as to why Stephen hates Cole. Cole reminds him of his brother, Thomas. Apparently, Stephen's mother doted a lot on Thomas trying to make up for her husband's ignorance and neglect. She didn't give the same attention to Stephen, which made him jealous. Stephen called his own brother an abomination, the same words his father used over and over on Thomas. The other reason is that Cole was also the main reason that cemented my decision to go back to Benjamin. In Stephen's eyes, my son took me away from him. Your father wants someone to blame, and Cole is the scapegoat.

"You have to break up with him, honey. You know very well, if your father puts his mind to hating something or someone, it's difficult to convince him otherwise. He will eventually hurt my son. I won't stand back and watch while he does that."

I imagine my life without Cole and I feel my heart falling, crashing with a resounding bang at my feet. My mouth opens and closes, but no words come out. I'm still trying to recollect my thoughts, words that will convince her that, our love will survive anything. Thing is, I'm not so sure about that. Maybe I should cut all ties with him. He'd be safe away from my father.

But what about me? A little selfish voice whispers to me. *What about us?*

My eyes smart with hot tears but I keep them lowered to the counter in front of me. How can she ask me to deny my eyes the sight of Cole, when they were made entirely for that purpose? Asking me to cut him loose is like forcing my heart to stop working. To yank it from my chest and throw it in a deep dark hole.

I mutter, "I'm sorry" over and over until I'm not sure what I'm sorry for.

Maggie's eyes move from me and over my shoulder, they widen at the exact moment a strong arm wraps around my waist, pulling me back to an equally strong chest.

Cole.

Oh, God.

Oh, crap.

I breathe his scent in and the flow of words stops immediately. Blinking away the tears, I paste a smile on my face and turn to face him. He looks just as breath taking as always, only this time, his eyebrows are scrunched up in what I can only guess is confusion.

"*I thought you were supposed to be in school,*" I sign, my fingers shaking

"*I wanted to check on you. You weren't in the house,*" he signs. "*What's going on?*" He glances over my shoulder to his mom and then back to me.

I look at Cole's mother, and pray that she can see how sorry I am. "This is not my story to tell, Cole, talk to your mom."

I lift to the tip of my toes and kiss his cheek, brush a thumb across his bottom lip. "I'll be waiting for you."

If the history between our parents doesn't scare you and make you break up with me, a soft voice whispers inside my head as I turn and leave Cole's house.

The sound of my phone ringing next to my pillow pulls me away from my sleep. I open my eyes. They feel heavy and swollen, a result of crying and I shift on the bed. Elon's arm falls away from my waist. She came to my room right after dinner, which I hardly ate, and curled up next to me on my bed.

I reach for the phone but something tumbles out of my hand and onto the bed. The penknife. I fell asleep last night, clutching it in my hand like a life line. I was so close to cutting when Elon walked into the room. I'd thought of sending her away but I couldn't bring myself to do it, because as much as I wanted some sort of release, I craved someone to hold me. Be with me.

I shove it under my pillow and grab the phone, swiping a finger across on the screen to answer without checking the caller.

"Eleanor?"

I bolt upright and swing my legs over the side of the bed. "Dr. Thorsten?" I whisper into the phone, darting a look over my shoulder to check if my sister is still asleep. "Could you please hold on a sec?

I'll be right back."

After my therapist's confirmation, I place the phone on my pillow then turn on the bedside lamp. I stand up, round the bed and scoop up Elon in my arms, careful not to jostle her. I head out of my room to hers, lay her on her bed and pull the covers over her body. I return to my room and close the door, my heart beating frantically in my chest at the thought of talking to Dr. Thorsten.

I snatch the phone from my pillow and grip it in my hands so it doesn't slip from my clammy palms. I've been waiting for her call and now that she is on the line, I'm dying to blurt out the words fighting to break free from my chest. "Hello. Dr. Thorsten?"

"I'm here, Eleanor. I got your message. Is everything okay?"

I scoot up on the bed until my back hits the headboard, and then draw my legs to my chest. "Not really." I drop my chin on my knees and inhale deeply, but my lungs can't seem to absorb enough air. "Today wasn't a great day. I wanted to cut so badly. . .I think I'm relapsing. God, I can't go back to cutting. Everything is going well and I'm scared I might lose—"

"Eleanor. Take a deep breath." I close my eyes and breathe in through my nose and out my mouth. I repeat this several times until the thudding in my ears fades. "Very good. Tell me what happened."

I give her a short version of what has happened so far since we moved to Florida. I tell her about Cole, Megs, Josh and Simon. She knows my entire life story so she understands the impact my new friends have on my life. She listens and stops me to ask questions. We fall silent when I'm done.

"Do you feel the urge to cut yourself now?"

My fingers slide under my pillow and wrap around the cool object there, and wait to feel *something*. "No."

"What do you feel when you are with Cole?"

"Like everything is right in the world," I answer without thinking and those words make me pause. I've been too busy riding on the rush I feel when I'm with him. What if something happens between us? Would I be able to handle it?

"You are over thinking this, Eleanor," Dr. Thorsten's gentle voice breaks through my thoughts.

"I'm way too deep in this," I whisper. "I'm so terrified of losing him. I'm scared of the kind of person I'll be, if I lose him. I don't want to be like my father. He is so obsessed. . .it's like a sickness."

"You are *not* your father. Your heart beats to a different rhythm than his. You have gone through so much. You are strong. Only you can teach your heart to be strong enough, to prepare for any inevitability."

Finally, I open my eyes and focus on the moonless night sky out the window through the parted curtains, breathing in the cool night breeze filtering through the window.

"I guess I better let you get some sleep," I sigh into the phone.

She chuckles. "Actually, I'm about to go out for a fundraiser. No sleeping for me. I'll talk to you in a couple of days, all right? Call me if you want to talk."

"Thank you, Dr. Thorsten." Peace settles inside me, the tension that holds my body captive melts away. She always had a way of making me feel lighter after each session.

After saying our goodbyes, I hang up the call and set the phone on the pillow next to my head, and scoot down the bed until I'm lying on my back, fighting the urge to text Cole.

It's almost midnight when Cole finally climbs through my window. I see his outline in the soft light from the lamp on the nightstand. He tiptoes toward me, kicks off his shoes and crawls up on the bed. I scrambled out of bed, head toward the door and lock it before returning to him. I shift and lie on my side, facing him and wait for him to talk because I'm too scared to open my mouth.

He rubs his eyes, looking exhausted, and then drops them to sign, "*Mom and Dad had a fight. I have never seen them fight like that before."*

This is all my fault. I wish I'd never caught my dad and his mom arguing. I wish I'd never confronted her. I wish the razor had gone for my father's throat, instead of his cheek.

Not every wish is granted, though.

"I'm sorry."

"You have nothing to be sorry about. It is not your fault." He assures me, running his fingers through my hair and resting them at the nape of my neck. He pulls me to him while moving his body toward me. *"I love you."* He signs with one hand before crashing his lips with mine, his breath warm on my skin. I pull away from him and sit up. If I can't comfort him, at least I have a little something I wrote for him a while back. "I have something for you."

He lets go of my neck. I leave the bed and cross the room, flip through the chaos on my desk and find what I'm looking for. I return to the bed and hand him the piece of paper. Then sit back and watch his face as he scans the paper which has words written on it. My attempt to focus on something other than the turmoil I was going through.

He licks his lips, leans forward, and scans the page.

Your eyes are my anchor.

They captivate me, quiet the restlessness in me.

Is it weird I feel so connected to you? My trust for you has no bounds. I know I can close my eyes, let myself fall and you'll be there to catch me. Even when I'm spinning out of control, confused, roiling in turmoil, I only need to feel your touch to make me breathe again. The past few days, the chaos in my head was too much, too intimidating. You were patient with me. You showed me it was possible to feel love louder than the chaos in my head, love harder to loosen the gripping fist on reality around my thoughts.

Kissed me so slowly I could still fill your lips on me when I fell asleep at night.

Kissed me harder and chased away my fears.

Every day with you is a day filled with butterflies and smiles. Every night while lying on the roof with you, is like the beginning of forever. You make me feel safe. You make me a better person. You silently entered my life, swept me off my feet and I fell truly and madly in love with you. I want nothing more than to fall back skyward with you.

Every day.

Every night.

Every second of the day.

I love you, Cole

He works his jaw and opens his mouth to speak but no words fall out. He covers his eyes with one hand but seems to decide otherwise and drops it.

"Come here," he orders. I shuffle closer on the bed. He drops the paper between us and cradles my face in his palms so gently. He kisses my lips. "I couldn't love you any quieter or harder even if I wanted to."

I bite the inside of my cheek. "Please be careful. I can't lose you. I know that my father is capable of making true on his threats and it terrifies me."

The look on his face fades, replaced by a hard look and the muscle in his jaw ticks furiously. "He won't keep me away from you. I can't wait to take you away from here."

"I can't leave my sisters and mother in his hands. You understand that, right?"

He nods. "We will work hard, get jobs then they can move in with us."

I crawl between his jean-covered legs to snuggle there. He slides his arm around my chest, and pulls me to him, kissing my hair and pressing his head on mine.

CHAPTER THIRTY

Nov

THINGS HAVE GOTTEN CONSIDERABLY BETTER THE PAST WEEKS right after that chat with Dr. Thorsten. I can look at a knife and not think of it as a potential tool to give me relief.

Today is the Winter Formal masquerade ball. It's also the day I give myself to Cole. I made up my mind a couple of days ago, and with every passing second of the day, I am more certain that I want him to be my first. Megs has been my cheerleader, preparing me mentally for what to expect.

Cole will be picking me up in less than thirty minutes. Elise has been working on making me look pretty. She finishes pining up my hair, holds the beautiful blue gown open and I slip inside.

"Cole is going to go crazy the moment he sees you, sis. He won't be able to keep his hands to himself."

My head jerks up, meeting Elise's gaze in the mirror. My cheeks heat up even more when I notice the pink around my cheeks. Gosh. My body is literally vibrating with excitement. Just thinking of the condoms in my clutch on the vanity sends a thrill down my spine.

I need to keep it together before my sister takes notice of my current state.

I smile and wink at my sister. "That's the whole point, isn't it?"

She giggles. "I love this playful side of you."

I bite my bottom lip to keep myself from grinning like an idiot and admire the dress in the mirror. Megs and I went shopping for gowns last week. I ended up choosing this one.

My gaze moves from the thin halter straps on my shoulder, down to the sweetheart bodice, embellished with little silver pearls. The chiffon material flows from the cinched waist, down to my toes. I turn around slowly to admire the back of the dress, which plunges low and stops mid back. I make a complete round then stop and stare at my reflection.

My sister leans over my shoulder and reaches for the mask from the vanity. She places it on my face, adjusting it around my eyes.

"The silver and blue blend so well with your gown." Her eyes move to the white scars—which look even whiter in this dress—and when she looks at me, the amount of love on her face humbles me. "Battle scars. You made it, sis."

I know what she means, but I can't bring myself to tell her how close I was to breaking down a few weeks ago. I can't stand seeing the disappointment replace the pride in her eyes. I nod and force a smile, pressing my hands down to smooth the invisible wrinkles.

"God, you look just like mom in that picture when she was seventeen. Remember the one on her dresser, wearing a white gown during her and Aunty Sabine's graduation party?" I miss not knowing about that part of my family.

Tears prickle my eyes. "I'll check on her in a bit," I say, untying the strap of the mask from the back of my head and placing it back on the vanity. And then pull my sister in for a hug. We step apart, and my sister wipes the tears now falling down her cheeks.

"God, look at us, crying like a bunch of babies," I say, laughing. I pluck some tissues from the box on the table and dab away the mascara trailing down my cheeks.

"No more crying. You're ruining my work," Elise scolds me with a cute, stern expression as she grabs the mascara and applies it again. "What time is Cole coming to pick you up?"

I glance at the clock on my nightstand. "Fifteen minutes. God, Elise, I'm nervous."

"Nervous?" she snorts, rolling her eyes. "You saw each other this morning. You two literally spend every second of the day staring into each other's eyes."

"No we don't. We also talk. And kiss. And talk." *And explore each other, Cole doing that thing he does with his tongue on my neck.*

She crinkles her nose and we laugh again. I pull her into my arms again, hugging her tightly, then lean back. "Thank you, Elise. For everything."

She shrugs, giving me that smile I love so much. The one that makes me believe in peace, love and unicorns. That the world is better because she is in it.

"I'll check on Mom now." I pick the skirt up in my hands and head for the door, and leave my room with Elise in tow.

We walk past Elon's room. A classical song with very heavy dark tones accosts us in the hallway, causing a shudder to slide down my spine.

"Wow, she's gone dark," Elise chuckles.

I shoot a playful scowl at her before stopping at the door and turning the knob. Elise murmurs that she's going downstairs to make sure the camera is working and skips off.

"Hey Elon," I say, entering the room.

Surprisingly, she jerks her head up, placing the book she's reading on the bed. Only Elon can listen to a song like this one while reading. She's always done this for as long as I can remember. Sometimes I think it's her way of blocking out whatever is going on around her, which includes my parents fighting.

She eyes my gown, a smile playing on her lips. "You look beautiful."

"Thanks." I reach the bed and crouch so we are at eye-level. "You okay, honey?"

She nods, but her eyebrows fold in a frown. "When will you be home?"

"As soon as I can. Elise will be here if you need anything. And you can always call me." I assure her. I raise my hand and tuck a lock of hair behind her ear. "I love you and Elise so much."

I always make sure to say that often. Assure her. My sisters hardly ever hear those words from our parents.

Those three little words seem to work the magic. The frown on her face disappears, replaced by a huge smile that seems to light up the entire room. She scrambles from the bed and wraps her little arms around me.

"I love you, Nor."

She lets go of me, climbs back on the bed and sits cross-legged. She seems so young, yet mature in some ways. I guess she learned to survive, living under the same roof as my father. I've tried to protect my sisters as much as I can, but I guess I can only do so much.

I straighten from my crouch and walk toward the door. I glance over my shoulder one more time but my little sister is already absorbed in her book, forgetting the world around her exists. Just her, the book and that song playing from her CD player.

When I enter Mom's room, the light is dimmed low. Music plays softly on the radio on top of the table next to the window, where she's sitting in a rocking chair, looking out. The curtains are parted to let in the moonlight, giving glimpses of the stars in the dark sky.

I know when I look at her I'll be met with eyes lost in their own imagination of whatever goes on inside her head.

I squat in front of her and lay my hand on her cheek. She blinks twice and then turns her head to face me, but her eyes aren't really focused on me, rather on the space above my shoulder. I know she can hear me though.

"Cole will pick me up any time now," I say, stroking her cheek with my thumb. She closes her eyes, a faint smile flirting across her lips. "What do you think of this dress?"

Her gaze moves slowly until it locks with mine. Tears fill her eyes. "You look so beautiful, honey."

"I know, right?" Remember when we used to talk about wedding gowns and prom dresses? Well, it's Winter Formal today. Elise says I look just like you. I'm so proud of that, Mom."

I stand up and twirl and right then I hear a sound, almost like a chuckle, but more pressed inside her throat. I halt, and the gown follows my movement.

"You like it? I knew you would."

The doorbell rings downstairs and her fingers twitch in her lap.

"That's Cole. I think I should go." My chest twists in pain. She is missing all this, moments a mom and her daughter should be sharing. I wish she was the one standing in the foyer, taking pictures instead of Elise.

I squat again, pressing my forehead against her hand. She turns it around to frame my cheek. I look up to see her eyes fully focused on me, tears falling down her cheeks. "I love you, Mom."

"I love you, Eleanor," her voice wobbles a bit.

The sound of feet shuffling in the hallway pulls me out of this rare moment. I quickly wipe my face and paste a smile on before turning around to face the door.

"Look who's here," Elise says in a sing song voice. "Cole fucking Holloway."

"Watch your language, Elise," Mom snaps, and my gaze momentarily moves from Cole to her, surprised by her outburst.

Elise laughs, and I turn back to face her, just in time to see her punch the air with a fist, and yell, "Success!" She shrugs and says, "I made her talk, didn't I? It's so good to hear your voice, Mom."

I shake my head, fighting a smile, grateful for her free spirit and energy because today, I need it badly.

Elise steps aside to let Cole through, and my world comes to an abrupt stop. Every snippet of air stolen from my chest at the sight of him.

God.

Cole.

His usually tousled hair is brushed back from his face but a few curls escape the perfection I'm sure he spent hours taming. He looks taller, his shoulders broader in his black tux, with a black bowtie. Seriously, I'm one lucky girl to be loved by this special guy. The enormity of it all sends my heart racing.

I clear my throat and face my mom again. "Mom. . ." I trail off, when I see her eyes have that blank look again, which tells me she's locked in her own world once more.

My body jerks with awareness as a large warm hand frames my lower back. That touch is tattooed in every cell of my body. Every part of me, even the dormant parts, wake up to that potent touch like they always do whenever Cole's skin is on mine.

I turn around and I'm automatically in his arms, my head hitting his chest. He bends and kisses my hair, his arms holding me, comforting me.

He pulls back and eyes me up and down in slow, deliberate caresses. I'm happy that he doesn't hide his appreciation and desire for me. When he meets my gaze again, his eyes say it all.

"*You look gorgeous.*" He swallows, tares his gaze from mine and faces my mother. He moves around me and drops on his knees at my mom's feet. "Mrs. Blake. Thank you for trusting me with your daughter. I'll make sure Nor is home by eleven."

Mom's lips quirk in a faint smile, but she doesn't meet his gaze.

We say goodbye to her and leave the room. After collecting my clutch—which I tuck in tighter under my arm—and mask we head downstairs, with Cole's palm on the small of my back. I slip on the silver heels at the door then pose as Elise takes pictures to her satisfaction. Ten minutes later, my sister seems content and we finally leave. Cole leads me to his car and after making sure I'm seated in the passenger seat, he rounds the car and slides onto his. Seconds later, we are driving out of his usual parking spot, Cole's fingers already linked with mine, and toward Fair Tree Hotel's ballroom with where the Winter Formal is being held.

Crap. My breathing is coming too fast. Heat pools between my legs and I have to press them tightly to squelch the craving there. We stop at a traffic light and Cole turns to look at me, frowning.

"Is everything okay?" he asks.

I nod too quickly and my head spins.

His eyes drop to my chest and he swallows hard before lifting my hand and kissing my wrist. "I love you." He murmurs on my skin and I'm a bird flying, soaring through the night sky.

"I love you too. And you look obscenely hot," I tell him when he lifts his head and stares at me with dark eyes, full of desire. Can he read my mind? Know what I'm planning for tonight? Oh God, I hope Megs didn't tell Simon and ruin my surprise.

The lights change to green, he doesn't say anything. Just focuses his gaze on the road. I exhale, relieved.

When we arrive ten minutes later, Megs and Simon are already there waiting in the hotel's parking lot. Simon looks handsome in his tux, his hair slicked back and a cocky grin on his face.

"You look great in Keds. But in these," Simon says the second his eyes drop to my feet, "You look phenomenal."

I grin up at him. "Thank you. You clean up well, Simon."

"Better than your boyfriend?" he points to Cole with his chin, who's darting looks around us, taking in the crowd of students and loosening his collar a bit.

"Nope. He looks spectacular," I say, wrapping my arm around Cole's waist and tugging him to my side. The look of uncertainty on his face fades. Warmth blooms inside my chest and my heart skips a thousand beats when he pulls me to him and holds me so tightly I can hardly breathe.

God, I love him.

After a round of hugs and kisses on the cheek, we put on our masks. Cole's is a black Phantom of the Opera, with gold gilding around one eye, and Megs' a cute red and gold butterfly mask, the colors resembling her gown, and Simon a black and white mask that covers his eyes only. Cole glances at the hotel entrance and bites his lip, taking a deep breath as if to prepare himself for something.

I touch my hand on his arm. He looks at me, and I ask, "Let me know if it's too much, all right?"

He nods and shakes his arms as though he is preparing for a fight before offering me one. I stare at him, worriedly. He straightens his shoulders and nudges me with his elbow. I hook mine around the crook of his elbow and we walk toward the hotel entrance, which is decorated with blue and white balloons.

The moment we step inside the ball room, I hold my breath, looking around. I feel like I'm in a dream. A band is playing a rock song on stage. Strobe lights blink on and off, illuminating the elegant, colorful gowns with equally colorful masks filling my vision. I tighten my hand around Cole's arm. A few people wave in our direction and I wave back. We stop on the edge of the dance floor. Simon and Megs excuse themselves and wander off. Cole and I stand awkwardly, watching the crowd in front of us gyrating to the song blaring from the speakers.

Cole drops his arm and shoves his hands in his pockets. His gaze darts around us, before looking down at me slightly uncomfortable. Or panicked.

"*Are you okay?*" I sign, turning my body to face him.

He scratches his head and then takes a deep breath before signing, "*Do you want to dance?*"

I giggle at the look on his face. He looks like he's ready to flee from this scene. "*Yes.*" I hold my hand out to him and he takes it.

Most of the students are dancing close to the stage, so we walk to a spot that's less populated with swaying bodies. We stop and turn to face each other. I slide my hands up his chest and link them around his neck, making sure my tiny clutch doesn't press into his skin and then push my body into his. Cole's arms settle on my waist, his hands pulling me to him, holding me tight.

Crap. He is really tense.

He leans down, aligning his lips to my ear and says, "I can feel the music vibrate beneath my feet. Are you ready to dance?" He lifts his head and beams down at me. I nod.

Cole's eyes never leave mine as the song ends and the band begins to play the next one. Our movements are not coordinated, but I don't care. He is here with me. He stepped out of his comfort zone for me.

Being in Cole's arms, swaying from side to side to the throbbing sounds of the fast song, is everything. I feel safe, cherished.

"Let's go get a drink," I tell him as soon as the song ends. I'm not used to wearing heels. My feet are killing me. The tension coiled around his body melts the further we move away from the dance floor and walk toward the bar. Simon is sitting on one of the stools at the corner and Megs is on his lap, laughing at something he tells her.

After grabbing a Coke in a glass for myself and Cole, we head to a deserted spot on the other side of the bar. Cole takes a swig from his glass and then starts to walk me backward without warning, his eyes blazing wickedly. I stumble back until I feel my back hit a stone column behind me. He undoes our masks, grabs the clutch and glass of Coke from my hands and sets them somewhere—I can't see anything beyond his broad shoulders. He curls his fingers around the nape of my neck, leans down and crashes his mouth on mine. My lips part automatically, welcoming him to claim my mouth like he always does. He doesn't disappoint. Pushing up on my tiptoes, I dig my fingers into his hair and tug gently, kissing him fiercely and savoring the sweet taste of Coke on his tongue. God, I love his mouth.

We pull back, panting, foreheads pressed to each other's, our eyes closed.

"Do you want to get out of here?" He asks and my eyes flip open.

Yes, I want to shout, but I end up nodding instead.

He reaches behind his back with his hand, retrieves my clutch and mask and hands them to me. And then lifts a thumb and presses it to my bottom lip. "I love your mouth."

There goes that tingly feeling in my tummy, sending heat pooling between my legs. "I want to kiss you everywhere." I blurt out without stopping to think. God, it feels good to say that.

His eyebrows shoot up and his eyes widen. Triumph soars through me as I watch desire flood his features. Finally, he grabs my hand and drags me toward the crowd but I pull back, causing him to stop.

"We have to let Megs and Simon know we are leaving," I yell above the music but then feel stupid for shouting because he can read my lips perfectly.

He huffs a breath and runs a hand through his hair, looking impatient to pick up where we left off but nods, and we head to the place we last saw them, the bar. My best friend and her boyfriend are dancing a few feet away, locked in their own little world.

After letting them know that we're leaving, Megs hugs me, and whispers, "Have fun and text me as soon as you get home."

"Definitely. Oh God. It's happening, Megs."

She grabs my shoulders. "You don't have to do this if you are not ready."

I take a deep breath. "I'm so ready. I haven't thought about anything the past few days, other than this. Honestly, I think I'll die if we don't do it tonight."

Megs belts out a laugh. "Well, then. I think you're good to go." She drops her hands just as Simon steps towards us and wraps his arm around her chest, pulling her to him.

After our goodbyes, Cole grabs my elbow and literally dashes out of the ball room. I stop at the hotel entrance, slip the heels off, and sling them around my fingers.

"My feet hurt," I tell him when he casts a questioning look at my bare feet.

Cole beams at me before leaning down and scooping me up in his arms. He strides toward the spot he parked his car, stops and kisses me before carefully standing me on the cool ground.

He looks at his watch and then back at me. "Do you want to come to my house for a little while? We still have about two hours until eleven."

I bite my lip and smile coyly at him. At least I hope I'm smiling coyly. "I have a better idea. A special place. Can I drive?"

He takes a step forward, pressing my body into the car, his hands gripping my hips. "As long as it is private. I have plans for this tight little body of yours."

I push my boobs into his chest, making sure he can read my lips. He sucks a deep breath, moves one hand up and wraps his fingers on the nape of my neck. "Call it a birthday gift, February twenty-eight is still a couple of weeks away, but I wanted to give you this gift in advance. So, can I drive?"

He nods quickly, his breath ragged and the bulge in his pants pressing into my stomach.

He wants me. I want him.

"Keys," I say, eyebrows raised. He puts them in my palm. I push his chest with my hand, causing him to take a step back. I turn around and open the car door, toss my shoes and clutch on the backseat, and then climb on the passenger seat and crawl across to the driver's seat. A pair of big strong hands grab my backside and knead with deliberate strokes. I glance over my shoulder to see Cole leaning inside the car, his eyes focused on me.

He bends down and nips my skin through the dress and I shiver. "I love your ass. Come on, hurry up."

God.

I hope we arrive at Chester's Hotel without causing an accident. My entire body is humming with the need to feel his hands on my skin. His face between my breasts, his warm breath feathering my skin there. I'm addicted to Cole, his effect on me is more than just a rush.

We arrive at Chester's, a private little comfy hotel ten minutes away from the Fair Tree. I booked it a week ago and paid the deposit by cash. I dart a glance at Cole and I swear his eyes almost pop out of his head they are so wide. I giggle and kiss his parted lips before grabbing my shoes and clutch and exiting the car. After handing the keys over to the valet, I slip on the heels and grab Cole's hand and walk toward the hotel entrance. He tightens his fingers around mine as he finally gets the gist of what's about to happen. Once we reach the reception, a young man hands me a key after confirming my details. I smile at Cole and tug him toward the elevators.

CHAPTER THIRTY-ONE

Nor

"Are you going to stand there the whole night?" I ask, smirking at Cole. He's standing a few feet away from the bed, his hands balled into fists in his pockets. I hope he can't see how nervous I am.

Doesn't he want this? Did I read his signals wrong? I felt his need for me when he pressed his pelvis to mine.

He stares at me for several seconds. The longer his eyes are on me, the more the hunger in his eyes deepens. I take a deep breath to ease the butterflies in my stomach. My skin is tight and too hot and tingling, desperate for Cole's touch. He nods, and licks his lips. He pulls his hands from his pockets and drags his fingers through his hair.

"God. Nor. I love you so much. Sometimes I don't know where I end and you begin. If we have sex, there is no going back. I'm never letting you go. I've wanted this so bad and I thought I'd wait until you were ready. I'm not sure I'll be able to control myself. I want this to be special for you. For me."

"I'm not planning on going back. I don't want you to ever let go. I love you, Cole. I want this with you. No one else, but you."

He starts to pace again, his eyes roaming everywhere as though

he's searching for something. When he doesn't find what he is looking for, his fingers go around his bowtie and attempt to loosen it. His
hands are trembling badly. So, I walk toward him and stop. I cover
his hand with mine and look into his eyes. His love and desire for me
shines so hot and bright I'm still wondering why I'm standing upright
when I should be ashes at his feet.

"I've wanted this for a long time, Cole. I've wanted this with no
one else, but you. It has always been you. Always you."

His lips part and his breath comes out faster. Cole cups my cheek
with one hand and wraps the fingers of his other hand around the
nape of my neck, brushing a thumb against the skin there. I moan
softly, breathe faster, and I'm five seconds from shattering. He groans,
his eyes bright with excitement. "We need condoms."

"In my bag." Megs and I went shopping a week ago and grabbed
different sizes. I ended up taking two from each pack and tucking
them inside my tiny clutch.

As soon as those words leave my mouth, his lips are on mine,
parting them wider as he plunges his tongue inside my mouth, claiming me in desperate passionate strokes. His hand leaves my cheek and
moves down to grab my hip, bunching my dress in his fist.

Suddenly he grins and I have to grab his forearms to stop myself
from toppling over.

"I'm going to show you more, Nor. I'm going to make you mine.
Just mine. Always and forever."

"Always and forever," I repeat the promise. I know we are young
right now, but with Cole, I feel everything. It can only get better from
here.

Finally, the black bowtie comes undone. Cole takes it from my
hands and bunches it up in his, then places his hands on my shoulders
and slowly spins me around. He plucks out the pins holding my hair
up and tosses them on the night stand then sweeps my hair over my
shoulder to one side. I feel his breath feathering my neck just before
his lips land there, placing soft kisses and tracing a path to the sensitive place behind my ear with his tongue. He nips my earlobe then

slips it into his mouth.

Oh my God.

Heat pools between my legs. In just a few minutes Cole and I will be joined like I've desired for such a long time. He moves that wicked mouth from my ear, leaving a trail of kisses that stop at the top of my back. I feel his fingers fumble with the zipper and slide it down and the soft whoosh is increased ten-fold by my sensitive hearing. Every sound, every touch is increased in magnitude.

I look over my shoulder to find his eyes focused on my backside. His breathing is no longer ragged. It's mega fast. He lifts his face and when he finds me looking at him, he winks at me and signs, *"Great ass."*

I laugh, my cheeks heating up. I reach down and stroke him through his pants. His eyes squeeze shut as if in pain but when he opens them, they are dark and hungry.

I move away and head for the dresser. After removing the condoms, I walk back to the bed. My knees shake and my stomach is a hundred definitions of fluttering. Cole is standing in his boxers, palming his erection through the material with no sign of reservations on his face.

Wow, talk about being ready. Is this the same guy who was reluctant just minutes ago?

I grin and toss two condoms on the night stand and walk toward him with the third one, then stand back and watch with fascination as his boxers drop to the floor and he rolls it on his rigid erection.

He closes the gap between us and grips my waist, pulling me to him unexpectedly and rather forcefully. I gasp and he grins before crushing his mouth on mine. He grinds himself on me, his erection pressed on my stomach. I'm not sure my feet will be able to hold me up much longer. This kiss is the mother of all kisses. He's kissing me as if he's marking me, feeding me life.

With his arm still around me, he walks us backwards until I feel the back of my knees hit the bed. I fall back and his body covers mine. Cole is not as gentle as he always is, and I don't want gentle. We've survived on gentle since we met. I want the wild Cole. The one I suspect hides behind that sculpted body and those gray eyes. I want everything he's willing to give me.

He places his hands on my knees and opens them a little wider. He moves between my legs and groans when his erection settles at my entrance.

Excitement pours through me.

He pulls back, lifts himself off me for a second and returns with the bowtie.

I raise my brow. "Are on planning on tying me up?"

He laughs and shakes his head. He motions for my right hand. Puzzled, I stretch it toward him and wait. He takes my ring finger and starts to wrap the material around it. When he's done, he leans back and meets my gaze.

"Always and forever. This is my promise to you."

Tears spring in my eyes and I'm at a loss of words. This is some sort of binding ring, or engagement ring or whatever. How thoughtful of my Cole

"Always and forever, this is my promise to you."

His face breaks into a huge smile. "You are officially mine."

I laugh out loud as his body covers mine once again. He nudges my legs wider with his thigh and I let them fall open to accommodate his hips. His fingers slide between us and he positions himself at my entrance.

"I don't want to hurt you."

"It will only hurt for a few moments." At least I hope it won't hurt for long.

He looks hesitant. I slide my hand down and wrap it around his fingers, pushing deeper. His eyes widen as the tip of his erection enters me. He pulls his hand away and wraps his arm around my shoulders, keeping his eyes on me as he thrusts slowly, pulls out and in again. He stops, his breathing coming out in pants.

I nod to let him know I'm okay. He starts to push again and this time I feel the beginning of pain and every muscle in my body locks, fighting the invasion. I breathe in and out through my mouth.

"Shit," he curses, lifting his body and starting to pull back but I tighten my hands on him and shake my head.

"I'm okay, I promise."

He glares at me. "You are not okay."

"Okay, I'm not. But I don't want you to stop. Please."

His expression softens. "You don't have to beg me, Nor. I'll always do what you ask me."

Melt.

God, I want this.

He takes a deep breath, clenches his jaw and this time he thrusts hard and I cry out. He drops his head to the crook of my neck, his breathing heavy and hot on my skin. I shut my eyes tightly, breathing in and out as my body learns the shape of his. I lift my hips slightly off the bed to create more friction.

"Don't move." His voice is muffled on my neck. His lips kiss my neck softly, my jaw, my cheek. He pulls back, his gaze roaming all over my face. "God. Nor. I'm inside you. You feel amazing."

Oh. My. God. WOW.

I take deep breaths and let my body adjust to him. He lifts his head a few moments later, and brushes my hair away from my forehead.

He leans back and stares at me softly, but I can see the storm brewing behind those eyes.

"I am about to make love to you, Snowflake. I don't want to hurt you. You feel so damn good wrapped around my dick like that. I might not be able to control myself once I start moving. I really want to make this special for you too."

"You are making it special," I tell him, brushing a finger on his brow to smooth the worry lines forming there.

He starts to move his hips and it takes a few seconds for my body to find the rhythm of his. Then my back is bowing, my body wanting more, eagerly. I close my eyes and feel my body tighten as it reaches a point of no return, seeking sweet release.

I open my eyes and nearly orgasm when I meet Cole's dark, intense gaze fixed on me. He grabs my legs and hikes them around his hips. I wrap them on his waist, holding him tight to me and I feel him sink deeper inside me. He lowers his body flush to mine and slides his arms around my shoulder. He increases the pace and his thrusts. Every time he plunges inside me, I suck a breath and release when he pulls out. His movements become more uncoordinated and desperate. My hands move up his back and circle his neck. I shut my eyes and smile, holding on for dear life.

Stars burst behind my eyes and I shatter, the world around me exploding into different colors behind my eyes. I scream Cole's name just as he calls mine, which comes out in a primal shout. We continue holding each other, our skin wet from the sweat, our ragged breathing and soft groans filling the room.

I open my eyes to look up at him and what I see before me steals whatever air is left in my lungs: Cole's head is thrown back, his body arched and veins popping on his neck. His body shakes with his release.

"Are you okay?" he asks.

I grin, using my hand to smooth the frown on his forehead. "I'm a million times better."

His shoulders droop in relief just before he nods, and kisses me softly. So softly I might have imagined it if I wasn't paying attention, then he pulls back to look at me. "Thank you for this gift. Everything about today is perfect. I love you so much."

"I love you too." I smile, my bones feel tired in a good way. My body is warm. Other than the slight ache between my legs, I feel wonderful.

He rolls over, removes the condom and heads for the bathroom. He returns with a cloth in his hands and crawls between my legs. My body tenses as soon as he starts to clean me but relaxes when his gaze meets mine with a troubled look on his face. "You must be sore."

I nod. "I am. It was worth it."

He heads back to the bathroom and returns minutes later with the same wash cloth. He cleans my tender skin and I just lie there enjoying the warmth and the way he is taking care of me. My eyes start closing. I feel him leave the bed. The sound of a toilet flushing in the distance. The bed sinking beneath me and then hands gently turning me to my side. His body drapes on my back, then he pulls me flush to his chest and wraps his arms around me.

I wake up to the feel of heat on my breast. I peel my eyes open to find Cole sucking my nipple while languidly rolling the other between his fingers. I sigh, move my hands down and sink them into his hair. His head comes up and his mouth drops from my breast in favor of my lips.

"I wish we could stay here forever," I say when we come up for air.

He flashes me a sexy smile. "Me too." He glances at the clock on the bedside table. "It's almost midnight. I promised your mom I would get you home by eleven. Come on, lazy bones."

CHAPTER THIRTY-TWO

Nor

Cole pulls up in front of my house at almost one in the morning. He turns off the engine, climbs out of the car and opens the door for me. The porch light comes on as soon as we hit the first step. He walks me to the door the proceeds to kiss me until my lips feel raw, loved, used by him.

"*See you tomorrow?*"

I nod, grinning blissfully. "*Tomorrow.*"

He starts to walk down the porch steps, but abruptly turns back. He grabs me around the waist and kisses me, dipping me backwards until I feel drunk with everything good in this world.

He swings me back up, steps back and tucks his hands inside his pocket.

"I couldn't have asked for a better Formal. Thank you for giving me that."

My chest hurts just thinking he'd never gotten a chance to enjoy his own prom because he couldn't find a girl who would go with him. At the same time I'm glad I was the one who gave it to him. His first. My first.

"*Thank you for giving me my everything,*" I tell him.

As soon as I step inside the house, I'm so high on my perfect night that I fail to notice the hunched form on the couch. I jump and shriek when the lamp is suddenly turned on, momentarily blinding me. I blink several times to adjust my eyes to the lighting.

I clutch a hand over my chest and stumble back. "Dad!" Of all the nights for him to come home, today had to be one of them?

He unfolds himself from the chair then staggers upright. Or sideways. He's still wearing his uniform, which makes me wonder when he came home and how long he has been lying in wait for me to come home.

"Did you have fun?" he asks, taking a step forward his hands on his hips.

I swallow hard and lick my lips. "It was okay."

"Hmm. What time did you tell your mother you'd be home."

My heart is beating so hard I can hear the thumping in my ears. Gosh, what time did Cole say he'd bring me home?

"E—eleven," I stammer.

He exhales through his mouth. "WHAT TIME IS IT NOW?!" He shouts so suddenly, I shriek and back away from him so quickly that I drop my purse in the process. "ANSWER ME!"

I dart a look at the clock although I already know the time. "One in the morning."

I hear a whimper coming from the stairs and glance over quickly. Elon and Elise are peeking through the bars on the stairs.

Crap. They shouldn't be seeing this.

"I'm sorry I wasn't here on time," I whisper, eager to appease him so he can let this go.

"You promised your mother you'd be here on time. She was worried."

As if he cares about my mother. This is all about him, throwing his weight around.

"I'm sorry," I whisper again, keeping my head low so that he doesn't think I'm confronting him.

"Were you with him?" He slurs the words, moving closer. "ANSWER THE FUCKING QUESTION!"

I nod, tears instantly forming. Elon or Elise, I don't know which one of the two, wails.

"Daddy please. You're scaring us."

He whirls around, his drunk gaze searching the source of that voice. He lifts a hand and points up. "Upstairs. NOW!"

"What's going on here? Stephen?" My mom appears from the top of the stairs. When my father doesn't answer, she climbs down the stairs. She sees me huddled on the wall, then glances at her husband. "What is the meaning of this, Stephen?"

My dad narrows his eyes on her and jabs his index finger at her. "Your whore of a daughter came in a few minutes ago. Did you know she has been sleeping with that. . .abomination?"

My heart ceases to beat. Everything in me locks in place. I take a step forward. "He is not an abomination, Father." I grit my teeth. "You are so judgmental you can't see anything beyond your prejudices. You hate everything that reminds you of your brother. You make me sick. Sick to my stomach." My body is on fire, my hands curled into fists at my side.

My words seem to enrage him even further. His face is turning an alarming shade of red.

"My brother. So you think you know me, huh? MY BROTHER WAS A DISGRACE. MY FATHER SHOULD HAVE KILLED HIM THE DAY HE WAS BORN!"

I gasp, falling back two steps.

Someone bangs three times on the door so loudly that I jump almost ten feet high. "Eleanor? Is everything okay in there?"

Maggie.

My dad swivels around so fast, his wide eyes on the door. I scoot to the side and twist the door handle. Cole barrels in with Maggie in tow.

He's at my side in a matter of seconds. "*Are you okay? Mom told me she heard some noises coming from here.*"

I nod at the same time Dad lumbers toward me, grabs Cole by the neck of his shirt and swings a punch. Cole doesn't have enough time to block the blow. It connects with Cole's jaw, causing him to stagger. One minute Cole is stunned by the punch and the next he's on his feet, his arm raised and fists raining down on my father. I'm so shocked that at first I just stare at the scene unfolding in front of me. My dad delivers a punch, but misses, which gives Cole an opening. He lands punch after punch, fury written all over his face. I catch a glimpse of my father, eyes wide and terrified as he looks around, cornered by my boyfriend's big body.

Maggie hurries forward to stop her son and I leap in action hot on her trail. Then everything happens at once. Josh sprints through the open door, launches himself on his brother and tries to get him off my dad. Police sirens fill the air and then they are there, holding off Cole and my father. Cole struggles against their hands, fighting to break free, his furious eyes centered on my dad. Another police officer joins the first one and grip Cole's arm, pulling him back. One of them slaps handcuffs around Cole's wrists, while reading him his rights. The words 'anything you say may be used against you' slam into me, jolting me and reminding me that this is not a dream. They drag him out of the house and inside one of their cars with flickering blue lights on top. I run after the police officers, wanting to explain what happened. But one of them shakes me off as if I'm a fly.

Dad is leaning against the wall on the porch, staring down at Maggie coldly.

"I warned you, Maggie," he says in a low voice that doesn't carry too far. "He stood between you and me. He is the reason you refused to come back to me. He had to go."

"God, Stephen. He's my baby. You started it. You hit him first. You can't do this to me." Tears are running down her face as she pleads with my father.

He sneers and speaks loudly, for the benefit of the police, I think. "He came to my house and he hit me first. Hell, I couldn't defend myself. I told you that son of yours would get in trouble one day. He has a temper. You should have dealt with him before it came to this."

What feels like a hundred pairs of eyes cast glances between my father and the car. But Cole is staring ahead, his jaw set in a defiant line.

"Hey Steve. We need you to come down to the station to record your statement about what happened here," a policeman with a protruding belly says to my dad.

My father nods and winces when he lifts his arm. "I will as soon as they check on me." He sounds friendly, easy going and I realize I don't know who this man is. Does anyone even know him?

"Are you okay, Sir?" A deep voice says. I follow the voice and see a paramedic jogging toward us, carrying a first aid kit.

Everything is happening so fast and I'm dizzy. My sight is blurry. I want to look away, but I can't. I'm nauseous and sweating and shaking.

Two more paramedics join the first one at my father's side with a stretcher as if he's dying. What the hell did he tell them? That is my passing thought. They load him on it and strap him down and then hurry toward the ambulance. The stretcher disappears inside the vehicle, but not before I catch a glimpse of my dad's face. The triumphant look on his bloody face as he cranes his neck to look out.

He did it. He has probably been waiting for an opportunity to seek revenge. Cole and I played right into his vengeful hands. He might not have orchestrated everything, but he won.

The cars start to pull off, the sirens piercing the dark night. I chase after them, trying to catch Cole's eyes. His jaw already has a huge red spot forming.

He doesn't lift his head to look at me.

He just continues to stare ahead, his chest heaving, his wrists shackled behind his back.

I finally give up, stop and stare as the lights of the car flicker, disappearing around the bend at the end of the street.

I turn and stumble back, tears streaming down my face. Maggie is weeping quietly, as she shifts her gaze to me, her face filled with so much regret and hate.

"I told you, Eleanor. You should have let him go." She stumbles a little as she turns and walks down the path. I watch her as she opens the door to her house, and disappears from sight.

Josh looks at me for a long time. His face filled with so much sadness, I'm not sure I'll ever recover from that look or the words his mother tossed at me. He follows his mother without looking back.

Glancing around, I realize most lights in the neighborhood are on, everyone surely awoken by the disturbance from our house.

I shuffle up the stairs, ignoring the sympathetic look on my mother's face, the twin expressions of pure horror on my sisters' faces.

I leave it all behind and enter my room. I don't cry. I don't cry until my head hits the pillow, and then it's just me and my sorrow.

Hours later, sleep still eludes me. My chest feels as if someone dug a hole, yanked my heart from my chest, and left it dangling. It's beating, yes. But the pain that tears through me rips every bit of strength away from me, leaving me numb. I just want to sleep and forget today ever happened. I want to stop feeling. . .dead.

I sit up from the bed and stare at the moonless sky out the window. Thunder rolls in the distance, but the crippling fear that always follows that sound doesn't set in. I stand up and shuffle robotically around the room and then sit back down.

I can't do this. I need some sort of relief. My hand moves under my pillow, grabs the penknife and flips it open. I pull my dress up and hover the sharp point of the knife on my thigh. I close my eyes and I see Cole's beautiful eyes bright with anger, his mother's look of contempt and blame toward me, my dad's triumphant expression. I press the tip into my skin and move my hand down. My heart beats faster, blood pumps loudly in my ears as the pain cuts through the numbness. I suck in a breath and open my eyes to look at my leg. Blood trickles down my thigh, soaking into my gown. I lift my hand off my thigh and fold the blade back. I tuck it under my pillow, pull my dress down and then lay back on the bed.

Finally, my body relaxes and sleep claims me, the sweet pain from the cut a lullaby to my shredded soul.

CHAPTER THIRTY-THREE

Cole

ACCORDING TO MY PARENTS, MR. RICHARD BARNETT, IS ONE OF THE best defense attorneys in Florida. I know the fees are high and that thought makes me feel even more miserable. They are very close to finishing paying the mortgage for our house, but this extra expense will prolong the process.

I've been in and out of this office for a week now. Stephen and my attorneys met and agreed to settle this case outside of court after advising us that if we went to court, it might take a long time until the date of trial. Plus it would end up costing us less if this was settled between the lawyers, avoiding court fees. I agreed wholeheartedly. I had already spent a week in jail and it was fucking hard. I couldn't imagine waiting for months to get my case in court, while spending more time inside that hellhole. This is the second time my attorney is meeting with Stephen's.

Stephen is sitting across the table from me, wearing a smirk and a victorious look on his face. My jaw tightens and I continue staring at him like I've been doing since we entered the room thirty minutes ago. I want to tell him how much I hate him, but I let my glare say it for me.

I pull my gaze away from the asshole and focus on the interpreter my parents hired for this case, just in time to see him sign, "*Your client was not on duty and according to the witness, he attacked the defendant first.*"

Loosening the tie around my neck, I close my eyes and wish this process would go faster. I don't regret what I did. I only wish I would have done more damage than breaking his arm and nose. Testimonies from various witnesses on both sides have already been presented. I'm not even sure how Stephen knew about those two dickheads from the swimming pool incident, but he did and they testified, but according to my lawyer, having the lifeguard and Nor's testimony helped a lot.

A touch on my shoulder prompts me to open my eyes and glance at Mr. Barnett. "Are you okay, Mr. Holloway? We could take a break if you want."

I shake my head. I don't need a fucking break, because it will only prolong this entire process. He nods once and settles back to continue the argument. I keep zoning out, letting my mind wander. At the end of the day, I'm certain of where I'm going. Stephen won't let me walk away, given the malicious glint in his eyes.

"*Three years and five thousand dollars in fines for assault and battery on a law enforcement officer. Don't forget he caused damage.*"

"*One year. Your client started the fight.*" Mr. Barnett replies. "*He wasn't on duty.*"

"*Two years and the fines. That's our last offer.*" Opposing counsel contends.

Looks are exchanged.

"*Can I talk to my client?*" Mr. Barnett asks.

Stephen's lawyer nods. My cold gaze flickers to Nor's dad, taking in that bitter look on his face. It hits me that he probably wanted a longer, harsher sentence.

I plant my fists on the polished table and lean forward. "You've taken me from her, but it's only for a while. You won't be able to stop us when this is over." I straighten and follow my lawyer out of the conference room, my interpreter in tow.

"Two years and five thousand dollars in fines," he says.

I don't bother to look at the interpreter for translation.

"Do I have a choice?" I ask him. I lift my hand and jab a finger toward the conference room. "That motherfucker should be the one going to jail for everything he has put his family through. Jesus, where is the justice? I wasn't the one who started the fight."

"I know," he says. "The evidence against you is indisputable. You barged into the privacy of his home and also caused physical injury. If there is anything untoward going on in that house, his daughter should press charges." He rubs his forehead in frustration. "Shit. I hate cops. Look, this is the best offer we have on the table right now."

I tug my hair back, pain smarting in my temples and a headache looking at the back of my head.

Fuck. More expenses.

I'll ask my parents to remove the five thousand from my college fund. I'll figure out how to compensate the loss later. I clench my fists tight, letting the pain wash through me. I'm exhausted. I don't have any more energy to keep on fighting. "All right. Let's take it."

We return to the room and Mr. Barnett announces our decision. Nor's dad scowls up at both lawyers and then at me. He stands up and storms out of the room. Two officers enter the room to escort me out of the room and out of the building. I lift my face toward the midday sunlight and cool breeze, soaking it in, because I have no idea when I will enjoy this again. In just a couple of weeks, I'll be turning nineteen in prison. This wasn't in my ten-year-plan and it fucking makes me sick.

Lowering my head, I feel the hate and anger for Stephen burn through my veins. Not only has he succeeded in thwarting my relationship with his daughter, he managed to destroy my life in the process.

I settle inside the police car and drop my gaze to my lap, blinking hard to force the tears back.

I swear he will pay for this, one way or another, but he will never break us.

I believe in us. I just hope that Nor does too. It's the only thing that will make it bearable.

CHAPTER THIRTY-FOUR

Nor

Two months have passed since Cole was led out of my house in handcuffs. Two months of me drowning in guilt. He couldn't hold up to my father. He had enough ammunition to put Cole behind bars.

Why didn't I listen to Maggie? Maybe if I'd broken up with him like she'd asked me to, he wouldn't have ended up in this predicament. The thought of my life without Cole is like a slash through my heart. There is no way I could have done it. Cole is the other part of me. The part that breathes air into me, the part that calms the demons that roam my mind.

Things are much clearer now. Even though the stars aren't aligned for us yet and fate seems to be working against us, I'm not going to give up. The tide will change soon. Cole and I will be together and nothing will ever stand in our way again.

Today is the day I get to see him after sixty days of missing him. His mother promised to take me with her. Things have been tense between us so she was hesitant when I first asked her if she could take me with her to visit Cole. Eventually Cole wrote me a letter and told me that he had put my name on the visitors list.

Taking a deep breath, I open the little kit on my lap and pull out the antiseptic cream. I apply it on the deep scratches on my thighs.

Today has been particularly bad and I couldn't stop scratching my skin. I'm nervous and excited to see Cole in equal measures. Does he blame me for what happened?

I've been trying so hard not to cut again since the night Cole was arrested. I even spoke to my therapist a few times. It seemed to help but sometimes I'd feel so helpless. Sometimes I'm terrified of my own thoughts, the little voice that urges me to find relief in a razor. I threw away the last one five days ago, but I can't seem to stop itching. Looking for relief. Every day is a battle and sometimes I feel like I'm losing it. Losing my grip on reality. I need to find my balance again. I should be stronger than this.

I close the kit and walk to the dresser, burying it where it has been living for the past two months—under the mound of socks, and then head to my vanity and finishing applying the lipstick. I stare at my reflection in the mirror, despising the eyes looking back at me. I hate how weak I've become. I keep promising myself that I'll get rid of the kit tomorrow. But the tomorrows come and go. I close my eyes and pray under my breath, because that is all I'm left with right now. I need strength.

"Cole's mom is waiting for you outside," Elon says quietly. I didn't even hear her walk into my room.

I turn to face her and force a cheerful smile.

"You look beautiful," my sister says, shuffling her feet toward me with a brown paper bag in her hands. She leans forward and reaches for something on the table behind me. When she straightens up, she's holding a yellow flower in her hand. This is the one we bought months ago, when my sisters, Megs and I dragged Cole and Simon shopping. It feels like years ago, though.

Elon pins it carefully on my upheld hair then stands back to survey me.

"Perfect." She digs a hand inside the paper bag and pulls out something wrapped in red gift paper. "Could you please give this to him? It's just a pair of wool socks I made for him. Just tell him they will keep him warm." She places the small package in my outstretched palm. I'm completely overwhelmed because Elon, this girl who keeps everything locked up in her chest, is opening up. She is gifting Cole something she made with her own hands. This is a huge step for her. I knew she liked Cole, but up to this point, I never realized how much. Closing the distance between us, I pull her into a hug, blinking back the tears threatening to fall. I lean back after that to thank her, only to realize she's wiping her eyes too.

"He is not allowed to keep them." I know this, Maggie told me the inmates weren't allowed to have personal stuff.

Disappointment flashes across her face. Nevertheless, she lifts her chin. "Cole is a good guy. He was just caught in a bad moment," she says. She is so wise for her age. We hardly ever talk about my dad, especially after that night when everything went to hell.

I nod and smile through the tears. "I'll be sure to let him know. Oh gosh, look at us. We should be happy and smiling, right? It's the first time I'm going to see him after weeks of worry."

I link my fingers with hers as we walk out of my room and downstairs. Maggie is chatting with Elise and Josh next to her car. She turns at the sound of our voices.

Josh can't come with us today because he has a doctor's appointment for a blood check. The last time he and I chatted, he told me that his parents were going through a bad time in their marriage after Cole's arrest. His father moved out and is now staying at a hotel in town.

I squirm on the passenger seat and glance out the window. The tension is so thick it's hard to breathe. I have no idea how to diffuse it. I turn to look at her, noticing the dark circles under her eyes.

"Maggie. . .I can't begin to tell you how sorry I am for everything. I—"

Her lips form a thin line and she looks away from me, but not before I see the anger fill her features. "It's already done now. Let's focus on today, all right?"

I nod and turn to watch the trees pass by outside of my window.

CHAPTER THIRTY-FIVE

Nor

Seeing Cole limping inside the visiting room is like a slap across my face. His usual wild hair is gone, replaced by a buzz cut. Despite his attempt to cover the pain, I can see him favoring the right side of his body.

He lifts his head and scans the room filled with inmates and their families. His search ends when his eyes land on us. I gasp and his gaze flickers to mine, then holds it. His mouth starts to widen in a smile and I feel all this fluttering in my stomach at the sight of his handsome face. His eyes. . .Jesus. They look more deep set than before, darker than before and even a touch cold as if he has seen a lot of things not worthy of mentioning in the past two months. And now those eyes are leveled on me with such intensity I'm wondering how I'm even sitting on the chair.

I wait until he reaches the spot where his mom and I are sitting before I stand up and give him a quick hug and a kiss on the cheek. I quickly pull back, afraid of doing anything that might be considered inappropriate according to the prison rules. After Maggie embraces him too, we settle on the chairs, the table separating us. I fold my hands on my lap to keep from reaching out and linking our fingers. I can't believe we are sitting in the same room. He is so close, yet so far.

There is so much I want to tell him, but I can't. Not in front of his mom.

Cole grimaces as he subtly adjusts his weight to lean more on the left side of his body.

"What's wrong?" Maggie and I ask at the same time.

He shakes his head a little too fast and signs, *"Nothing."*

No, no, no. This cannot be happening. "Are you hurt, Cole?" I ask, my voice unsteady.

His face turns angry. "Don't do this, okay?"

"Did something happen? You are hurt, aren't you?"

"Cole—" Maggie starts but Cole stops her with a glare.

"Let this be," he insists.

He glares at me for a few moments. "*I thought you guys came here to visit and not for doctoral duties.*" he signs scowling.

I keep my unyielding gaze on him.

"Who did this to you?" Maggie asks.

He shrugs. "Just some guys who thought they'd introduce me to the system of how things work around here. How's everyone doing?" he asks.

Maggie goes ahead to give him updates of what is happening, but my thoughts are spinning in circles. My eyes can't get enough of him. She pauses and darts a glance my way, but ends up telling him about his dad moving away from home.

It's painful watching Cole's face fill with sadness.

His mom excuses herself to go to the bathrooms.

I swallow around the lump in my throat, unfold my hands from my lap and place them flat on the table.

"What happened, Cole?" I ask, as a tear rolls down my cheek.

He rubs his forehead, and when he meets my gaze again, his eyes look tired, tortured. He moves his hand inch by inch in my direction. I meet him halfway, glancing around to make sure we are not being watched. He quickly brushes the tip on his index finger on my pinkie finger twice before pulling back.

"It's nothing. I promise." He bites his bottom lip, studying me.

"You have lost a lot of weight, Snowflake. This is not your fault. I knew what I was doing when I raised my fist to punch him. I would do it all over again, if it meant keeping you safe, Nor. I did this and not you."

I shake my head. "I should have known he would never stop until he destroyed us. You. Sometimes I wonder if I have that trait in me. I don't ever want to hurt you, Cole. I would rather lose you than turn out to be like him. His obsession is a sickness."

He leans forward, his eyes flashing with anger. "Don't talk like that, Eleanor Blake. You are nothing like your father. You will never lose me. Your father is a sick bastard. You are not him, do you hear me?" He lifts his hands and signs, "*I love you so much.*"

"*And I love you so much.*"

"Miss Eleanor?" A deep voice says, pulling me away from Cole and his wound.

Startled, I look over my shoulder to find Mr. Taylor, walking toward us. He smiles wide, stretching his hand in greeting. "I thought it was you."

I climb to my feet, surprised to see him here. I extend my hand to him and smile. "Mr. Taylor. How have you been? How's your mom doing?"

He shakes my hand, then steps back, his gaze switching over to Cole and I swear his gaze softens slightly.

"My mother's not doing so bad. Did you stop working at the center?"

I nod. "School has taken up most of my time. But I'll come back in summer." I pause, looking around the room. "Are you here for a visit?"

He shakes his head. "I work here. I'm the warden of this facility." He looks at Cole and offers his hand in a handshake.

"You remember Cole. You two met when we dropped by at Grandma's house a few months ago."

"I remember him. Your grandmother speaks very highly of him." He turns to Cole. "I heard about what happened. The people in here are messed up sons of bitches. Lie low and keep your head down, son."

He purses his lips, opens his mouth to say something but stops and directs his gaze at me.

"It was great to see you, Miss Eleanor." He shakes our hands before leaving.

Maggie returns and we continue chatting. I can't shake off the fear swimming in my belly.

Our visiting time comes to a close and we say goodbye.

I turn around to leave, my heart heavy and feeling sick to my stomach. Cole calls my name. I stop and turn around to face him.

"I need you to do me a favor, Nor," he says, his gaze intense to the point of feverish.

"Anything."

"Don't come back. Please."

I feel as if someone ripped my heart through my chest. "What?"

He braces a hand on the table as if he's about to collapse and tears brim in his eyes. "I don't want you to come back."

Sweat beads my forehead and I'm getting a little lightheaded. "Cole, don't ask me to do that. God, please don't do this," I beg him as tears start to burn my eyes. I blink back furiously. "No. You don't get to tell me not to visit you." I declare stubbornly.

He's wearing this tortured look on his face now, as if whatever he's about to say will cost him his life and his hands are balled into fists at his sides. Veins pop up along his arm. "Nor. I'll request your name to be removed from the visitor's list."

"Cole! You can't do that to her," Maggie says, desperation in her voice. "Think about it, sweetheart. You don't really want to do that."

"Cole, please. Don't do this." I plead again. When he continues to stare at me, I finally let the tears fall, which is his undoing.

He wipes his face with his hands. "I don't want you to see me like this. This is killing me. If you love me, stay away. Write to me. Wait for me. Don't give up on me."

He turns and walks away before me or his mom can say another word.

Once we step out of the room and we collect our belongings,

Maggie puts her arm around my shoulder and we walk to her car.

When we arrive home, my father is standing on the lawn, his hands on his hips. He usually doesn't spend his weekends around the house. He finds any excuse to stay away from home. The rumor flying around the neighborhood is that he was seen with a woman in town. It's no surprise, though. The thought of my father having an affair has crossed my mind in the past. I don't even care. He can do whatever the hell he wants.

Maggie doesn't even justify his presence with a greeting or a look. She mumbles a goodbye to me, and strides toward the door of her house.

I don't bother greeting my father either. As far as I'm concerned, he doesn't exist, even though he makes sure I know he does by his mere presence.

"I hear you went to visit him." His voice is casual, but it doesn't hide the underlying threat.

I stop and finally face him, feeling hate pour through my pores. "You put him there. But you will never take away what he and I have," I say calmly, which surprises me given the hate I have for this man.

I walk away, feeling defeated instead of victorious for standing up to him. I still can't believe that Cole banned me from going to see him.

I feel my dad's foot falls thudding behind me so I hasten mine, eager to get away from him as fast as I can.

"Is that what you think, huh? That I can't take him away from you?" His voice is still calm, cold. Taunting.

I whip around to face him, preparing my words for my last blow, then freeze as I watch him looking at me with narrowed calculating eyes.

"I put him where he is. I have the power to end his existence."

Blood roars in my ears. Oh God, please don't let him do this to Cole.

"Didn't he tell you what happened? Or was he too much of a coward to admit that I am winning?"

What the hell is he talking about?

"Be careful, daughter. That boy's life is in my hands right now. I say he jumps, and he fucking does."

Blood drains from my face and pieces of what might have happened to Cole start to click in my head. "Oh, God. What did you do? Did you hurt him?"

He suddenly grins wide, triumph filling his features. "Atta girl. You're getting it now."

"Cole has never done anything to hurt you. Is it because he reminds you of your brother? Or did your father brainwash you, so you can't see anything beyond hate?"

His gaze flickers to the Holloway house, softening a little and lingers for a few seconds. When he swings back to face me, his face is calculating. Hard.

He swivels around and stalks out the front door. I rush upstairs, the impact of his words swirling in my gut.

I can't get enough air into my lungs. My thoughts run wild inside my head. Surely, he will have Cole killed in the name of revenge. He must have paid someone to hurt Cole. Maybe Mr. Taylor could really help him. Protect him.

But how? What happens when those officers don't do their job? Maybe they are the same people who beat up my boyfriend.

When I get to the bathroom, I drop in front of the toilet and finally vomit, tears running down my cheeks.

For the first time in a long time, I feel truly hopeless and helpless.

CHAPTER THIRTY-SIX

Cole

"You're a jerk, Cole. A big one. I can't believe you had Nor's name taken off the visitor list." Megs glares at me.

"That's tough shit, man. Do you have any idea what the girl is going through?" Simon speaks the words for Megs' benefit. He shakes his head.

I clench my jaw. Flex my hands to loosen the pain lodged in there as a result of a fight that happened three days ago between me and The Behemoth. A tall Hispanic guy with three missing front teeth and a Bronx accent. The last words he spat out before landing a blow in my gut were, "A gift from Stephen."

I rub the right side of my jaw and flinch as my fingers move over the huge bump there. "Do you think I enjoyed telling her not to come back? You think I enjoyed watching her stricken face when she saw me limping toward her? As much as I hate her father, I couldn't bring myself to tell her that he was the one who was paying people to take care of The Freak. She already blames herself for what happened. I'm locked in here like a caged animal. I can't bear to see the look of pity on her face."

Megs throws her hands up in frustration. "Pity? That girl has never looked at you with anything less than adoration."

Simon stares at me as if I've lost my mind. Maybe I have. "Aren't you worried she'll ditch your ass for treating her like that? Maybe some dude has been waiting in the wings for a chance like this, waiting to activate their stalker mode, swoop in and sweep her off her feet. She's got that innocent vibe on her. Wickedly sexy. Guys love that shit." He leans back in his seat, satisfied that he's made his point. He cringes when I shoot him a glare. "What? She's got them porn tits. She's hot."

Megs grabs her purse and whacks Simon on the head with it. "Really, Simon? Porn tits? You're so not getting any tonight. Or ever." She scoots her chair away from my best friend, glowering at him.

I close my eyes and pinch the bridge of my nose with two fingers. I tip my head back, open my eyes and glance up at the ceiling, which was probably white at one time, but is now almost gray.

Simon just hit me with my worst fear. Losing Nor. What the fuck was I thinking?

Someone touches my arm. I tip my head forward and meet Simon's eyes.

"So what happened to the Behemoth?" He stares at my knuckles, which are raw and red from the fight.

"Someone let him in my cell. Luckily, I have picked up a few moves while inside this hell. I have learned to fight dirty. I won. I have my medals to prove it."

I subtly lift the bottom of my T-shirt. "Just one broken rib this time."

"Yeah. That and a black eye." Megs stares at me with wide eyes. Her eyes lower to my covered midriff, then up at me. "This looks bad. Are you in too much pain?"

I shake my head. "It was worth it. I broke Behemoth's jaw and a couple of ribs." I grin. She grimaces. Simon locks his jaw and averts his eyes from me. "Do you understand now why I didn't want Nor to see me like this? I don't know how long Stephen will do this. I don't have any proof to show he's been sending them."

"So, what are you planning to do with Nor? She's getting desperate. You know how determined she is when she gets that way. She will turn every rock to look for a way to see you."

My back straightens and I narrow my eyes are on Megs. "What is she up to? Has she told you anything?"

She scowls at me. "I'm not even going to justify that with an answer. Do you think you can ban my best friend and then expect me to tell you anything?"

I glare at her. Jesus. Nor is definitely up to something. I glance at Simon. He shrugs.

"Don't look at me for answers. I'm with Little Miss Sassy over here. You had better be very good at apologizing when you leave this place."

I purse my lips. "I will fucking woo her. I will compose a damn sonnet if I have to, just as soon as I murder her father first." Rage burns through my veins and my hands curl into fists.

"That sonnet had better be fucking stunning. Better than Shakespeare."

The visiting time draws to a close and my friends leave. Afterwards, when I get to my room, I lay in bed obsessing over Nor being swept off her feet by some guy. I fucking hate my best friend for putting those images in my head.

Turning on my side on the hard mattress, I close my eyes and imagine wrapping my hands around Stephen's neck, squeezing and watching life fade from his eyes. And I feel peace settle over me.

CHAPTER THIRTY-SEVEN

Nor

THE LAST TIME COLE ASKED ME NOT TO GO SEE HIM, I HAD A HARD time accepting his orders. Really, how can you tell someone you love they shouldn't come to visit you? How do I even begin to not see him for the next eight months? I've gone through the first three stages of grief. Denial, anger, bargaining. Well, I'm not going to let myself get depressed and accept his decision in any way. I want to see Cole more than anything I've ever wanted in my life.

I have a plan. I just need to find Mr. Taylor first.

I glance down at the letters on my lap. I hadn't received Cole's letters in a while, so I was pleasantly surprised when I open my mail box and found two letters inside.

My gaze flickers to the antique wooden box that holds the other letters he sent. About nine so far. The title on the envelopes is, "Open Me When. . ."

I pick the one closest to me and flip it open, reading his words written in confident scrawl. My heart crawls up my throat immediately and I have to blink hard to keep the tears at bay.

My Snowflake, When you feel like we need to break up, remember the silver lining. I'm an ass for asking you to stay away. Wait for me just a

little bit longer. Just a little longer.
I love you.
Cole.

I smile, and carefully open the next one.

Open me when you need to know how much I love you. Go to the
mirror. That girl staring back at you with big green eyes and freckles on
her nose. . .that is the girl I love.
I love you.
Cole

God.

Cole.

I wipe the tears from my cheeks and fold the letters, then rearrange them inside the antique wooden box I bought a while back to
keep gifts and letters from Cole. Then look up in the mirror directly
opposite to where I'm sitting on the bed.

I miss him so much I need to see him soon. Lately, Grandma
has been feeling ill. I paid a visit to her last Thursday, and Mr. Taylor
dropped by for a visit. I asked him how Cole was doing. Someone beat
him up again. Taylor has asked a few trusted guards to keep an eye on
him, but somehow the attackers find a way to get him alone.

A few weeks ago, I overheard Maggie and my dad talking downstairs in the foyer.

"*Stephen, please. You need to stop hurting him. You said you love*
me. Do you hurt the person you love? Cole is a piece of me."

My dad growled and said, "*He took you away from me. If you*
weren't pregnant with that. . .him. . ." *he stopped and took in a long,*
deep breath. The next words that came out of his mouth made me re-
alize that my father had gone mad. "*You and Benjamin are no longer*
together. But you still refuse to come back to me."

"*We were kids, Stephen. We didn't know what we wanted.*"

"That's where you're wrong!" he bellowed.

Maggie had tried to talk to him, to dissuade him, but he'd gotten angry and shoved her out of the door.

My father had spat something in a low voice before slamming the door shut.

I clear my head to get rid of that memory and focus on a plan to see Cole.

PART THREE

PRESENT

"Life breaks you, dismantling every part of us into pieces. It's just a way to prepare us for what we are meant to be. Who we are meant to be. Survivors."

~ *Caroline Blake.*

CHAPTER THIRTY-EIGHT

Cole

I STARTLE AWAKE, THE STIFFNESS IN MY ARMS SENDING PAIN THROUGH my body. I try to stretch my arms but some sort of weight holds them down. Lifting my head, I squint in the dark to see Cora and Joce snuggled at my sides. It was almost ten o'clock at night when we finally arrived home from the hospital. Nor didn't want the girls to sleep alone, so they ended up in her bed. As soon as Joce's little body hit the mattress, she held up her arms for me and I fucking cried as I scooted between her and Cora. I pulled them to me so that their heads were on my chest. I held them as sobs racked their bodies until they fell asleep. I must have dozed off as well, unaware when Nor left the room.

Carefully, I slide my hand out from under the girls' bodies and inch out of bed. The room is dark so it takes a while for my eyes to adjust to the darkness. Nor must have decided to turn off all the lights and went to sleep elsewhere in the house since I took up her place on her bed.

Once I find my bearings, I shuffle to the door, turn on the light in the hallway and pull my phone from my pants pocket. I turn on the camera and set it to night mode, tiptoe back to the bed and snap a picture of my daughters. They look so adorable, sprawled on the bed with their faces relaxed in sleep.

According to the clock on the nightstand, it's past one o'clock in the morning. Turning around, I head out of the room and walk downstairs. My breath stalls when I see Nor's petite frame curled on the couch, her focus on the shopping channel running on TV. Suddenly, she lifts her head and looks over the couch but then averts her face quickly, wiping her cheeks. She twists her body slightly to the side and turns on the small lamp on the side table.

Shit.

I can't stop looking at her. Even when crying, she looks so damn beautiful.

"The girls are asleep." I shove my balled up fists inside my wrinkled pants pockets to stop myself from walking over and pulling her into my arms. She looks so heartbroken, so scared. I glance around for her sisters. They arrived a few hours ago after we came home from the hospital.

"Elon and Elise are already in bed," she says, as if reading my mind.

I nod, my thoughts momentarily wandering to Stephen. My hands clench tighter and I want to bust some balls with my fist, just thinking about that sick son of a bitch.

He completely ruined my life and made Nor's life a living hell. I really need to know what happened, then I can track down that bastard. When I was in prison, I tried to stay away from trouble as much as I could. But if trouble followed me, I dealt with it without hesitation. I learned fast how to use my fists. I also learned how easy it was to choke the life out of someone. Watch life fade from their eyes. I never killed anyone, but it didn't stop me from showing them I could do it without blinking an eye. I came so close to losing my own life several times. I learned that respect had to be earned.

I earned it.

Pain shoots from my cheek and I realize my jaw is clenched too tight. I pull my hands from my pockets and sign, "*I have to go.*"

Nor nods once. "*Thank you for today.*"

We stare at each other for several seconds, the air heavy with our loss. My brother. Her husband. I turn and walk toward the door.

After putting on my shoes, I glance over my shoulder one more time and my fucking chest explodes with pain.

I can't leave her like this. Her shoulders are shaking and her head is bent, her hair covers her face, hiding the pain tearing her apart. She'd held herself together the entire afternoon after Josh died, never allowing herself to show any weakness.

Pushing away from the door, I stride back and sit on the couch before pulling her in my arms. I expect her to push me away, but she doesn't. She wraps her arms around my waist, hugging me tight and then tucks her head into my chest.

Jesus. Feeling her body shake against mine breaks me. I wish I could absorb her pain through my skin.

"I got you, Snowflake," I say, kissing her hair. "I got you."

My words unlock something in her. She lets herself go and she cries. I continue to hold her, tightening my hands around her and comforting her with words. Holding Nor like this fills my heart, reminding me how good we used to fit together.

Leaning back, I comb her hair back and just stare at her, taking in her tear-filled eyes, pink nose scattered with freckles. Flushed cheeks and snot running down her nose. My fucking heart trips on itself, overriding my brain.

She has never looked more beautiful.

"Tell me about my brother. I feel like I missed out on knowing him these past nine years."

She bites her cheek, softly smiles then wipes her cheeks with her nightgown.

"*He loved the girls so much. He taught them how to fish,*" she signs. She tells me how Josh freaked out when her water broke, that he fainted when he saw Joce pop out of her. Woke up and fainted again when he saw Cora. She laughs. I tighten my hands, a lump forming in my throat. I should have been the one there welcoming my babies in to this world. "*He was the best friend I could ever have asked for. He was so good to me and the girls, even though staying with us meant him losing any chance of meeting someone who loved him as he wanted to be loved."*

Then she starts to sob again. I have so many questions running through my mind, but I push them to the back of my head and tighten my arms around her.

"Shhh. It's okay. I'm here," I say, rubbing her back in circles.

Nor lifts her head from my chest and looks at me. She raises her hand and softly touches my jaw. Every nerve in my body is centered on her fingers, lessening the ache of losing my brother, of missing out on my children's lives, of losing Nor. I fucking hate how much I crave her touch. We still have a lot to talk about, but no one has ever touched me like she just did seconds ago, since her.

Nor shifts on my lap, leaning forward without breaking eye contact. She kisses my jaw, my cheek. When her lips brush against mine, her eyes fall shut and she exhales hard. My fingers are gripping her hips, moving up to cup her face. I shudder and groan when she sucks my bottom lip into her mouth.

"Fuck, Nor," I breath into her. My heart's beating fast inside my chest. Her hands are touching me everywhere, fast, desperate.

She leans back and stares at me. "Kiss me, Cole. Just, please kiss me. I need to forget for just tonight what I lost. What we lost."

I'm so eager to erase the crippling pain in my chest. Eager to feel Nor again. So I give her what she wants because it's what I want too. What I frantically need. Her lips on mine. Her skin on mine. Quenching the hunger that is still buried in me even after all this time. Within seconds, I'm kicking my shoes off and she's lying horizontal and I'm on top of her. I wedge my leg between her thighs and throw her arms over her head, arching her lower body up, grinding her covered pussy on my jean-covered crotch.

Jesus fucking Christ.

"So damn sexy," I say, as she moves beneath me, her lips parted. I lean forward, slide my hand up her throat and wrap my fingers around the nape of the neck. My thumb moves along the column of her neck. He skin vibrates and my cock presses harder on my zipper.

I need to bury myself inside her or I might die. Our legs tangle, my fingers fighting to get more of her. They remember the map of her body as if we've never been apart. I can't remember the last time I felt a hunger this deep. My mouth trails down her neck, across her chest. I take her nipple between my lips and suck it, then move to the other one and do the same thing. Her body writhes under me, her mouth parted.

I lift my head to look at her as my hand slides under her white flimsy nightgown, I brush her pussy and push a finger inside her.

"So wet," I say.

Her hooded eyes meet mine and I'm three seconds away from jerking off in my pants.

She opens that mouth and I can't stop watching those lips. "Make me forget, Cole." I know she wants me to fuck her into oblivion, because I want that too. I want to forget everything. I need to forget for just one night. "No one has ever touched me like you used to. No one else has been in there since you. I want to feel again."

My finger inside stops. "What?"

She startles, stares at me with wide eyes and licks her lips. She probably didn't intend for those words to slip out.

This is probably not the right moment to ask, but I do. That animal part of me that claimed her eleven years ago needs to know. "You and Josh never. . ."

She shakes her head. I remove my hands from below her dress and sit up. Drag my fingers through my hair and lower my head.

What the fuck am I doing?

I stand up from the couch, glance up at the ceiling. Shit. Shit. Shit.

I slide my gaze down to Nor, who's staring at me with something like fear in her eyes.

"I'm sorry. I can't do this. This is not right. . ." I shove my feet inside my shoes, spin around and stalk to the door. I step out without looking back and close the door. I lean back on it and my squeeze my eyes shut.

That memory of the first time I made her come is a reminder of how much I enjoyed watching her fall apart. Something holds me back though. She mentioned that she and Josh had never slept together. I know their marriage wasn't real. But with Josh being gone less than twenty-four hours, I need to keep a lid on my feelings for now.

Digging out my phone from my pants, I scroll through my contacts and tap on Megs' number. I promised her I'd text her when I left Nor's house to let her know how Nor and the girls are doing. When I'm done, I head for my car, fighting the urge to turn around and go back inside the house to finish what we started on the couch.

As soon as the door clicks shut, I drop my head back on the couch and stare at the burgundy curtains across from me.

Shit.

What the hell is wrong with me? I shouldn't have tried to kiss Cole. And then I opened my mouth and told him that Josh and I were never intimate. I just wanted him to know that it has always been him.

He pushed me away and left.

I cover my eyes with my hands and groan.

Nip those feelings at the bud, Eleanor. It's been a long time. Cole is one in a million and has an amazing heart. Any girl would be lucky to have him. Oh gosh. Maybe he has a girlfriend and I threw myself at him. My heart twists in my chest. I double over and squeeze my eyes tight as pain steals the air from my lungs.

Would he kiss me the way he did if he had a girlfriend?

Plus, Josh died. Who kisses another man when her husband has just died? Even though Josh and I married for reasons other than love, he still deserves respect.

He'd been my best friend for these past years. It has been eight years and fifty days since I last cut. The journey to healing hadn't been easy. He was there when I relapsed. Held me when I cried myself to sleep after the wedding, pep-talked me on days that the thirst to cut became too much. He and Megs took turns to hold my hand before and after each therapy session. Dr Thorsten had referred me to a therapist here in Willow Hill. I was too weak, too messed up. I despised myself for falling off the wagon after Cole left.

Josh was the best father any child could ever ask for. And when my dad left—good riddance—I took that chance to get mom the best therapy care, after years of living with depression. Josh was everywhere, and yet he never pursued any sort of intimacy between us because he knew. He knew that my heart was in New York and would always be. On days when I felt discouraged that Cole never replied to the letters I sent him, Josh would sit me in front of my desk and hand me a pen and paper. Our marriage was a union to save the person we both loved, which doesn't mean that he didn't have women lining up to fulfil the part of our deal I couldn't perform. He always said that he wasn't the kind of person to settle down. But now that he did, he could 'get some ass without strings attached' or have some woman stalking him home.

Then he started becoming sicker and sicker. My life revolved around Josh, my daughters, my mom and sisters. My Bachelor's degree in Music Therapy took a back seat. My regrets are many and one of them is that Josh got tangled up in this entire situation.

Now, Cole is back and I've reverted to that eighteen-year-old girl. Butterflies in my stomach, weak knees and stars in my eyes.

I groan again and flip to my side on the couch and try not to die. I'm equal parts embarrassed and rejected. My phone trills on the glass table. I crane my neck long enough to see who the caller is and then reach for it.

"Hey you," Megs greets. "How are you and the girls?"

I close my eyes and sigh. "Cora and Joce finally fell asleep."

"Is everything okay? I can drop by as soon as my shift is over."

"Oh no. Get some sleep first. Elon and Elise are here in case of anything."

She sighs, silence filling the conversation. "You and Cole?"

I open my eyes and focus on the fan whirring round and round on the ceiling. I smile, despite the current circumstances. "Cora and Joce cried so much they slept in the car. He carried both of them up to my room. The girls adore him. God, Megs. You should have seen them, cuddled on my bed together. Cora and Joce's little legs tangled up with his."

"Of course, they do. Blood is thicker than water, right?"

I nod. "Yes, it is," I whisper. "I miss Josh so much. It hurts, Megs. It hurts so much, even though I knew the time would come when he'd leave us. But I'm also happy he's no longer in pain."

"So, do we need to hire a mediator or something?"

I laugh. "No, but thank you for the thought. It's awkward. And Megs—" I inhale deeply, "—I kissed him."

Silence, then, "You did what?"

I groan. "We were on the couch and he was comforting me. I couldn't stop myself. . ."

"Did he kiss you back?" Megs asks in an excited whisper.

"Yes," I say, breathless.

"And?"

"And then he left. Things were getting a bit heavy. He stopped and left. I'm so embarrassed Megs. I threw myself at him without even thinking. Maybe he has a girlfriend—"

"Nor? Stop it. Take deep breaths. This was bound to happen. You two are like fuel and fire. Just say, keep a safe distance until things cool down. Do you think your lady parts will behave?"

I giggle. "I'm keeping my distance—and my lady parts in check—that's for sure."

"Good. Okay, girlie. I have to go. I'll talk to you tomorrow, okay? Love you."

"Love you more."

I hang up the call, smiling and sit up. I turn off the TV, turn off the lights, climb upstairs, and head to the bathroom. After brushing my teeth, I head to my bedroom, crawl on my bed, and finally lie down on the little space that is not occupied by my daughters. Taking a deep breath, I close my eyes and wait for sleep to claim me.

CHAPTER THIRTY-NINE

Cole

THE PAST WEEK HAS BEEN BUSY, PREPARING FOR JOSH'S FUNERAL. Soon I will be saying goodbye to my brother. I've been trying to keep myself busy just to stop from breaking down. I spend most of my nights at Nor's house, sleeping on the couch and figuring out how to be a dad. If I wasn't floundering around and Googling every piece of advice in a panic, I was smothering them with attention. I was having a hard time finding a balance, but Cora and Joce didn't seem to mind. In fact, they welcomed it. Being close to my daughters makes things easier.

Simon arrived last night. Simon is currently staying at my parents' house in the guest room downstairs. Last night we stayed up late catching up.

Right after the funeral, the crowd disperses heading for the row of cars parked twenty feet from Josh's grave, ready to drive to my parents' house for the wake. Elise and Elon wave at us as they head toward Elise's Prius with Nick's arm slung around Elon, holding her close. I've seen the way he looks at her, and I know he hasn't gotten over his childhood crush on her.

Megs and Simon hang back to chat. They still seem awkward around each other. I watch as Nor and the girls walk slowly toward my parent's car. After informing Megs and Simon that I'll meet them at my parents' house, I stride toward Nor. Just as she ushers Joce and Cora to my parent's car, I grasp her arm. She stiffens and looks over her shoulder at me, her red-rimmed eyes wide, and frowns. Her face looks too pale and thin. Stress from the past years, being a care-taker and a mom rests heavily on her face. I don't like seeing her like this. As much as I know how weird this sounds, I don't care for the look on her face. Every time she looks at me with those eyes filled with pain, I feel a sharp sting stab me inside my chest and go straight to my heart. I can't stand it anymore. That look on her face has to go.

"What's wrong?" she asks, averting her gaze to my chest. Nor has been avoiding looking at me since that night we made out on the couch.

"I want you and the girls to ride with me in my truck."

Her eyes flash with irritation and her cheeks flush, wiping off the desolate look of before. This is the first time I've seen her look alive in the past week. She has a right to mourn for him. She has done a good job, distracting the girls. As soon as she thinks no one is watching her, the curtain falls. But I see everything. In fact I think it's a little disturbing how much I watch her, which is why the little flash of anger on her face makes me feel some sort of victory. Damn it, I'll do anything to see that kind of passion again.

Her gaze flickers to my truck a few feet away and then back to me. She shakes her head and opens her mouth, most likely to protest. My grip on her arm tightens slightly.

"It is not a request, Nor."

Her lips tighten and she mutters something under her breath. Joce and Cora whip around to stare at their mom in what I can guess is shock, then cover their mouths with their little hands, snickering.

"*Mama said a bad word,*" Cora signs. She slaps a hand over her mouth again, her shoulders shaking with laughter.

I don't have to guess what Nor said, given the girls' laughter and Nor's blushing face. But I'm glad the somber mood is gone.

At least for now.

"*Get in the car. I'll talk to Mom and Dad.*" I jerk my chin toward the truck. Cora and Joce scramble on the passenger seat, looking all too happy.

But not Nor. She thrusts her chin forward, her jaw locked and arms crossed on her chest. She glares at me, and I return the look, my hands propped on my hips.

She huffs. "You—you brute."

My lips twitch and seconds later my shoulders are shaking with laughter. I think saying the words 'Fuck you' would make her spontaneously combust.

"*Don't fight me on this, Nor,*" I sign when I'm calm enough to face her without laughing. "*Get in the car.*"

Shoving my hands inside my pants pockets, I whirl around without waiting for her response and stride to the spot my parents are waiting inside the car. Fighting the urge to look over my shoulder as the weight of Nor's angry gaze bores into me.

I used to love the fierce look on her face when she got angry. So full of fire.

Mom rolls down the window on her side and watches me as I walk toward them. My aunt, Madge, her husband Ray and my cousin Abe are seated in the back of the car. They arrived last night from Portland to attend my brother's funeral. Aunt Madge flashes me a wobbly smile, wiping her eyes with a handkerchief.

After letting Mom know that Nor and the girls will be riding with me, I straighten and huff when they exchange smug looks. Shaking my head, I spin around and stalk back to my truck and notice Simon getting inside Megs' car ten feet away.

Once everyone is seated inside my truck, I hop in and then follow behind my parents' car as we leave the cemetery.

I needed a moment alone, away from the guests downstairs, which is why I'm standing inside Josh's old room. I shove my hands inside my pants pockets and slowly swivel around on my heel, taking in the shelves stacked with books, two footballs in one corner. A stack of magazines filled with random shit are piled neatly on top of a box on the floor. On top of the dresser is a framed photo of my brother, Cora and Joce are snuggled into him, their faces screwed up in cute funny expressions. Looks like my mom never got around to clearing his room just as they never cleared mine.

Someone touches my arm softly. I turn around and see Elon, dressed in a knee-length black dress. She has grown up a lot from the girl who spent most of her time practicing cello in her room. We've spent a few nights this week catching up so I know she's pursuing a Bachelor's of Music program in classical and modern music with special concentration on cello.

"Are you okay?" she asks, stepping forward and wrapping her arms around me. Then she steps back to look up at me.

I nod. "I'm trying. How are you?"

She glances around the room and brushes her fingers down her cheek. "It's hard to accept that he is gone. Your brother was amazing. I didn't get a chance to say good bye. To thank him for what he did for my Nor. If something would have happened to you, it would have killed my sister."

I open my mouth then shut it again as a wave of pain cuts through my chest.

"Cole, I'm sorry for how my father treated you."

"You don't have to apologize for him. Your father was ruled by a kind of sick obsession and prejudice. He was looking for someone to blame for how his life turned out. I was the scapegoat."

She inhales deeply and folds her hands in front of her. She reminds me of Joce. "I'm happy Cora and Joce never met him."

"They didn't?" I ask, taken aback by this news.

She shakes her head. "After the. . .um. . .wedding, Nor and Josh moved in with Grandma. She never brought the girls to visit my dad. He left town a few years later."

Thank fuck. I don't even want to imagine my children in his presence.

"Well, I'll go downstairs and help out."

"Thank you for telling me, Elon."

She nods and leaves the room, leaving me reeling with the news she just delivered. Walking to the dresser, I lift the framed photo and stare down at the people in it and a smile tugs on my lips. A soft nudge on my arm jerks me from my thoughts. I open my eyes to find Nor standing in front of me.

"*Hey,*" she signs. "*Elon told me you were up here.*"

I nod. "*Hey.*" I set the frame back on the dresser and run my fingers through my hair.

"*Can I get you anything?*"

I blow air through my mouth. "*Can you take this fucking pain from my heart?*"

She blinks twice before dropping her gaze on the beige carpet. She pushes a lock of hair behind her ear.

Shit. Why am I being such a dick?

"I'm sorry."

She lifts her head, glares at me, and signs, "*You're not the only person who lost Josh, Cole. I did, too. Your parents, Nick, Cora and Joce. We all lost him.*"

She turns on her heel and walks out of the room. I run my fingers through my hair.

Fuck.

I swing my clenched fist back and punch the wall across from me. I shake my fingers as pain sears through my brain.

Nor is right. We all lost Josh. And here I am behaving like a selfish motherfucker.

I need to apologize to Nor and I also need a strong drink to calm me the fuck down. I leave the room. As soon as my foot hits the bottom step, I stalk toward the kitchen.

Halting at the counter in the kitchen, I reach up and fling the cupboard doors open and scour through the random shit. Then I remember my dad keeps his scotch in the living room cabinet. I stride back, ignoring the curious looks being thrown in my direction. I stop in front of said cabinet, throw the door open and reach for the bottle of scotch. I return back to the kitchen with my prize.

I'm in the process of pouring a shot in a glass when someone taps my shoulder. I whirl around, scowling.

"*Easy, Man,*" Simon signs, taking a step back. "*What the hell's crawled up your ass?*"

I glare at him, turn around and grab the scotch. I toss the contents down my throat and grimace as the liquid burns a trail down my throat. Reaching out for the bottle again, I pour another shot and toss it back. I tip the bottle, ready for another shot, but Simon's hand on mine halts my progress.

I shoot him a scowl. "Take your arm off me before I rip it from your body."

He grins, undeterred by my threat then drops his hand. "Talk to me, man. One minute you and the girls are heading here in your truck looking all sad and shit and the next you look like someone took your favorite toy or something. Talk, bro."

I down another shot and slam the glass down on the marble counter.

"*I have to leave,*" I sign, brushing past him and heading toward the door then stopping abruptly when I see Nor, standing a few feet away from us, talking to an old couple I have never seen before. Her cheeks are still flushed and her eyes look brighter than they have been since I arrived in town a few weeks ago.

As if sensing me, Nor stops talking, scans the room until she finds me. Her mouth tightens in obvious irritation before looking away. Simon appears in my line of sight and stares at me incredulously.

"*You fucked her,*" he signs. It's not a question, more of an observation.

My gaze flickers to Nor and I watch as the couple leaves, and my cousin Abe saunters towards her, then back to my best friend, but I don't answer him.

"What's wrong with you? Couldn't you have waited until, say, to-morrow? Or at least until the guests left? This is some twisted shit, bro."

"Fuck off, Simon." I don't bother to correct his assumption and head for the door, but catch something at the corner of my eyes. I whip around to see Abe leaning down, that dirty mouth of his edging toward Nor's cheek. That same mouth that kisses anything in a skirt. Forgetting I need some fresh air, I stalk toward them. She sees me bearing down on her and takes a step back, her eyes wide.

"Abe," I grit out his name, at the same time my hands circles Nor's upper arm and I focus on her. "Can we talk? Please."

She gives me an exasperated look then shakes her head. "Later."

"Now." I don't give her a choice. I mumble "excuse us" and herd her to the kitchen. Most of the guests are outside, chatting with my parents or catching up anyway. The chances of making a fool of myself are minimal. I drag her inside the little alcove that serves as the pantry, and finally drop my hand.

"What the hell do you think you're doing?" she signs, her eyes greener and angrier.

My heart is racing fast as I sign, *"I want to apologize."*

"Did you have to drag me all the way here to do that?"

I shift on my feet. Yeah, that was a stupid move.

"All right. Apology accepted." She skirts around me but I grasp her hand, pulling her back.

"Cole. Stop it."

I stare down at her. *"Stay away from Abe. He is a womanizer."*

She stares at me, frustrated. *"Jesus, Cole. He was not doing anything. We were just talking."*

"I don't trust him."

She blinks. *"He is your cousin."* I grit my teeth. She rolls her eyes and smirks. *"You do not trust anyone. You've been staring daggers at any man who stopped to talk to me or the girls."*

"I don't like the way he's looking at you."

She narrows her eyes at me. "Are you jealous? Oh my God. You are jealous."

Yes, I am. But that's not it. Abe practically sniffing around her has me seeing red. I can't believe she can't see it. My cousin is shameless. He has always been a shameless manwhore and broke every girl's heart within a two hundred mile radius when he was sixteen. He looks like he wants to eat Nor alive and he's just waiting for the perfect opportunity to do it.

I glare her down. I'm not even sure what point I'm trying to prove or get across. I don't even know why I'm doing this. She is a grown-ass woman. She can handle anything.

She wrinkles her nose and I fucking want to kiss the freckles there. Each and every one of them. *"Move and stop manhandling me."*

I smirk. *"I haven't even started to manhandle you, Snowflake. I promise you if I do, you'll be begging me to do it over and over again."*

Her cheeks flush pink as she opens her mouth and closes it, and then huffs and says, "You are impossible. . .ugh. . .what the hell!"

She grabs my face without warning, yanks me to her and kisses me.

Holy fucking shit. I wasn't expecting that.

I lift my hands, and slide my fingers to the nape of her neck, grabbing a fistful of red hair in my hand. I hold her to me as she assaults my mouth with hers. Then her tongue parts my lips, fucking my mouth. She slides her hand between us and grips my cock through my pants. I jerk my hips, groan, walk her backwards until her back is pressed to a wall but she pushes me back, somehow flipping me around on my back and I let her. I let her because I know she needs this. I need this too, and for once, I see the little firecracker I left behind all those years ago. She's still fierce and I love it. Then she pulls back, her cheeks flushed, lips swollen and eyes bright, breathing hard.

Shit. That was fucking amazing. I grab her hips to pull her back, eager to let her consume me as I want to consume her, but she pushes against my chest with trembling hands, her chest heaving up and down fast.

"You think you're the only one who lost something? I lost you. I lost

my world. You were my world but I couldn't let anyone destroy my everything. Not even my father. You, Cole, were my everything." She steps forward, her eyes narrowed at me. "*Stay away from me, Cole. If you're ready to talk, come and see me, and I hope to hell your Batman won't be doing the thinking next time. Pull your head out of your ass for more than three seconds and listen.*"

She pats back the tresses of red hair that have escaped the bun after my manhandling and adjusts the front of her dress where her breasts are eagerly calling for me. She opens her mouth and says, "I'm leaving now."

"We are not done talking." I step around to block her way.

She looks up at me, one eyebrow raised. "Well. Boo-freaking-hoo. Don't. Follow. Me. You big brute." She adds the last part with a swift lift of her chin, and then she spins around and strides away.

Whoa. I feel like a tornado just whooped my ass, and instead of destroying me, it left me wanting more.

After taking deep breaths, I'm hot on her trail as she rushes toward Abe—the whoring motherfucker—as though Satan is after her ass. The magnitude with which I crave that cute little ass is immense, Satan has nothing on me. Simon intercepts me, causing me to stop.

"*Can I speak with you? Alone?*" Simon signs, staring at me meaningfully.

"*Get out of my way, Simon.*"

"*Not going to happen. Unless you want to continue entertaining the guests with your He-Man tendencies, then, by all means.*" He smirks, wagging his eyebrows.

I scan the room, my heart still racing after that hot little session in the kitchen. My parents are standing near the front door, staring in our direction. Mom is frowning and my dad is rubbing his chin as if he's contemplating something.

My gaze flickers to where Nor is staring nervously in my direction. She gives Simon a look of relief and then shoots me a grimace. Her chin juts out and she turns back to face Abe.

I follow my idiotic best friend while gritting my teeth.

"You're treading on very dangerous grounds, Simon. What do you want?"

He stops and turns to face me. "Jesus, Cole. What kind of fore-play was that? You and Nor literally eye fucked each other in front of everyone. And then you dragged her out of the room, looking like you were about to kill her. Or fuck her. You need to dial down whatever you're going through. I thought you hated her."

I clench my jaw. "What do you want?"

He rolls his eyes. "Fred Kiplinger wants to meet with you and Tate as soon as possible. Tate will meet you in Boston."

Fuck. "I can't leave Nor and the girls just yet."

He stares at me hard. "I agree with you. They need you. But you are not in a position to be here for them acting the way you did. Dude, that shit would be hot if it weren't for Josh being dead."

"Stay the fuck out of my business."

He raises his hands in surrender and takes a step back, grinning. "Look at it this way. That trip to Boston will be you putting things into perspective. And when you come back, you can go and get her before you drive everyone crazy with your shitty attitude, you moody bastard."

CHAPTER FORTY

Nor

My phone on the wooden table beeps and then lights up with a text message. I reach for it, squint at the screen, and smile as I tap on the yellow envelope.

Megs: How are you and the girls?

Me: Girls are sleeping. I'm on the roof.

I press send and then grab the glass of Bailey's and Coke, and take a sip. I set it back on the table just as my screen lights up.

Megs: I'm coming over.

Crap. I'm not sure I am up for company tonight. Megs has been amazing as always. After Cole left, her friendship had been my life vest keeping me from drowning those first years. It's unfortunate that she and Simon broke up after he moved to New York with Cole. They'd have been together if it weren't for me.

Me: Please don't worry about me. I'll be fine, I promise. I just need to be alone tonight.

Megs: What happened at the wake? That kind of tension was off the charts. Have you told him yet?

Me: Not yet. God. He was being such a cave man. We kissed again upstairs. What the hell am I doing, Megs?

Megs: You are Nor. He is Cole. It's a given.

I huff a breath of frustration.

Me: **He might have a life in New York for all I know. A girl-friend or a wife**.

Megs: **He doesn't.**

Me: **How do you know?**

This time she takes longer to reply. A thought tickles my mind and I feel excitement soar through me.

Me: **You little vixen! Have you and Simon been humping like rabbits? Did he tell you that while he was reacquainting you with his Batman?**

My phone beeps.

Megs: **Simon told me. And no. There hasn't been any reac-quainting going on. I need to sort out the mess in my life first. Plus, I kind of hate men at the moment.**

I chuckle under my breath. Yeah, right. Anyone with eyes could see how those two affected each other.

Me: **Want to bet how long you'll hate men?**

Megs: **I'm not even going to dignify that with an answer. Good night. Call me if you need me.**

I smile and reach for my glass then gulp down its contents before I set it back on the table. I look around, taking in the string of lights hanging low above me. After moving in with Grandma, she had given me free rein to redecorate the roof terrace. We celebrated the twins' birthday here on the roof last year.

I snuggle deeper into the loveseat, the fire crackling in the fire pit. I sigh and continue star-gazing. Cora and Joce fell asleep two hours ago, exhausted and emotionally spent. Lying here like this, re-minds me of Cole and the nights he and I used to sit on my roof for hours. Sometimes the pain is just too much but I've learned to em-brace it over the years. To turn it into something positive. Something peaceful.

One thing is for sure. My desire for Cole hasn't waned. You'd think after nine years of being away from each other we'd be more reserved. But no. Our broken souls stirred awake the moment we set eyes on each other at the hospital. And now they thrive, nourished by being in each other's presence. Every touch and each look stitches those parts in me I thought would never mend.

Crap. Stop it, Nor. Don't torture yourself like this.

Cole and I still need to talk. The question is, will he forgive me after he knows the truth?

Earlier today, my mother called from Phoenix where she's now living with her boyfriend, Pete. She couldn't make it to the funeral, which I guess, is okay. They will be visiting in two months or so. She said she'll call to confirm the exact date. She sounded happy, much more than when she lived at home. I'm glad for her. My father had done a lot of damage to her, he almost broke her completely. I feel content that Pete is taking good care of her. The last time I saw them was over a year ago when they came to visit us. He doted on her, held her, made her smile. They met a few years ago in group therapy. Pete was the attending therapist. It was love at first sight, that's what she says.

My phone vibrates on the wooden table, forcing my gaze to leave the starless sky. I reach for my phone and click on the message flashing on the screen with my finger. Goosebumps trail down my arms and I squeeze my thighs together to ease the tingling between my legs. He isn't even here and my body is responding to him with a vicious need.

Cole: **I'm outside**.

I don't have the strength to deal with Cole right now. He's too intense. Too everything. And that terrifies me and excites me at the same time.

He doesn't have a girlfriend.

Me: **Go home Cole. The girls are sleeping**.

Cole: **I'm not here to see the girls. We need to talk.**

I sigh. Now is not the right time to talk.

Me: **We'll talk when you come back from Boston.**

Seconds pass.

Cole: **Nor.**

Cole: **Please**.

I drag my body from the couch and shuffle down the steps. When I reach the front door, I remove the door chain, flip the locks, and peek out. Cole's standing on the porch. His forehead is pressed on the wall. He's not wearing his trusted beanie so his hair is on full display: wild and wavy. He tilts his head to look at me. I suck in a breath, taking in the tortured look on his face. The muscles on his shoulder and stomach flex as he pushes himself off the wall with his hands and straightens.

How can I turn him away, when he looks like this?

"*Come on in.*" I step aside to let him in.

He takes a step forward and stops in front of me. He dips his head into the crook of my neck. Inhales long and hard. I shiver. Warmth spreads across my skin and I'm dizzy, dying. He exhales even harder, pulling me back to life. I'm drunk from having his body so close to mine.

Oh.

God.

I can't move. I need to move something. A hand. My legs. My mouth. Maybe kiss him and take those wasted breathes into my lungs.

Behave, my brain tells my body, my heart.

I stumble back and step aside to let him in. I close the door and follow him into the living room, my gaze on his backside. My feet guide me forward, my palms itching to grab a piece of his—

"Ooomph!" I hit a wall of muscle and stagger back. Two strong hands grip my shoulders, righting me.

"Are you okay?" Cole asks, frowning at me.

Heat explodes across my face but I manage to bob my head. Oh wow, that Bailey's went straight to my head.

"Want a beer?" I ask him, my pulse thudding in my ears.

He nods. I hurry to the fridge and grab a bottle before I end up groping him. The cool glass startles me, knocking some of the haze from the Bailey's from my head. I return to Cole's side and shove it in his hands, then stand back to watch as he twists the cap, slants his head back and takes a long drink. He lowers his arm holding the bottle and then wipes his mouth with the back of his hand.

Sexiest thing ever.

"Can I see the girls? I won't wake them. I promise." He breaks through my thoughts with those words.

He looks so broken. If seeing the girls will take away that look of hopelessness from his face, then so be it.

I nod and lead the way upstairs. Halting in front of Cora's room, I push the door with my fingers. Snores drift from where Cora and Joce are sprawled on the bed, sleeping. The light from the hallway faintly illuminates the angles of their faces, while the other side is cast in shadows. We stand there, watching our daughters. Joce jerks her hands, startled in her sleep but quickly calms down and goes back to sleep.

"They are beautiful. You and Josh raised them well." I nod, a lump forming in my throat. Cole takes another sip from his bottle. He looks at me, tears brimming at the corner of his eyes. "I miss him so much." He squeezes his eyes and the tears fall down his cheeks.

"Oh Cole," I murmur under my breath as I close the distance between us and wrap my arms around him. He returns my embrace with a tighter one, his face buried into the crook of my neck. His body shakes against mine. I can't take away the pain, but I can hold him at least. I rub my hand down his back, and kiss his bowed head. He shudders as his tears subside and raises his head from my shoulder.

I cup his face in my hands and wipe the lingering wetness on his cheek. "He loved you so much, you know. He never stopped talking about you to the girls."

"Fuck. He died thinking I was mad at him. I was angry with him for a long time. It took fucking cancer to knock some sense into me."

I push the locks of hair falling on his forehead. "He knew you loved him."

He shakes his head as if to deny my words and turns away from me. He props one elbow on the door frame and bites his bottom lip, his focus on our daughters.

I lean on the wall behind me and close my eyes. I try to sort out what I'm feeling. Warm lips brush against mine. My eyes flip open, colliding with Cole's intense, dark gray eyes. A frown mars his brow as he continues to study me. I'm trapped by the sudden rush of bliss his mouth stirred up in me.

"It is wrong to kiss you like this, Snowflake. But I can't stop myself. Why does it feel so right? I should have known we would end up in each other's space sooner or later."

His mouth presses on mine again, sucking my bottom lip inside his mouth, nipping it. I wince a little, but lift my arms and dig my fingers into his scalp. I take a fist full of hair and tug it.

He hisses, groans. That sound hits me low in my stomach, ricocheting all over my body. He leans to the side and I hear the sound of glass thud softly on the floor. He straightens, and then he's kissing me and I'm moaning, the sound bouncing on the walls.

Crap. We're going to wake up the girls. I pull back, ready to duck under Cole's arm, but he seems to have other ideas. He slides his arm around my waist and walks me backward toward my room, his heated gaze never leaving my face. I want this so badly, even an earthquake wouldn't stop me from taking what he is offering.

He stops and cups my face in his hands. He crushes his mouth on mine, kissing me wildly, desperately, needy. He pulls his head back abruptly, stares at me. "I need you so much. I want to bury myself inside you." He removes one hand from my cheek, trails it down my shoulder, my breast. He squeezes it hard before kneading it and pinching my nipple. My body jolts and I whimper. I try to move away from his grasp. I want to grab his hand and drag him to my bed, but he seems to have other ideas. His hand continues its descent, in slow deliberate touches and by the time he rounds my thigh and cups me between my legs, I'm writhing against his hard body.

"I need to stop feeling like this." His speech is more labored, rough. "Please make the pain go away. I want to bury my cock in here. This sweet pussy. Fuck, Nor. I cannot believe no one else has been in there."

His words heat my body. No one has ever spoken to me like that. Well, other than Cole himself. His words always had that kind of effect on me.

I'm ready to beg him to make me feel better. Fill this hollow feeling in my chest. I pull back enough for him to see my mouth. "I need you too. So freaking bad. Please, Cole. Make me feel whole again."

We still have a lot to talk about, but those issues are minute at the moment, compared to the hunger tearing us apart. I don't care if he doesn't touch me again after today. All I know is that my body has been waiting to reconnect with his all these years. I'm not about to push him away.

He takes my hand and pulls me into my room and then kicks the door shut with his foot. My body is being pushed against a hard wall, and an even harder body presses into mine. It's dark in the room. I'm not even sure how he knows where the wall is. Maybe men have a feel for these things. Like their inner "sex-against-the-wall" compass activates the second their brains switch to sex mode. His large hands grab my backside and lift me up. His mouth is on my neck, kissing me, nipping me, sucking me.

Oh holysweetmotherofbabyjesuspleasepleaseplease! I'm three seconds from spontaneous combustion and I haven't written my will yet. Whoa. I can't breathe. I need to breathe. I wiggle out of his arms and dart away in the dark.

Stumbling around in the dark, my knee hits my bed and I fall forward, roll around and sit up. Now that I found my bearings, I tap the surface until I find the night stand, the lamp switch and turn it on. I blink several times to adjust my eyes to the sudden light.

Cole is still standing near the door, his chest heaving. "*Nor?*"

"*Give me a damn second. I just need a second to think without your hands on me.*"

He shifts his weight to his right foot. Doesn't say a word for about five seconds. "*Do you want me to go?*"

Do I? The Bailey's and Coke made me feel good. But Cole's kisses made me feel great. For those ten seconds his mouth was on my skin, I felt alive. I forgot *everything*. Just him and his talented lips and tongue.

I shake my head.

"*Come here.*"

I fight the urge to roll my eyes. Apparently, demanding Cole never left the building.

"*Nor. I won't tell you again.*"

His face is dangerously dark. There's so much lust in his eyes, so much pain. Hunger. I can't tell where one emotion ends and the other begins.

I crawl out of the bed and go to him.

"*Did you ever even love me?*"

Whoa! Where is this coming from? It started as desperate need to fill a void in each other, but now we are talking about feelings.

I stare at this man standing in front of me. Hurt and uncertainty have joined the turmoil in his face.

I did that to him. As much as I wanted to save him, I broke him and took away the trust he had for me. He'd once saved me and ended up in prison. I saved him but ended up with the wrong brother. But while we did that to keep each other safe, it drove a wedge between us, separating us. Taking a deep breath, I nod and shift my gaze to stare at my feet. I can't afford to let him see how much I miss him.

How much I need him.

How much the past years have created a crater so deep inside my soul it would take a lot of forgiving on his part to make me whole.

I shut my eyes, gathering the courage I need to tell him what I've kept locked inside me all these years. It might be too late for us, but I want him to know. I need him to know.

A firm grip around my chin jolts me and my eyes snap open to find his face mere inches from mine.

I lift my hands to sign, but they're shaking too much. I give up and angle my face, making sure he can read my lips. "I didn't just love you, Cole. I worshiped the ground you walk on and I never stopped. I know you think I stopped loving you. But you're wrong. How could I stop loving that big part of me that makes me who I am today?"

His face goes blank. His entire body goes still. Everything about him screams "Run, Nor". The only reaction I get from him is his eyes, slowly moving down my body. He doesn't need to touch me with his hands. His stare is doing all the touching I need to bring my body back to life.

Pride is a thing of the past. When it comes to Cole, I have none.

Suddenly, he pounces swiftly. I yelp in surprise. His strong hands are on my shoulder, walking me back until I feel my back hit a wall again. His fingers slide down my arms in firm strokes and finally rest on my hips.

"What the hell are you doing?" I ask, squirming against his tight hold, wanting out at the same time, needing his touch on me more than I need to breathe.

His hands leave my body long enough to sign, "*Unless you want to wake up the girls and have them find you flat on your back with my cock inside you, you need to keep your mouth shut.*"

Jesus, why am I turned on by his words?

My body jolts when his fingers lift my dress, his callused palms moving up my thighs. He continues to touch me, his eyes holding mine captive and I'm burning with every touch, panting when his fingers wrap around my neck, his thumb stroking the length of it as he absorbs the vibrations caused by my moans and groans. He'd always had a habit of touching my neck because feeling the vibrations turned him on even more.

He pins me harder with his body as his breathing becomes heavy. Leaning forward, he buries his face in my neck, inhaling me deeply. He traces his tongue along the vein beating erratically there, and I nearly come when he sinks his teeth in my shoulder. His lips latch on that spot, licks it and I jerk when I feel a sharp pain on my butt.

I pull back and glare at him. Did he just spank me? Oh, God, why do I like it so much?

Cole steps back, taking the warmth of his body with him. I bite my cheek to stop my greedy hands from pulling him back.

He lifts his chin and looks at me through hooded eyes. He lifts his hands and signs, "*Show me. Show me how much you worship me.*"

My thoughts explode into images those words evoke. I start to shake my head.

"Cole—"

His mouth tightens and anger flashes through his face. I snap my mouth shut and inhale deeply, closing the distance between us until we're standing toe to toe. His body is shooting off some serious heat. He's coiled tight, I can see his chest rise and fall through the shirt. I lift my head and meet his gaze, my fingers itching to touch him, run across his hair. Closing my eyes, I focus on bringing my raging arousal over this man under control. I've missed him so much I'm afraid if I act on what I'm feeling I might not let him go. I don't realize my hands are touching him until I hear Cole hiss followed by a groan so potent it leaves my legs shaking. My eyes snap open to find him leaning his cheek into my hand, his mouth parted in pleasure. Gone is the furious look on his face.

God, he is beautiful.

I continue tracing my fingers around his face, down his throat, reacquainting myself with his body. When I reach his chest, my hand freezes at the feel of something hard and round attached to his nipple. His eyes peel open when my fingers stay there too long and he raises a brow at me. Is he wearing a nipple ring? That's hot. I pluck it to see his reaction. He groans deeply, biting his bottom lip, breathing erratically. He grabs my hips and flips me around, pushing his front to my back. He lowers his head, licks my neck from the base of my throat to the sensitive spot between my ear and neck. I'm nothing more than a bundle of nerves.

Something catches the corner of my eye. Josh's cologne. Shit. Crap. Shit. Josh. I don't want Cole to keep on thinking his brother is the villain in the story.

I spin around and push at his chest with my hands. "We need to talk first."

"I didn't ask you to talk. You said you worshiped me. Show me."

"No." I step back, raising my chin "I'm not going to show you anything."

I whirl around to leave the room and head for the bathroom on the other side of the bedroom. Wrong move. I should have known Cole wouldn't let me walk away. Strong hands grip my hips and I'm flung around and slammed into a body that's hot, hard and unforgiving. He grasps my wrists and yanks them up, shackling them with one hand while his free one moves around to cup one breast, roughly squeezing. My heart triples its pace and I buck my hips to throw him off. I never thought I'd ever feel anything but love for this man, but right now, fear is ripping through my veins as I fight to get away from him. The more I squirm to get him off me, the harder he pushes me to the wall. I can feel his erection, huge and unyielding on the small of my back as he thrusts his pelvis into me. Heat settles between my legs as memories of him inside me bombard my head. I remember the last time he was inside me, he'd taken me roughly, his teeth latching on any places they could find as we hid inside the prison warden's bathroom. When I got home that night, I'd shed down my dress and gone to the shower. I'd nearly come again when I saw the red marks caused by his teeth and rough beard on my breasts and thighs.

I close my eyes, shuddering, letting that memory wash over me. Cole seems to sense my body's reaction. His fingers around my wrist tighten, his mouth latches on my earlobe and sucks it as his other hand leaves my breast and slides down my body, under my dress and cups me between my legs. He moves his finger back and forth before pushing my underwear aside and slipping a digit inside me. I moan just as his hand leaves my wrist and circles my neck, his thumb pressing along the vein. He groans, thrusting his fingers deeper into me while his mouth leaves my ear and he drops his forehead on my shoulder, his breathing ragged.

Does this turn him on? Forcing me to submit to him? And the big question is, why on earth is it turning me on? Why am I fighting this? My pre-prison Cole had been gentle, yet demanding. This post-prison Cole is nowhere near gentle and a whole lot of demanding to the point of ruthless. And God, I love it. Maybe I'm still suffering from the dry spell I've been in for nine years. The last person to ever touch me intimately was Cole. It has always been him. I lift my forehead from the wall and try to turn around, wanting to tell him this. Wanting to do something to calm him the hell down. He spreads my feet slightly apart with one of his. Shoves a hand under my dress. Thrusts another finger inside me and I get even wetter. He sweeps my hair over one shoulder, which has come undone after all of Cole's manhandling, before he sinks his face into my neck and traces his tongue upward, bringing goose bumps to life all over my skin. He pulls his fingers out of me abruptly, swings me around to face him and his mouth is on mine even before I can draw in my breath. I don't fight him. I give in, circling my hands around his neck while raising to the tip of my toes to return the kiss. Now his hands are running all over my body again, touching me as if we've never been apart. They remember every part of me, what made me sigh, what made me writhe in pleasure, and his mouth still remembers how to play with mine. He pulls back, his chest rising and falling in exertion, and looks at me with dark eyes. Gone is the tortured look he was wearing when he arrived here. In its place a lust so furious and dark, it reminds me of the way the sky looks right before the storm descends.

With his gaze still on mine, he hooks his fingers around my panties and yanks them down.

Shit. I'm so confused. Why am I so conflicted? I want what he's about to give me, but I wanted it on my terms, and not his. He taps my ankle for me to lift my leg. I stare down at him.

He sighs. "We both know you will do it sooner or later. I prefer sooner. Lift your legs or I will do it for you."

I want a release badly. After years of loneliness, emptiness, I need him to fill me. Take away the ache and pain, the loss in me. Sometimes feeling lonely is not because you don't have friends, or someone to snuggle with. Sometimes feeling lonely is when you don't have someone who can touch you in places you've never been touched before. Places only the person who owns your soul can reach, fill you, calm you.

"You love it when I talk to you like this. You are breathless and your pussy is dripping for me. And when my fingers were inside you, you clamped down on them so hard I felt it in my dick. This is my last warning. Lift your legs."

I do as I'm told. Cole bunches the white cotton panties in his hands and brings them to his nose. He inhales them deeply before shoving them into his pocket.

Oh. My. God.

That is the most arousing thing I've ever seen. My face is a thousand shades of hot as I gape at this man in front of me.

He grabs my hips again and he slides me down his body. His eyes flicker to the door then back to my lips.

"Go lock the door."

Yes, Sir.

I stumble toward the door and flip the lock shut. When I shift around to face him and gasp to find him standing close, so close the bulge in his pants rubs against my stomach. He grasps my hand and drags me to the bed. Then he turns me around, pressing his hand on the small of my back and urges me to bend forward. Cool air brushes over my backside as my skirt is thrown over my back. The sound of the zipper being lowered zings through the air and my breath hitches in anticipation. I look over my shoulder, making sure he can see my lips.

"Crap. Condoms. And don't you dare tell me you'll pull out."

His ears and cheeks turn pink. "Are you on birth control?"

I nod. I'd started taking the pills right after the birth of Cora and Joce. I love my daughters and will do anything for them. But I wasn't going to be caught unprepared again. Birth control pills became my religion.

"I don't have a girlfriend. I haven't had sex in five years," he confesses unabashedly.

"What? Your—" My gaze moves down to see his crotch, his erection long and hard, pointing toward his stomach, "—Batman hasn't had action all these years?"

His lips twitch. His big hands move down to take himself in his hands, running his palm up and down in firm strokes.

Jesus.

"Are you still calling my cock, Batman?" He shrugs. "I'm clean. I got tested after leaving prison and right after my last relationship. I like to get a handle on things."

As soon as I nod my head, he bounds forward. I'm on my back in two seconds flat and his erection is teasing my opening. He slams into me without warning and I scream, my body overloaded with bliss and slight discomfort. He grabs my arms and slides them above my head, and then drops his forehead to mine. Our hot breaths mingle, our bodies coiled, waiting for release.

Holy shit.

He feels so good. Nine years without him, without his touch and suddenly he is there, blowing my world to pieces. I'm gulping for breath. His hands on my wrists grip me and he groans when he pushes himself inside me excruciatingly slow, hissing when he pulls out. His bottom lip trapped between his teeth. Sweat beads his forehead. Veins popping on his neck. The muscles hidden beneath his shirt bunch up and flex with his every movement. He focuses his gaze on mine. The longer we stare at each other, the more intense he takes me, fast and rough. Unable to hold his hot gaze and the pressure building inside me, I feel my orgasm rushing forward. It builds up and my breath becomes rougher. Cole stops moving, hooks his arm around my waist and lowers us on the bed. Then he buries his head in my neck and I feel his teeth on my shoulder as he commences the kind of torture that's leaving me breathless. I come hard, pressing my mouth on to his arm and scream. He picks up his pace, desperate, jerky thrusts of his hips. His hands tighten around my body as he comes hard.

He pulls out and stands up, before proceeding to tuck himself back in his pants. The dark look on his face is gone, replaced by a look I can only call indifferent. I can't look at that face, especially after the sex we just shared. I roll out of bed as decently as a person who isn't wearing underwear can do and I pull up my dress.

"Give me my underwear."

He shakes his head. "I'm keeping it."

I gape, watching him stalk to the door and unlock it. He stops and glances over his shoulder at me. "I'll see you when I return from Boston."

He leaves.

With my underwear in his pocket and no goodbye.

I guess we both got what we wanted. This wasn't a souls reconnecting kind of sex. I'm not about to complain though, because I needed this.

I turn my head and meet my reflection in the closet mirror. Gone is the pale, stricken look that has been a constant on my face since Josh's condition worsened, replaced by flushed cheeks and bright eyes. A woman who has been thoroughly taken and had a good time while at it.

CHAPTER FORTY-ONE

Cole

I'VE BEEN THINKING ABOUT MOVING BACK HOME. I'M NOT SURE when I came to that decision. Probably between finding out I was the father to the prettiest girls in the world and having my misconception about my feelings for Nor blown to pieces. The electric current between us, the rush of kissing, the euphoria I felt when I was buried balls deep inside her. It's fucking everything. The night when I dropped by her house before flying to Boston, I thought I'd feel relief after fucking her. I was a complete mess.

Fuck.

I was an animal to her. I fucked her, feeding on her pain and her feeding on mine. I'd been so caught up in her. Feeling her sweet pussy wrapped around my cock made me forget about Josh and soothed my confused state of mind. As soon as she opened the door, and I saw her in the same black dress she'd been wearing during the funeral, her eyes red from crying, I wanted to make it better. The second my cock touched her pussy, I knew there was no going back. Two weeks away from her, and my hunger for her skin on mine is enormous. It's a miracle it hasn't swallowed me alive.

I miss who Nor and I used to be. Being away from her and the girls is complete torture. I can't stop thinking about them. I miss them so much, even though the girls and I have been chatting on Skype every night since I left.

All I know is that, there is no fucking way I'm staying away from my girls again, which is why I've been looking for apartments to rent close to Nor's house. Earlier today, I called the realtor who is in charge of the property and made all the arrangements to visit the place when I flew back home. I finally feel confident enough to be a dad without running to Google every time panic sets in. I realized that being a parent doesn't come in a manual. You just have to accept it in your heart and the rest will slide in place.

Also my dad and I have been talking about the possibility of me working in his firm. I've already spoken to my boss at Lawrence and Barnes and explained my situation. We'll be discussing how to go about handing over my pending projects to the other architects in the company during the coming weeks.

Simon is meeting a new client today, so he flew back to New York yesterday to prepare for the meet. Our work here in Boston is almost done and I will be out of this hotel and flying back home soon. Tate will let me know if he needs me for this particular project again.

After hopping out of the shower, I dry my body and quickly rub my hair with a towel and leave the bathroom. I pull on a pair of jogging pants and T-shirt, before settling down on the couch in front of the laptop on the table to Skype with my favorite girls. I contemplate the past few weeks since I went back home up until I left Florida. I was in a shitty mood and I regret how rough I was with Nor. At least my time away has worked wonders on my attitude and put things into perspective. I feel more like a human being and not an animal, ready to piss a circle around her to warn everyone to stay away.

I shake those thoughts away and focus on Cora's little face when she appears on the screen, grinning at me.

God, I make beautiful babies.

Correction.

Nor and I make beautiful babies.

I grin back and wave at her just as Joce scoots up next to her sister and wraps her arms around Cora's neck.

"*Hi Uncle Cole,*" Cora signs.

My fucking heart shatters as it always does every time I hear that name.

Uncle Cole.

I feel as if a goddamn knife has been thrust inside my chest. I flex my hand to tamper down the pain searing through me.

I swallow the lump of pain choking me and settle down for the chat. Joce, who has intentionally been keeping one side of her face away from me, slants her head to the side. I suck my breath and gape at the dark spot, right below her chin. My body tenses at the thought of someone hurting her.

"*What happened to your jaw, Joce*?"

Her body jerks, startled by my question. She thrusts her chin forward, eyes flashing with anger. "*She started it. Abigail. She said mean things about my dad.*"

"*And. . .*"

"*I punched her in the nose. She hit me back. Then I hit her again.*"

What? Prim and proper Joce punched a girl in the face? Cora is most likely to punch someone in the face, but Joce? No. Whatever this Abigail said must have been bad. The worst thing is losing Josh is still a fresh wound that might never heal.

My heart aches for them and my first instinct right now is to get on a plane and deal with this child that hurt my daughter. I sigh and inhale deeply, tampering down that feeling.

I clear my throat. "*Baby, I'm so sorry Abigail said the mean thing about your father. Josh was the best father ever. And also the coolest brother.*" I pause. Let the words sink in. That fierce look on her face softens and she nods. "*Using your fist to solve problems is not the best way to go, though. Did you try to talk to Abigail first?*"

Joce shakes her head, her bottom lip quivering. "*I was so angry, I couldn't stop myself.*"

Damn it. I wish I could comfort her.

I lift my hand and press it on the screen, and wait. She seems to understand my intention. She places her tiny hand parallel to mine, her lips tugging into a smile.

I pull my hand back and sign, *"Do me a favor please?"* She nods. *"If someone ever says something bad about your father, try to ignore them. Remember all the good things about him. The coolest things he ever did."*

She wiggles her freckled nose, so like Nor's. *"You mean like teaching me and Cora how to fish?"* I nod and smile. *"Do you know he would let us win when we played basketball? He'd lift me up so I was high enough to throw the ball inside the hoop."* She grins wide.

Cora bounces on the seat beside Joce. *"Yes. He used to lift me up too. Sometimes I felt as if I could touch the sky when he did that."*

Shit. I'm three seconds from bawling. Josh did well, raising my girls. *"See? Good memories. I'm sure there are a lot more. And you know what? I'd love to hear about everything when I return. Deal?"*

They nod, grinning identical smiles.

Cora's face falls after a few seconds. *"I'm sad he couldn't finish the tree house on the terrace though."*

"What tree house?"

She sighs. *"Papa started to build a playhouse for me and Joce, but he became too sick he couldn't finish it."*

I bite my lip. *"I have an idea. How about you pretty girls and I work on it when I get back?"*

Cora beams and she claps her hands. *"We would love that!"* She turns to look at something that's out of my view then back at me. *"Mama says we need to take a bath then go to bed. I can't wait to see you again, Uncle Cole. Love you."*

"Love you too."

Joce stares at the screen, a little crease forming between her brows. *"Do you think Papa can see us wherever he is? Mama says that Papa is in Heaven and he never sleeps. He's always watching over us. Like an angel."*

I nod and smile softly. *"Yes, he is. Always."*

The troubled look on her face fades. She smiles and she stands up. *"Love you, Uncle Cole."*

"Love you, baby."

"I told you," Cora signs. *"Daddy sent that unicorn in my dream last night."* She laughs.

God, these kids are a riot.

After promising the girls to take them to the carnival next week, they blow kisses at me before dashing from the living room. I shake my head smiling.

I fucking can't wait to see them.

Nor appears on the screen and my breath leaves my chest.

Christ. She's fucking beautiful.

I focus on the stunning woman on the screen, smiling softly.

She tucks a lock of hair behind her ear. Her face is so pale and her eyes are surrounded by dark circles. *"Hi."*

"Hi." My hands flex on the table, missing the feel of her skin. Guilt slams into me as I take in the faint worry lines fanning the corner of her eyes. I should have been more considerate. *"I'm so sorry for being such an asshole. I shouldn't have treated you the way I did the night before I left."*

She drops her gaze quickly, but not before I see her eyes cloud with pain. Hurt. Her chest rises and falls, and she lifts her eyes back to meet mine. She looks exhausted. *"You made me feel like I was nothing, Cole."*

Anger storms through me. Shit. I really messed up. I rub the nape of my neck, grimacing, then I sign, *"You're not nothing. You are so much more. I wish you'd see yourself the way I see you. I'm sorry for making you feel like that, Nor."*

The frown on her face is replaced by a soft smile. *"I know. God, I'm so tired. I just want everything to be okay."*

She should be angry with me, instead she lets it go. I'm a jackass.

"You and the girls. . . Are you okay?"

Her face clouds over and she looks away, blinking fast. Biting her bottom lip she turns to face me and shakes her head. *"I miss him. The girls miss him. They are having a hard time coping. Joce got into a fight today.*"

"*She told me. She'll be okay though. I promise.*" I feel fucking helpless. Knowing they are going through this and I'm too far away to offer them the comfort they need.

"*You were amazing with Joce. I tried to talk to her about what happened but I could not get through to her.*"

Those words send warmth inside my chest. I didn't realize until this moment how much Nor's approval means to me. How much her words lift me up. My throat closes up with emotion.

"*I miss him too.*" I know I can admit this to her without feeling weak because she knows me. She always has. Before Nor moved in next door, she and I had been living in our own little bubbles, our lives so different yet similar, somehow. I never thought I'd ever find someone who'd understand me. Whose heart would beat to the same rhythm as mine. Then I found her and my fucking heart soared.

I miss that connection.

We stare at each other across the screen, across the distance.

"*Are you coming home soon?*" she asks, jolting me from my thoughts. I wasn't expecting that and my first instinct is to raise my fists and beat my chest.

She fucking missed me.

I'm not about to turn into a cocky bastard when we still have a huge gap to fill in on what happened nine years ago.

"*I should be done with everything by tomorrow afternoon. I'll be home the day after.*"

"*Good.*" She purses her lips, rubs her eyes and yawns. "*I need to talk to you.*"

"*I would like that,*" I sign. I remember the conversation I had with Elise two days ago when she texted me, concerned her sister was turning into a scarecrow right in front of her eyes. "*So I hear you've not been eating well.*"

Her lips move and she scowls. Fire lights up her eyes as irritation flashes across her face. She looks so damn cute, all fired up and shit.

My lips twitch, fighting a smile.

I really missed that.

"*Who told you that?*"

I shrug. "*Someone who cares about you.*"

Suddenly, she slumps forward, the fight leaving her body. She doesn't say anything and I won't push her to talk until she's ready. But as much as I want to see that spark of life behind her eyes, I realize for once, I need to give her a break. For now. All bets are off when I get home.

"*I have to go and finish up some details for the meeting tomorrow.*"

"*Right. Okay.*" Her shoulders rise a bit higher and she straightens on the seat, looking relieved. She must have been bracing herself for a fight. She straightens her dress with nervous fingers and signs. "*See you soon.*"

"*See you soon.*"

CHAPTER FORTY-TWO

Cole

By the time Nick picks me up from the airport and parks the car outside Nor's house, my head is in chaos. Different emotions run through me, and I'm not sure where one emotion ends and the next begins.

The car stops vibrating beneath my feet, jolting me from my thoughts. I glance out the window and squint through the dark night to the house illuminated by the street lamp. I'm surprised we're already at Nor's house. I turn to face my brother, who is staring out the window, while tapping his fingers on the wheel. He shifts on his chair to face me.

He lifts his hands from the wheel and signs, "*You have been twitchy the entire ride from the airport. I thought you would hop out of the car as soon as we got here.*"

I massage the back of my neck with my fingers. My brain is a jumbled mess and I can't think straight.

"*If it is any consolation, Nor was just as nervous when I dropped by earlier to babysit the twins while she went grocery shopping.*"

I exhale in relief. At least I'm not the only one feeling this way.

"*She worships the ground you walk on,*" he continues. I cock a brow at him. "*She looks at you like she wants to absorb you inside her.*"

It is the same way she used to look at you when we were kids."

I purse my lips. "*You were just a kid."*

"*I wasn't blind,"* he counters. "*You probably do not want to hear this shit, especially after the past. But I am your brother. Brothers give each other advice, whether it is needed or not. She is a keeper. Do not let her slip away."*

I shake my head and smile. "*Wow, bro. You are like Yoda."*

He laughs. "*It is all about The Force, man."* Playfully, he punches me on my shoulder with his fist. "Absorb what you can from me right now. I might not be feeling so wise in a couple of hours."

I chuckle and turn to look out the window again. Suddenly, I'm not sure if I'm ready to learn the truth. I want to walk inside that house and start fresh. But my conscious won't allow me to.

I need to know.

Taking a deep breath to still my nerves, I look at my brother and say, "I fucking missed them the last two weeks. I feel like I've known Cora and Joce my entire lifetime, even though I missed most of theirs."

He leans over the console, over my lap, flips the lock of my door, then straightens on his seat. "Get your ass out of my car. Sappy conversations are not my super power."

Laughing, I step out of the car.

"*Would you like to hangout over the weekend?"* I sign.

"*I have a deadline to finish a project that's due next week. How about the next one?"* he asks, a hopeful look on his face.

"*Sounds great."* I can't wait to spend more time with my little brother. After requesting him to take my luggage to my parents' house, I walk up the little path flanked with daffodils toward the front door. I stop and turn around, searching in the dark for the little apartment I will be moving into in just a couple of days. I inhale deeply and spin around slowly to face the door again and ring the bell.

Nor

My body tenses as the sound of the doorbell ringing ricochets inside the house. Taking a deep breath, I wipe my clammy hands down my dress and walk to the door.

Cole is here. It's finally time to finish this. He might hate me after all is said and done.

When I open the door, Cole is standing in front of me, with one hand shoved inside the pocket of his pants, while the other rests on the nape of his neck. He raises his eyes from the ground to meet mine. His expression instantly softens, then darkens as his gaze roams down my body, staying a little longer around my boobs and mouth. In that tiny slip of time, my heart beats rapidly in my chest and warmth spreads all over my body, finally settling between my legs. He clears his throat and then tugs the beanie from his head.

God, I've missed that look.

"Hi."

"Hey," I manage to cough out the words and step aside to let him in. After locking the door, I push off it, brush past him and walk into the living room. His body is like a warm shield as he trails behind me. I stop in front of the sofa, clasp my hands together, and face him.

"Where are the girls?" he asks.

"At your parents' house. I thought it would be easier for us to talk without distraction."

He nods, his intense gray eyes never leaving mine.

God, I'm so nervous. "Can I get you anything to drink?"

"No, thank you."

Right. I motion for him to sit down and then I sit on the farthest corner of the couch. Being close to him puts me off kilter and I need all my thoughts in a neat little pile for this conversation.

He drags his fingers through his short hair, glances at the couch to the side and lowers his tall frame on it before he stares up at me expectantly.

I clear my throat and bite the inside of my cheek. "I need you to understand something first. Whatever I did nine years ago, I did it to protect you. I didn't set out to hurt you."

He leans forward, matching my pose but doesn't say anything. Damn it. I don't know what he's thinking right now.

I have no idea where to start, so when I open my mouth words just flow out. "You asked me not to visit you in prison. I couldn't do that. I had to look for a way to see you. I went back to Mr. Taylor—the warden at the prison—and asked if there was a way he could help me. He informed that it was against the rules and he didn't promise me anything. But I held hope and prayed that he would find a way. Somehow. During those months, Mr. Taylor and Grandma became very close. He was like a son to her. I think he filled the void in her that my dad couldn't. During that time, Mr. Taylor's mom passed away and he stopped visiting Grandma for a while. The only thing that kept me going was your letters, taking care of my sisters and my mom, and school. The college work load was getting too much and the therapy sessions were more intense. I wanted to be better before your release from prison.

"I didn't hear from Mr. Taylor until a couple months before your release. I was helping Grandma finish up an urgent delivery one Saturday afternoon when he walked into the shop. After chatting for a while he asked me to be in his office on Monday at ten o'clock in the morning. That was two months before your release, but I didn't care. The opportunity to see you was there, right in front of me. Two months to see you again was a long time."

I pull up my legs on the couch, wrap my arm around my knees and rest my chin on top of them, angling my face so Cole can see my mouth. And then I start to tell him how our lives drastically changed nine years ago.

PART FOUR

PAST

CHAPTER FORTY-THREE

Nor

By Monday morning, though, I'm a complete nervous wreck. I'm excited and anxious to see Cole. He will probably be angry when he sees me. How could he ask me the impossible, to stay away from him? I can understand he didn't want me to see him behind bars, all beaten up by the thugs sent by my father. I couldn't let him push me away and I was determined to do what I could to see him. My heart was his heart and nothing was going to change that.

I make sure my clothing complies with the dress code—not too fitting or provocative. I'm wearing a simple knee-length, black dress with sleeves that stop slightly above my elbows. I finish the look with my blue Keds with little light blue and yellow hearts on them. Satisfied, I leave the house. After texting Megs to let her know that I'm on the way to visit Cole, I get inside the Old Station Wagon and drive away.

I arrive at the correctional facility with just about thirty minutes to spare. After reporting to the reception area and letting them know I have an appointment with the Warden, one of the guards asks me to follow him down a hallway and to the north side where the offices are located. He deposits me in front of a receptionist with white hair, blue eyes, and a grandmotherly smile. But I know that behind that smile, there's a tough woman. You can't work in a place like this without being some sort of ninja or something.

I sit on the offered chair. Nervousness sets in and my fingers fiddle with the edge of my skirt as I wait. How does Cole look now? I haven't seen him in one year and six months. He never says much in his letters, most likely to avoid worrying me. I still can't forget the night I wept for him after Megs told me about his injuries.

My heart skips several beats. Is my father still paying the inmates to hurt him? What if they hurt him badly? Maggie would have told me if that were the case. Or maybe not. I'm certain Cole would have asked her not to tell me anything.

I straighten in my chair when the warden steps out of his office, scowling.

He flicks his wrist to look at his watch, and then faces his secretary. "Ask the guards on Block C to bring inmate C two hundred and eighty to my office," he barks the order to his secretary, and as soon as he sees me his face softens. After exchanging pleasantries, he asks me to follow him into his office. He sits on the leather chair behind his desk, props his elbows on the wood surface and steeples his fingers.

"You understand this is against procedure," he repeats the same warning he told me months ago, I nod.

About twenty minutes later, someone knocks on the door. A guy with dark hair, even darker eyes and rugged features pushes the door in and steps in. I'm hypnotized, staring at the door, waiting to see Cole. The second he comes in, I exhale long and my pulse picks up. At first, he doesn't notice me and then his eyes wander lazily around the room until they land on me. He gapes, his eyes widening. His shocked gaze darts between Mr. Taylor and me.

"*Nor? What are you doing here?*" he signs, taking a step forward, his eyebrows scrunched up in a worried frown.

"Twenty minutes, Holloway," Mr. Taylor says, shooting a stern look at Cole, then to me. "Don't make me regret this."

Cole and I nod.

The warden stands up from his chair and leaves the room. I feel the tension in the room pick up as Cole's gaze tracks down my body with deliberate strokes, and by the time his smoldering eyes meet mine, my breath is coming out fast.

"*You never follow orders, do you*?" he signs, prowling closer and I have to stand up fast. God, he looks bigger. He still has the buzz cut. Somehow being in here has given him a rougher edge, which makes him look a little dangerous, especially when he is scowling like that.

I drop my purse on the chair as he edges closer. "You left me no choice."

He takes one huge furious step and suddenly I'm scrambling backward and my hands are flailing around, searching for purchase.

"*You're scaring me, Cole.*"

His expression softens at my admission, but not entirely. He is still wearing that dangerous look and his body is coiled tight, ready to snap at any second.

Suddenly, his hands shoot out and grip my hips. He pushes me back, and my back slams into a wall behind me. I'm suddenly excited and panicked at the same time.

"Cole," I say, my voice shaking.

His gaze is stuck on my mouth. He shakes his head once and that is all I get before his lips come crashing down on mine. His hands slide down until he reaches my thighs and yanks them up, settling them around his lean hips. My dress rides up as he settles his hard body between my legs and he starts to thrust his pelvis forward. I shake my head and forcefully pull back.

"We can't do this here. The warden will come back any second now. "

"You shouldn't have come here, Nor," he says, his voice hoarse as if he hasn't used it for long. "As soon as I saw you sitting here, I wanted to do this. Kiss you. I cannot think of anything I would rather do right now, so if you want to stop me, do it now. Otherwise shut up and let me kiss you. Your mouth is my weakness and I want to feast on it. Let me kiss you, Snowflake. Please."

God.

I couldn't deny him what he wants even if I tried. His words, his hard body, everything about him makes me feel desired. He makes me want to climb inside his skin so I can feel him.

He lifts a brow in question, waiting, but my mind is still trying to come to terms with this new Cole. He is no longer the boy who walked into this institution months ago. He's somehow hardened, having become even more demanding than he was. It's different.

I like different.

"Am I scaring you, Nor?" he smirks and I see my Cole in there. The sweet, sexy boy I fell in love with. The boy I'm still helplessly in love with.

I shake my head and as if that is his answer, his mouth descends on mine, one hand coming to my neck and framing it while caressing the vein pumping blood there. I groan, and I feel the thumb press slightly and his kiss becomes intense. Oh my God, talk about intense. He's kissing me hungrily and I'm returning it. He yanks his head up and looks around with wild, dark eyes. I feel his chest inflate at the same time he grabs my bottom and whirls me around. I have no idea where he is going until I realize we are in a small room.

The bathroom.

"What are you doing Cole?" I squeak, squirming to get down. "We can't do this here."

"Yes we *can*. We just have less than thirteen minutes. Do you want to waste that time arguing? Because either way, I'm burying myself inside you. I haven't had you in a long time. I cannot. . .I need something to keep me going, Nor. I need my fix."

My heart races and my heart beats louder and louder in my chest until I'm breathless with want and need and anticipation. "I didn't bring any condoms with me. If I knew this was going to happen, I'd have—"

"I'll pull out. I promise. I just want to feel you, Snowflake. Just want to show you how much I have missed you. How much my cock misses your warm heat."

His body is hot, literally vibrating with need, sweat is beaded on his forehead. His erection pressing against my stomach and suddenly the urge to feel him inside me is strong. I remember how he felt in me. I've never been a risk taker, but now. . .

God, I want to do this. With him. It's wrong, doing it in the Warden's office. He has been so kind to me. But I want it bad. I want to swim in the sea of its wrongness if it means having Cole inside me. I've missed him so much.

I hear the sound of a door open and close on the other side of the bathroom's door, and I freeze.

"What?" Cole asks, picking up on my body language.

"Someone is out there." His eyes cloud with fury and he puts me down. He stalks to the door, opens it and ducks his head to look, then pulls back seconds later and flips the lock. He grabs my hand and yanks me flush to his hot, hard body while walking us backward to the wall. His large, calloused hands are hungry, desperate as they slide under my dress and circle my hips. His fingers press on my skin as if he's trying to leave a mark there before gentling.

""I really love dresses. So accessible," he says as he hooks his fingers around my panties, pulls them down, bunches them and shoves them in his pocket. "I'll need to keep these."

Oh, God.

I shove my hand inside his pocket but he clasps his fingers around my wrist. "I can't walk out of here without underwear."

"I *dare* you." The words bounce off the walls in the tiny room.

I groan. Crap. He has no idea how loud he is. We might be discovered any second. I pull back and meet his dark gaze and whisper, although it's more for my benefit than his. "So I'm supposed to walk out of here commando?"

"Yes." He grins while his fingers work on the zipper on my dress. He tugs the bodice front down and bows his head and sinks his face between my breasts. He inhales deeply and groans, that sound sending shivers all over my body. He lifts his head to look at me.

"I fucking love your tits. You smell like my best decision ever. I missed touching you so much." His fingertips slide across my lower stomach. My heart stops beating when his palms skim the raised scars along my thigh.

Shit. With my brain overloaded with the feelings Cole's invoking in me, I completely forgot about the new scars there.

I try to pull back while forcing my dress down, but Cole's grip around me tightens. Without shifting his gaze from mine, he bunches the dress in his hands and shoves it up. I break the eye contact by shutting my eyes and tilting my head to the side, not ready to see his reaction. After what feels like a lifetime, suspended in silence, I feel his fingers on my chin tugging my head to face him.

"Open your eyes, Nor."

I shake my head and wiggle my body free. I stop as goose bumps begin trailing up my arms and down my neck as he nips at my bottom lip and he pushes his body against mine, trapping me.

"Open your eyes," he says again.

Taking a deep breath, I do as I'm told. I expect to see disappointment, anger. Hell, even revulsion. But what I see knocks the breath out of me. He swallows violently and drops his hands from my body. The loss is immediate.

"*Why, baby?*" he signs between the space separating our bodies.

I shake my head and drop it on his shoulder. Oh man. How will I make him understand the numbness I felt, the emptiness that had taken over me both physically and emotionally without sounding like a broken record?

"I'm not judging you," he says. My eyelids flutter open. "I'll never judge you. I told you before and I'll say it again. Your scars don't scare me. You once asked me, who would love a girl with scars. I told you I do and always will for as long as you'll have me. It would take a monumental effort to get rid of me." He pauses and bites his bottom lip as he studies me with dark, hooded eyes. "I'll say this over and over again until every word is imprinted in your soul. Your scars don't make me love you less. I fucking love you. What I feel for you is not just an emotion, Snowflake. It's alive and breathing. Knowing I'll see you when this is all over is the only thing that keeps me going. Looking at you is like looking into a mirror."

He finishes this declaration in a rather loud voice, but I'm beyond caring if we'll be heard at this point. Tears roll down my cheeks at the same time I'm smiling hard, and pulling his tousled head down towards my mouth.

"I love you with every broken, messy piece of me."

"Good. Now give me your mouth, Snowflake." He stands still, waiting for me to bridge the small space between us. I lean forward and touch my lips with his. His restraint explodes and suddenly his fingers are wrapping around the nape of my neck, his thumb pressing and stroking my windpipe, absorbing my moans and groans into his skin.

He stumbles back, pulling me with him. His free hand shoves between us and fumbles with his pants. He pushes them down in hurried tugs. He switches our positions without breaking stride, flips the toilet seat down and plops on it. He grips my hips with both hands and parts my legs with one of his, then tugs me forward to straddle him.

"Come on, Baby. Sit on my cock"

I do, biting back a groan as I feel him stretch me. He shudders as his hold on my waist tightens.

"God, I've missed this. You feel so good."

He pounds into me desperately and all I can think about is that the warden trusted me to just talk. . .or maybe not. Why would he leave us alone?

Cole pinches my nipple while his mouth sucks on the other one. My orgasm hits me hard and I'm falling, clutching on to Cole as he pounds into me. His body coiled tight. I can feel his release coming and I can feel a second one rising from me. His arms band around me as he buries his face into my chest and his body shakes and I'm too far gone to remember he was supposed to pull out.

Crap.

Oh God.

No.

I stand up on shaking legs, swing a leg over his hips and start to straighten my dress.

After putting ourselves to rights, we exit the bathroom. Footsteps shuffle on the other side of the door.

"*Someone is coming,*" I sign quickly. The door opens before he can reply. Mr. Taylor waddles in, his gaze darts between Cole, who has somehow managed to get to the other side of the room, and me. His hands are shoved inside his pocket and his face unreadable.

"Everything okay?" My Taylor asks me, just as the same guard who brought Cole strides in, heading for him.

I nod, but my eyes are on my boyfriend. We don't have time to say goodbye properly. The guard jerks his chin toward the door. Cole winks at me and mouths 'I love you'.

"*See you soon,*" I sign. "*I love you with everything I am.*"

I don't tell him how worried I am.

He doesn't mention it either.

I pray under my breath that everything will be okay.

CHAPTER FORTY-FOUR

Nor

THANKSGIVING WEEKEND ARRIVES. MY PERIOD SHOULD HAVE BEGUN two days ago, but it didn't. I decided to wait a few days before I took the next step.

Now, dread is filling every part of me as I stare at the white stick in my hand. The third pregnancy test I have done in the past thirty minutes. My pulse is racing madly. I take several deep breaths to keep the panic at bay. I need to think.

I grab my phone from the night stand and call Megs, but then I realize that she and Simon made plans to go camping. There is a chance she won't be able to get to my calls until they drive back to Willow Hill.

I walk to the window, fighting the urge to cry and stare outside. What the hell am I going to do? God, what a mess.

I wipe my eyes with the back of my hand. Cole will be here in a few weeks. I'm twenty-years old, I don't have a job. I'm a recovering cutter and I'm not even sure if my mind is in the right place right now. My mom is practically a zombie. My sisters still need me.

Oh God.

I drop my head in my hands and whisper over and over that I'm strong. I can handle this.

The sound of a car pulling to a stop outside my window startles me and I lift my head. I watch as Josh leaves his car with a girl trailing behind him, giggling. They head toward the front door, open it and disappear inside the house.

I stand there, my eyes stuck on that door. I need to talk to someone before I go mad. I leave my room and head down the stairs.

Two minutes later, I'm standing in front of Cole's house, ringing the bell.

"Can I talk to you?" I ask as soon as Josh answers the door. Laughter and voices fill the air from somewhere behind Josh and my heart aches at those sounds. I wish my family was as happy as Josh's. You'd think that Thanksgiving would brighten things up in my house.

Josh eyes me for a few seconds, his usual wide, cheery smile fading. "You okay?"

Unable to hold his gaze, I drop mine to the ground and shake my head. "Just, please. . ." My voice shakes and I have to stop talking. I need to be strong to talk to Josh. I brace myself for his reaction after I deliver the news.

Clearing my throat, I raise my head and face him again.

He darts a look over his shoulder, then steps onto the porch, closing the door behind him. Walking ahead of me, he heads toward the swing on the porch but stops when he notices I'm not following him.

"Not good?" he asks, jerking his head to the swing. When I shake my head, he retraces his steps back to where I'm standing, hugging my waist.

"Let's go for a walk." My voice is strong, despite the fear devastating every trace of who I am. But that fear fuels my decision.

I straighten and lead the way down the path and out of the gate. I see him shove his hands in his pants from the corner of my eye, see him spare a glance my way.

When we reach the fenced playground that Elon loves, I bypass the swings in favor of the bench. I'm not feeling queasy anymore. The ginger ale seems to help the nausea.

Josh sits next to me, stretches his long legs and tucks his hands inside the pockets of his hoodie. He doesn't say anything, just sits there and seems to wait for me.

I take deep, long breaths, willing my heart to calm down. Wipe my palms down my pants and lean back on the bench.

"I'm pregnant."

Silence. It stretches for long seconds.

Did he hear what I said?

I shift on the bench and directly face him. "I'm pregnant, Josh. You are the first person I've told."

He stares at me incredulously. "How? Are you—Do you have another boyfriend? Is that why you're coming to tell me this?"

I shake my head quickly. "No! No, no. Josh. It's Cole's baby."

He snorts. "Cole is in prison. Unless his dick somehow got to your—"

"Ugh, Josh. Stop. Please stop." I take a deep breath and tell him about my meeting with his brother.

He pulls his hands from his pockets, leans forward and props his elbows on his thighs. He looks at me, his eyebrows dipping low. "Does my brother know?" he asks quietly.

My eyes prickle with tears. Tears I've tried hard not to let fall. "No."

He sighs. "Wow."

We stay silent for a few seconds.

When he turns to look at me again, his blue eyes are dull, his mouth pulled down in a frown. He clears his throat, and his face turns neutral before he stands from the bench and begins to pace.

"Jesus. Nor. Jesus fucking Christ," he mutters to himself, his fingers interlocked on the nape of his neck. He stops suddenly and swings around to face me. "Your father, your dad—" he doesn't need to finish that sentence. We both know what my father will do. But worse, I know what my father is capable of doing. He hates Cole with a passion unrivaled by anything I've ever seen before.

"I know," I whisper. "I know." I bite my lip, gathering courage to say what I've been planning since I heard my father making plans to make Cole's life harder.

Josh sits next to me, slides his arm across my shoulder and pulls me into him. He wraps the other arm around me and I fall into him, taking in a long trembling breath. He kisses my hair, and even though his kisses don't come close to the comfort Cole's offer me, I soak it up. I need the comfort he is offering me. I soak it up before I bring his world crashing down in confusion.

It's the only way to save Cole.

"He's coming home soon." I hear a smile in his voice. "Just a few more weeks. He will be fucking happy. I know he will." He ducks his head to meet my eyes. "I don't see you hopping up and down with joy, soon to be momma. What's wrong, Nor?" He ducks his head to look at me closely. "Shit, Nor? What's wrong? Don't you want this? I know that you and Cole are still young. But, it's already happened. I'm not going to criticize you or my brother."

"If my dad knows, he won't let Cole walk out of prison alive. I'm stuck. I've thought of ways to do this. I've thought about leaving town, but I can't abandon my sisters and mother in the hands of my father." The tears I've been holding back finally fall free. His arms tighten around me, and he begins to run his hands down my back in soothing circular motions.

He kisses my forehead. "Shh. It's going to be all right. I swear to you, Nor. I won't let anything happen to you or Cole. I promise you, Nor. You hear me?"

His words only serve to make my tears fall faster. He continues to hold me until the tears stop falling. Until I feel all that's leaving my chest are shallow breaths.

I pull back, sit up and wipe my face with the back of my hands.

"Crap! Look what I did to your shirt. I'm sorry I hit you with that information. I didn't know where else to go or who else to tell. Megs left for Georgia. I'm scared to tell my grandmother because I can't bear to see the disappointment in her eyes. I wanted someone who knows me and Cole. I want everything to work out. I want my father to stop hating Cole. I can't understand how someone can hate another person without reason. I want to protect my sisters and mother from my father's influence and fury. Does that make me selfish?"

"Nor, no. No it doesn't. You care too much about everyone to be selfish."

He takes my hand, links his fingers with mine and stares at my wrist. He turns it over twice, his face soft as he studies the cuts on my skin.

We sit in the park until night chases daylight and all that's surrounding us is the dark night. The wide expanse of a sky that normally soothes me, now makes me feel as though I'm being swallowed by it and there is no way out. But there has to be a way out. There just has to. I need to clear my head and think.

"I need to go home and check on everyone. Thank you for listening to me. I'm not going to let him hurt Cole."

When I get home, Josh walks me to the door. My body stiffens as my father's voice comes crashing through the heavy door from somewhere inside the house. He shouts a question and I hear Elon answer in a small voice. Elise yells to him, asking him to leave her alone. Somewhere in there is my mother, most likely curled up in her chair with her hands covering her ears.

My heart is beating hard in my chest when I burst through the door. I round the corner, stop and blink as my eyes readjust to the light. Elon is curled up on the couch and Elise is on her knees in front of our sister in a protective stance. My father is standing next to the fireplace, glaring at my sisters. From somewhere inside the house, I hear my mother's keening, getting louder with every passing second.

"What's happening?" I ask, my heart thumping hard in my chest.

My father, having not heard me come in swings his enraged eyes at me, his face flushed in anger. He drops the hand from the wall, straightens and advances toward me. Suddenly I feel a warm body behind mine. A quick look over my shoulder alerts me that Josh followed me inside the house.

I focus on my father as he raises his hand. He unfolds his fist, shoving his palm to my face. My heart stops beating as my gaze drops to the object in his hand.

Bile rises up my throat.

"Do you know anything about this?" he asks, his eyes narrowed as he scrutinizes my face.

The white object mocks me from his large palm. The pink line laughing at me. I threw it outside with the trash. How the hell did he find it?

I can't speak. Every part of me is locked in place. But I have to say something.

He glares at my sisters as if that look will make them spill. But they are innocent. No one knows but me.

I straighten my back, ready to face him.

"Yes, I do."

He sucks a deep breath, his face flushing more.

"What did you say?"

I feel Josh's hand grasp my elbow, squeezing it gently, whether to lend me some of his strength or encourage me, I have no idea. All I know is that, hell just broke loose.

"I'm pregnant." I say, the taste of those words which at first was foreign now sounds familiar. Comfortable. My body and mind have accepted the situation.

He stalks forward, bringing his angry face into my space. Eliminating any confidence I'd felt before.

"You stupid girl, sleeping around and getting knocked up. Who is the father? That abomination of a man in prison?"

Suddenly, rage unlike any other I've ever felt fills me. I stand up straighter and lift my chin up in defiance.

"His name is Cole," I shout. "He is perfect. I love him with everything I am and he loves me. You will never tear us apart." My chest is heaving with furious breaths and tears burn my eyes. "I don't know what I did to deserve a father like you. Your narrow-mindedness astounds me. Most times I wish you'd just die and rid the world of your filth. You break everything that stands in your path. You're a waste of oxygen and if God could grant me a wish right now, I'd ask him to throw you in hell. I hate you with every part of me. If I could rip out those parts of you that are in me, I'd have done it the first time I realized you were nothing to me but a sperm donor."

My cheeks burn with hot tears and my throat feels like it's on fire.

Dad's mouth has fallen open and his eyes are wide in shock.

I should have set him straight a long time ago. Maybe I'd have earned some respect from him.

Air whooshes past me at the same time my body is pushed aside without warning, jolting me out of my fury. I look around, my head spinning. Josh is standing in front of me with his arms raised toward my father, whose fist is suspended in the air.

The shock of what almost happened slams into me. I shudder, clutching a hand to my chest.

"It's. . .it's mine." Josh stammers and clears his throat. "It's my baby." His words are louder this time and confident.

I gasp, completely stunned by Josh's confession.

What?

I swing around to face Josh, shaking my head, pleading with him not to put himself in my father's war path.

This is my battle.

"Josh, no," I whisper, still shaking my head. "You can't do this. Just no."

"Anything," he murmurs under his breath, his gaze now fully focusing on me. "Anything for you and my brother. We'll sort this out later." The fear that was present seconds before vanishes, replaced by reassurance and confidence and love. The kind of love that has always been lurking and he couldn't hide it from me. The kind of love I haven't been able to reciprocate.

I can't let him do this. I change my focus to my dad. His face is cloaked in disbelief and rage and he's wearing murder like a second skin.

"Father—"

"Shut the hell up!" He shouts at me, his eyes filled with a kind of madness I've never seen before. Those brown eyes shift above my shoulder, narrowing on Josh, whose grip on my arm is right now cutting off any blood circulation. "Are you responsible for this?"

I feel Josh breathe as he exhales slowly behind me and coughs once. "Yes, sir."

Stupid, utterly stupid but brave boy.

I open my mouth to negate Josh's claim, but he slides a hand around my waist pulling me to him and kissing my hair. My father watches us with narrowed eyes.

"Please don't, Nor," his voice trembles in my ear. "Don't say anything. He's going to kill my brother if he learns the truth. Save my brother. Please."

I feel wetness on the side of my cheek. I turn and meet his gaze and my heart stalls. The pulse pounding in my ear halts and I hold my breath as I see the magnitude of his fears splayed across his face. The impact of his words hit me and everything inside me jump-starts. I'm breathing hard now, fighting for breath.

Save Cole. Save Cole. Save Cole.

I give him a subtle nod. I know what he means.

My father stands up, eyes both me and Josh, turning those wild eyes on my sisters then back in our direction.

He jabs a finger in our general direction. "You. In my study."

I take a step forward, but his glare freezes me on the spot. He sneers, eyes me up and down and shakes his head. "Not you. You." He points at Josh.

I feel Josh's fingers shake, getting clammy as he slides his arm from my waist. He follows my dad to his office without a backward glance.

I rush in the direction they disappeared to, and begin pacing in the small hallway. My heart is beating hard and I can hardly get enough air in my lungs.

Shit, shit, shit.

My feet give way. The blackness hovering on the edges, swoops in. I can't fight it anymore.

I'm going down. My head hits a hard surface and everything goes blank.

CHAPTER FORTY-FIVE

Nor

MY EYES FINALLY OPEN SLOWLY. I BLINK FAST TO ADJUST MY SIGHT and narrow in on Josh, sitting next to my form lying on the bed. He leans forward, his eyebrows furrowed in worry and whispers, "Nor? Can you hear me?"

I try to sit up but a sharp pain on the left side of my head halts my progress, forcing me to fall back on the bed as I feel his fingers twine with mine, squeezing gently.

"You hit your head pretty hard. Just lie down for a few minutes, okay?" He pushes my shoulder down when I try to sit up again. "Jesus, you scared the shit out of me. Are you okay?"

I close my eyes, trying to remember what happened and why Josh is in my room. I swing my legs out of the bed as everything comes rushing back, causing his hands to drop away from mine. Clutching my stomach, I double over, tittering on the edge of the bed.

"Oh God, he knows. What did he say? You were in his office. What did you two talk about?"

He leans forward, bracing his elbows on his knees and drops his head into his hands and mutters, "Fuck!" under his breath.

"What?" My arms fall from my waist and I grab his forearms. "Josh, what does that mean? What happened in there?"

He raises his head and drags shaking fingers through his hair. His eyes meet mine and I feel my world narrow to this moment. I've never seen anyone appear so deeply broken like Josh does at this moment.

"Josh?" I call his name again to get his attention.

He squares his jaw. "He wants us to. . .your father wants us to get married as soon as possible."

"NO! We can't. Shit. This isn't how it's supposed to be," I whisper.

He sucks in a deep breath. His nostrils flare and he clenches his fists on his lap, opens his mouth and closes it again. When he finally speaks, his voice shakes, whether it's from anger or the aftermath of meeting with my father, I can't tell.

"How was it supposed to be Nor, huh? Did you think your father would be okay with this? Did you think he'd fall at my brother's feet and thank him for getting you pregnant?"

Every single word is like a knife to my stomach, jabbing and jabbing until I can't breathe.

I slide off the bed and stagger forward. Josh's hand shoots forward to catch me, then he drops it after making sure I'm okay. I walk to the window overlooking the street and stare out. Mrs. Robins is on her knees, working on her garden. Little Katherine wobbles her way to her mother's side and drops on her little knees. I feel my lips tip up as I imagine my child—Cole's and my child—tottering around the lawn. Cole and I sitting on the porch steps or on the swing. But that dream is about to be ripped from under my feet.

"I'm sorry," I whisper. "I'm so sorry I involved you in this. I shouldn't have come to you. I wasn't prepared for my father to find out so soon." I leave the window and return to stand in front of Josh. "Thank you for standing up for me before my father. Thank you for being my friend. There has to be another way. I will sort this out."

He closes the distance separating us and ducks his head to meet my eyes. "I can't do that even if I wanted to."

My body stiffens. "You can't seriously be thinking of doing what he told you to do. I wouldn't let you do that. This is mine and Cole's baby. This is my problem." I shake my head and touch his clean-shaven jaw. "You shouldn't have told him the baby is yours. Look. I will talk to my dad."

He sighs, digs his hands into his hair and tugs it back. "Sweetheart, you know your father. You know what he is capable of. He's the devil. You don't want to cross him. Not this way." He tips up my chin so our eyes are locked. His are dull, filled with regret. "He told me if I don't convince you to do this, he will take everything away from you. Your sisters and mother. You crossed him the moment you chose Cole over him."

He brushes his fingers on both of my cheeks, making me realize I'm crying.

"Between your father hurting you and my brother, two of the people I love the most, and walking away, I choose you and Cole, Nor."

Tucking my head into his chest, I fist his shirt in my hands as tears fall down my face.

There has to be a way to solve this, work it out so Josh doesn't end up bound to me.

It's Cole. It has always been him. He promised me forever. I promised him forever and a day because if he were to leave this world before me, I'd be lost. How would I survive?

When the tears have dried and all that is left is emptiness in my chest and my thoughts are the only thing roaming my mind, I pull back from him and push my chin forward.

Once Josh leaves, I climb the stairs on weary feet and head for my room, numbness cloaking my body. I change directions and shuffle down the hallway toward the bathroom.

"Eleanor." My dad's voice freezes me on the spot. Wiping the tears from my cheeks with my palm, I shift around to face the man I've come to hate with every single bone in my body. Bile rises up my throat at the mere sight of him.

I raise my chin and stare at him with what I hope is a brave look on my face. I won't allow him to see how defeated I feel.

"One more thing." His voice is cold, brimming with loathing. "You will not visit that boy in prison. You will not tell him about the child." My eyes widen and my bravery facade disintegrates a little. "Yes, I know. Do you think I'm stupid to not realize that Josh never had a chance with you? I know the warden arranged a meeting with you and Cole in his office. Your conversation with his brother confirms that child is Cole's. Defy me and you won't like the consequences."

Shock washes over me. "Please, stop. Just stop," I whisper, terrified by his words. I've seen the horrors my dad unleashes when he's defied or angry. I can't even begin to imagine what he will do to Cole.

He sneers. "You should have listened to me when I asked you to stay away from that boy."

I should have, but I couldn't. The more determined he was to keep Cole and me apart, the harder we fought to be together.

I've never understood the mechanical workings of my father's troubled brain or his actions. But one thing is for sure; I'll heed his warning.

I thought I'd found my mental balance after the last few months of therapy, but I'm not sure about that anymore. I feel it slipping away. I'm drowning in guilt, praying for a miracle. My mornings are full of morning sickness and my nights are spent crying myself to sleep. I can't handle school, so I dropped out, I don't think I'll be going back after Christmas break. I'm breaking. I don't want to. The doctor said I have to take care of myself or I might lose the babies.

Yes. Babies. She confirmed that I was carrying twins. I'm caught between wanting these babies so much that my entire being aches with need, and fear because I'm too young to be a mom. I'm also terrified of bringing them into a world where my dad exists.

And then there's Cole. He still doesn't know I'm carrying his children. Any chance of telling him was destroyed after Josh's last visit to the prison. When he returned home, he told me that Cole had a broken nose and a sprained ankle. My monster of a father confirmed it later that evening with a smirk. His message was loud and clear.

Josh and I decided to talk to his parents about our current situation right after my dad's ultimatum. His father had words with my father, but it didn't go well. We didn't even have any proof that my father is responsible for the kind of brutality Cole has endured while in prison. And after Josh's visit, the decision for us to get married was cemented. My father had won in that aspect. Cole was coming home soon. Getting married to fool my father was the only way to go until my boyfriend was safe at home. Josh and I planned to annul the marriage on the grounds of marriage under duress.

We had it all planned. What we didn't expect is that, our plan would be blown to pieces. My father's plan for revenge was in full momentum as he set the date for the wedding, coinciding it with Cole's release from prison. It was time for the woman who had rejected him, and the boy my dad blames for the said rejection to pay.

We just had to make sure we got to Cole in time before he got the news.

CHAPTER FORTY-SIX

Nor

When I was a little girl, I used to dream of finding a man who would sweep me off my feet and take me away from my sucky life. Far, far away from my father. He'd drop on one knee and ask me to marry him, and then we'd get married in a big church. I'd wear the most beautiful white gown with a train that goes on for miles.

That illusion shattered when I was a teen and I realized that no one could love a girl full of scars, both inside and out, and a messed up mind. A mind that terrifies her sometimes. I lived that dream by watching romantic comedies while eating ice cream and popcorn.

Then I met Cole, and that part of me that believed in fairy tales, unicorns and fairy dust stirred to life. He saw *me*. He looked past my scars and saw the frightened girl I was. He embraced me. Desired me and he never attempted to hide his feelings from me. He loved me so hard, so desperately, so fiercely I literally burned bright from inside out with his love. And I loved him and still love him so violently my heart twirls and spins and does all these dangerous things that would be harmful under different circumstances. Our love is the kind of love that would make Romeo and Juliet stand up and applaud. The kind you feel in your bones. Every time I closed my eyes, I saw Cole and me, walking down the aisle, smiling and looking into each other's eyes.

I never expected my life to turn out this way.

I'm standing in front of a mirror in an empty room at St. Christopher's Church, the place that used to bring me peace, is now wreaking havoc in me. I'm wearing a simple white dress, holding a bouquet of roses, getting ready to walk down the aisle toward the wrong brother. I close my eyes and see my mother like I saw her last night, smiling sadly at me. She's lying in bed, wasting away in a mess of abandoned dreams, rejected love and heartbreak. She murmurs that I'm doing the right thing to save the boy I love. I want her to hold me so badly. To comfort me. But she can barely lift her head Her body is riddled with antipsychotics and I keep wondering if she'll ever be the same woman who brought me in to this world; vibrant, caring and full of laughter. I swear to myself that after this is over, I'll get her the help she needs.

I open my eyes and find my best friend's brown eyes staring back at me worriedly. Pain lurks in them.

"I'm so, so sorry, Megs," I tell her, guilt writhing inside me. She and Simon aren't talking at the moment. Simon is currently doing his internship in Miami, so he has been in the dark about what is happening. He's very loyal to Cole and I knew he'd tell him about me being pregnant. Simon suspects something is wrong and she refuses to tell him.

She shrugs. "It's not my place to tell Simon what is happening. If Cole has to hear it from someone, it has to be you and not my boyfriend."

I love this girl. I adore her for her relentless loyalty to me, even though it led to her breaking up with the love of her life.

She cups my hands in hers, squeezing them tightly. "I know you're sorry, honey. I don't regret my decision for even a second. Everything will work out, okay? Let's get this wedding over with. Cole's parents are on the way to pick him up. I'm sure he will understand the situation here. You and Josh didn't have a choice. Both of you are pawns in a game that has no rules."

Megs hugs me tight before she pulls away and looks at me with tears in her eyes. "You look beautiful."

"Thank you. Thank you for being my corner stone," I say, tears running down my face.

The door opens and Elise and Elon step inside the room. They look stunning in matching lavender dresses, but the look on their faces dulls the beauty. My father made sure his show was spectacular and went all the way.

"It's time, sis," Elise says, offering me a comforting smile. "Everyone is waiting."

I nod and force a smile. "Let's do this." I walk toward the door and stop to hug my siblings. "I love you both so much."

"We love you too," they say in unison.

"Let's show The Monster that he hasn't won in any way," Elise says, tugging the strap of my dress back over my shoulder.

Minutes later, I'm standing at the back of the church, watching through the veil that covers my face as my sisters walk down the aisle. Soon, the Wedding March song fills the air. My father appears at my side. I feel his hand on my elbow and I jerk mine away.

"Don't touch me," I snarl under my breath.

His hand falls away. We start to walk toward Josh, who is standing stoically before the pew. His eyes hooded in the pain caused by what he has to do. Glancing to my side, I see a few people, some wearing police uniforms. They stare at me as I pass and I wonder if they know the kind of man they work with. The man they respect. The Monster among them.

My gaze shifts to the other side of the aisle and I meet Grandma's eyes. She dabs her eyes with a handkerchief using fingers ridden with arthritis. She shakes her head as if she can't believe what is happening. I pull my gaze from her and focus on the man standing a few feet away. Josh tugs at his tie and then coughs into his hand. His lips quirk to the sides even though that smile doesn't reach his eyes.

Suddenly, his entire body freezes. His gaze lifts above my head. Fear washes over his features. I halt mid-stride, my pulse picking up a furious beat in my ear. Only one thing can make him react this way.

Cole.

The hairs on the back of my neck rise in awareness and I feel his eyes on me even before I turn around.

"Cole," I breath out when I turn around, pushing the veil over my head. My heart soars and tears of joy burn my eyes. I can't believe he is here. He's wearing a gray T-shirt that hugs his tight chest, framing the lean muscles he's obviously earned in prison. He looks ridiculously hot and dangerous at the same time.

Thank God, he is safe and sound.

He eyes me up and down, as confusion enters his face. "What's going on, Nor?"

I blink, puzzled by his question. Didn't his parents explain to him in the car what was going on?

I crane my neck to look over his shoulder, but I can't see Benjamin and Maggie anywhere.

"Nor?" he says my name again.

"Your parents. . ."

Cole's gaze abandons mine and raises over my head. "Josh?" His eyes dart between me and his brother, as the pieces of the puzzle move around inside his head.

I watch as disbelief fills his features as the pieces click in place.

I watch as anger, then hurt form a path of destruction on his face.

"Nor!" He says my name and signs it at the same time.

I'm sorry. I whisper the words in my thoughts. "I'm sorry," I say them a little louder. "I'm so, so sorry, Cole. I thought your mom and dad told you by now." I say his name on a broken sob.

His eyes move to Josh, and then to me. Cole shakes his head, his eyes narrowed.

"Talk to me, Nor." Torment crowds his face.

Anguish splits me in two. I wish I could give him more than my tears. I wish I could give him words that will make him understand, as much as this decision is wrong on so many levels, it's also the right choice.

His hands curl into fists and a muscle twitches in his jaw. Ten steps forward and he's standing in front of me, begging me with his eyes. "Why, Nor?"

"Is there a problem here?" My dad drawls in a bored voice, reminding me he is standing beside me.

His gaze bores into mine, a smug look on his face. He's enjoying this. He's absorbing the scene with greediness, it makes me nauseous. He looks at Cole, and then me.

I ignore him and focus on Cole. I need five seconds to talk to him and explain what is happening. Five seconds to crush his world, along with mine to save him. To save my family. To save me, because if anything ever happens to him, I will cease to exist. I would rather have Cole safe and him hating me, than dead.

Can I talk to you?" I finally manage to sign with shaking fingers.

Cole shoots me a hard look I've never seen before on his handsome face and nods. He starts to move toward me, past me. I exhale in relief, but the sickening sound of bone connecting with bone robs air from my lungs. I spin around and the sight before me stops my heart from beating, freezing me on the spot.

I've never seen Cole like this. Rage is splashed across his face, dispatched into Josh with every punch that connects with his ribs.

Punch after punch. He doesn't defend himself. He lets his brother hurt him. Josh is on his knees.

Then I'm running forward, I grab Cole's shirt from the back and yank hard. He whirls around, his eyes black with fury.

"Please stop!"

He doesn't. He jerks away, ready to unleash his wrath on Josh. This time, Josh's hand shoots up and grasps Cole's. Blood runs down the side of his face but he doesn't let him go.

"Go!" Josh yells. "Get out of here, Cole!"

His orders don't make sense until I hear sirens piercing the air. I look around, searching for my father and see him pacing at the church doors with a phone stuck on his ear.

The bastard called the police.

Recognition hits me hard. This was a trap and some sort of revenge rolled up into one. Megs was right. Josh and I are just pawns in my father's twisted game. The ultimate prize is getting rid of Cole completely.

I grab Cole's shirt again, pummel my fists on his back until he whirls around and glares at me.

"*You need to leave. The police are coming.*"

His chest heaves with heavy breaths. Fury rolls across his coiled muscles. He glances around, then back at me. Understanding dawns on his face.

"*I hate you.*" His words punch me in my chest, tearing a hole in my heart. "*I wish I never met you.*" He turns to face Josh. "*And you. . .my brother.*" He sneers. "*I hate both of you.*"

The sirens are closer.

"*Please leave. Now!*"

The fire in his eyes dies, replaced by a dreary gray.

I did this to him.

I broke him.

I watch as he turns and sprints down the aisle and through the door that leads to the pastor's chambers.

I straighten, collecting the slips of dignity and confidence I have left and inhale deeply.

I need him as far away from my father's hands as possible. For now.

His parents arrive fifteen minutes later, panic written all over their faces. When they arrived at the prison, an officer told him that Cole hitched a lift in a delivery truck.

That evening, I lay in bed, my body curled as I hold in the pain, knowing I deserve it. I press a hand on my stomach, rubbing it in circles.

Cole. Oh my God. Cole please forgive me. I chant the words over and over, seeking absolution in them.

The bed dips as Josh climbs on it, his face a mask of sorrow that mirrors mine. We spent the past two hours apologizing, talking, me crying as I tried to pick up the pieces of whatever was left of my heart after I threw it away. Now there's nothing left to say, yet my chest aches with words I still need to say.

He lies beside me and takes my hands in his. He leans forward and kisses my forehead, and then pulls me to him, tucking my face into his chest. He just holds me and I weep for Cole. For our unborn babies. The lives I've destroyed and saved.

Most of all, I cry because I can feel myself losing balance again and I need to fight hard to keep my sanity.

PART FIVE

PRESENT

CHAPTER FORTY-SEVEN

Cole

I FEEL AS THOUGH SOMEONE HIT MY RIBS WITH A HAMMER.

Jesus fucking Christ.

I knew Stephen hated me. He'd tried to hurt me several times when he sent his thugs to beat me up in prison.

The man was fucked up in the worst way. How could he hate his brother so much he'd transfer those feelings on anyone that remotely reminds him of his own flesh and blood? This shit is incomprehensible. He'd succeeded in separating us just like he'd been doing since they moved in next door.

I sit back on the chair, drop the beanie on my lap and drag my fingers over my head.

"Nick told me your father left."

"He did when I turned twenty-two. No one knows where he is."

I bite my bottom lip, studying the woman sitting in the corner of the couch, watching me with cautious eyes. God, she went through so much in her life. She wasn't lying when she said she wanted to protect me.

Dropping her gaze to the ground, she takes in a deep breath and seems to hold it for ages. She exhales and lifts her gaze to mine. Her tiny hands clench into fists, causing veins to pop out beneath her skin. I'm overpowered by the instinct to go to her, comfort her. She was too young to disobey a father who held all the cards in his hands. One wrong move would have either been the end of me, or have her family ripped out from under her feet. Her mother and sisters, people she's been fighting hard to hold onto.

Shit.

Watching pain tearing through her is like someone is slowing ripping a bandage off old, deep wounds inside me. Wounds that have barely healed.

But I can't. Not yet. I have a feeling if I go to her, I will end up doing more than comforting her and that's not the point right now.

I shift on the seat and turn my body so that I'm directly facing her this time because I want to see her truth when I ask her the next question, something I've wondered about since I returned back home a few weeks ago.

"Your father left. You stayed married to my brother, even though you said you didn't love him. At least not the way a wife should love her husband. Shouldn't you have put an end to the whole charade already?" She opens her mouth to speak, but I quickly put my hand up to stop her. "I have nothing other than respect and love for my brother. In fact, as far as I'm concerned, he was a martyr. I will never understand why he went to that extent, knowing he'd be bound to a woman who doesn't feel the same way he does. Why did you stay?"

A soft smile plays on her lips. "Because he asked me to. My life was Cora and Joce. I couldn't bring myself to raise the two girls on my own, and it's not because I was afraid to do it. I needed help, a father figure who was around. We needed him as much as he needed us. I missed having a father to look up to while growing up. I didn't want the same thing to happen to the girls. Besides, having someone to talk to, other than our daughters, was amazing. Josh's health started deteriorating and I wanted to be there to take care of him."

"Your brother did all that because he loved you," she says and signs at the same time, something she always did when she got angry with me. Or to get her point across. "God, he was so terrified when we got home from the walk after I told him and we found my father shouting at my sisters. He didn't even take a second to think about what he was offering. All he wanted to do was keep you safe. Keep me and the babies safe."

Her body is shaking badly and tears are streaming down her face now. My resistance crumbles to dust.

Ah, fuck it.

I scoot over on the couch and pull her in my arms. She wiggles, trying to shake me off but my hold on her tightens as I feel my heart break for everything she has gone through without my knowledge. Holding her, though, is like being home. Every piece of my heart glues itself together as her shaking body calms down with every soothing stroke of my hand on her back.

"I will fucking kill him for hurting you."

She raises her head and flashes me a wobbly smile, full of tears. Our lips are seconds away from touching and all I can think about is claiming that mouth over and over again. I need space and time away from her overpowering presence to think about this.

Snatching my beanie from the floor where it fell when I moved to comfort her, I shove it over my head and stand up. Panic flashes through her eyes before she averts them, hiding whatever is going on inside her away from me, which is okay. For now.

"I have to go."

Her head jerks up and her legs straighten as she stands up from the couch. She nods, her fingers fiddling with the edge of her blouse.

I'm at a loss for words so I turn and stride to the front door, without checking to see if she is following me or not. I don't need to, though. Her scent is like a blanket, surrounding me. I feel the familiar pull she's always possessed when our bodies were close.

I turn around and stare at her, taking in that innocent look. Even after everything that has happened, she still looks like my Nor. The seventeen-year-old girl with freckles on her nose and wide green eyes. The girl that changed my world the minute she moved in next door.

The nervousness that surrounded her when I walked in through the door is gone now, replaced by acceptance.

Peace.

Even her shoulders have loosened a little. I can't even begin to imagine how it would feel, carrying all that weight, full of secrets, on my shoulders. I search for the anger and rejection I'd been carrying around the past nine years, but it somehow dissipated between her telling me what destroyed us and now.

"Will you be all right?" I ask her, my hands shoved so deep inside my pockets I'm certain they will tear the fabric, just to keep my hands to myself and not end up grabbing her and doing everything I've wanted to do since returning back home.

"Will *you* be all right?" she asks.

My hand moves of its own accord, sweeping the hair off her shoulder to her back and wrapping my fingers around her neck, stroking the vein pulsing there. That little movement there eases the loss and anger that has been storming inside me all these years. Finally, I let out a long breath.

"I don't know." But, God, I hope I will be okay. I'm tired of being angry. I'm tired of holding back. I'm just tired and I want everything to be okay.

I need everything to be okay. "I just need some time to think."

I tuck a lock of hair behind her ear, wrap my fingers on the nape of her neck and kiss her forehead.

I drop my hand and step back. "*Goodnight, Snowflake.*"

Those green eyes search my face, with uncertainty, and then subtly nod. "*Goodnight, Cole.*"

After leaving her house, I drive my car for hours and end up parking in front of my parents' house. I need some time alone to think. I couldn't do it with Nor's tortured eyes on me.

I get out of my car and walk past the two-story house, heading for the gate in the backyard. I retrace the path that Nor and I walked on years ago until I reach the tree house. After flipping on the switch, I head for the wooden ladder, which has aged due to non-use. It's chipped in places due to lack of maintenance. The solar panels and part of the roof hang low.

I grip the first step and hoist myself up, climbing up the rest of the way. As soon as my foot lands on the floor, dust motes rise, floating in the air. The interior looks smaller than it was when I was eighteen. Cobwebs hug the ceiling, tiny spiders crawling along the delicate threads.

I lie down and shut my eyes, remembering the last time Nor and I were here. I lose myself in that memory, embracing the comforting silence surrounding me, taming the anger raging through me.

My eyes snap open and I groan as pain stabs my back.

Fuck. How long have I been lying here? One minute I was reminiscing about the old days and the next I'd fallen asleep.

I glance at my watch and realize I've been here for almost two hours. Sitting up, I stretch to get rid of the kinks around my neck and back, and then climb down the tree and turn off the lights.

Seven minutes later, I walk up the porch to my parents' house. The door is unlocked, just like it always was growing up. Some things never change.

The smell of cinnamon and vanilla teases me as soon as I step inside and I follow its trail. Mom looks up from pouring the batter inside the baking pan as soon as I step inside the kitchen, a grin quickly replacing the look of concentration on her face. It falls quickly, her gaze scanning my face.

"Is everything okay, honey?" she asks, setting the mixing bowl on the counter and hurrying toward me.

I shake my head, my throat burning. I raise my hands and sign, *"Nor told me what happened."*

The worried look on her face disappears and she wraps me in her arms, hugging me tightly.

She pulls back and pushes the hair off my forehead. "I'm so sorry."

I tuck my hands in the pockets of my pants. "Jesus. He was a fucking psycho. How can someone do that to his own daughter?"

She scowls at me. "First of all, stop cursing. Jesus and fucking don't belong in the same sentence. Ever."

My ears are burning, hearing that word, 'fucking' leaving my mom's mouth. Mothers shouldn't be allowed to utter things like that.

I pull my hands out of my pockets. "*Sorry.*"

She cups my cheek, her eyes softening. "Let me put the cake in to bake and then we can talk. It's for tomorrow's knitting club."

I nod and head to the living room. I start to pace, unable to stand still. I feel the hate for Stephen rise inside me, potent and overpowering. He literally tore my life apart with no regard for collateral damage. He punished his own daughter for loving me. Was I that appalling in his eyes? Jesus. I couldn't even protect Nor from him like I'd promised her. I've lived with people's prejudices all my life, but Stephen's was the worst kind of narrow-mindedness ever.

I fist my hands and swipe at my cheeks. Bitterness rises in me. Fury blinds my sight. I sit on the couch next to me and drop my face in my hands as the past twelve years come bearing down on me.

A touch on my arm stops the flood of memories. I wipe my face and look up to find Dad standing in front of me.

"*It's over,*" he signs. "*I'm so proud of you, Son.*"

Those words touch me deeply. I stand up and grab him in a hug. He pats my back and just holds me. I don't feel strong right now. I'm exhausted, feeling empty. I want everything to be fucking okay.

He pulls back, holding me at arm's length. "Do you remember when you were arrested? I was so angry with your mother and I blamed her for everything. I left her after you were sent to prison. Leaving her for the second time in my life was a very difficult decision for me. One evening, I was sitting in my hotel room, thinking about her. I loved, and still love, her with everything that I am. I came back home and we talked. We fought, and at the end we made up."

His gaze wanders over my shoulder and he smiles as Mom joins us from the kitchen. "In your case, things got really messed up. But you cannot let Stephen win. If you love that girl as much as you say you do, nothing will stand in your way. Nothing should stand in the way of true love."

My mom pulls me down to sit on the couch. "Do you know what Josh told me a few years ago after he was diagnosed with cancer? His mission in life was to keep you safe. Sometimes things happen in life for different reasons. For him, it was life's way of giving him a family he knew he'd never have. And for you and Nor, it was a test of time. A test of love. Please don't let his sacrifice go to waste."

I drop my head and finally let the grief I've been holding back sweep through me. My parents' arms around me offering me comfort I desperately need.

Fuck, Josh. You wise-ass. I could never repay you for everything you have done for me.

Eventually, after a long talk with my parents, we settle down and Mom puts together a chicken sandwich for me.

Later, I lie in bed and try to sort out my thoughts. I have no fucking clue where to begin, but one thing is for certain. I'll do everything in my power to make sure Nor and the girls have the kind of life they deserve.

CHAPTER FORTY-EIGHT

A WEEK HAS PASSED SINCE I TOLD COLE WHAT HAPPENED. HE HAS been coming to the house ever since and spending time with our daughters. It's been awkward as we tiptoed around each other, trying to find a middle ground. A sense of balance where the past nine years didn't loom above us like a nightmare. I'm grateful for his strength, for being there for our girls.

A book slams on a wood surface, jolting me out of my thoughts. I look over my shoulder to Elon. She frowns and huffs, her movements jerky around her knitting needles.

Sighing, she picks up the book from the floor and shoves it inside the basket at her feet with more force than necessary.

"Hey Elon, is everything okay with you?"

Her hands freeze. She jerks her head up from the red and white sweater she's knitting and looks at me.

"Yes. Everything is just perfect," she replies, prolonging the 'r' in perfect. She clears her throat. "Do you need me to deliver those to Mrs. Fredericks?" She's pointing at the bouquet of flowers in my hands while folding the sweater and arranging it inside the basket beside the book.

"Holy crap. Your pants are on fire, Pinocchio." I narrow my eyes at her. "Stop changing the subject. Mrs. Fredericks doesn't need them delivered until later on tonight. Everything going well in school?" She nods, climbing to her feet and stretching her arms above her head. "Nothing exciting? Like maybe a hot guy?"

She bites her cheek and bends down at the waist to pick up her basket. She's been spending more time at home the past three weeks, which is something she hasn't done since she started school two years ago.

"Nope. Nothing that exciting," she mutters, marching toward the counter and tossing her bag under it. "I should be asking you that. We haven't had time to talk since Cole came back."

The tiny bell on the door dings, announcing a customer's arrival.

"Be there in a minute!" I yell, heading to the other side of the room where five bouquets of pink carnations lay and add the one I've been working on to the bunch.

"Cole!" Elon says, sounding almost relieved. "It's so great to see you again."

Shit.

I can't breathe. I press my shaking hand on my chest and take deep breaths to bring my breathing under control.

"Alright, Nor. Call me if you need me," Elon yells, sounding all too happy. Her footsteps echoing around the shop as she walks toward the door. The bell dings, announcing her exit and leaving Cole and me in silence. A silence that's very quickly filling with heavy tension and the sound of my thudding pulse in my ears.

CHAPTER FORTY-NINE

Cole

As soon as I step inside Phoebe's, I spot her, surrounded by pink carnations. Her red hair is tied up in a loose braid, and my fingers itch to undo that knot. Set that braid free. I know the moment she senses me because her body stiffens and she clutches her chest as it rises up and down quickly. She doesn't look at me, though, which is fine with me. I need a few seconds to take her in, strategize the ways to add weight on her bones and her cute little ass.

As soon as Elon leaves, I walk back to the door, flip the sign from OPEN to CLOSED, and then turn and walk toward Nor. Immediately, she drops her eyes, a red flush filling her cheeks.

I tip her chin up and then drop my hand and sign, "*Keep your eyes on me because you and I have a lot to talk about and I need those pretties focused on me. Starting today you and I will work on that. I will cook for you and my daughters. You will eat. I will take care of you, all right?*"

Her eyes narrow at my words and she takes a step back. I follow her, invading her personal space, letting her know without words that I'm not leaving. If she wants to be stubborn, I'm all for it. Hell, every part of me is made of stubborn.

"*All right?*" I ask again.

Her eyebrows shoot up and she crosses her arms on her chest. "So, your word is law now. Aren't we going to talk about this?"

"Yes, we will. I want to make sure we are on the same page first."

She purses her lips, a little frown on her face. I duck my head to be eye level with her.

"One more thing, Nor. I'm not leaving. I don't care how long it takes for us to work on this. I'm not leaving."

She bites her lip. She's worried about something and I need to find out what it is.

"Talk to me," I say.

"Do you think this—" she points between us, "—is too soon?"

My determination falters at the worried look on her face. "Snowflake. The only people that matter to me right now are you, Cora and Joce. If you feel that you are not ready, I will respect that. But I won't keep my distance. I need you to understand that."

She rubs her forehead and nods. "Can we continue this conversation later at home?"

"Sure." I stare down at her mouth. Restraint is such an alien feeling when it comes to this woman. Glancing at the door to make sure there are no customers waiting outside, I turn and stalk forward. Her eyes widen.

"Cole?"

I reach for her hips and walk her backwards until we make it to the small hallway that leads to the storeroom, hidden from the public eye. I wrap my fingers loosely around her neck, running my thumb on the vein pumping furiously beneath her skin, I feel vibrations from her soak into my palm and I know she moaned or groaned. Angling her face up, I crash my mouth on hers and she doesn't resist. Her breath fans my face as she tries to catch her breath, her arms going around my neck. I drop my hand and tug her wrists, shackle them in one hand and pin them on the wall above her head. Her chest pushes forward, her lips parting and she peeks at me through her lashes.

"You look incredibly sexy like this. So inviting. . ." I take her mouth with mine, slipping my tongue inside hers and exploring her sweetness and warmth. I finish the kiss with a slight tug on her bottom lip and then raise my head, watching her as her eyes slowly open. Her cheeks pink, her chest rising and falling quickly.

Fucking perfect. I unshackle her wrists and run the pad of my thumb along the soft skin on her jaw.

"That is my apology for being a jerk before I left for Boston," I tell her.

She rubs a finger on her lips, looking dazed, then smooths her hair back "You already apologized."

"It wasn't enough. I wanted to show you how sorry I am."

She rolls her eyes, her lips twitching and drops her head back on the wall before shutting her eyes.

"Will you be all right?" I ask her, feeling way too cocky about that kiss.

She nods, her eyes closed. I turn to leave the shop, but pause mid-step and turn around to face her again.

"What time do you close?" I ask.

Her eyes slowly open and she signs, "*Six*."

"*I'll pick you up at six. Be ready.*"

She straightens, pushes away from the wall, and walks toward me. "*I can't Cole. I need to go home—*"

"Nor? Mom is babysitting the girls." She snaps her mouth shut and scowls up at me. "Be ready at six."

I came to a decision last night, and I'm not going back. I'm on a mission. Feed her, make her angry more often, and make her smile more often. Give her time, I have all the time in the world. Claim her as mine once again. I'm a stubborn son of a bitch and if I set my mind on something, I go for it with everything I have. Right now, I want Nor and the girls. I've spent my entire life wanting more, but returning home made me realize all I needed was her. She is my more.

I tuck my thumb under her chin and tip her face up. "Chin up, Beautiful." I kiss her forehead, and head for the door, flipping the sign from CLOSED to OPEN on my way through.

CHAPTER FIFTY

Cole

AFTER LEAVING PHOEBE'S, I FIND MYSELF DRIVING TOWARD THE cemetery. I park the car a few feet away from Josh's grave and glance out the window to the rows of tombstones until I find his. My hands tighten around the wheel, allowing his loss to sweep through me until it settles snugly in my veins. Pulling the keys from the ignition, I step out of the truck and weave my way to the spot covered with roses in different colors and sunflowers. I brought the later the last time I was here three days ago. I have no idea the kind of flowers he liked, but I remember he once said Nor was like the sun. Sunflowers had seemed like a good choice.

I spend the next five minutes sitting across from Josh's grave, trying to look for the words I need to tell him how grateful I am. How much I miss him. And just like the previous times, I fail miserably. Some sacrifices are too big for words. So, I go ahead and toss in a joke.

"I forgot to bring fresh flowers. Please don't smite me with lightning or some shit like that. I don't know what kind of super powers people get up there." I smile. "So, what do you guys do up there? I bet dudes have to work hard to get their wings, huh? Wait, is that shit for real? If it is, then there is no one who deserves it more than you do. That and a halo."

"Yeah, I do bro," the voice in my head says—Josh's voice when he was seven and I was five before I lost my hearing.

I close my eyes and lift my face to the sun filtering through the trees. "Cora and Joce miss you so much. Our little Joce punched a girl in the face."

I imagine him saying that my little girl got that trait from me, and I laugh.

"I know I've thanked you before for taking care of Nor and the girls. For being there for them. I know I'm stubborn, but your words finally sunk into this hard skull of mine. I'm going to try to mend things with Nor. Dad and I have been talking. I'll finish my internship at his firm and then see how things go from there."

I close my eyes and just enjoy the feel of being at such a peaceful place. It's weird because it's a place of the dead. But it calms me.

Half an hour later, I leave Josh, get into my car and drive away, feeling more at peace than when I came here.

I pick Nor up as promised. She doesn't fight me. In fact she looks as if she's been looking forward to six o'clock. She's even wearing makeup, something I haven't seen since I returned home. It's minimal, but it's there which makes me think she made an effort. Her eyes light up when I step into the shop. Then she tries to cover that look by quickly busying herself with shutting down the computer. What she doesn't know is I'd give anything to see that look again. She steps around the counter and I suck a breath.

Fuck.

My gaze moves down her body, taking in the little black dress that hits slightly above her knees and hugs her ass and tits perfectly. The braid is undone and her hair falls in waves to her lower back. A pair of red heels, the straps tied around her shins, completes the little sexy package.

She wobbles a little before righting herself, then looks up at me, her bottom lip trapped between her teeth.

"Elon made me wear them," she smiles nervously, walking toward me as if she's treading on a tight rope.

Elon, thank you for this wonderful vision. As much as I love Nor in Keds, seeing her in red heels has my blood roaring in my veins. When she reaches for her purse, I quickly readjust my erection in my pants. This night is going to be torture.

"Elon is home a lot lately. Isn't she supposed to be sleeping in the dorms? Is everything going ok in school?" I ask her when she turns around to face me.

"She shares an apartment with her friend." Nor shrugs. "Elon doesn't say much. She started coming home a lot after she told me they got a replacement professor. She doesn't seem to like him a lot."

I frown. "Do I need to go knock around this guy?"

She laughs. "You know Elon. She will talk only when she wants to."

After closing up the shop, we head to the spot I parked his car.

We've been driving for a while now. I glance at Nor from the corner of my eye. Nor has been quiet since we left. Her gaze is focused on the passing scenery outside of the car window. It's not very impressive so I know her thoughts are a million miles away, lost in her own head. I glance at the bones sticking out around her collar and I feel a scowl forming on my face. I quickly tamp it down.

The only things she is surviving on are guilt, stubbornness and air. Even after telling me what happened, I still see guilt in her eyes whenever she looks at me. I have to look for a way to show her we were both at fault. If anything, I am to blame. I should have avoided crossing her father. I should have kept my dick in my pants until my time in prison was up. I never should have fucked her without protection. But, I won't regret Cora and Joce. Just like I won't regret beating the crap out of Stephen. The thought of that worthless piece of shit harming Nor, any of her sisters, or her mom, makes me want to track him down and finish him off.

I park the truck in a spot outside the cafe and watch her side profile. I reach over the console and cover her hand with mine, squeezing it gently. Her head snaps up to face me, searching my face.

I pull my hand back and sign, *"Are you okay?"*

She blinks, the emptiness in her gaze fading. She nods, her lips stretching into a quivering smile. *"I'm getting there,"* she signs back. *"Are we going in or are we spending the rest of the night out here, chatting?"*

Ah, there she is. The girl I remember before shit went to hell.

I laugh and it feels damn good. This time when she smiles, it's genuine and her eyes light up.

I open the door on my side, round the car and open hers, then guide her toward the entrance of Spinners Cafe with my hand pressed on her lower back. We step inside the softly lit interior and I look around. The wooden floor beneath my feet vibrates to the sound of the music coming from the jukebox at the far end of the room. One couple seated in a booth facing the door are heavily making out. The man dips his head and says something to his partner. She throws her head back and laughs.

Shit. That was us when we were teens.

Nor and Cole. Once named the couple that would go down in history as unbreakable.

But we broke up.

Memories of my time spent in here with Nor bombard my head. Nor touches my arm and looks at me curiously. I jerk my chin toward an empty both. Two steps into our destination, I feel her stiffen against my palm. She spins around to look at me, her eyes too big for her beautiful face, which seems to have paled within the last few seconds.

I can't tell what caused this sudden change in her. I glance around at the same time I feel the beats of a song vibrate through the floor and seep into my body.

"Which song?" I ask.

She smiles shyly, her cheeks turning pink. *"This girl's in love with you.*"

"*Our song.*" I smirk, remembering it from the first time I saw her play it on the piano in her living room.

Nor eyes me warily while biting her lip as if she doesn't know where to go from here. I reach for her hand and I feel her tense.

Her eyes couldn't get wider even if she tried. Her gaze dips to the place where my fingers are wrapped around her skin, then back to my face. She seems to read the intent in my eyes and for one split second her gaze softens, a smile touching her lips. Then she shakes her head once as though to clear it of some sort of haze. She tugs her hand from mine. Mine wraps tighter.

"Dance with me," I mouth the words to her.

She opens her mouth but nothing comes out. There's a war raging in her eyes as she quickly looks at the table we were aiming for and back at me. So I make the decision for her.

Taking a step forward, I slide my free arm around her waist and cover the remaining distance between us. She plants her hands on my chest, pushes me away a little, and then curls her fingers on my chest.

Air rushes out through her parted lips. She stumbles on her heels as we continue dancing. I hoist her up, pressing her body to mine, taking more of her weight into my body. Her hand relaxes around my shirt and she circles her arms around my neck. Her finger tips graze my skin and I fucking shiver, unable to suppress it.

I've missed that touch.

I tighten my arms around her waist and hold her close. So close that no air passes between us. She tucks her head into my chest. I can't resist, I drop mine into her hair and inhale deeply.

Her scent is a comfort. Familiar. How have I survived so long without her in my arms? Without this familiar scent.

Unable to resist, I push the amber locks over her shoulder and bury my face in the crook of her neck. She shudders and presses her body into mine, laying her head on my shoulder. My hands shake and my grip around her tightens as I continue to mouth the words of that song. I have no idea if I'm out of tune or not. I press a kiss on her hair and murmur the words, 'Don't let my heart keep breaking'.

I feel the weight of her head leave my shoulder and she taps me twice on my arm.

"The song is over," she says, smiling shyly. "Thank you for the dance."

I fucking love that look on her face right now. She looks innocent, like she did when I first met her.

With her hand in mine, I walk her to an empty booth and we sit together on one side. We place our orders when the waitress arrives, then sit back in our seats. The awkward feeling that was present when we walked inside the cafe is gone. Nor kicks off her heels and pulls her legs up. Before she can tuck them under her ass, I grasps them and set them on my lap. She peeks up at me and I notice her shoulders loosen as if letting go of the weight she has been carrying since God knows when.

CHAPTER FIFTY-ONE

Cole

AFTER OUR DINNER, I DRIVE HER HOME, PARK THE TRUCK IN FRONT of her house and walk her to the door. This dinner wasn't planned. It was impromptu but that doesn't mean I won't treat it like a date.

I lean forward, lifting her chin with my thumb and lower my mouth to hers. She licks her lips, pulling back a little and raises her head to look over my shoulder.

"What's wrong?" I ask, searching her face. Is she afraid of kissing me? Or maybe being seen by people kissing me. "Are you worried about what people will say when they see us kissing?"

She bites her cheek, sneaks a glance up at me then drops her gaze to stare at my chest.

I sigh in frustration. "Fuck what people think, Snowflake. This is about you and me." I take a step back, dropping my arms to my side. "I'm not going to beg or force you to kiss me. It's up to you, Nor. No one should be allowed to dictate what you should or shouldn't do. That decision is all yours."

But it's only a matter of time before I take that decision into my own hands. She'll just have to deal with it.

I spin around, walk down the path and out of the gate before I cross the street. I dig my keys from my pocket and unlock my door.

Once I'm inside, I flip on the lights, toss my keys on the table in the hallway, kick off my shoes and stride into the living room. Sirius, who's sprawled on a pillow on the sofa, lifts his head. As if he considers me not worthy of any welcome, he drops his white head back on the pillow and shuts his eyes.

I head to my room and change into a pair of training pants and nothing else, and then leave and climb down the stairs to my basement which is also my gym room. I stalk to the punching bag, curl my hands into fists and work on getting the stress out of my body. Ten minutes later, I'm far from cooling down. I bound up the stairs and out the front door barefoot. Seconds later I'm knocking on Nor's door. The moment she opens it, her eyes widen slightly, tracking the rivulets of sweat down my chest. I pounce forward, slip my arm under her knees and throw her over my shoulder, before whirling around to stalk back to my house, my back absorbing the blows from her tiny fists.

I've officially gone insane.

I toss her on the couch, and take a step back, my chest heaving.

"*Are you insane, Cole? You can't just haul me from my doorstep and drag me here without my permission, you. . .you big savage.*"

Sirius sits up all of a sudden, stretches his body. He blinks a few times, then hops onto Nor's lap. I scowl down at him as he settles in, rubbing his stupid head on her chest. I clench my jaw, flex my hands.

Fucking hell. I'm jealous of a cat.

CHAPTER FIFTY-TWO

Sirius

COLE IS BEING STUPID AGAIN. AND JUST TO SHOW HIM HOW MUCH his foolishness is going to cost him, I wait until Nor settles nicely on the couch then I hop onto her lap. I curl up in her lap, tucking my legs under me and purr, my eyes falling shut. Seriously, I would live here if I could. Marry a kitty and have a few kittens. Not only does she smell like catnip, her fingers are magic. Cole is missing out on this big time.

I force one eye open and peek at Cole. He's scowling at me, his gaze moving from Nor's captivating fingers stroking my fur, and back to me. He probably wishes he was me. I've never seen him this affected by a woman since he adopted and took me home with him from the animal shelter five years ago.

Tough shit. A cat has to be selfish sometimes. Cole left the house huffing and sweating, a scowl on his face. He came back a few minutes ago with Nor over his shoulder. He tossed her on the couch then stood back and glared at her.

Nor is right. My master is a savage. My savage. It doesn't stop me from showing him what he is missing.

I climb to my paws and knead Nor's lap, but I'm completely side tracked when she starts to rub the back of my ears distractedly. My purring motor picks up when she strokes my chin and I forget all about teaching Cole a lesson.

This shit is dope. Yeah, we're keeping this girl.

CHAPTER FIFTY-THREE

Cole

"*I just have a few questions. Did you have fun tonight?*" I ask,

She stares at me incredulously, shakes her head. Nods.

"*Did you want me to kiss you tonight?*"

She licks her lips and nods again.

"*Are you scared of what people will say? Does it really mean that much to you? If it does, I'm willing to give you time.*"

She stops breathing. "*Give me time for what?*"

"*To accept this. You and I are going to happen. Josh was right. He gave me a push in the right direction. You and I never stopped happening. Just because a wedge was forced between us to stop the momentum doesn't mean we stopped.*"

Her chest expands as she inhales, her fingers rubbing Sirius' neck. "Okay."

"Okay what?"

"We are happening. Did you have to drag me all the way here to make a point?"

I tug my hair with my fingers and shake my head. "You are as frustrating as you are beautiful."

She rolls her eyes, trying to hide the smile fighting to break free. "Can I go home now? I kind of need to get some sleep. I have an early delivery tomorrow morning."

I nod, glance down at her bare feet. Reaching down to her lap, I pick Sirius up and put him back on the couch. I take Nor's hands in mine, pull her up and scoop her in my arms. Her lips part and I feel air brush my cheek. The urge to kiss the living shit out of her kicks in, but I know if I do, I won't stop.

I pick her up in my arms, stride across the street and set her down on her door step. She stares up at me, searching my face. She lifts a hand, cups my face and I lean into her palm. I kiss the soft skin of her inner wrist, deeply inhaling her scent. Fighting the need to grasp her by the nape of her neck and kiss the shit out of that perfect mouth of hers.

"*Good night, Nor,*" I sign.

"Night, Cole," she says.

Then she drops her hand and steps back. She opens her door, steps inside the house and closes the door without a backward glance.

CHAPTER FIFTY-FOUR

Nor

It's Friday evening and Megs and I were supposed to hang out tonight, but she was called in to work because one of her colleagues fell ill. We haven't spent a lot of time together since Josh's death. Everything seems to be happening too fast, plus her crazy shifts at work don't make things easier.

Cora and Joce are playing upstairs. They spent most of the afternoon on the terrace, helping Cole finish building the play house. Then he ordered me to sit on the couch and put my feet up. He made dinner for us, which consisted of burgers and fries. He left afterwards to visit with his parents.

I have been putting off packing up Josh's clothes for a while now because I feel like if I do that, I'm getting rid of him, pushing him out of my life. But at the same time, I can't postpone it any longer. After grabbing some boxes from the basement, I drag my feet up the stairs and inside my room. I open the door on Josh's side of the closet and stand there for a few moments, twirling the ring on my finger around.

You will always be here with us. Always in my heart and thoughts, Josh.

One hour later, I finish taping up the last box containing Josh's things. I glance at the top of the dresser where I put a few things I wanted to keep to remember him by and my chest hurts just taking in the last of what belonged to him. I've been holding back tears for the past two hours. Finally, I let go and crumple on the floor. I'm crying for my best friend and the man who had become a very big part of my life. Our lives. Our relationship had begun as a way to save us, but ended up being the best of friendships with no strings attached.

Taking in deep breaths, I carry them down to the basement one by one until everything is gone. I haven't decided what I will do with them, but I want to check with Cole and his parents if they would like to keep a few things.

Speaking of Cole. . .I have been thinking about telling the girls that he is their father. I have no idea when would be the right time to do this and I have no idea how they will react. They adore Cole, but watching his face fall every time they call him, 'Uncle Cole' is tearing me apart. His name is on their birth certificates, which was the first thing I told the doctor to do once my daughters were born.

I pull my phone from the pocket of my jean shorts and open a new text.

Me: **I'm planning on telling the girls tonight**.

My phone buzzes immediately. Oh, that was fast.

Cole: **Telling them what?**

Me: **About you. It's high time they knew.**

His reply doesn't flash on my screen immediately. Minutes later, when I don't hear from him, I inhale deeply, my fingers poised on the screen.

Me: **I know this is awkward and not easy. I'll understand if you think we should wait—**

The screen flashes with a text, momentarily blocking the one I was typing.

Cole: **I'm outside. Open the door.**

What? I spin around, rush to the door and swing it open.

He must have been leaving the shower when I texted him. His hair is still wet. His hands are tucked inside the pockets of his faded jeans and he's wearing a gray Henley shirt that clings to his toned body perfectly. His jaw is covered with light scruff.

He scans my face intently until I feel heat fill my cheeks. I wet my lips and his gaze drops to my mouth, following my tongue but then goes further and drops to my chest. There hasn't been any other incident since the "haul-me-over-the-shoulder-toss-me-on-the-couch" move he pulled when we last went out for dinner. As much as his behavior infuriated me, it was also the most exciting thing that has happened to me in a very long time. It was such a huge turn on.

Shit. My nipples are hard just thinking about that night.

He lifts his eyes to mine, his eyebrows raised as if to ask me, "Are you going to let me in? or what?"

I stumble aside and sign, "*Please come in.*"

He brushes past me, his scent wrapping around me.

I need to keep my tingling lady parts in check.

After closing the door, I lead the way to the living room, absorbing the heat from his body on my back.

"The girls?" he asks when we reach the living room.

I turn to face him, watching as he lowers his long frame on the couch. "Upstairs." I'm extremely nervous so I opt to remain standing. "Thank you for coming."

He nods, eyeing me as I continue to pace and wipe my hands down my jean shorts.

"I'll go upstairs and get the girls." I turn and go for the stairs.

"Nor." His voice stops me. I whirl around and, as always, my heart is beating hard in my chest. "I'm here. I'm always here for you and the girls."

I nod, spin around and start to climb the stairs. I pause, turn and walk back to stand in front of Cole. I take a deep breath and exhale the little pride left in me because I'm about to beg. Badly. Sometimes your first love comes back to you and you get a second chance. "If there is a second chance for us, no matter how small it is, I'll take it. Love is what makes people fight harder for something they want to hold on to. I'm ready to fight for us. Whatever it takes. I will do anything to show you that you and I are not coincidental. We are more than that.

We are Cole and Nor. Us."

He cocks a brow and signs, *"Aren't you concerned about what people will say?"*

I raise my chin, look him in the eye. "I don't care what people will say. Everything you said. . .you were right."

His arm lifts without warning and he wraps his fingers around my thigh, burning me with his touch. He drags me to stand between his legs and cups my backside firmly in his hands. He yanks me forward at the same time he leans his forehead to my body and kisses the tiny slip of skin peeking out between my T-shirt and shorts.

He tips his head up, meeting my gaze. "You and I are far from coincidental."

He drops his hands from my body, leaving me tingling with need and hungry for more than a touch.

Framing my heated cheeks with my hands, I turn around and head for the stairs. The girls are not in their rooms, so I follow their voices to my room and stop to stare as Cora ties a knot on the blanket fort made of white bed sheets, with strings of lights dangling around it.

The first time Elise and the girls made a fort, Cora and Joce had argued about which room it would be built in. Eventually, we decided mine was the neutral ground. At that time, Josh was spending days on end in the hospital as the doctors tried to save him through chemo. So it was a comfort to have the girls in my room. Even though Josh and I shared a bed, we never got intimate. It was more for putting up appearances to the girls. Before Josh became really sick, he'd been seeing a girl he'd gone to college with. Then he stopped when he got too weak to go out. Megs and I made a plan to take him dancing or to a bar, just to hang out with a different crowd every once in a while, whenever he was well enough.

"Hey honey," I say to Cora, scanning the room for Joce. "Where's your sister?"

"She just went to her room to collect some things we need."

"Can I talk to you two for a few minutes?"

Her hands holding a string of lights pause. She looks up. "Oh Mom! Can't it wait? We're almost done," she whines.

"Cole is here."

She drops the lights and grins wide. Gray eyes so like her father's flash, hopping from one foot to the other. "Really? Oh my gosh. Joce! Uncle Cole is here!" she shrieks then darts out of the room. I trail after her and stop in the hallway.

Joce yells something from inside her room, then she's zipping past me in the hallway and bounding down the stairs. I can't believe that's my always cool, calm and collected daughter. And it's not like they don't talk to him every day. Even on days he doesn't drop by for a visit, which is extremely rare, he still chats with them on Skype. I'm grateful for that, because somehow, he has become a fixture in their lives. I suspect it also eased their pain of losing Josh.

When I reach downstairs, I take the seat directly across the couch from Cole and the girls and then fold my hands on my lap.

I wipe my clammy hands on my shorts, and sign. "*Girls. I need to ta—*" Cole's eyes narrow on me. "*Cole and I need to tell you something.*"

Joce leans forward, propping her elbows on her knees and Cora settles herself on Cole's lap. They stare at me expectantly.

Right. I inhale. Hold my breath. "So, you know Cole and your dad—Josh, are brothers."

Cora rolls her eyes and laughs. "*Of course, Mama. Is that all? Because Joce and I want to make plans with Cole about the carnival.*"

Cole lifts his hand and grasps the nape of Cora's neck. The gesture is so possessive, it sends my heart fluttering inside my chest. "Patience, sweetheart."

Crap. This is so hard. "Sometimes things happen in life and we are unable to control them and. . ." I blow out a breath and rub my forehead. The twins squirm impatiently and Cole stares at me, a question clear in his eyes.

I shake my head subtly. I can do this. His lips quirk at the sides in encouragement.

"*Cole. . .Cole is your real father.*"

Joce frowns. Looks to the floor, and then at Cole. She leans back in her seat.

"What?" Cora squeaks and scrambles off her father's lap in favor of sitting next to him with her tiny legs crossed.

Taking the 'rip the bandage off approach', I proceed to tell them a watered down short version of what happened nine years ago.

Cora's eyes twinkle, a dimple appearing on her cheek. "*So, you and Cole are like Cinderella and the Prince, and your father was the stepmother?*"

Cole's lips twitch. "*Yes.*"

Cora bite her lip, seeming to contemplate something. "Did you love Daddy too?"

I nod. "*Yes. Very much. I loved your Daddy and Cole, but very differently.*"

Her eyebrows scrunch up. "*How can you love two people differently? I thought there is only one kind of love.*"

"*It is possible to love people differently,*" I try to explain and hope I don't end up confusing her even more.

Cole mouths, "let me try" and I nod.

He scoops Joce up and over his lap and sits her next to Cora, and then he angles his body so that his entire focus is on the girls.

"For example. *You love Joce and your mama. And you love your best friend, Lara or any of your friends at school.*" He pauses and watches them intently to make sure they're following his logic.

"*So Mama loved Daddy the way I love Lara?*"

Cole nods and Cora falls silent, mulling over the words. She seems satisfied for now, but I'm sure she will be back with more questions. Our story is complicated and probably confusing to Cora and Joce. Or maybe I'm underestimating their power of understanding.

Joce hasn't spoken yet. She's wearing a look I can't read, which reminds me of Cole. It's pretty worrying.

"*Honey, do you have any questions?*" I ask her.

She bites her bottom lip, stares at Cole for a long time. "*You lived so far away. You never came to visit even after Mama's father went away. Didn't you want to be our father?"*

Cole sucks a sharp breath, and starts to shake his head. His stare is fiery, darting between the two girls. *"Nothing would have kept me away from you if I had known about you. Your mama wrote me a letter and told me about you. I didn't open the letters on time. I regret that a lot, because I would have seen you sooner. I'm so sorry."* He pauses and kisses the top of their heads. *"You two are my forever girls. Nothing will stop me from wanting you."*

Joce nods, her tiny shoulders slumping forward in relief, but then frowns again. *"It's kind of weird having two dads. What about Daddy? Does it mean he won't be our daddy anymore?"* Her lip quivers when she lifts her gaze to mine.

My chest hurts just seeing the panic on her face. *"Oh God, no, baby. He will always be your papa as long as you want him to be. No one will ever take that away from you."*

She turns to Cole. *"I love you too. Like really, really love you."*

Oh Joce, my baby girl.

I shake my head, smiling. Cole's mouth is slightly parted. He looks a little stunned too. Cora, on the other hand, is just her happy self, climbing on her knees and playing with her father's hair, which has grown considerably longer since he came back home.

"You want to know a secret too? I love you too. Like really, really love you and Cora." He pulls Cora down for a kiss on the forehead and does the same with Joce. *"You want to know something else. Josh is still your papa and he always will be. You have two papas who love you so much."*

Cora's face lights up even more. *"I can't wait to tell Lara. She has two papas too, but both of them are alive. She and her little brother and mother now live with the new papa. But the old one visits them every two weeks."* She stops and takes in a huge breath. *"So, is it okay to call you Daddy Cole?"*

Cole grins. *"You can call me anything you want."*

"Cool." Cora hops off the couch to the floor. *"Are you two going to get married? I've seen you kiss Mama. You love her, don't you?"*

Cole and I stare at each other, a look infused with hope, reconnection, lost and found love.

I shift my gaze to my daughters. *"We haven't spoken about that yet."*

Cora bounces on the soles of her feet. *"Okay. Can we go now? We really need to finish the fort."*

"Sure," I say.

She quickly hugs Cole, and then does the same to me. Then she dashes up the stairs. Joce stands up, leans forward and hugs her father, then kisses him on the cheek. After giving him a shy smile, she walks toward me with a huge grin, embraces me and kisses my cheek.

"I'm sad that Daddy is not here anymore. But I'm really happy that your prince came back. I'm happy Cole is here," she says, before trailing after her sister.

And then I burst out in tears at her words. The couch sinks as Cole settles next to me and wraps his arm around my shoulder, pulling me to him. He just holds me to his chest and rubs his palm on my back until my sobs turn to sniffles.

I place my hands on his chest and push away from him. "I'm such a mess, aren't I?" I try to smile but it feels like a grimace.

He nods, smiling. "You actually look really cute. A cute mess."

I chuckle and sit up. "Thank you for being here. You are so good with the girls. You are a natural."

He shakes his head. "I'm always afraid that I might be doing the wrong thing. You and the girls are patient with me, so thank you." He pulls me to him and kisses my forehead, and then tucks a loose strand of hair behind my ear.

I bite my lip and look away. After Cole left, I never thought, even for a second, he would come back home.

I'm really happy that your prince came back. Joce's words give me confidence and I lift my face.

Cole cups my jaw and tugs it gently to face him. "What is it?"

I clear my throat. "I thought I'd never see this day. You sitting here next to me, or Cora and Joce finally getting to know who you are. I wouldn't have been surprised if you hated me or didn't want anything to do with me."

Cole leans forward, his gaze holding mine captive. "I could never hate you. I said those words in a moment of anger, but it wasn't true. I will always regret not opening those letters. It was stupid of me. There is something my dad said to me a few weeks ago. Something that Josh said. Things worked out the way they did for a reason. You were there for Josh when he needed you the most. He was there for you and the girls when you needed someone to lean on, and I'm thankful for that." He shrugs. "Life is never meant to be easy."

He is right. Life is never meant to be easy, otherwise, there wouldn't be any challenges to face.

I lift his hand to my lips and kiss his palm. "Tell me about New York, your tattoos, everything." I trace the 'Silver lining' tattoo and lift my eyes to his. "I can't believe you did this one. How did you even get the image?"

He grins. "I took a photo from your doodle book. I had no idea why I did that. I just know that every time I looked at the photo, it gave me courage. I had it tattooed on my skin after I left prison."

I sit across from him as he fills me in on the years we were apart. By the time he is done, I feel gratitude and respect for this man. He hasn't let anything stand in the way of his dreams, he even didn't let the lack of money to finance his education pull him down.

Finally I ask what has been simmering in the back of my mind. "You said that you are not leaving. What will that do to your internship program at Lawrence & Barnes?" I don't want him to give up his dreams just to take care of us.

"I'll finish it in my dad's firm. I just have a couple of months left, then I'll be done and after that, take the exams to get my licence. So you see, I'm not leaving. Ever. You and our daughters are my dream." He grips my shoulders and kisses me softly, before pulling back.

"I'm glad. I'm sorry for everything that happened."

He shakes his head. "I am sorry for believing that you'd hurt me intentionally and for ignoring those letters. Forgive me?"

"How about we forgive each other?" We laugh and fall silent.

I purse my lips. "I was thinking about something. Josh's birthday is coming up on May ninth and I wanted to check with you first. We could invite a few friends and your parents, and have a get together in his honor? How does that sound?"

He stares down at me, tears gleaming in his eyes. "I think that's a brilliant idea. Josh would love that." I take in a deep breath. "Tate and Simon were supposed to fly in in a week or so for a visit. I will ask him if it is possible for them to postpone the trip until the birthday."

"That would be great," I say, climbing on his lap and settling in for a kiss. I figure that, if I want to take this a step further, I should be the one to make the next move. He already told me what he wanted and I need to show him we are on the same page. "Maybe we should put the girls to bed and continue this later?"

He groans, shifting lower on the couch to take in my weight and then grips the back of my head. He pulls me down, taking my mouth in a hot searing kiss before rolling his hips.

I lean back and grin at him, feeling his erection rubbing between my legs. "Batman doesn't need a take-off countdown, does he?"

He smirks. "I'm always hard for you. He's like a soldier, ready at all times. A goddamn fine soldier."

I laugh and kiss his mouth one more time before climbing off him. "Let's go herd the girls to bed. I have some plans for Batman."

"Shit. I love your kind of dirty talk," he flashes me a teasing smile and then reaches out and spanks me on my rear, grinning up at me. "The soldier has been anxiously waiting to play."

I shake my head, laughing. The girls are ready and tucked in their own beds forty-five minutes later.

Cole takes my hand when we hit the hallway and pulls me inside my room. As soon as the door shuts behind us, his hands are all over me, tearing at my clothes and his lips kissing my mouth, neck, anywhere he can reach. His hands fumble with the button of my shorts while mine hurriedly undo the belt of his pants. When it's undone, I push them down, then hook my fingers around the waistband of his black boxer shorts, and yank them down. Heat spreads inside me and my heart races as I take in his erection, his need for me. The sound of our heavy breathing fills the room and I want nothing more than to rip the shirt off his chest, press my body flush to his. His fingers push the shorts down my legs impatiently. I lift my legs and untangle the shorts from my feet, kicking them to the side. Our shirts join the pile on the floor next. We stand back staring at each other, chests heaving.

Then we're moving forward again, pulled toward each other like two neutron stars heading for a collision. Unstoppable. Our bodies collide and everything around us explodes in a flurry of insatiable fingers and hungry lips. Breathless moans and deep groans. Something tangles around my legs and I stumble back, but Cole's arm bands around my waist and pulls me back to him. He kisses me, drinking me in. I gasp when his hands squeeze my breasts and my mouth parts. His tongue moves past my lips and inside my mouth, tasting me. I whimper, he groans, rolling his hips with his erection trapped between us, hot and ready. He scoops me up, strides to the bed and lays me down. My flaming body hits the cool sheets and I gasp again, welcoming the cooling effect. Cole's hard body is on mine, covering me with his heat, his mouth is on my neck, kissing and licking and nipping. Sucking as if he can't stop himself from tasting me. His thigh probes between mine and my legs fall open, welcoming him home.

I grip his hair in my hands, arching my body, too greedy for more. I try to push him off me but he is too heavy. I gently pull the locks of hair and he moans. I tug it again and his head leaves my neck, his eyes, so dark and stormy, collide with mine. Now that half of his weight is not on me, I untangle my fingers and lift up on my elbows, then press forward until he is no longer lying on me. I give his chest a little shove. Understanding dawns in his eyes and he falls onto his back.

Sitting up, I put a hand on his chest, and the ring on my left hand glints against the room's lighting. Taking a deep breath, I pull it off my finger, lean forward and open the night stand drawer. I lay it inside and with another deep breath, slide it shut. I turn back to focus on Cole, noticing the way his eyes soften as his eyes lower to my hand.

He doesn't say anything, just takes my hand and kisses the faint scars on my wrist. I swing a leg over his body, straddle his thighs, and then take him in my hands. A hiss passes between his teeth, veins popping in his neck and his fingers digging into the skin on my hips.

"Fuck. I want my cock inside your pussy. Now."

"Patience," I tell him.

He lifts his hands and signs, *"Fuck patience."* He grabs my waist and flips us around. I'm flat on my back in two seconds and he's pushing inside me.

He stops and takes deep breaths. "Jesus, Nor. You are so wet and tight," his voice is hoarse and the words heavy on his tongue. He thrusts forward, burying himself to the hilt. Wrapping his hands around me, he holds me to him tightly as I do the same, ramming inside me with abandon, his face buried in my neck. And I close my eyes tight, letting my emotions take over as I give myself back to Cole all over again. And when we finally come, we rise together, riding on the wave and then falling into a blissful surrender.

CHAPTER FIFTY-FIVE

Nor

COLE TOOK THE GIRLS TO THE CARNIVAL EARLIER TODAY. WHEN they came back a few hours ago, Cora was scowling and sending daggers in her father's direction. She stomped upstairs and slammed her door shut. Apparently, Cole glared at a few boys from Cora's class which ended up scaring them away. Cora had initially bragged to her classmates and told them that her new daddy was taking her and Joce to the carnival, so she was extremely eager to introduce Cole to her friends. When I asked Cole about it, his jaw tightened and a vein throbbed viciously as he told me the boys were looking at his daughters inappropriately. I pointed out that the kids were only nine years old.

Honestly. How can a child that age stare inappropriately?

Obviously not amused with my question, Cole crossed his arms on his broad chest and scowled at me.

I laugh under my breath. I really pity Cora and Joce's future boy-friends.

This evening we're having a get-together at my house in honor of Josh. I prepared the rooftop terrace for this occasion earlier today but it started to rain, and I ended up moving everything back inside the house.

Cole mentioned that Simon and Tate arrived last night from New York. They are staying at Cole's house and they will be here soon. Elon left for school earlier this morning. She has mid-term tests and she was so nervous about that. She still hasn't opened up to me about the reason she's been spending more time at home than in her apartment. Elise will drop by later as well.

Megs squints up at me, tears running down her face. "Where's that man of yours? He needs to finish cutting these onions. He survived prison. He can survive this."

I gape at my best friend. "Oh my gosh. Megs! What's wrong with you?"

"What? It's true." She drops the knife and rushes to the sink to wash her hands. "Damn it. Little shits sucking my eyeballs."

I laugh. "Cole went to take a shower after working on the play house on the terrace." Pain tugs in my chest, just thinking of Josh. But this is a happy day. A day to celebrate his life. "You'd better be done soon. The snacks should be ready before everyone arrives."

She rolls her eyes. "Let's order Chinese. Anyway, what's the deal between you and Cole? Someone saw him dragging your ass to his house. Are you guys playing the Tarzan-Jane thing? That's kinky. Tell me it's true, though. I'm living vicariously through you. My divorce is wringing me dry so I only have you to entertain me. Did he toss you on his bed? Did he let you play with his magic stick? I bet his dick is like Batman."

My cheeks are on fire. "What?"

"You know, all scowling and demanding like Batman. I bet it sprang up and said—" she clears her throat and screws up her face into one meant to portray intimidation. "*It's not who I am underneath, but what I do that defines me.*" She winks. "I bet his penis showed you what it's made of."

"Oh. My. God. Only you can make that quote sound dirty."

She laughs, picks up the knife again, and attacks the onions brutally.

Megs' heart has always belonged to Simon. When Cole left town,

Simon packed up and followed him. That kind of friendship is quite rare. I completely admire the kinship.

"Cole won't be going back to New York to finish his internship. He has already worked things out with his dad so he will continue interning at BH Architects." I sigh, my thoughts on Cole. I smile, feeling happy. Peaceful. "Sometimes he is stubborn and possessive—"

"So he hasn't changed a lot in the past nine years. Dude, Cole is the man."

"—and I wouldn't change him for the world." I finish the sentence.

The doorbell rings. Cora yells she'll open the door. My heart does this wonderful thing in my chest, pumping faster and faster. Before I can turn around, I feel him, our connection crackling in the air. His arm circles my waist and he kisses my neck. My heart slows down its erratic beating. It's like his presence and his touch are the only things that can race and calm my heart. Simultaneously.

"Dude, let up. It's my turn."

I look over my shoulder to see Simon, grinning wide. I spin around and throw myself at him and he catches me, hugging me tight. I pull away grinning, lift my gaze and see a tall hot guy walk into the kitchen. He's really hot, like GQ cover model hot. He flashes me an easy smile that has most likely won awards for the best smile, displaying a row of straight white teeth and deep groves on the side of his mouth.

"*Eleanor? It's really good to finally meet you,*" The hunk signs without preamble.

Oh, this is *the* Tate. "*It is great to finally, officially meet you,* Tate," I sign, extending my hand toward him in greeting.

"*Any family of Cole's is mine as well.*" He ignores my hand and wraps me in a hug, then takes a step back. "*How are you and the twins doing?*"

"*Great, thank you for asking.*"

"*I bet they are great,*" Simon says and I look at him, grinning wide at me. He winces when Megs smacks his arm and scolds him.

After the introductions are over, I finish up cooking, while Simon and Megs do this kind of awkward dance filled with unforgotten memories and missed opportunities. I hope Simon comes to his senses and sweeps her off her feet. They are so good for each other.

When everything is ready, I dash upstairs to freshen up, strip out of my little shorts and T-shirt, then hop in the shower. I'm out five minutes later with a towel wrapped around my hair and another one covering my body. I rush to the closet, grab a white dress and a set of black cotton panties and slip them on. I remove the towel on my head and give my hair a thorough rub. By the time I'm ready, my body has been moisturized, my hair finger-combed and curled around the ends. I turn to leave the room, but freeze in my tracks. Heat washes over my body, responding to Cole's intense perusal. He's leaning one shoulder on the doorframe, his arms crossed on his chest.

"*How long have you been standing there?*" I ask, shifting on my feet. I press my thighs together to get some friction between my legs.

He drops his arms to the sides, steps into the room and pushes the door shut with one hand, trapping me inside with him. "*Long enough for me to want to bite your ass and lick it. Taste you. Eat you.*"

Oh.

God.

I'm still frozen in place. He ambles closer, the look on his face so dark, hungry, needy, it defies his calm pose. My brain is yelling for me to move. Run. My body is nothing more than a mess.

He lifts his hand and cups my cheek. "You are so damn beautiful, Snowflake." He skims his thumb lightly across my bottom lip. I pant, whimper. My tongue sneaks out, brushes along the pad of his finger. I nip the skin there just a little. He hisses. A moan rumbles in his throat. His eyes are more black than gray. A storm ready to break and destroy whatever lays in its path. I want him to destroy me, then put me back together.

He pulls his hand away only to curl his fingers on the nape of my neck, with a thumb on my throat, stroking the vein there. Then his mouth is on mine, kissing me, his tongue invading my mouth without asking for permission. His kiss is untamed, feral, starved. Brutal. I'm delirious and drunk, electrified. His free hand lifts my dress and grips my thigh. Inches up and cups me between my legs. He slides one finger inside me.

Cora's voice seeps through the door, reality slapping me in the face. I jolt, try to break free.

"We have guests waiting for us downstairs, Cole. Someone might walk in on us."

He blinks. "*Well, you'll just have to hurry up then.*"

"Hurry—" Suddenly, the finger inside me is gone and my body is being pressed against a wall before I can finish the sentence.

Cole hooks his fingers on the band of my underwear, slides them down. I lift my legs and he pulls them the rest of the way, tossing them on the floor. He drops to his knees, pushes my dress up and buries his face between my legs. He grasps my thighs and hooks my legs over his shoulders, thrusting his tongue inside me. My hands fly out, searching for something to hold on to. I grab his hair in my fists and pull. He groans deeply, sending vibrations skittering all over my body. Cole is on a mission and just because I'm skittish about being found doesn't make him abandon his task. He pushes a finger inside me, then another while his talented tongue continues to lick me, burn me, and consume me whole. My back arches. I can feel the climax rushing through me. Then it hits me, forcing a scream out of my lips. I slap a hand over my mouth, my eyes closed, panting, panting, panting. I can't seem to get enough air in my lungs. I'm completely and utterly ravished.

Cole kisses my inner thigh before unhooking my legs from his shoulders and standing up. With his gaze locked on mine, he cups my face in his hands and once again kisses me. This time the kiss is languorous as if we have all the time in the world, gentle as his tongue tangles with mine. Powerful. Tasting myself on him is pure bliss. His lips worship mine reverently, as if he's sealing me to him. Then he pulls away and brushes the pad of his thumb on my bottom lip. My gaze takes him in down his broad chest and all I can think about is, I want to see him naked. Suck that nipple ring. I look down and inhale sharply. He's so hard the zipper on his jeans looks like it might pop open any second.

I bite my cheek, meet his gaze. "Um. . .your—"

"What?" his raises a brow at me.

"Batman. He's still—"

He rolls his eyes. "It's 'cock.' I'm not leaving until you say it. In fact," he prowls closer. "I might just toss you on the bed and fuck you until you say that name. Cock."

I straighten on the wall. Narrow my eyes at him. "You wouldn't dare."

"Want to bet?" He has this determined scary look on his face.

"All right, all right. Sheesh. Don't get your panties all bunched up." He laughs. I roll the word in my head. Feel my cheeks heat up as I open my mouth and say, "Cock. Satisfied?" I'm surprised I haven't exploded or something. It's not a bad name though. Why was I having trouble saying it? "Batman sounds cooler though."

He steps back laughing and smacks my butt. "*All right woman. Feed me.*"

After dashing back to the bathroom to straighten my appearance, I cringe when my gaze falls on my flushed cheeks. Everyone is going to notice. Megs will be dying to lock me in a room so I can give her the details. I rush out and scuttle around Cole, dart for the door and bound downstairs before he can think twice and haul me over his shoulder to carry out his threat.

Cole

We are all sitting around the table, our wine glasses poised in the air, ready to toast to the most amazing brother. Dad nudges my mom's arm, passing her a handkerchief as tears run down her face. She leans to the side to kiss my dad's cheek. I feel my own tears burn my eyes when my parents turn to look at me and nod. Dad mouths, "You did great" and I have to blink several times to stop myself from bawling my eyes out.

Nick waves his hand to get my attention. "*What time did Elon say she would be here?*"

I glance at my watch and back to him. "*In twenty minutes. Keep your cool, bro. Your lipstick is showing.*"

He scowls. "*Fuck you.*"

He startles and swings around when Mom smacks him on the head. "*He started it, Mom.*"

Mom glares. "*Mind your manners, Nick.*"

I laugh and he looks at me, shaking his head. "*I will get you for that one, big bro.*"

After Nor takes her seat next to Cora and picks her glass up, she glances around the table, a soft smile on her lips.

"To the most wonderful, selfless man in the world, my best friend and a great father," Nor says, her eyes finally finding mine, and I smile at her.

I swallow around the lump in my throat and say, "To my brother, my hero. A great son."

After the toast, bowls of food are passed around. I pause and look around the table. My family and friends. Every one of them means the world to me. I couldn't be any more blessed or happy.

The lights flicker several times, indicating someone is at the door. As soon as Nor leaves the table to answer the door, I notice the way Tate trails after her with his gaze. I nudge shoulder and glare at him.

"*Stop staring at my woman before I punch your face,*" I sign, glaring at him.

He sets his cutlery on his plate in favor of rubbing the spot on his shoulder, and then signs, "*Calm down man. She's a knock-out, I'll give you that. But I wouldn't risk our friendship like that.*" He sneaks a look in Nor's direction and turns back to face me. "*Do the scars bother you?*"

I shake my head. Most people don't understand what I see in Nor. What lies beyond those white scars. *"It's simple. I see the beauty in her broken soul. I see a fighter who wears her battle scars with pride. I see my soul mate."*

He holds my gaze for a few minutes before blowing out a breath. *"Dude, I think I'm crushing on you."*

"Sorry, man. I'm already taken."

He grins at me. *"You mentioned you might be working on a new project? In Jacksonville?"* Tate asks. He picks up his knife and fork and continues wolfing down the food.

He looks away from me as his attention is claimed by the return of Nor, with Elon and Elise in tow. Tate straightens in his chair, subtly puffing out his chest. I can't wait to teas the shit out of him. I go ahead and introduce him to the sisters. He keeps on staring as they settle in their respective seats across the table. His gaze lingers on Elise a little longer before he peeks at me and mouths, "Wow."

I laugh, watching him dart a look in her direction again.

I touch his arm to reclaim his attention. *"We'll talk about this project without distractions,"* I sign, smirking.

Later, when everyone has gone home, I slip between the sheets next to Nor and wrap my arms around her, then bury my nose into her hair. She shifts on the bed, and snuggles into me, her legs tangled with mine. I close my eyes and drift into sleep, a sense of completion filling me.

EPILOGUE

Summer

Nor

THE PAST FEW MONTHS HAVE BEEN AMAZING. COLE FINALLY MOVED in with us and the transition has been smooth.

I've been thinking about going back to school to pick up where I left off years ago, but I haven't decided if I want to apply for Music Therapy or Psychology. Plus, the tuition is a bit higher than what is left in my college fund. I'll need to check if the schools offer a scholarship or apply for a student loan. I managed to pay part of the hospital bills with the help of Maggie and Benjamin.

The four of us went to visit Josh today. Cora lit one of her scented candles that we made last week, and then placed it in a glass candle holder beside the headstone. She sat cross-legged on the grass and told him about the play house and that she, Joce and Cole were working on it. She also talked about Sirius, the cat. I teared up when she told Josh about his birthday party-get together which we had weeks ago. Cole took me in his arms and held me while I cried, unable to hold back the tears.

Joce was her usual quiet self as she lay a pair of black and white knitted gloves—she knitted them in her crafts club at school—beside the headstone on the grass. She was worried Josh was cold wherever he was.

We arrived back home three hours ago. The girls dragged Cole up to the roof terrace to put the final touches on their house and they have been up there since then.

Things have finally calmed down. Every time I think of Josh, I am so thankful to God that he blessed me with such an amazing friendship. He might not have lived his life to its fullest, but I'd never seen him more content. He had once told me that he couldn't have asked for a better life.

I wipe the tears trailing down my cheeks with my hand and smile. "I could never repay you for what you did for me, Cole and the girls," I whisper under my breath. "You are loved and will always be in our thoughts."

After setting a beer for Cole and three bowls filled with vanilla ice cream with pieces of orange fruit tossed in on a tray, I head out to the terrace, my thoughts on the call I've just had with my mom half an hour ago. She and Pete will be arriving tomorrow before dinner. I'm really excited to see them.

Cole is sitting in a corner inside the house, his knees pulled up and his elbows planted on his thighs, listening to Cora and Joce discussing their plans for the house. Sirius is lying on a black and white pillow the girls set aside for him on the floor when Cole brought him over the first time a few weeks ago.

God.

That look on Cole's face leaves me breathless. His entire world is right there in his eyes. His gaze shifts to mine and his lips tip up at the corners in that special Cole smile, spreading across his features until it reaches his eyes. Tingles sweep through me and I grin at him.

"*I brought refreshments.*" I point to the tray.

There's a burst of clapping as the girl's dash out of the house, heading for the little table.

Cole unfolds himself from the floor, and walks toward me. He looks so sexy, with the tool belt hanging low on his hips. The gray

T-shirt frames his chest, outlining the nipple ring and the toned muscles beneath.

"*That look on your face, Snowflake.*"

I squint up at him. "*What look?*"

"*You look at me like that every time I'm wearing this tool belt. Do you get off watching me wearing it?*"

I grin. "*You know I do. You drove me crazy when you took me to your father's company and I had to watch you walking around while carrying heavy stuff and building things.*"

"*Say it.*"

I quirk my brow at him. "*Say what?*"

"*That I'm good with these tools. You wouldn't know what to do without me.*" He pokes my ribs without warning.

"Ow! That hurts," I yelp.

"Admit it, and I'll make you feel better."

I laugh, shaking my head. "You're too cocky for your own good."

He grins wide and bows at the waist. "Thanks for noticing." He grabs me so fast I don't see it coming and pulls me into his chest for a hug. The Cole kind of hug.

He kisses my neck and then smacks my rear, and signs, "*God. I am in love with a girl who gets horny when she sees me wearing a tool belt.*" He leans forward, his lips brushing my ear. "On a scale of one to ten. How wet are you?"

I turn and start walking backwards. "*A hundred. And I am in love with a man who turns me on just by looking at me.*" I bite my lip and slant my head down, looking at him through my lashes. "*A man that drives me insane with every command that leaves his mouth. I am in love with you, always have been, and always will be, Cole Holloway.*"

The smile on his face slowly fades as he closes the distance between us. "I love you, Eleanor Holloway." He cups my face in his hands and leans down to kiss my forehead. "I will never ever let you go."

I shiver and sigh as his lips leave my skin. "*Dinner is almost ready. Come inside when you and the girls are done?*"

"Cool. I will clean up first."

I wink at him and smile coyly. "Oh, don't clean up. You look so hot when you are dirty and sweaty."

His jaw drops and his eyes darken. "Fuck."

I dart a look at the girls and back to Cole. "Watch your mouth, baby."

"Sorry." He leans forward and grips my hips. "You love it when I do dirty things to you?"

I lift on my tip toes and nip his chin. "You have no idea. I want you in my bed after the girls go to sleep."

"I wasn't intending on sleeping anywhere else."

"Good." His hand drops as I turn to leave. I feel his eyes on me, hot and needy. My stomach tightens and heat pools between my legs at the memory of his hands on my skin, his eyes focused on me as if I'm the center of his world.

I turn and catch him subtly readjusting himself in his pants. I've become braver during the past few weeks after realizing my man loves it dirty. So after making sure Cora and Joce are distracted, I place a finger on my lips, suck on it and then blow him a kiss. He takes a step toward me, his body coiled tight but halts mid-stride, darting a glance at the girls. He coughs into his fist.

"*You will pay for that, Snowflake,*" he signs, his chest heaving with ragged breaths.

I giggle and sign back, "*Is that a promise or a threat?*"

He narrows his eyes at me. "*A promise.*"

"*I'll make sure you follow through on it.*"

He shakes his head, props his fists on his hips and looks at the evening sky as if he's praying for strength.

After dinner, Sirius hops up on the couch, and stares at me as though to tell me he is glad to be here, and then curls up in the corner and shuts his eyes.

I fucking love being here too. This is everything I've ever wanted. Everything I will ever need. My life is in a great place right now. I still need to fly to New York to wrap up any pending issues at Lawrence and Barnes, and also pick up my things from the apartment Simon and I shared.

Last week Dad and I finally drove to Jacksonville to meet with the client who was interested in working with BH Architects. He was looking to buy a property overlooking St. John's river in the central business area.

Right after dinner, the girls clear the table and then focus their attention on me.

"*Daddy Cole? Stay here until we come and get you.*" Cora signs, squinting up at me. "*We have a surprise for you.*"

"*Sure.*" My chest warms every time they call me Daddy Cole, knowing they are getting used to the idea of me being their dad.

They turn and dash upstairs without a backward glance. I smile, turning around and stroll into the kitchen. I stop at the counter, taking in the sight in front of me. Nor has added on a little more weight and she looks fucking amazing.

She's elbow deep in bubbles, her head bowed as she washes the dishes. She has a thing for washing them by hand, even though she has a dishwasher. She says it's relaxing and helps to sort out her thoughts.

I grab the dish towel from the counter and walk to her. Stopping behind her, I feel her body shiver with awareness, but she doesn't turn around. I fist the tresses of hair flowing over her shoulder and lift them to the side. I press my mouth on her skin. So soft I just want to bite her, mark her. I inhale her scent deeply, and unable to help it, nip that luscious flesh with my teeth. Goose bumps pop along her arm. She leans her head back on my chest, giving me half her weight.

"You teased me," I say, stroking my thumb against her throat. I know she's moaning or groaning given the vibrations seeping through my fingers on her neck. I push my pelvis forward, grinding myself into her curvy little ass. "I should bend you over and fuck you right here for teasing me."

Pink color flushes across her neck and the side of her cheek. She turns around to face me. Her mouth is parted, her quick breaths feathering my chin, and her perfect tits brushing against my chest.

She takes the dish towel from me, dries her hands, and then slings it over my neck. She tugs it a little, bringing my head close to hers and slants her face so I can read her lips. "Where are the girls?"

"Upstairs."

She purses her lips, staring at me with those huge green eyes, which seem too big for her heart-shaped face. "Do you think we could get away with you doing that to me?"

"Do what? Fuck you?" I tease.

Her pupils dilate and her knees buckle. I use my thighs to support her weight. I'm so turned on right now, knowing that my words have that effect on her.

Her head bobs up and down quickly.

"Probably not. One of them will be coming down soon. Apparently they have a surprise for me."

She drops her head on my shoulder and her body quakes with what I think is laughter. I pull her close and rub circles on her back.

"Do you mind sharing the joke?" I ask, amused. My hands skim the sides of her body and rest on her breasts, kneading them in my palms. I brush the pad of my thumbs over her nipples and I feel a shiver race through her body.

She lifts her head, her eyes dancing with laughter. "I hadn't had sex in years. And then you came back to Willow Hill and I cannot stop wanting it every freaking second of the day. With you. And not just normal sex, the dirty kind."

I raise an eyebrow. "So you just want me for my cock? I feel so used."

"And your body. Don't forget your abs." She winks at me.

My gaze drops to her chest, my cock unbelievably hard as I take in the exposed, flushed cleavage. Tugging the top of her dress down,

I lower my head and suck her nipples through the material and then bury my face between her breasts.

"Fucking gorgeous," I say into her chest, not even caring if she heard me or not. I'm in heaven.

Her hands grab my hair and tug it urgently and my dick grows impossibly hard.

Jesus Christ.

She pulls again. I finally lift my head and stare at her, intoxicated by her scent. I blink several times to get rid of the haze covering my vision and catch the word 'Cora' leaving her lips.

I straighten up, feeling as though cold water has been dumped down the back of my shirt, sobering me up. My hands hasten to rearrange her clothes just as someone tugs on my shirt behind me.

I look over my shoulder to see Cora watching us curiously.

She adjusts the waist of her Hello kitty pajama pants, then signs, "*We are ready, Daddy Cole.*" Her gaze shifts beyond me. "*Are you okay, Mama?*"

I glance at Nor, her face now flaming red. Her mouth opens and closes again before she signs, "*Yes, honey. I hear you have a surprise for Daddy.*"

I press a fist to my mouth to stop from laughing. She looks so flustered it's cute.

"*Are you coming too, Mama?*"

Nor shakes her head and smiles softly to our daughter. "*I want to finish up reading the brochures I received today.*"

Wrapping my fingers around the nape of her neck, I pull her to me and kiss her on the forehead.

"*What was that for?*" she asks me when I let her go.

"*I am so proud of you.*" And I am. She's fighting hard for what she wants.

I'm staring at this woman who literally owns my heart, when I feel small fingers wrap around mine. I focus on Cora as she tugs me toward the living room. Right before we climb up the stairs, I glance back and see Nor leaning against the sink, a hand on her chest. I fucking can't wait until the girls go to bed and I have Nor to myself. Uninterrupted.

The minute Cora and I step inside her room, Joce, dressed up in similar Hello Kitty pajamas as her sister, jumps up from the floor and takes my other hand. She leads the way toward the blanket fort, drops my hand and ducks inside the tiny entrance, flanked by two white bed sheets with lights dangling on the sides.

I drop on my knees and crawl through the entrance, careful not to destroy my daughters' hard work, and settle on one of the pillows in the middle of the fort. I hunch my shoulders, hoping to make myself small and then look around the space decorated with tassels in different colors and more lights. A laptop sits on a small wooden table at the far corner of the 'room'. A tray holding several shades of nail polish and another with makeup sits a few feet away.

Cora plops next to her sister. They both beam at me with twin expressions of pride. "*Do you like your surprise?*"

God, I love them so much.

"*Very much.*"

Cora claps her hands and reaches for the two trays. She hands one to Joce and they begin their work.

My daughters have been working on making me pretty for almost thirty minutes, asking me "would you rather" questions.

Joce pauses and lifts her head, the nail polish brush poised above my big toe. "Would you rather be a giant squid or a mermaid?" Her gaze hopping between her sister and me, waiting for our answers.

"A mermaid," Cora says.

"What? No merman?" I scowl playfully.

Joce's mouth quirks up in a small smile and she shakes her head.

I sigh. "All right. Mermaid."

"Your turn, Daddy Cole." Cora points at me with a finger.

I search my head for appropriate questions but my mind has been wandering to Nor every so often, images of her writhing beneath me as my cock owns her pussy.

Fuck.

I need to focus on the here and now. My dick is already having a hard time calming down.

I clear my throat twice and force my mind to focus on PG questions. "Would you rather eat your own hair or lick the bath tub?"

"Ew, Daddy!"

We all laugh.

"*Let me give you the mirror,*" Joce signs before twisting around and reaching for the mirror behind her and shoves it in my face.

I take it from her hands, meet my reflection and press my lips together to stop grinning. My lips are painted in scarlet red lipstick, my eyes and eyelashes lined with black shit. I tuck my chin down to get a look at my hair and finally grin, unable to hold back any more. Clumps of my hair are tied together with colorful hair bands. The look is completed with a shiny silver crown on my head.

Cora touches my shoulder to get my attention. "*Do you like it?*"

I nod. "*I would make a very beautiful princess.*"

Joce puts a hand over her mouth and giggles, while Cora beams, happily.

"*Oh wait, I forgot something,*" Joce signs and plucks the red nail polish with glitter from a tray and orders me to splay my hands on one of the pillows. When she is done painting them, she returns the bottle to the tray, leans back and smiles, satisfied.

"*Much better.*" I flutter my hands like they showed me to do for the nail polish to dry faster and then blow air on my nails.

Joce yawns and shifts around to lie on the mass of pillows and her sister follows suit.

"Time for bed. Thank you for the awesome surprise." They nod sleepily. I lean down and kiss their hair, taking in the strawberry scent from their shampoo. "Good night, my little princesses."

They wave at me, their lips moving but I can't read them because their faces are slightly turned away from me.

I lift the crown off my head and put it inside one of the trays, then crawl out of the fort. After turning off the lights, I head downstairs. Nor is curled up on the couch asleep, a couple of brochures scattered around her and another one on her chest. Those delectable full lips parted in slumber. After gathering the leaflets and setting them on the table, I scoop her up in my arms and carry her upstairs and to her room. Using the hallway light to guide me, I kick the door shut with my foot and navigate my way to the bed. She doesn't even stir when I lay her on the bed.

I sweep the red locks of her hair from her temples, tuck them behind her ear and kiss her forehead, her cheek, her neck.

"Wake up, Snowflake," I murmur into her shoulder. My hand trails around to cup her breast. My thumb swirls her nipple in deliberate caresses and then I skim my fingers to her waist, down between her legs. I push her panties to the side and part her folds, stroking gently while sucking the column of her neck. I feel her stir awake, wiggling her ass to my erection. I lift off the bed and shift down her body, parting her thighs as I go. I pull my fingers away and replace them with my mouth. I blow hot air through the material then suck her.

She moves on the bed, letting her thighs fall open. Her hips raise off the bed, chasing my lips when I lift my head to look at her. Pressing a hand on her stomach, I hook my fingers around the panties and pull them down her legs. I toss them away, dip my head down to kiss her inner thighs, and keep inching forward.

Jesus. She smells amazing. I want to taste her now, make her come with my tongue and watch as she falls apart.

Fingers sink into my hair and tug.

Good. She is awake.

Holy freaking hell!

My eyes snapped open at the feel of fingers thrusting inside me. Slightly confused, I raised my head and glanced down between my legs. Squinting in the dark, and from the little light seeping in from the street lamp, I see knots of hair held together by colored hair bands. I make a move to close my legs but then the purposeful lick of a tongue stops me. I know whose mouth is on me. The only person that has the power to render me into mush. I drop my head back on the pillow and shut my eyes tight and try to catch my breath.

Cole is trying to kill me with his mouth. I yank the hair in my fists and only manage to pull out a few hair bands. I clutch his hair again, desperate to get his mouth on mine at the same time eager for the promise of release. He puts his strong palm on my pelvis and holds me down while his mouth works its magic on me, beckoning my orgasm. My hands leave his head, flying to my sides to clutch at the sheets and hold on for the ride. Cole makes a sound, sort of like a grunt, in his throat. It vibrates between my legs, up my spine and I'm spiraling out of control. I squeeze my eyes tight and yell his name as the wave hits me hard, leaving me trembling in the aftermath.

I slowly open my mouth to find Cole hovering above me, smiling, his teeth bright in the darkness.

"I am about to keep my promise." He doesn't wait for me to answer. He flips me around and in two seconds flat, I'm on my stomach. He hooks his hands behind my thighs, yanking them up so my rear is in the air. His big, calloused hands knead my cheeks roughly, then I feel a sharp pain on my skin. I glance over my shoulder and find his face inches from my buttock, his teeth barred, ready to take another bite.

He freaking bit me.

I wiggle my backside, but his grip tightens as his mouth lowers on my skin. He lifts his gaze to meet mine and I suck in a breath when I see the possessive, needy look leveled my way. He dips his head and kisses my flesh and then does the same to the other cheek before nipping a bit.

Crap. I can feel my orgasm building again. I slide my hand between my legs and urgently rub my clitoris, eager to find my release. Cole seems to sense it. He flips me around fast, sits back on his haunches and drags me to him.

"You will come with my cock inside you. Sit on me." His words are barely intelligible now. He leans his back on the head board and fists his erection, moving his hand up and down in slow movements.

As soon as I straddle him and put my hands on his shoulders, he lets go of himself and grabs my hips with both hands. He lowers me down, impaling me to the root, filling me completely. I inhale deeply and hold still. I want to tell him how good I feel, how much I love him, how perfect we are together. But I don't want to move to switch on the light so he can read my lips. I don't want to break our connection. So I take one of his hands and place it on my neck so he can feel what he is doing to me. I wrap my arms around his neck, concentrate on watching his face in the dark, memorizing each feature. We don't talk as our breaths mingle, our hearts speak to each other and our souls merge over and over.

The fingers on my neck tighten a little before releasing me and moving down to cup my breast. Pinching my nipple. I dip my head to kiss his neck, trailing my lips down his shoulder and nip with my teeth. Down to his chest. I suck on his nipple and then do the same to the other one, tugging at the metal ring. He groans and grabs my head in both hands and pulls me up to his mouth, kissing me brutally, passionately. His hips buck up. I bear down on him hard, matching his furious thrusts, feeling him go deeper. Deeper than I've ever felt before. His hands move to my hips and hold me in place as he thrusts in and out. In and Out. In. Out. I press my forehead to his, our lips so close to touching. We don't kiss. Just keep on breathing. Breathing each other's air. Feeding on the intensity of our union.

God, Cole.

Cole.

I love you.

The sound of my phone ringing penetrates the lusty haze. I shut my eyes tighter, throw my arms around Cole's shoulders and grab him harder.

I feel the wave rise inside me. My body shakes against Coles. He seems to sense how close I am to coming. He wraps his strong arms around my waist and buries his face into my breast. The orgasm rips through me and I'm flying. I feel him join me and we both fall over the edge together, my mouth pressed on his shoulder.

When we are calm enough to move, he slumps back on the headboard, taking me with him and stretches his legs beneath him and just holds me. His heart beats wildly against my chest.

I feel him move beneath me and seconds later the room is bathed with the soft light from the lamp on the nightstand.

"*That was mind-blowing,*" I sign. "*God, you are incredible.*" I squint at him then burst out laughing. "*You are wearing makeup.*"

He grins, the sexiest thing ever. "*I was a princess and it was amazing,*" he signs, then cups my neck in his hands, the pad of his thumbs skimming across my jaw as he kisses me softly. A whisper of a kiss. A promise of forever.

The phone starts to ring again. I groan, annoyed that I have to move my well-loved and used body.

"What is wrong?" he asks, sliding his hands to my shoulders.

"My phone is ringing. Who could be calling at almost midnight?" I reach for the phone on my side of the bed and squint at the screen. I frown at the unfamiliar number flashing on my screen. I'm about to press the 'call end' button, but I pause.

What if it's Elon or Elise and something happened, and they couldn't use their phones?

I quickly swipe the screen to answer. "Eleanor Holloway."

There is a pause on the other end of the line, then "Mrs. Holloway? My name is Charles Witkson. I'm calling from Chicago." A pause, then a deep intake of breath. "I'm a friend of your father's. Your name and number were in his wallet. I didn't know who else to call."

"My father?" I ask, trying to wrap my mind around the stranger's words. Then a chill runs down my spine and I tense. My mind is still stuck on 'Your name and number was in his wallet'. My first instinct is to ask if he is okay, but suddenly the anger that has been buried inside me all these years rears its head.

"What do you want, Mr. Witkson?" I ask coldly, watching Cole's expression darken as he reads my lips.

The man coughs. "He has been arrested for attempted murder—"

My brain shuts down. Everything after that is background noise. Bile burns my throat and I want to vomit. My body locks down and I feel hot and cold and I can't breathe. Thoughts fly inside my head, thoughts of my father, the hell he had put us through. . .

I jolt when hands grab my shoulders and shake me violently.

"Nor? What is wrong?"

I shake my head, tears burning my eyes. "I don't have a father. I never have," I declare over the phone. "Good bye Mr. Witkson. Please, don't ever call me again."

I end the call with shaking fingers and clutch the phone in my hand.

"Your father?" Cole asks, his face transformed from bliss to thunder. "What does he want?"

"He was arrested for attempted murder. In Chicago," I reply, but I don't really feel anything at all. I was used to not having him around, and suddenly he is there, his presence looming around me like a nightmare.

My father. The monster. He destroyed me and my family without even a second thought.

Cole pries the phone from my hand then cups my face and forces me to look at him. "Nor, look at me." I do. He brushes his thumb across my cheek. "Take deep breaths. Stephen is not here. He cannot hurt you. Or me." I take deep breaths and finally nod. "He would have to kill me first to get to you."

"Come on." He slides down on the bed, and I turn around to face him and snuggle into his chest. He holds me, rubbing circles on my back until I fall into a dream full of monsters.

I woke up hours ago, unable to sleep after last night's phone call.

I glance at the phone for the hundredth time, anxious to hear from my sisters. I sent them a text one hour ago after debating for most of the night if I should tell them about the disturbing call from Chicago.

Dragging my hands through my mused up hair, I pull my legs up on the couch and prop my chin on top of my knees.

I hate him for showing up in my life again.

I close my eyes and focus on shoving those thoughts from my head.

A hand cups the back of my neck and lips press warmly on my forehead. I open my eyes and see Cole standing shirtless in front of me, the gray pants slung low on his hips. His lips are smeared with red lipstick and his eyes circled with kohl and mascara.

I pull him down for a kiss on his cheek and laugh, momentarily forgetting my problems. "You look so hot, baby." I wipe my thumb on his lips and show it to him. "I love this look on you. So edgy."

He chuckles and shakes his head. "I woke up and you were gone. How are you?"

I shake my head and drop my hands from his face. "Angry. Terrified. I know he can't hurt us, but that phone call brought back bad memories—"

Cole puts his index finger on my lips to stop my words. "He will never hurt you again. He will have to go through me first, okay?"

I nod. "Okay."

"Good." He kisses my nose. "Time to make my woman and my daughters breakfast."

He turns and walks toward the kitchen. I stand up and follow him, and then sit on one of the stools so I can watch him to distract myself.

God, he is a fine specimen of a man. Those abs, that tight, tight rear. . .my eyes zoom in on his crotch and I swallow hard at the bulge. He was right. He doesn't need a take-off countdown.

Yes. Batman. I love Batman.

Mom and Pete arrived one hour ago. I still can't believe how healthy and peaceful she looks. She hasn't asked about my father, which is a big step for her. She used to ask about him every time I spoke to her when she was undergoing therapy.

She slips her hand in Pete's and smiles at him, and then stands up and kisses him on the lips.

She turns to face me. "Need help clearing the table, baby?"

I startle on my chair, slap Cole's hand away from my thigh and shoot up, my cheeks on fire. "Sure."

I glare at the father of my children, then proceed to clear the table. Cole's fingers have been lingering on my body the entire evening. Caressing the back of my knee, gripping my thigh, brushing a finger up my inner thigh. . .It's like he can't help himself.

"So. Cole, huh? I assume things worked out?"

"Yes, we did." I smile

"Good, because you two were meant to be."

I bite the inside of my cheek, fiddling with the dish cloth in my hands. I feel resentment burning a hole in my chest.

"Mom, why did you stay? Dad was so bad to you. To us. It was unhealthy, actually. Why did you stay?" I finally ask the question I'd asked her years ago.

She stares at the counter for a long time before raising those radiant green eyes to meet mine. "Remember when you asked me the same question and I told you that it was complicated?"

I nod.

"My parents thought that your father was only interested in marrying me for the money. They suggested he sign a prenup, which could only be nullified in case one of us died or if I filed for a divorce. If I did the latter, your father would end up getting half of my worth. Things got interesting when my parents died and I inherited everything. He became more desperate. He did everything he could to force me to file for divorce. I'm not even sure why I held onto the stupid notion that he'd change in time. He never loved me. It took me a couple of sessions before I finally saw the truth.

"I loved Stephen at first when we met. After meeting Pete, I realized my parents were right about him. I hadn't really loved your father. I had been lying to myself. Waiting for him to change. He'd shown me a smidge of attention and my world imploded. We met at a time when I wanted someone who'd love me for me. Not because they were impressed with my dancing skills, or my money. Or worse, because they only wanted a rebound.

"Before I met him, my life was all about pleasing my parents and dancing. Success was the only way to win my parents affection. My twin sister, Sabine, who was also my best friend, was a grade A student. My parents were proud of her so I had to fight to achieve that kind of love. Your father and I went to different schools. We met at a football game held at our school. It was love at first sight for both of us. Or so I thought, until I found out about Cole's mother."

I'm shocked by this entire revelation. Mom hardly ever spoke about her family, her past. The first time I asked her about her sister and her family, Mom broke down and cried. It took her weeks to get over that low. I learned my lesson and I never made that mistake again.

I take in a deep breath and then exhale, letting go of the past, the negative emotions and quickly send a prayer up above. Count my blessings instead of ticking off a list of everything bad that has happened.

I wrap my arms around her in a hug. "I'm very glad you are okay, Mom."

She returns my embrace and then pulls back to study me with

eyes full of tears. "Do you know what I learned in all those years? Life breaks you, dismantling every part of us into pieces. It's just a way to prepare us for what we are meant to be. Who we are meant to be. Survivors."

Tears run down my face. "That is so beautiful. And I completely agree. We are survivors."

Pete walks in, carrying the girls in each of his arms. He is a big guy, about two hundred and thirty pounds, with white hair and sky blue eyes. Lines curve the corner of his mouth, a sure sign that he laughs a lot.

"How about we take the girls for ice cream, Carol?" he smiles wide.

We step apart and Mom walks toward her boyfriend.

"Sure. I haven't spent time with my little angels in a long time. Let's go have fun." She turns and winks at me, before turning and leading the way out of the kitchen.

I smile after them and pull out my phone from my shorts pocket. My sisters have been texting the entire day, checking up on me. After letting them know that we are okay and Mom is in town, they promise to drop by tomorrow and spend the next three days together with Mom.

After the dishes are done, Cole scoops me up in his arms and climbs the stairs to the terrace. He lays me on the love seat and then crawls beside me and takes me into his arms.

I shift a bit to make sure he can see my mouth. "What is the best thing that has ever happened to you?"

Those beautiful gray eyes linger on my lips until I feel my breath leave my lungs. "You. Josh. My parents. Nick. Cora and Joce. You." He falls quiet for a few moments. "What about you?"

I bite my lip, fighting a smile. "I survived. You. Josh. My sisters and Mom. Cora and Joce. You."

He brushes his lips on mine but doesn't kiss me. Instead, he slants his head away from me.

He sighs. "We haven't had an ordinary life, have we?" He squints his eyes thoughtfully. "What I feel for you isn't ordinary. What we share was complicated from the start. But, our souls knew long before we met. That this is a once in a lifetime thing. And if it's up to me, I'm going to make sure I'm in your life until my dying day. You're not just my ordinary, Eleanor. You're my extraordinary. My everything."

Tears gather in my eyes, but I'm not ready to let them fall yet, otherwise I won't be able to finish what I want to say. "I don't want ordinary with you. I want extraordinary. I want to drown in your passion and kisses, Cole. I want to be the only thing that lives in your mind long after you leave my side. I want our souls to marry each other and stay in love.

"Before I met you, I'd been running from myself. Running in different directions, without any destination in mind. I couldn't find my balance in life, my anchor. For nine years, I've been drowning and only came up for air for Cora and Joce, but deep down, the part that needed you was being dragged under, day in day out. Then you came back after receiving those letters. That part of me lying dormant stirred to life. You kissed me, setting my body on fire. You pulled me to the surface and made me breathe again. I've been waiting nine years to exhale and now that I have, I'm going to make sure I keep breathing."

I lift my hand and wipe the tears falling down his cheek and smile at him. "I promise you darkness and light. I promise you a love so deep, so profound you will feel it even when we're apart. You good with that?"

He nods and grins through the tears in his eyes. "You have given me everything. A love that consumes me. Cora and Joce. You. You gave me a reason to fight when I thought I couldn't. I promise to keep your heart and love safe for always. Are you good with that?"

Instead of answering him, I slide my hand around the nape of his neck and pull him to me, mesh my mouth with his.

When we finally come up for air, I say in a breathless voice, "I'm going to marry you one of these days, Cole Holloway."

His entire body shakes with laughter as he holds me flush to his body.

Finally, he looks into my eyes with a look that tells me I'm wanted. I'm desired. I'm everything he has ever, and will ever, need. "I will hold you to that."

Love is when you accept each other's weirdness and faults and demons, without judging them. Without trying to change them.

It's unconditional.

It's fearless.

It's powerful.

And for me, love is Cole.

He is my once in a lifetime. My happily ever after.

PLAYLIST

Beneath Your Beautiful - Labrinth
How To Save A Life - The Fray
Little Wonders - Rob Thomas
Mirrors - Justin Timberlake
Where I Stood - Missy Higgins
This girl's in love with you - Steve Tyrell
Make You Feel My Love - Adele
When I Was Your Man - Bruno Mars
Heaven - Bryan Adams
I Don't Want To Be - Gavin DeGraw
I Will Wait - Mumford & Sons
Bring Me To Life - Evanescence
Cut—Plumb
Broken Vow - Josh Groban
You're Still You — Josh Groban
I Was Born To Love You — Queen
Fall Into Me — Brantley Gilbert
Fearless — Taylor Swift
Set Me on Fire — Bella Ferraro
You Are The Best Thing —Ray LaMontagne
Down —Jason Walker
A Drop In The Ocean — Ron Pope
Dream a Little Dream of Me—Yiruma
River Flows in You — Yiruma
What Is Love — Empire Cast (feat. V Bozeman)
Because I Love You —Yiruma
You to Me Are Everything —The Real Thing
Jealous—Labrinth
Ten Feet Tall —Wrabel
Breakeven—MAX
Walking Blind—Aidan Hawken

Never Let Me Go— Florence + The Machine
Taking Chances—Glee Cast
Have You Ever Really Loved A Woman—Bryan Adams
Running' (Lose it All) featuring Beyonce, Arrow Benjamin - Naughty Boy
Growing up (feat. Ed Sheeran) - Macklemore & Ryan Lewis
See You Again (feat. Charlie Puth) — Wiz Khalifa
Iris — Goo Goo Dolls
Fall For You—Leela James
Scars — James Bay

ACKOWLEDGEMENTS

I wish I could find the words to thank everyone who has been involved with this book.

My two children. Two of my most favorite people in the world. You're amazing. Your patience and unconditional love floors me. Thank you for the laughs and for believing in me. You are my silver lining.

To the ladies in the Autumn's Minxes Group. I love you! Thank you for being so incredibly wonderful, encouraging and supportive. You're my happy place. I'm honored and feel lucky you're in my corner.

I experienced all kinds of emotions while writing this story. I'm grateful for my wonderful beta readers—Amy Bosica, Ella Stewart, Sejla Ibrahimpasic, Selma Ibrahimpasic, Polly Lynne, Elaina Lucia, Katie Monson, Marian Girling, Emma Louise, Mg Herrera, Vivian Freeman, Maiwenn (I hope I didn'T forget anyone)— who stuck with me from the first draft to the last draft of this story. Thank you for your wonderful feedback and encouragement. Every word, every suggestion, is ALWAYS appreciated. To Cora Brent, Cecilia London and Sidney Halston. I can't thank you enough for your help during my research on prison and laws, and for being there to provide answers to all of my questions. I learned so much from you. I'll forever be grateful for that.

Thank you Elaina, Selma and Sejla for the last minute reread of the final proof and for your notes. I can't tell you how grateful I am that you did this for me.

I'm so thankful for the C.O.P.A. girls and Indie Chicks. You ladies are amazing! I love how positive and inspiring you are. Thanks for your support and love.

Ella, you're such an inspiration to me. Thank you for always having time for me, for being my sounding board, and for introducing me to mind-melding. ;). Vivian, our chats are proof that neither time difference nor distance can keep us apart. My favorite twins, Selma and Sejla, I really enjoy our FB & Starbucks chats. It's always great to just kick back and have fun with you. Maiwenn, thank you for your help and suggestions, and encouragement. Don't forget our chats. :) Elaina, you've been amazing and a wonderful friend. We haven't known each other for long, but I feel like I've known you for a long time. Karen Ferry, #GlitterChick I can't wait to be your roomie in Dublin. It's always a pleasure to chat with you. Thanks for being such a wonderful, supportive friend. Amo Thomson, I believe that you and I are meant to be :). Mg Herrera, you have a beautiful soul, my friend, and are a fantastic teaser maker. I'm very lucky and honored to such wonderful friends.

To the bloggers who work tirelessly to read and review books, and promote authors without expecting anything in return. There are not enough words to let you know how appreciated you are. Thank you.

To Give Me Books. Thank you for organizing the release blitz.

Vanessa Bridges, thank you for taking my words and making them shine. You're amazing and thorough. Thank you for always being ready to answer my questions. To two amazing proofreaders, Fiona Wilson and Jessica Descent. Thanks for making this story better.

To my cover designer, Sarah Hansen (Okay Creations): You blew my mind. Thank you for this breathtaking cover. I can't wait to work with you on the next one.

Megan Baxter, Marian Girling and Rachelle Marie, thank you for giving *Spinners Book Emporium & Cafe* (Fall Back Skyward) a name. Also thanks Elaina Lucia and Tobi Spalla-Beaty for contributing to the playlist.

Thank you Stacey Blake of Champagne Formatting. You have a great eye for detail and you blow my mind with your beautiful work. It's always a pleasure to work with you.

And to you my amazing reader. . . Thank you for taking a chance on me and my stories. I thank you from the bottom of my heart.

xoxo

Autumn

ABOUT THE AUTHOR

Autumn Grey is the author of *Havoc, Obliterate, Mend* (Havoc series). And just like her characters, she is quirky, sometimes funny and definitely flawed. She writes sexy contemporary romances full of drama, steamy kisses and happily ever afters.

Author links:
Facebook: www.facebook.com/AuthorAutumnGreyAG

Twitter: twitter.com/AutumnGrey26

Pinterest: www.pinterest.com/autumngrey75

Goodreads: www.goodreads.com/author/show/7337710.Autumn_ Grey

Instagram: www.instagram.com/authorautumngrey/?hl=en

OTHER BOOKS

Printed in Great Britain
by Amazon